More Praise for *As Husbands Go*

"A rollicking caper."

—*Good Housekeeping*

"There's a trick to mining comedy from tragedy, and bestselling novelist Susan Isaacs knows exactly how to make it work."

—*The Miami Herald*

"A laugh-out-loud mystery."

—*The Star-Ledger*

"Since this is a Susan Isaacs novel, we can be reasonably sure the good gals will win. . . . The characters are fun to meet, and the accretion of detail makes the book nice and chewy."

—*The New York Times Book Review*

"Isaacs brings it all together in this fast and furious ride through wanton greed, fragile relationships, and love worth fighting for."

—*Publishers Weekly* (starred review)

"Isaacs's latest Jewish-gal-under-stress adventure purrs along perfectly—sharply funny, all-knowing, and marvelously diverting."

—*Booklist*

"Nobody but nobody skewers vanity with the daring yet big-hearted wit of Susan Isaacs. *As Husbands Go* is mandatory reading for anyone who's married, not married, was married, or is thinking of getting married. I laughed my head off. And I was profoundly moved. That's what Isaacs does. And she does it better than anyone else on earth."

—Patricia Volk, author of *Stuffed* and *To My Dearest Friends*

Also by Susan Isaacs

Novels
Past Perfect
Any Place I Hang My Hat
Long Time No See
Red, White and Blue
Lily White
After All These Years
Magic Hour
Shining Through
Almost Paradise
Close Relations
Compromising Positions

Screenplays
Hello Again
Compromising Positions

Nonficton
*Brave Dames and Wimpettes: What Women Are Really Doing
on Page and Screen*

As Husbands Go

A Novel

SUSAN ISAACS

Scribner
New York   London   Toronto   Sydney

Scribner
A Division of Simon & Schuster, Inc.
1230 Avenue of the Americas
New York, NY 10020

First Scribner trade paperback edition April 2011

SCRIBNER and design are registered trademarks of The Gale Group, Inc., used
under license by Simon & Schuster, Inc., the publisher of this work.

For information about special discounts for bulk purchases,
please contact Simon & Schuster Special Sales at 1-866-506-1949
or business@simonandschuster.com.

The Simon & Schuster Speakers Bureau can bring authors to your live event.
For more information or to book an event contact the Simon & Schuster Speakers
Bureau at 1-866-248-3049 or visit our website at www.simonspeakers.com.

Designed by Carla Jayne Jones

Manufactured in the United States of America

10 9 8 7 6 5 4 3

Library of Congress Control Number: 2009052241

ISBN 978-1-4165-7301-2
ISBN 978-1-4165-7308-1 (pbk)
ISBN 978-1-4165-7984-7 (ebook)

To St. Catherine and Bob Morvillo with love

Here, take this gift,
I was reserving it for some hero, speaker, or general,
One who should serve the good old cause, the great idea, the
progress and freedom of the race,
Some brave confronter of despots, some daring rebel;
But I see that what I was reserving belongs to you just as
    much as to any.

—Walt Whitman, "To a Certain Cantatrice," *Leaves of Grass*

Chapter One

Who knew? It seemed a perfectly nice night. True, outside the house, the wind was whoo-whooing like sound effects from a low-budget horror movie. The cold was so vicious that a little past seven, a branch of the great white spruce on the front lawn that had been creaking all afternoon suddenly screamed in pain. Then a brutal *CRAAACK*, and it crashed to the frozen ground.

But inside our red brick Georgian in the picturesque Long Island town of Shorehaven, all was warmth. I went from one bedroom to another to kiss the boys good night. Despite the sickly yellow gleam of the SpongeBob Squarepants night-light in his bedroom, Mason, the third-born of our triplets, glowed pure gold. I stroked his forehead. "Happy dreams, my sweetie." He was already half asleep, thumb in mouth, but his four other fingers flapped me a good night.

A flush of mother love reddened my cheeks. Its heat spread. For a moment, it even eased the permanent muscle spasm that had seized the left side of my neck seconds after Jonah and I gazed up at the sonogram and saw three little paisley curls in utero. My utero. Still, a perpetual neck spasm was a small price to pay for such a wonderful life, one I had hardly dared dream about as a little girl in Brooklyn.

Okay, that "wonderful life" and "hardly dared dream" business does cross the line into the shameless mush of Mommyland, where "fulfillment" is all about children, not sex, and where mothers are jealous of each new baby-shoe charm on their friends' bracelets. Feh.

Sure, sure: Sentiment proves you're human. Feelings are good, blah, blah, blah. But sentimentality, anything that could go on a minivan bumper sticker, makes me cringe. Take this as a given: Susan B Anthony Rabinowitz Gersten (i.e., me) was never a Long Island madonna, one of those moms who carries on about baby Jonathan as if he were Baby Jesus.

What kind of mother was I on that particular night? A happy one. Still, it wouldn't have taken a psychologist to read my emotional pie chart and determine that the sum of my parts equaled one shallow (though contented) human being. One third of that happiness was attributable to the afterglow of the birthday present my husband had given me two weeks earlier, a Cartier Santos watch. Another third was courtesy of Lexapro (twenty milligrams). A little over a sixth came from the pure sensual gratification of being wrapped in a tea-green Loro Piana cashmere bathrobe. The remaining sliver was bona fide maternal bliss.

Maybe I'm still shallow, just deluding myself that after all that's occurred, I've become a better person. On the other hand, even at my superficial worst, I wasn't terrible. Truly, I did have a heart.

Especially when it came to my immediate family. I loved them. So I gloried in that moment of mommy bliss. I remember thinking, *Jonah and I have some lucky star shining down on us.* Along with our three boys, my husband, Jonah Paul Gersten, MD, FACS (picture a slightly older—and significantly shorter— Orlando Bloom, with a teeny touch of male pattern baldness), was the light of my life. Naturally, I had no clue about what was happening with Jonah twenty-six miles west, in Manhattan.

How could I possibly know that right at that very instant, he was stepping into the Upper East Side apartment of a call girl who had decided a month earlier that the name Cristal Rousseau wasn't projecting the class-up-the-ass image she had been aiming for. Lately, there hadn't been much of a market for the refined-type fuck, so she'd changed her image and her name to something still classy yet more girl-next-door—Dorinda Dillon.

Why would a man of Jonah's caliber bother with someone like Dorinda? Before you go "heh-heh," think about it. It's a reasonable question. First of all, Jonah never gave me any reason to believe he wasn't devoted to me. Just a couple of months earlier, at the annual holiday party of his Park Avenue surgical practice, I had overheard the scheduling coordinator confide to one of the medical assistants, "Dr. Gersten always has that look of love, even when Mrs. Gersten is standing right beside him in those four-inch heels that—I hate to say it—make her *shockingly* taller."

Also, being a plastic surgeon with a craniofacial subspecialty, Jonah was a man with a sophisticated sense of beauty. He had the ultimate discerning eye. No way would Dorinda Dillon's looks have pleased him. Objectively speaking, I swear to God, she looked like a ewe in a blond wig. You'd expect her to go *baa*. Genuinely sheepy-looking, whatever the word for that is. All my life I've read much more than people ever gave me credit for, and I have a surprisingly decent vocabulary—though obviously not decent enough.

Anyway, Dorinda had a long, wide sheep nose that sloped down straight from her forehead. It took up so much room in the middle of her face that it kept her eyes farther apart than human eyes ought to be. Despite her loyalty to some hideous blackish-red lipstick, her mouth came across more as dark two-dimensional lines than actual lips.

Not that I was gorgeous. Far from it. All right, not that far. Still, most people saw me as . . . well, fabulous-looking. I guess

I should apologize because that sounds arrogant. Okay, obnoxious. A woman who comes right out and says, "Hey, I'm stunning!" (even when she is) is violating what is probably the real First Commandment, the one that somehow got replaced by the "I am the Lord thy God" business, which never really made a lot of sense to me because how is that a commandment? Anyway, the true numero uno of human conduct is "Thou shalt not speak well of thyself."

Because of that, every great-looking woman has to apologize not only by acting nicer than she really is but by showing she's paid her dues, à la "I had major zits when I was fourteen and was totally flat-chested and, like, so self-conscious nobody even knew I was alive. I'm still, like, really, really shy deep down."

So let me get with the program. For most of my life, whenever I looked in the mirror, I honestly did feel insecure. In fact, throughout my childhood in Brooklyn, I kept waiting for someone to shout "Hey, Bucktooth!" which would inevitably become my nickname until I graduated high school. Weird: No one ever did. Years passed without any cruel mockery. My confidence grew—a little. And after Jonah came into my life, it flourished. Someone like him genuinely wanted someone like me! Yet I always knew my overbite stood between me and actual beauty.

Braces would have fixed me up, but I didn't get them. With perfect clarity, I still see myself at age ten, gazing up at Erwin Monkarsh, DDS, a blobby man who looked like he'd been put together by a balloon-twisting clown at a birthday party. Even though he didn't seem like a guy who could answer a maiden's prayer, my young heart fluttered with hope. I put all my energy into willing him not to do . . . precisely what he now was doing: shaking his head. "No, her bite's actually okay," he was telling my mother.

In that instant I understood I was doomed. No orthodontia. "However, I'm not saying she couldn't use braces for cosmetic reasons," he added. "She definitely could."

At that time my mother was in her Sherry the Fearless Feminist and Scourge of the Frivolous stage, and she responded with a single humorless chuckle. "'Cosmetic reasons'!" Then she snorted at the notion that she would spend money on a treatment that would aid in transforming her daughter into a sex object.

For the next ten years of my life, I spent thousands of girlhours on self-criticism—gazing into mirrors, squinting at photos, having heart-to-hearts with my girlfriends and department store makeup artists. What I finally concluded was that my overbite was clearly not a plus. The good news was that it made me look a little dumb but not unappealing. Sometimes after I changed my hairstyle or got a new coat, I'd catch myself in a mirror. In that fraction of a second before I realized it was me, I'd think, *Great look, but double-digit IQ*.

Still, as I explained to Andrea Brinckerhoff, my business partner as well as my official best friend (you're not a true woman unless you have one), men liked what they saw when they looked at me. I still got frequent second and, once in a while, third looks. Naturally, no guy ever went—I demonstrated by pressing both hands over my heart and gasping—"Omigod!" the way a guy might if he bumped into an indisputable, acknowledged beauty, a Halle Berry or Scarlett Johansson. On the other hand, Halle and Scarlett weren't rolling carts down the household-detergents aisle of a Long Island Stop & Shop.

"Why do you even waste two seconds worrying about your appearance?" Andrea demanded. "Look who you're married to. A plastic surgeon. Not just any plastic surgeon. A plastic surgeon who made *New York* magazine's top doctors. You know and I know, way before Jonah even went into medicine, he had a gut understanding about what 'stunning' meant. He couldn't marry a d-o-g any more than he could drive an ugly car. With all he has going for him, he could have had almost anyone. He has a good family background. Well, not Social Register, since they're ... you know. But still, he is Ivy League. Then he stayed at Yale for medical school. And he's hot in that Jewish-short-guy way. He could have picked a classic beauty. But he chose you."

Andrea may have been irritating and snobbish, but she was right: I was close enough to beauty. Take my eyes. People called them "intriguing," "compelling," "gorgeous." Whatever. They were very pale green. At Madison High School in Brooklyn, Matthew Bortz, a boy so pasty and scrawny that the only type he could be was Sensitive Artiste, wrote me a love poem. It went on about how my eyes were the color of "liquid jade mix'd with cream." Accurate. Sweet, too, though he got really pissed when I said, "Matty, you could've lost the apostrophe in 'mix'd.'"

It wasn't only great eyes, the kind that make people say a real woof is beautiful just because she has blue eyes and three coats of mascara. I also had world-class cheekbones. They were prominent and slanted up. Where did I get them? My mother's face was round, my father's was closer to an oval, but both their faces were basically formless, colorless, and without a single feature that was either awful or redeeming. My parents could have pulled off a bank heist without wearing masks and never have been identified.

I was around thirteen and reading some book about the Silk Road when I began to imagine that my facial structure came from an exotic ancestor. I settled on a fantasy about a wealthy handsome merchant from Mongolia passing through Vitebsk. He wound up having a two-night stand with one of my great-great-grandmothers. She'd have been the kind of girl the neighbors whispered about: "Oy, Breindel Kirpichnik! Calling that green-eyed minx a slut is too good for her. They say she's got Gypsy blood!"

It's a long story I won't go into here, but I was twenty when I sought out and actually found where my looks came from: my no-good grandmother who'd taken a hike, abandoning not only her boring husband but her eight-year-old daughter—my mother. Grandma Ethel was tall, willowy, with liquid-jade-mixed-with-cream eyes. She was me minus the overbite. She told me I could thank her for my hair, too, light brown with gold highlights. She was pretty sure hers had been my color, but she'd become a blonde in 1949 so couldn't swear to it.

But back to me. My mouth was better than Grandma Ethel's, but "better" is mostly luck, since I'd been born into Generation X, a global slice of humanity that tolerates fat only in lips. Other women were forever asking me, "Did your husband inject collagen or some new filler into your lips?"

My body was good, which made me one of maybe five females within a fifty-mile radius of Manhattan who did not have a negative body image. I was blessed with an actual waist, which came back (though not 100 percent) after the triplets. Long legs and arms. Enough in the boob department to please men without having them so cantaloupish as to make buying French designer clothes an act of willful idiocy.

My mind? No one would ever call me brilliant, unless those MacArthur people gave grants for genius in accessorizing. Still, I was smart enough not only to make a beautiful life for myself but to be grateful for my incredible blessings. Plus, to get people to ignore any "she's dumb" thoughts courtesy of my overbite (also so they wouldn't think I was all style, no substance), I listened to *The NewsHour* on PBS five nights a week. Jonah helped, because having gone to Yale, he went for subtitled movies about doomed people, so I saw more of them than any regular person should have to. I read a lot, too, though it was mostly magazines because I never got more than fifteen minutes of leisure at a shot after Dashiell and Evan and Mason were born. Still, there was enough stuff about books in *Vogue* that when all the women at a luncheon talked about, say, *Interpreter of Maladies,* I'd read enough about it to say "exquisitely written" and not "hilarious." I did like historical fiction, but more the kind that got into eighteenth-century oral sex, or the marchioness's brown wool riding jacket with silver braid, and didn't linger on pus-filled sores on the peasants' bare feet.

So, okay, not a great mind. But I definitely had enough brains not to let my deficiencies ruin my happiness. Unlike many wives of successful, smart, good-looking doctors, I didn't make myself crazy with the usual anxieties: *Ooh, is Jonah cheating on me? Planning on cheating on me? Wishing he could cheat on me but not having the guts or time?*

To be totally truthful? Of course I had an anxiety or two. Like knowing how fourteen years of marriage can take the edge off passion. We still enjoyed gasping, sweaty intimacy now and then. Like one starry Long Island evening that past August. We did it in a chaise by the pool after three quarters of a bottle of sauvignon blanc. Also in a bathtub in the Caesar Park Ipanema Hotel during an International Society for Aesthetic Plastic Surgery convention.

But with three four-year-olds plus two nineteen-year-old live-in Norwegian au pairs (twins) and a five-day-a-week, eight-hours-a-day housekeeper, our chances for hot sex were close to zero—even when Bernadine wasn't there and Ida and Ingvild had a weekend off. After "Sleep tight, sweetie" times three, Jonah and I were rarely finished being parents. We still had to deal with Evan's nightmares about boy-swallowing snakes, Dashiell's nighttime forays downstairs to play with remote controls, and Mason's frequent wakenings. So even ho-hum marital hookups weren't as common as they had been. On those exceptional nights when I still had enough energy to feel a tingle of desire, Jonah was usually too wiped from his ten-hour day of rhinoplasties, rhytidectomies, mentoplasties, genioplasties, office hours, and worrying about what the economy was doing to elective surgery to want to leap into bed for anything more than sleep.

Even though I was clueless about what my husband was doing when he was actually doing it (though now I can picture

Jonah stepping onto the leopard-print carpet of Dorinda's front hall, his milk-chocolate-brown eyes widening at the awesome display of lightly freckled breasts—which of course he would know weren't implants—that rose from the scoop neck of her clingy red tank dress), I do remember sighing once or twice over how Jonah's and my private time lacked . . . something.

Fire. That's what was lacking. I knew I—we—had to figure out some way to cut down the noise in our lives so we could once again feel desire. Otherwise? There could be trouble down the road.

Not that I didn't trust him. Jonah was a one-woman man. A lot of it was that he had an actual moral code. Not just the predictable DON'T SHOPLIFT AT BERGDORF'S MEN'S STORE. Seriously, how many super-busy, successful guys in their thirties were there who (like Jonah) absolutely refused to weasel out of jury duty because they believed it was a citizen's obligation to serve?

Also, Jonah was monogamous by nature, even though I hate the word "monogamous." It always brings to mind a nature movie from eighth grade about a mongoose that had dried-out red fur and brown eyes. Just as I was thinking, *Oh my God, it looks like the Disney version of my mother!* the mongoose gave a gut-grinding shriek and *whomp!* It jumped on a snake and ripped it apart in the most brutal, revolting way.

Okay, forget mongoose and monogamous. Jonah always had one girlfriend at a time. We met standing on line in a drugstore when he was a senior at Yale. I was a freshman in the landscape architecture program at the University of Connecticut at Storrs but was in New Haven for a party and had forgotten lip gloss. The weekend before, he'd broken up with a music major named Leigh who played the harp. That we actually met, going to schools sixty-five miles apart, was a miracle. Right from the get-go, I became the sole woman in his life. I knew that not only in my head but in my heart.

And in the years that followed? At medical school, lots of the women students were drawn to him. At five feet eight, Jonah couldn't qualify as a big hunk, but he was a fabulous package. He looked strong with that squared jaw you see on cowboy-booted politicians from the West who make shitty remarks about immigrants, which of course he never would. Plus, he was physically strong, with a muscled triangle of a body. And the amazing thing was, even though Jonah was truly hot in his non-tall way and had that grown-up-rich-in-Manhattan air of self-possession, he gave off waves of decency. So his female classmates, the nurses, they were into him. But he had me. He never even noticed them. Okay, he knew he was way up there on lots of women's Ten Most Wanted, which couldn't have hurt his ego. But my husband was true by nature.

However, a girl can't be too careful. Since I wanted Jonah more than I wanted to be a landscape architect (which was a good thing, because with the department's math and science requirements, my first semester wasn't a winner), I quit UConn five minutes after he proposed. There I was, eighteen, but I knew it was the real thing. So I moved in with him in New Haven. At the time I was so in love—and so overjoyed at never again having to deal with Intro to Botany or Problem Solving—that dropping landscape architecture seemed all pros and no cons.

I transferred to Southern Connecticut State in New Haven as an art major and wound up with a concentration in jewelry design, an academic area that evoked double blinks from Jonah's friends at Yale (as in *Could I have heard her right?*) followed by overenthusiastic comments of the "That sounds sooo interesting!" variety.

Much later, it hit me how sad it was, my tossing off my life's dream with so little thought. From the time of my third-grade class trip to the Brooklyn Botanic Garden, when I gaped at the thousands of roses covering arches and climbing lattices, the bushes laid out in a plan that had to one-up the Garden of Eden,

and inhaled the mingling of roses and sweet June air, I understood flowers were somehow my ticket to a world of beauty.
Those scents transformed me from a shy kid into an eight-year-
old live wire: "Hey, lady!" I hollered to the guide. "What do you
call someone who thinks all this up?"

"A landscape architect."

Strange, but until I talked to my guidance counselor in my
senior year at Madison, I never told anybody this was what I
wanted. No big secret; I just never mentioned it. The librarians
knew, because two or three days a week, I walked straight from
school to sit at a long table and look at giant landscape books.
When I got a little older, I took the subway to the garden itself or
to the main branch of the Brooklyn Public Library. The librar-
ian in the Arts and Music section there, a guy with a face like a
Cabbage Patch doll's, would always ask, "What do you want to
look at today, garden girl?"

Though I did turn out to be a quitter, landscape architecture-
wise, I wasn't a loser. First of all, I snagged Jonah. I got my BA
in art from Southern. Also, from the get-go in New Haven, I
proved I wasn't going to become one of those burdensome, useless doctors' wives. I moved my things into Jonah's apartment
on a Saturday while he fielded hysterical calls from his parents.
By late Monday afternoon I had landed a late-afternoon/week-
end design job at the crème de la crème of central Connecticut
florists by whipping up a showstopping arrangement of white
flowers in milk, cream, and yogurt containers.

Why am I babbling on like this? Obviously, I don't want to
deal with the story I need to tell. But also because I never bought
that business about the shortest distance between two points is a
straight line. What's so great about short? Too often it's the easy
way out. Plus, a straight line is minimalist, and my work is all
about embellishment. Any jerk can stick a bunch of thistle into
an old mayonnaise jar, but what will people's reaction be? *Why
couldn't that thistle-pulling bitch leave the environment alone?*

But I take the identical thistle and jar, grab a few leaves or blades of grass, and voilà! create an arrangement that makes those same people sigh and say, *Exquisite. Makes you really appreciate nature. And so simple.* It really wasn't simple, but if your design shouts, *Hey, look how brilliant I am,* it's not much of a design.

Anyway, after Jonah graduated from college and then finished Yale med school, we moved on from New Haven. With time ticking away like that, a lot of men who marry young start thinking, *Do-over!* Not Jonah. Even after ten years of marriage (along with two failed attempts at in vitro), when some other deeply attractive senior resident in plastic surgery at Mount Sinai might have dropped a starter wife for a more fertile number two (maybe one from a Manhattan family even richer and more connected than the Gerstens, one who could push his practice), Jonah stayed in love with me. Never once, in word or deed, did he communicate, *It's not my fault you can't conceive.*

Once we were settled back in New York, I began realizing my chosen career shouldn't have been chosen by me. I did not love jewelry design: Finding brilliant new ways to display pyrope and tsavorite garnets in Christmas earrings wasn't a thrill. Living in Manhattan made me want to work with something real, and I yearned for the smell and feel of flowers.

So I wound up with a design job at Bouquet, which billed itself as "Manhattan's finest fleuriste." While I was still finding myself, Jonah was already a success, and not just in the OR. He was surrounded by enamored patients. Housewives and advertising executives, beauties and battle-axes. So many had crushes on him. They would have given anything for a taste of his toned pecs, his status, his obvious decency. Except those women only got what they paid for—a first-rate surgeon and a caring doctor. Not that I was complacent. Throughout our marriage, I saw what happened to other doctors' wives as well as to some of our neighbors when we moved to the North Shore of Long Island. I understood: Marriage is always a work in progress.

On that particular night, I was too wiped to be inventive about how to turn up the romantic heat. In fact, I was too wiped to do anything. So instead of calling Andrea to discuss what seasonal berries would be right for Polly Kimmel, who wanted ikebana arrangements for her daughter's bat mitzvah, or exfoliating my heels, or reading *The Idiot* for my book club because Marcia Riklis had said, "Enough with the chick lit," I flopped onto our Louis XV–style marriage bed without my usual satisfied glance at its noble mahogany headboard and footboard with their carvings of baskets of flowers and garlands of leaves. Almost instantly, I fell into an all-too-rare deep, healing sleep. Sure, some internal ear listened for any sound from the boys' rooms, but one thing I'm certain of: I would have been deaf to the soft tread of Jonah's footsteps as he climbed the stairs.

If he had.

Chapter Two

"What?" I mumbled about ten hours later. I didn't want to exchange the pleasure of French lavender sprayed on my pillowcase for the daily blast of triplet morning breath, which for some reason reminded me of the cheap bottled salad dressing my mother bought, the kind with brown globules and red pepper flecks suspended in a mucous-like vinaigrette. The boys were fraternal, not identical, triplets. Yet not only did they smell alike, they also had that multiple-birth juju, sharing some magical connection, like their triplet alarm clock that rang only for the three of them at the same instant each day, right before five-thirty.

Jonah always said if he'd known about the five-thirty business, he wouldn't have agreed to get them big-boy beds for their third birthdays. But he knew we really didn't have any choice. Dash and Evan had inherited my height and all three of them had variations on Jonah's solid musculature. If we hadn't gotten the beds, we'd have had to deal with three little King Kongs breaking through the bars of their cribs or climbing over the rails.

That morning, like every other, the boys raced toward our

bedroom. Outside our open door, as usual, they merged into a single wild-haired, twelve-limbed creature that climbed up Jonah's side of the bed. The game never changed: He would grab them one by one and bench-press them up from his chest to arm's length. Then there would be the usual breathless laughter and shrieks of "Daddy, Daddy, I'm flying!" As he finished with each one, he'd set him down between us.

So I knew that within a minute, Evan, Dash, and Mason would be climbing all over me, wild from their high flying, to yell into my ear: "Cocoa Krispies!" "My Band-Aid came off! I need a new one!" "Put on *Rescue Heroes* now!" When I wouldn't respond, one of them, usually Mason, would remember there was a concept called politeness and scream, "Please!" which would bring forth an earsplitting chorus.

Except that morning they woke me with something completely different: a quiet question. "Where's Daddy?" My mind started to reply, *Probably downstairs getting a cup of coffee,* but before the words made it to my mouth, I turned my head.

The white duvet over Jonah's side of the bed was like a pre-dawn snowfall, immaculate. The sham on his pillow with its subtle off-white monogram, SGJ, was pristine. The hideous plastic digital clock with its cracked red and gray Camp Chipinaw medallion that he insisted on keeping on the hand-tooled leather top of his English Centennial nightstand read 5:28.

"Where's Daddy?"

"Where's Daddy?"

My gut must have understood something was terribly wrong before I did, because I reacted so primitively. My eyes darted across the white linen field, and an instant later, I took the same path. Like a snake with prey in sight, I slithered over the undisturbed duvet at amazing speed and grabbed the phone on Jonah's side of the bed. The optimist in me took over. I pressed it to my ear, ready for the beep of a voice-mail signal. I even shushed the children so I could key in our password and hear Jonah's message. Yet when all I heard was the standard steady dial tone, some small, shadowed thing inside me was not surprised.

"Where's Daddy?"

Say anything, I commanded myself. Don't let them see you panic. Because there's no reason for panic yet. Cause for discomfort? Yes. Fear? Of course. But say something Mommyish. Lighthearted or at least reassuring, like "Daddy had to—" The sentence would not finish itself in my head, much less emerge. I vaulted out of bed and ran toward the bathroom. The boys followed, calling out, "Mommy?" With each step, each second without a response, their voices rose.

As I ran, I tried to think what could have happened to Jonah. A freak accident? Maybe last night, when I'd poured my Dramatic Radiance TRF cream into my hand, a tiny blob had dropped on the floor. When he'd gone in there as I slept, he'd slipped on the blob and cracked his head against the white onyx counter! The image was so vivid: him on his back on the Carrara marble floor, eyes closed. No, wait. Eyes open, blinking, because even though he had been unconscious the whole night, he was now coming to. Aside from a slight headache and an ugly red bump on his left temple, he was all right! In my mind I was kneeling beside him, crying out, "Oh Jonah, oh God, oh my God," then calming myself so I could turn to the boys and say, "See? Daddy's fine."

Except Jonah wasn't there. My mind went blank because fright took over and pushed everything else out. It got hold of my body, too. All I felt was that scary internal vibration from nonstop adrenaline, like a running engine that couldn't be turned off.

I braced my hands on the strip of countertop in front of the sink. My back was turned to the boys. All of a sudden, some basic animal instinct for keeping the nest intact momentarily overcame my fright. It seized control, forcing me into action, if not rationality. I grabbed the Bio-Molecular firming eye serum I'd left by the faucet the night before and put it back in the medi-

cine cabinet. Then I yanked a hand towel off the rack and polished the fingerprint I'd just made on the mirror. I folded and
refolded the towel lengthwise into thirds and hung it up again.

Since Evan, Dash, and Mason rarely asked a question without each of them repeating it at least three times, I was still getting pounded with "Where's Daddy?" There was no fright in
their voices, maybe discomfort over my leap from the bed, some
concern, but mostly bright curiosity over this intriguing change
in the morning's routine.

I was about to charge over to the linen closet and get a
fresh bottle of L'Essence de Soleil liquid hand soap when
the endangered-animal-trying-to-get-control nesting instinct
exhausted itself and the terror returned. I whimpered, a high
sound in my throat. In the movies it would have built into a
shriek of pure terror, but since it was me in my bathroom, I
made myself turn and face the boys. "I'm not sure where Daddy
is." Evan, more fearful than his brothers, always on guard
against any monster beyond a closed door or inside a toy chest,
cocked his head and watched me through narrowed eyes. "Probably . . ." I threw out the word, stalling until I could come up
with something that would pacify not just Evan but me. "There
was an emergency at the hospital and he had to go there. Maybe
he was in the operating room all night. He could still be there."
The marble floor was ice that rose through my feet. I knew I
hadn't been standing there that long, but the bones of my feet
felt frozen; my ankles ached from the cold. At the same time, my
hands perspired. I wiped them on my nightgown, but the apricot
silk charmeuse wouldn't accept anything as déclassé as sweat.
"Breakfast time!" I announced in an upbeat tone. I guess I was
trying to come off confident, like one of those TV-commercial
microwaving moms whose brains lack despair neurons.

Instead of following the boys downstairs to pour out Evan's
and Mason's usual additive-rich, dye-laden cereal (for which,
truly, I did feel guilty) and hand Dash his unvarying choice, a

container of vanilla yogurt, I rushed past them, through the bedroom, down the long hall to the other side of the house, and banged on the door of our au pairs. "Ida! Ingvild!" My voice ascended to whatever pitch was one notch below hysteria. I tried to pull it down an octave. "I need both of you right away!"

I commanded myself, *Stop overreacting.* A normal woman discovering her husband had not spent the night at home wouldn't be on the brink of psychosis. She wouldn't be so sick with dread that she wanted to puke up last night's fusilli primavera: *wanted* to, as a purge from the horror poisoning her. At most, a normal wife would be frantic—*Oh my God, maybe he was in a terrible car crash!* Or super pissed off—*How stupid is he that he thinks I'll believe some stupid excuse: He got so sick from E. coli nachos at a sports bar that he passed out for eight hours?* Already I was miles beyond that. I pounded on the girls' door as if my clenched fists were racing each other. "Ida! Ingvild!"

Every other second it hit me how important it was that I didn't lose control. The boys, right behind me, would absorb my fright. I couldn't hold back: Terror was appropriate. Jonah was unfailingly dependable: the ever-responsible Dr. Gersten. A man of routine. A man of decency, too. Would he ever willingly leave me open to this kind of fright? Not in a billion years.

If there had been some horrific urban emergency that had pulled Jonah into Mount Sinai for unscheduled surgery, he'd have had someone call me. Later, right from the OR—surgical mask in place, skin hook in hand—he'd have demanded someone double-check that the call to his wife had been made. If he'd been in an accident, it would have occurred hours before, on his way home, and someone would have phoned.

Ingvild, who had plucked away her nearly invisible blond eyebrows and who, by day, replaced them with penciled circumflex accents, opened the door so fast she nearly got punched by my pounding fists. Fresh from sleep, her round, browless face showed about as much emotion as a picture drawn by one of the boys in the first year of preschool: a big circle with minuscule circle eyes and nose plus a crooked line for a mouth.

I could definitely read the alarm on her sister's face. Ida was standing a little farther back, and I felt her apprehension: *Has something awful happened? Did we do anything wrong? Is this some bizarre American holiday nobody told us about that begins with waking people before sunrise on a Tuesday in February?* The two of them wore pajama bottoms and T-shirts with the names of bands I'd never heard of.

"Maybe it's nothing," I began slowly. But then I couldn't stop my words from rushing out. "My husband didn't come home last night! It's definitely not like him to do something like that. You know him well enough to know that." The girls seemed to be getting the gist of what I was saying. They weren't sophisticated Scandinavian types, students whose English was so flawless that they comprehended every nuance, who spoke with such slight accents that they might have come from some far corner of Minnesota. Ida and Ingvild were from a small farming community near the Arctic Circle. As they stared at me—watching my eyes dart insanely from one of them to the other, at my hair, which I suppose was sticking out scarecrow-fashion—they were probably pining for the security of the old chicken coop back home. I tried to slow myself down. "I'm worried about my husband. I need to make a few calls."

Though no doubt longing to shoot *What the fuck?* glances at each other, they both managed to keep their eyes on me. I forced my shoulders into a more relaxed position, since I realized I must look like I was expecting blows from a blunt instrument. I didn't want them to think I was out of control. The two of them, at least, should stay calm so as not to communicate any more fear to the boys. "It's probably nothing," I said. "Please take the boys and give them breakfast. And then—whatever. Keep them busy downstairs."

"Okay," Ingvild said.

"Mrs. Gersten," Ida finished. They divided a lot of what they said into halves. I once told Jonah I worried the boys would assume this was some practice of multiples, and they'd wind up splitting whatever they had to say into thirds. If they went off to separate colleges, they wouldn't be able to complete a sentence until Thanksgiving vacation.

The triplets were eyeing me, probably hoping what they feared—Mommy thought something *bad* was happening— wasn't true. They wanted Mommy to be okay and everything to be wonderful. I flashed them my razzle-dazzle smile, the one I employed at medical conventions. It always worked.

Except Evan saw through it. His Mommy radar was picking up bleeps of phoniness. Now he would be agitated all day. When the girls took them all down to the kitchen, he'd still be so rattled by the mere fact of my falseness that he'd puke up his breakfast. That would set off a chain reaction: Mason would gag at the pink and yellow blobs of Froot Loops on the polyurethaned bamboo kitchen floor, then Dash would have to display how tough he was by mimicking Mason's retching sounds. Evan would vomit again, this time from overstimulation.

The five of them headed to the stairs. Ida, who had the crowd-control instincts of a collie herding sheep, rushed ahead so she could set the pace of the boys. Ingvild descended slowly, not holding the banister, like a bride making her entrance. Racing back toward the bedroom, I fell down flat as my nightgown slid around my legs and hobbled me. I managed to push myself up to my knees but couldn't catch my breath to take in enough air and propel myself to a standing position. Alone, I was hit again with panic. Where could Jonah possibly be? I was no longer befuddled from sleep, but my fear so overwhelmed me that I could barely manage to get up off the floor. Thinking things through was beyond me.

When my feet left the sturdy hallway carpeting and felt the soft rug in our bedroom, I relaxed enough to let my mind escape into fantasy: *Oh! Wait! I know: Maybe our phone's ringer is off. Yes! That could definitely be it.* Maybe Jonah had an accident, and someone in an emergency room had called to tell me. Not wanting to leave a frightening message, that nurse had left a note for the chief resident on the next shift: *Please notify wife of traumatic brain injury, bed 7. Collapsing scaffolding in front of building on Madison Avenue. (FYI his ID from Sinai/he's MD!!). Tell her he's here.* I hiked up my nightgown and hurried around the bed to the phone.

The ringer was on. To double-check, I raced back to my side of the bed and grabbed my BlackBerry from my nightstand. My hands were trembling so uncontrollably, it took me a couple of tries to press the speed dial, H for home. As our phone shrilled its first ring, I jumped, then ran back around the bed, fleetingly forgetting I had just dialed myself. *It's Jonah, and he feels absolutely terrible because he forgot*—then I glanced down and saw my cell number on the regular phone's caller ID readout.

I wanted to heave my BlackBerry across the room, hard, and create a vicious bruise on the Venetian-plaster finish on the wall opposite the bed. But my shaking hands decided to obey some barely conscious command from my brain: I brought up Recent Calls on the little screen of the phone. Hope lived under a second. My last incoming call had come at 6:47 P.M. the night before: Aurora Hartman saying, "It would be a major blessing for the community if you'd co-chair the Trike-a-thon event for Tuttle Farm nursery school, because this could be a huge, huge fund-raiser for Tuttle, and you do *everything* with such style, and oh my God, your energy—I'm always in awe—and, Susie, this is our chance to make a major difference in our kids' lives."

What had sounded so comfortably familiar the night before—Aurora failing to be charming yet again—now, because of its ordinariness, felt like a smack in the face. My heart couldn't keep up with its own pounding; it slammed against my chest wall so hard . . . how could it not explode? I pictured pieces of cardiac muscle pierced on the shards of my shattered ribs.

Jonah hadn't come home the night before. He hadn't reached out to me. Therefore, something unthinkable had happened. Absolutely. Sure, I could imagine him walking in the door and running upstairs shouting, "Susie, Susie, you're not going to believe what happened to me!" But it was getting harder each minute to take off on any flight into fantasy.

My husband was missing. Then I thought, *Missing? If I'm lucky.*

Chapter Three

✂ ──

I sat on the edge of the mattress. Instead of doing what I meant to—covering my face and sobbing—I started sliding and almost landed on my ass. My nightgown again, and the perils of the good life: Everything was so smooth, there was hardly any friction between the gown and the Egyptian cotton sheet. My bare feet saved me with an up-down, up-down step, like in one of those folk dances performed by people trailing ribbons. When at last I got steady, I was panting, almost gasping, from the effort. This was crazy. I was strong, fit, well coordinated if not brilliantly athletic.

Except the bottom had dropped out of my life. Ninety-nine percent of me believed that. But that other one percent was almost afraid to call Jonah's cell: He would answer with his cold, busy voice: "For God's sake, Susie, there's an emergency here! Dammit, don't you think if I had a free second—if anyone here had a free second—you'd have gotten a call?"

I called anyway. Three rings and then "This is Dr. Gersten. I can't answer the phone right now. To leave a message, please wait for the tone. If this is an emergency, please press the number five and the pound key."

"Jonah, sweetheart, I know something's happened—your not coming home at all last night—and I'm terribly worried. Please call me as soon as you can, or have someone call me to let me know how you are. I love you." Right then it hit me. Maybe something had happened in the city during the night and I didn't know about it yet. I rushed for the remote. But my hands started shaking again, so it took four tries to turn on the TV. I didn't care whether it would bring terror or relief. I just needed to know what was out there. That was what I'd done for months after 9/11, turning on the TV every few hours, ready for the worst but hoping for the sight of Nothing Catastrophic. I'd longed for boring weather forecasters standing before maps, McDonald's commercials. And that was exactly what I got now: normality as presented by News Channel 4. Darlene Rodriguez was asking Michael Gargiulo if he knew why people used to eat oysters only in months that had an R in them. The sports guy glanced up at Darlene and Michael from his papers. From his grin, it looked like he'd been born with double the normal number of teeth; all of them gleamed with pleasure at his knowing the oyster answer.

I switched off the TV and paced back and forth on the carpet, trying for grace under pressure—or at least enough self-control so I wouldn't howl like a dying animal. I leaned against the footboard. Considering all the crap I'd read in my life, how come I'd never come across a magazine article entitled "What to Do When You Wake Up and Your Husband Isn't There"? It would have had a bullet-pointed sidebar of suggestions that could flash into my head.

The only information I could imagine in such a sidebar was "Phone police." No, that probably wasn't right. I remembered a TV show on which the wife called the cops and the guy on the phone asked, "How long has he been missing?" When she said, "Well, he didn't come home last night," the cop told her, "Sorry. We can't take any action until he's gone for three days. Try not to worry. Nine times out of ten, they just show up." The cop had an edge to his voice—world-weary, snide—as if he were picturing a staggering-drunk husband, or one with the lousy luck to fall asleep after having sex with his bimbo girlfriend.

I walked across the bedroom toward the window that faced the front and sat in Jonah's favorite chair in the world, a Regency bergère with gilded wood arms and legs. It was upholstered in creamy silk with a ribbon motif. When I'd spotted the bergère at an auction house, an embarrassingly loud "Ooh!" had escaped me. It was a beauty, fit for British royalty—and okay, suburban Jewish doctors, too.

Because I wasn't the only one blown away by its beauty; Jonah had wanted the chair way more than I did. He'd sat on it and noted in his objective clinician's tone that it wasn't comfortable. You didn't see it, but you could feel its back angled in a bizarre way. Instead of sitting straight, you felt pitched slightly forward, as if you were examining your knees. But he added in his deeper-than-usual, I've-got-a-refined-aesthetic-sensibility voice, "It's a splendid piece." Also a decent investment. But there was more: I could feel the chair's power over him. It made him feel not just well-off—*Hey, I can afford this exquisite objet*— but incredibly refined. If George the Whatever had needed a court plastic surgeon, Jonah knew he would have been tapped. In a flash of marital ESP, I caught all this in under a second. We bid. We bought. For both of us, sitting in that chair always made us feel elegant and rich. Protected, too: *We've made it. We're upper-class, and therefore things go the way we wish them to go.*

Even in that instant, petrified that life was about to give me the cosmic smack in the face that would make every woman on Long Island tell her best friend, "Thank God I'm not Susie Gersten," I knew if I were sitting in a repro Regency covered in polyester damask, I would feel worse.

A second later, as I glanced back at my cell phone, the chair vanished from my head. I got up and called information. When the computer said, "City and state, please," I told it, "New York, New York," then enunciated "Donald Finsterwald" even while knowing the computer wouldn't get it, having obviously been programmed not to comprehend New York accents by some hostile Southern Baptist; except for twice in my entire life, I'd always had to wait for an operator.

Even though it was not yet six in the morning, Donald Finsterwald, the administrator of Jonah's plastic surgery practice, sounded not just alert but primed, up on the toes of his orthopedic loafers, ready and eager to handle the day's first crisis. "Hello!" His extreme loyalty to Manhattan Aesthetics always creeped me out because it resembled patriotism more than simple dedication to work. Jonah said I didn't have an organization mind-set, that every decent-sized office needed a Donald.

"Hi, Donald. Susie Gersten. Sorry to call so early." My voice came out squeaky; plus, I was still breathless. I tried calming myself by taking a Lamaze breath through my nose and exhaling it through pursed lips as silently as I could so he wouldn't think, *Partner's wife breathing hysterically. Watch what you say!* "I'm concerned . . . I am worried about . . . Jonah didn't come home last night. I didn't get any messages from him."

"Oh, I'm sure—" He always strung out his vowels—"Ooooh, Iiii'm suuure"—so even in the best of times, it took practically a week till he got out a sentence. Also, he had one of those unisex voices, so nearly every time he called, if he asked for Dr. Gersten and didn't say, "Hi, Mrs. Gersten, it's Donald," I'd wonder if it was a patient with a question about her new chin implant who'd managed to get Jonah's home number, or the Irish dermatologist who always sat at the Manhattan Aesthetics table at any Mount Sinai fund-raising gala.

I said, "Listen, Donald, something is really wrong. Jonah doesn't not come home. And before you think—"

"Mrs. Gersten, I would never think—"

"I know. Of course you wouldn't." Truthfully, I had no idea

what he would think. Despite his almost pathetic eagerness to please, Donald Finsterwald had always repulsed me. I know I was being unfair, but I couldn't help it. I saw him as (like antimatter and the Antichrist) the Anti-style, a man who always picked the most heinous clothes and accessories and wore them with total seriousness. What would make someone have his thick prescription lenses stuck into narrow black frames that made him look like he was Peeping Tom checking out the world? Why would he wear strangulating turtlenecks that pushed up his double chin until it hung like a feed bag? Donald's inner life—he must have one, since everyone was supposed to—was a mystery. "Sorry. Forgive my manners," I apologized. "I'm so beside myself, Donald. In all the years we've been married, Jonah's never not come home. I mean, if he's going to be over a half hour or forty-five minutes late, he calls. Or has someone call."

"Don't I know it," he said. "There have been a fair number of times I got word from Dr. Gersten, 'Have someone call my wife.' The very moment I get an order like that, it's carried out."

"Jonah tells me about the great job you're doing," I said. "And I know if you'd heard from him, you'd call me immediately. What I'm wondering, though, is if you heard . . ." The phone was in my right hand; I used my left to massage my temples with my thumb and middle finger. "Have there been any calls from the police? Or from the office's alarm company? Maybe a hospital? I mean, not about one of his patients but about something happening to Jonah?"

"No. Of course not. I would have called you immediately, Mrs. Gersten."

"I know, but I just wanted to be sure you weren't, whatever, protecting me or waiting until, like, around seven o'clock, before calling me or Dr. Noakes or Dr. Jiménez." Jonah's partners, Gilbert John Noakes and Layne Jiménez, would have called me right away if they'd heard anything.

"Oh no, no. I wouldn't have waited to get in touch."

"Okay, fine. I just wanted to be sure before I started making any other calls."

"Oh. Who were you thinking of calling? I mean, could it be better to wait, it being so early? Dr. Gersten, maybe if he had some sort of emergency at Sinai, he might have gone to one of those rooms where residents can rest, because he wouldn't want to disturb you at this hour."

I was on the verge of saying, "Oh no, he knows I'd be up because the boys always wake us at five-thirty." Then I realized Donald was buying time so he could figure out if Jonah's not coming home could be a potential catastrophe for the practice. Was Jonah sick or dead or God knows what? Or was his absence the result of some marital misunderstanding that could end in either tears and kisses ("Oh, sweetie, I was so worried!") or else in a gargantuan retainer to a matrimonial lawyer? Maybe Donald was stalling so he could call Gilbert John Noakes, the practice's senior partner, and get some guidance on dealing with a hysterical wife.

Except I wasn't hysterical. In talking with Donald Finsterwald, I had concentrated on sounding calm. Calm was good, wasn't it? Under normal circumstances, I came across like a calm person. Pleasant, friendly. An excellent doctor's wife, with just enough sex and sparkle to keep me out of the ranks of Xanaxed zombie ladies or sugarplum spouses who smiled in lieu of talking. I had my own career, but I didn't bore the crap out of people by carrying on as if floral design were the answer to the world's prayers.

And just now with Donald, I'd been courteous, balanced. Totally nonhysterical. Good, I'd paid my dues to Manhattan Aesthetics. So instead of agreeing to wait before making any calls, or telling Donald that I appreciated his input and would give it the serious consideration it deserved, I dropped the nice and snapped, "I've got to go."

Then I hung up and called the police.

Chapter Four

It wasn't only that I had what in the flower business is called "a great nose," a highly sensitive sense of smell: Anyone with two nostrils would instantly know that Detective Sergeant Timothy Coleman's body odor was over-the-top. And his generous application of synthetic lime cologne did nothing to camouflage it.

"Please excuse me, Mrs. Gersten," Nassau County's finest said after he cleared his throat. His manners were exquisite, as if to apologize for his pungency. Maybe as a child he'd been beaten and forced to memorize *Emily Post's Etiquette;* his politeness was as aggressive as his BO. "Are you sure it's all right if I sit down?"

"Of course," I said, fast as I could. "Please." I couldn't wait to get to the couch. The chemical reaction of his smell added to my ever escalating fear was so explosive that—*ka-boom!*—I got dizzy two seconds after I'd opened the door for him. Now I almost dove onto the couch so I wouldn't risk swooning into it.

"Thank you *so* much," he said.

We had already spent twenty minutes talking at the kitchen table, but then my housekeeper had arrived, toting a bag of her own microfiber cloths. Driven as Bernadine was by her obsessive-compulsive need to empty the dishwasher before she took off her coat, the detective and I couldn't stay in the kitchen. However, bringing Coleman into the living room hadn't changed the environment. He stank. And his excessive courtesy was simultaneously exhausting me and making me a nervous wreck. *What's his game? What does he want from me?*

"The reason I'm asking for all this information now, ma'am, is so I don't need to keep having to come back to you for more. I hope you understand and can bear with me."

"Of course. I appreciate . . ." Besides the dizziness, my mind kept veering off in a hundred directions. It didn't seem like I'd offered any helpful information about Jonah that Detective Sergeant Coleman could use. Not one single "Good, I see, right" had escaped his lips. So I felt doubly pressured to make a positive impression. I wanted him to think I was a fine, deserving person so he'd work day and night to find my husband. But he wouldn't think I was so fine if I went berserk, which I felt I could do at any second. If I started screeching hysterically—"I want my husband! I want my husband!"—while grabbing the detective's lapels and shaking him, he would get sidetracked. Maybe he'd decide I was one of those "She seemed so nice" wives who, three days before her period, axes her husband and shoves him into a calico-covered Container Store box with the croquet set and pool toys—then saunters back to the kitchen to make zucchini bread.

The tension was too much. Also, from the minute I opened the door, I was afraid he'd be hostile because of my height. Tall women get to some short guys, and not in a good way. And Coleman was short, like he'd been zoomed down to 75 percent. With me at five feet nine inches, I didn't want him to feel I was the type who didn't take mini-men seriously, even though he'd never see the five-five he probably lied about on his driver's license. I wasn't hung up on height. Jonah was shorter, but not dollhousey like Coleman. Jonah was solid and strong.

Then I got upset with myself: *It's not about you or Detective Sergeant Smell-o-rama. It's about Jonah.* I hung my head with shame—not a good idea, because the sudden shift of position made me want to throw up.

Coleman, perched on the edge of the seat of a carved Sri Lankan chair, kept the questions coming. I suppose I answered. Images kept flashing inside my head and overpowered any thought: Jonah writhing on the floor in some obscure men's room at Mount Sinai, delirious with fever from a superbug he'd caught in the hospital. Jonah carjacked, bound and gagged in the black, near airless trunk of his BMW.

"I hope you don't mind my asking," Detective Sergeant Coleman said, "but has Dr. Gersten ever, uh, not shown up before? Not come home?"

"Never. Jonah is completely reliable. I can always count on . . ." The tears I'd held back in the kitchen started to spill. I wasn't actually crying; my eyes just became full and overflowed, like a stopped-up sink. "He's so responsible." It came out as a froggy sound because I was choked up. "That's why I think it must be something bad, because . . ." The tears cascaded down my cheeks. Coleman sat there. Instead of averting his eyes, he watched. A tiny spiral-bound notepad rested on his knee. Its size seemed grossly inadequate for recording the huge facts of Jonah's vanishing.

Finally, I found the energy to propel myself up. "Excuse me," I said. I rushed into the guest bathroom, blew my nose, wiped my eyes.

When I returned to the living room, Coleman was still at the edge of his chair. "I didn't know whether to call the police this soon," I told him. "I remember from movies when detectives say they have to wait forty-eight hours or three days until they can look into a matter."

"Oh no, ma'am. If someone who keeps a regular pattern suddenly doesn't show up, we should know about it. A lot of times the local precinct only sends in regular officers to take the initial report, like if it's a teenager who's probably with a friend, or if it's someone with a history of instability. The next day, if that sort of person is still unaccounted for, the department follows up with a detective. But with someone like Dr. Gersten, what with his position in the community, well, you know."

"Right."

"Now, when we were in the kitchen, you mentioned your last conversation with your husband was yesterday afternoon."

"Yes."

"Can you recall what each of you said in that conversation, ma'am?" I was examining a medallion of roses and laurel leaves on the needlepoint rug. He repeated "Ma'am?" louder, which made me jump.

"I don't know. Let me think. It was a regular late-afternoon phone call. Jonah still had a couple of post-op patients to see. Then he had some odds and ends to do in the city before he came home."

"Did he happen to say what they were, ma'am?"

"The only thing he mentioned was maybe going to Tod's. It's about twenty blocks downtown from his office. A shoe store."

"To . . . ?"

To have a martini, shmuck. "To try on a pair of shoes," I said. "Brown suede lace-up shoes. He'd seen them in the window. But he was pretty tired, so chances were he wouldn't bother."

"He said he probably wouldn't bother, or was that your sense of things?"

"He said it."

"Had he been under any special pressure lately?" I must have given him a *Duh* look because he added, "That he was tired from a more-than-usual workload? Or maybe family pressure?"

"No. I mean, he's in a great surgical practice. Well, it's been less than stellar lately, the economy being what it is, but they're doing better than most of their colleagues. So far, so good." Coleman blinked. I noticed he had no sign of beard, as if he used Nair instead of a razor. Imagining stroking a hairless, almost poreless man's cheek was so repulsive that I forgot I was in the middle of answering his question. When Coleman uncocked his head and looked into my eyes straight-on, I quickly said, "Sorry, I lost my train of thought."

"You were saying your husband wanted to build up his practice," he said.

"Right," I said. Coleman wiped the tip of his pen on the pad. He seemed ready to jot down some significant detail. "A lot of his business comes from referrals from other doctors, so he needs to stay active in the medical community. Like if a woman asks a doctor she knows, 'Can you recommend someone for . . . ?'" I patted the underside of my chin with the back of my hand to demonstrate. "Jonah says if that doctor has run into him in the last week or two, he's likely to say, 'Jonah Gersten. Definitely. He's first-rate.' Which he truly is. If you're not well trained and gifted, no one's going to risk recommending you. But Jonah knows being out and about is important, too. And he's big on PR. If he's quoted somewhere, like in O or *Allure*, he'll get calls for the next few months. All that takes time and planning. Plus being a surgeon, he has to keep up professionally. So his hours are incredible. And since the triplets were born—"

"They're how old again?"

"Four. They're usually asleep when he gets home. They go to bed at seven. We decided that instead of family dinner, we'd have family breakfast. But I know Jonah wishes he could have more time with them, not just mornings and weekends. I guess you could call that pressure, too."

"What about financial pressure, ma'am?"

"We're okay." Early on in my marriage, I'd overheard my mother-in-law telling one of her friends that it was très LMC— lower-middle-class, a heinous crime—to say "X is rich." "God in heaven," she said, "'rich' is so crass." She meant saying it, not being it. Anyway, within a month after moving from New Haven to New York, I'd come to understand that "rich" was fine to describe Rembrandt's colors or a veal stock. But when it came to even really big bucks, I knew to say "X does nicely." Detective Sergeant Coleman was fingering his hairless cheek, trying to figure out what my "we're okay" meant. So I added, "Jonah's making a very good living."

Coleman's fast 180 scope of the living room apparently gave him confirmation because he started nodding like a bobblehead. "You mentioned earlier he has partners in his plastic surgery practice," he said.

"Yes."

He didn't hear me because he was busy flipping through his little pad, stopping every couple of pages. Maybe he was fascinated by notes he'd made. Or he couldn't read his own writing. "I hope you don't mind my asking, but do Dr. Gersten and his partners get along?"

"Yes."

"No financial disagreements? Egos? That sort of thing?"

"They're fine," I said.

"If I might ask, how are things within your family?"

"Fine. Great. He loves the children, loves me. And vice versa."

"The two girls you say are living here?"

"Our au pairs," I said. His lids fluttered. "Mother's helpers. They're here from Norway." More flutters. "They're all legal and everything. They have valid work permits and—"

"Dr. Gersten has no issues with them, ma'am?" He wrote something on his pad.

The dizziness that had eased sneaked back, maybe because I could almost hear Coleman thinking, *Two Scandinavian girls. Blondes, I bet.* True, they were blondes. But Ida and Ingvild bore such a resemblance to Miss Piggy that I was waiting for their visas to expire before buying the DVD of *The Muppets Take*

Manhattan for the boys. "No issues at all. Jonah thinks they're great with the boys. Listen, my husband is, you know, easygoing. Friendly but polite. Respectful." He underlined whatever he had just written.

"Ma'am?" he asked.

"Yes?" I had to raise my head slightly to look at him. Dizzy again, like the floor had switched places with the ceiling.

"When we're called in on a case, we're put in the position of having to ask questions that may seem, you know, not polite. But we have to ask them anyway."

"I understand." He was going to ask me if Jonah screwed around.

"So I hope you don't mind if I ask you . . . You said your husband loves you, and I'm sure he does. But some men do have a midlife-crisis thing."

"Jonah's thirty-nine. I don't know if that qualifies, but—"

"Is it possible that there is someone else—"

"I'm absolutely sure there isn't."

"Maybe a patient—"

"Jonah says any surgeon who takes up with a patient has a fifty-fifty shot at a malpractice suit, and no sex in the world is worth that."

He smiled and nodded at Jonah's remark. But what doctor wouldn't say that to reassure a suspicious wife? "What I meant to ask was if there has been any patient calling or stalking him in any way. Sometimes with doctors—"

"No. Our home number is unlisted. And he knows how to deal with patients who get emotionally dependent or pushy or a little crazy."

Coleman flipped to a clean page in his pad. He held the pen against his upper lip, just south of his nostrils, and took a deep breath, like he was working on an ink-fume high. "Are Dr. Gersten's parents still alive?" he asked.

"Yes. Clive and Babs—Barbara—Gersten. They're still very

active, professionally, socially. They live in the city." I saw he wanted more. But I was so wiped from all the frantic hours I'd spent since I'd woken to "Where's Daddy?" that it was getting too much to think up more words and then push them into speech. Coleman rotated his pen near his nose a few times. Even though I was looking at my wedding ring, I could feel him gazing into my eyes. Finally, I got it together enough to answer.

"His father's a radiation oncologist in Manhattan. Clive Gersten." To look at my father-in-law, you wouldn't think he was in that field. He smiled all the time. Or at least the corners of his mouth turned up. I sometimes wondered if he'd had a stroke early in life because his personality was un-smiley. Not morose. Just bland. If he were ice cream, he wouldn't even be vanilla. But his patients adored him, clearly taking the rising corners of his mouth as either an optimistic smile or a compassionate one, depending on their diagnosis.

"Oncologist is cancer, right?"

"Right. Jonah's mother is marketing director of Gigi de Lavallade Cosmetics." Babs Gersten was the person who, back in the eighties, had convinced millions of white women all over the world that they should wear brown lipstick and bronze blush. In the nineties she got millions of black women converted to maroon cheeks, not red. Currently, she was working on a major campaign to get Asian women out of rose-tinged foundation, to open themselves up to the untapped potential—the actual brilliance!—of much maligned yellow.

"Does your husband get along with his folks?"

"Yes."

"Does he see a lot of them?"

"We usually see them every couple of weeks. They have a place in Water Mill, in the Hamptons. They sometimes stop here on their way out or back. It's easier that way. Having the triplets running around their apartment is a little much for my in-laws. They collect pre-Columbian art. Lots of clay figurines. We do visit them at the beach, but even that's pretty chaotic if the weather's not good."

Coleman wrote what appeared to be a long sentence in his pad, then turned back a page and made what looked like three dots. "Any other children? Your husband, I mean. Does he have any brothers or sisters?"

"He has a younger brother. He's a casting director."

"Do they get along?"

"Jonah and Theo?" His brow furrowed, which was what usually happened when people first heard it, because it sounds more like a lisp and diphthong than an actual name. Whenever I had to introduce him, I fought the urge to say "Thith ith Theo." "T-h-e-o," I spelled. "They talk on the phone . . . I guess about once a week. Whenever they see each other, they have a good time. It's a solid relationship."

He closed his pad and stuck it in the outside pocket of his jacket. "Would you mind taking me for a look around?" he asked as he stood.

"Of course. I mean, I'll be glad to show you." Coleman didn't seem the house-and-garden type. I assumed he had some sort of checklist he needed to go through in a missing-person case. Suddenly, those words, "missing person," hit home. They ricocheted around my brain and grew more powerful with each repetition as they brought home the reality: I not only didn't know where Jonah was, I couldn't even guess.

Now that Coleman was no longer seated, some hostess gene made me pop up from the couch. Not the best idea. I swayed sideways and made a stupid grabbing gesture with each hand as I tried to get hold of something to steady me. There was only air. It was scary, not being able to distinguish between up and down.

He rushed over and braced my elbows until he was sure I could stand perpendicular to the floor. We spoke at the same time: "Are you okay?" "Sorry, I got dizzy."

That was followed by a couple of eternal seconds of silence.

Coleman moved himself out of the narrow space between couch and coffee table with the klutzy sidestep slide of someone who should not bother trying tennis. "Are you okay to take me around the house?" he asked.

"Yes. It'll be fine."

I'd sent the boys off to preschool to get them out of the way. Ida and Ingvild would hang out there in the mommies' room in case of—whatever.

So it was just the two of us, me and Detective Sergeant Coleman. The dizziness was gone, but I definitely didn't feel normal. Every few minutes my heart banged with an almost audible boom. *But listen,* I told myself, *considering everything, I'm functioning.* Leading him to the basement, then through all the rooms on the first floor, I was at least reassured I could control myself sufficiently to go through the motions.

Only after we climbed the stairs and he opened the linen closet outside our bedroom did I comprehend that he wasn't just hunting for some subtle clue to Jonah's whereabouts. When Coleman had peered in cabinets and armoires and opened the tops of the benches that ran across one wall in the basement playroom, he'd been searching for Jonah's dead body.

"Do you ever find the person somebody says is missing right there, in the house?" I asked. "Or do you just find clues?"

"Sometimes an individual writes a note," Coleman said carefully. "He's in a rush and winds up leaving it in the weirdest place." He must have decided I was thinking, *Note? Does he mean suicide note?* Not wanting me to tilt and maybe pass out, he said real fast, "'Dear So-and-so, I have to go to . . . whatever, someplace . . . for a few days' and so forth." I noticed he wasn't answering my question about discovering the missing person right there at home.

We went through Jonah's closet and then the bedroom. Other than gaping at the lineup of Jonah's tassel loafers—which admittedly was a little excessive, the same shoe over and over,

as if some weird form of asexual reproduction were going on—
Coleman didn't seem to find anything worth noting. In the bedroom, he didn't cringe at the plastic Camp Chipinaw clock on
Jonah's nightstand the way I did, and completely ignored the
book lying beside it, *Einstein: His Life and Universe,* not even
saying something like "Hey, Dr. Gersten really must be a genius
to be reading about a genius." He didn't pick it up and shake it
the way detectives do on TV—where paper falls out that's inevitably a clue. So I picked up the book and pretended to be pag-
ing through it. Nothing fell out because Jonah didn't even use a
bookmark, just bent down pages. He was up to page 104. I held
it against my chest, closed my eyes, and told myself, *He's going
to get to finish this book,* even though I dreaded he wouldn't. But
I didn't say that out loud because I wasn't the plucky-heroine
type. As I was laying it down again, I quickly leafed through it.
Nothing: just his name, written in his graceful, non-doctorish
script, and his usual underlinings and margin notes, as if he'd
never gotten out of Yale. Inside the back cover, he'd even written a shopping list: *Mach3,* his razor blades, *black shoe polish,*
and *check red cap,* probably something to do with capsules.

Then the phone rang. I knew it was Jonah's office because all
the calls from there and his answering service rang with a special
bing-bing-bing tone. A little Tinker Bell–ish, I'd told him. Now
it sounded beautiful. A burst of hope propelled me to the phone.
It wasn't until I was almost bellowing "Hello" with desperate
eagerness that it hit me it might be someone else and not Jonah
finally, finally calling to explain why—

"Susie?" Not Jonah. It was Layne. "I'm here with Gilbert
John on speakerphone."

Layne Jiménez was from New Mexico, so she had that no-
accent all-American accent television journalists have. Her tone,
though, was doctor-gentle rather than reporter-crisp. "We hate
to bother you, Susie. Donald told us about Jonah," she said.
"We kept going back and forth: Should we call, shouldn't we

call? You've got to be waiting for the phone to ring. But we're so concerned. Have you heard anything?"

I shook my head for a few seconds until the shuffle of shoes coming through their speakerphone made me realize they were nervously waiting for my response. "No. No calls." I put my hand over the mouthpiece and murmured to Detective Sergeant Coleman, "Jonah's partners."

"Susie?" Gilbert John Noakes this time. He had that gorgeous bass voice you'd expect to be singing "Ol' Man River," in his case, without the customary African-American inflection. Gilbert John had a grand accent, slightly more British than Boston. He sounded like he'd been born on some elitist island in the mid-Atlantic. His pronunciation of my name was "Syu-see?" His appearance matched his voice. Handsome, like one of those manly actors with thick white hair who played rich, potent older men on daytime soaps.

"Yes. I'm here."

"How are you holding up, dear?" he asked.

"All right."

Over the years, I'd come to believe that Gilbert John's supercilious delivery was a minor case of snobbishness made much worse by shyness—and dullness. He never had much to say about anything except the most tedious surgical matters—or in migraine-inducing detail, his latest mosaic. He made his compositions from found objects. That had the potential to be interesting, but Gilbert John didn't understand how not to be boring. Listening to him, you wanted to gasp for air. He'd go on (and on) about smashing up a souvenir plate from the 1989 Philadelphia flower show, and about how half of creating mosaics was getting the right-sized shards. Even if you were backing out of the room, he'd stay with you step for step to give you his secret for getting the proper consistency of grout. The weird thing was, in spite of his aggressive tediousness, his mosaics were fresh, even lively.

"Has either of you heard anything?" I asked. "Anything at all?"

"Not a thing," Layne managed to say. She had a catch in her gentle voice. I tried to think of something to comfort her so she wouldn't burst into tears and then feel terrible because, by crying, she'd made it harder on me. But she was able to go on. "We have the whole staff calling hospitals, but no one like Jonah has come in," she said. "You know, Susie, I've been thinking. Maybe you should call the police. Or Gilbert John says you might want to think about a private investigator. You know, if you don't want word getting around."

"Up to you entirely," Gilbert John said. "We simply want you to know we'll do anything we can if you need us."

"Absolutely," Layne said. "Whatever you want done—or not done—you only have to ask."

That instant I started second-guessing myself. Had I been stupid to call the Nassau County police when Jonah very well could be in the city? Should I have called the NYPD instead? He could be anywhere.

Maybe he would wind up being one of those vanishing husbands who turned up decades later, living a different life in some other country. Years from now, when the triplets were in high school, or later, when I was on my deathbed, we'd learn Jonah had been living as Dottore Giovanni Giordano, treating the poorest of the poor in the slums of Naples, not taking even a *lira* for his work.

Except that wasn't what happened.

Chapter Five

"I know you came here to keep yourself from staring at the phone, trying to will it into ringing," Andrea Brincker-hoff said brightly. She picked up a speck of floral foam from our worktable and flicked it into the green plastic trash can. Andrea rarely said anything non-brightly. She seemed to have modeled her personality on one of those debutantes in 1930s movies: a martini in one hand, a cigarette holder in the other, laughing in the face of doom. "Though I'm assuming you call-forwarded so it would ring here."

"So it would ring on my cell. Car, bathroom: I could be any-place and I'd be able to hear it."

"Excellent!"

I understood Andrea's over-the-top brightness on this morn-ing was an effort aimed at keeping up my spirits—though her detractors might claim she simply wasn't touched by other peo-ple's sorrow.

She headed for the coffeepot, her head swiveling slowly back and forth as she walked, searching for stray bits of stem or leaf on the concrete floor. Not that I watched her every step. I was flipping through the pocket-sized brown leather phone book I'd brought with me, the one Jonah had used until two years earlier, when he finally surrendered to a BlackBerry. I finished his A's and B's and began the C's, copying down names and numbers of anyone who might be in his life currently, people he could have seen or spoken to in the last couple of weeks.

Andrea handed me coffee in one of her L'Objet porcelain mugs. She'd chosen the Aegean-green style; its handle was twenty-four-karat gold. "If I might suggest . . ."

I listened. Andrea was thorough. While we both did the same jobs—floral design, client development, running the business— we both accepted reality and roles. She was the efficient, let's-create-a-system one. I was the more imaginative and (despite Andrea's copy of the Social Register that leaned against *Contemporary Approaches to Floral Art* on the shelf above her desk) had the more upmarket aesthetic. Not that Andrea was Miss Azalea Plant in a Green Plastic Cachepot, but she had too many musts and no-nos to be an exciting designer. She stuck to the old tired-out rules, like no bear grass or carnations ever or that heritage roses and English ivy in Grandmère's 1780 silver teapot were the ultimate word in elegance.

"Instead of writing a list," she said, "put a mark next to each name. That way you can tell at a glance who you need to call."

"Good idea," I murmured. Was it? I hadn't a clue, but she sounded authoritative. My thoughts were dark and swirling, like a tornado. The mere idea of a system was soothing.

"See? Make a dot on the left side of the entry. After you speak to that person, put a check mark on the right."

I either knew or had heard Jonah mention about half the names I'd gotten to in his phone book. That I didn't know the others wasn't particularly meaningful. Like many surgeons, my husband was meticulous to the point of being a pain, or worse. When he hung a tie on his pull-out rack, the pointy bottom of all the ties had to be at the same level. If he was in the kitchen when I was cooking and overheard me mumble to myself, "Where the hell is the dill?" he'd stare at me not just in disbelief but with displeasure, as in *How can you go through life and not have a precise place for everything?* I'd told him the need for a precise place for things was a definite plus for a guy who reconfigured faces. He had to be finicky about detail: like *Where are the sutures?* or *How many millimeters to the right do I move this nose?* And the proof was right there in his phone book. Nearly all the entries I didn't recognize had a teeny P above the name. Patient. Well, I assumed P meant patient, as Jonah's universe wasn't peopled with peony growers or philosophers.

"One more suggestion?" Andrea said. I nodded. "Drink your coffee. You need some . . . you don't want to sound so" — she combed her straight blond hair off her forehead with her fingers — "so down."

"I am down. I'm terrified."

"Susie, I know that. You know that. But if your cell rang and it was Jonah saying, 'My car went over a cliff — '"

"Where are there cliffs between Manhattan and Long Island?" I snapped.

"I'm talking in, you know, whatever that stupid fucky word people always use — something terms."

"Metaphorical terms?"

Andrea was hostile to words over three syllables. "Right," she said. "So let's assume he'll be fine. And if he is fine, you don't want him saying, 'I hear you called Dr. Schwartz' — I'm sure there's always a Dr. Schwartz — 'asking about me. Schwartz said you sounded totally down, like you'd lost all hope.' I mean, if I know Jonah, he wouldn't be thrilled."

"No. He'd be humiliated." I came close to smiling at the thought of Jonah clapping his hand to his forehead, jaw dropping, when he heard I'd called the names in his phone book. Then it hit me that he might be not embarrassed but proud I'd taken such initiative. On the other hand . . . Angry, definitely angry. *I know you must have been frightened, Susie. But call-*

ing everyone . . . God! Can I ask you one simple question? Why couldn't you have waited twenty-four hours? What the hell am I going to say to all these people?

"Humiliated?" Andrea said. She had seen Jonah's flash of temper—rage, almost—when I'd said or done something to hint that maybe he had a flaw or two. "No. He'd be pissed beyond belief. But it's not just about Jonah getting mad that you called his entire phone book sounding like the 'Before' in an antidepressant commercial. You need to get some caffeine into you so you don't sound like you mainlined Ambien."

I picked up the mug. Andrea had paid for them herself because she believed clients should know that Florabella had a profound understanding of what beautiful was. L'Objet mugs were, in her view, irrefutable proof. I'd vetoed them, telling her yes, they were gorgeous, but Bergdorf's could get four hundred thirty-two bucks for six coffee mugs from someone else, not us. But they did get it: from Andrea herself. Self-indulgence came easy for my partner, because she'd married a hedge fund. Well, technically, she'd married Hugh Morrison, whom most people called Hughie. She called him Fat Boy. I'd pointed out to her that "Fat Boy" was cruel as well as pointless; anyone seeing a three-hundred-pound guy whose ankle flab hung over his Italian driving moccasins could figure out his nickname wasn't Slim.

"You might want to start phoning the people you've marked off already, because some of them will have to call you back. Especially the doctors."

"Do you think I should leave my home phone number when I call? If I'm on my cell getting an important lead, I don't want to be interrupted by call waiting. But if the police want to reach me, or if Gilbert John or Layne hear something, I need to know right away." I set the mug on the worktable as a wave of the morning's dizziness came back. Not a tidal wave, but I pictured myself saying, "I was wondering if you'd spoken to Jonah recently . . ." to some snooty ENT guy while my cell vibrated with another incoming call and I wound up cutting off the ENT and missing the other call, which would turn out to be Jonah, and in the end all I'd have were his final inexplicable words on my voice mail: "I love you, Su—" Then silence. "And there's another problem. When I'm talking and a call comes in, I know I'm supposed to push the Send button, but half the time that doesn't work."

"Calm down," Andrea said. She jerked her head back. Apparently, I'd gone from being emphatic to yelling.

"*Why?*"

"Because you need to stop fixating on phones and think clearly." I found myself nodding slowly, like what she said was wisdom so dazzling it couldn't be absorbed all at once. "This is what you should do: Give them my cell number, okay? You'll take my phone. Don't even think of arguing with me. I want to get a new one anyway. That Vertu Rococo." I struggled. "I can't believe you haven't heard of it. It would be the Rolls-Royce of cells if the Rolls didn't suck. Listen, this makes sense for both of us. You take my cell because then I can get a new number and not tell my mother-in-law. She has me on her speed dial as A. Every time she shoves her phone into her handbag—it's as full of shit as she is—it dials me. Just don't answer any call that comes from Palm Beach."

Andrea lifted her hair with both hands and let it fall back. It covered her shoulders like a short cape made from the fur of a gleaming blond animal. An unkempt animal. Though she'd never admit it, she thought having scraggly ends was cool. She saw herself as an aristocrat and looked down on the nouveau riche as trying too hard with their pricey blunt cuts or exquisitely scissored layers.

In an era where there were (maybe) a hundred people left in New York to whom pedigree mattered, hardly anyone gave a rat's ass that one of Andrea's Brinckerhoff ancestors had come to New York (Nieuw Amsterdam then) in 1559. From the way she sneered at most of humanity, it was clear her lineage was the central fact of her existence. It offered her a reason to feel superior. It gave her (she'd decided) license to transgress any social or moral law—like a lady should have a good haircut. Like it's tasteless not to mock one's obese husband in public. Like it's seemly to refrain from committing adultery with members of your husband's family, country club, and church.

"Okay, I'll take your cell." Then I remembered to add, "Thank you."

"You're welcome." She paused. "Are you going to make those calls?"

"Now?"

"Why not now? Do you need six more months of therapy to work through your Brooklyn accent anxiety?"

I rubbed my forehead as if that would encourage an idea or two. It didn't. "It's not about that. It's that I won't know what to say if someone takes the call. I'll end up going, 'Uuuh, uuuh, I'm Jonah Gersten's wife. I don't know if you remember me, but now uuuh, uuuh.' And if I get their voice mail, do I say, 'Hate to bother you on a workday, but I'm Susie and my husband, Jonah Gersten, vanished from the face of the earth, and did you . . .'"

"Go on," Andrea said. "Did you what?"

"I don't know. Speak to him recently? Have any idea where he might be? Listen, calling people is stupid. God knows why I even thought of it. Everything was fine with Jonah. No one out there knows anything about him I don't know. He's not a secret-life kind of guy."

"You believe that."

"Yes!"

"I do, too, actually," Andrea said. She spoke so slowly that for two seconds she forgot her brightness. "But some men with a secret life really want to keep it that way—not like the assholes who leave Amex receipts on top of their dresser. Fat Boy used to do that, before he got too fat to fuck anybody but me, probably because he's afraid he'll drop dead from excitement and crush the girl and it'll make *The Financial Times.* Anyway, if Jonah wanted to keep a secret, you wouldn't know, and neither would I. And no, I don't think he has any secrets worthy of the name."

"He paid a scalper a fortune for Giants play-off tickets. But then he told me about it."

"But someone in here"—Andrea tapped his phone book with her index finger—"might know something you don't. Or it doesn't even have to be a secret. Maybe someone heard him say, 'There's a store up in Litchfield that has fabulous antique chronographs—'"

"What?"

"Those watches with all the little dials on the faces. Classics. Très popular right now. And maybe that means you should be calling hospitals in Connecticut because—"

"Do you honestly think that after a hideously long day, he'd drive up to Connecticut?"

"No. I was just making up an example."

"Jonah would never collect—"

"Susie, listen to me." She set her elbow on the table. Instead of resting her chin on her hand, like most people do, she stuck out her thumb and put the deep cleft of her chin on it: Andrea's "I'm deep in thought" pose. Finally, she said, "If you keep saying Jonah wouldn't do this or that, you're closing your mind. Am I right?" I didn't answer. "Am I being logical?"

"Yes."

"So you shouldn't decide not to listen to something that could be useful simply because it doesn't jive with your version of your husband."

"But my version is the right one." I said it in almost a whisper.

I shuffled into the small office that took up part of the space between our reception area and the workroom. Then I returned with a pen and a piece of our billing stationery. *Make it first-rate with Florabella,* it said along the bottom. When I got back, I jotted down a few talking points along with Andrea's cell number. I knew I'd be needing a script.

After a half hour, I got good at leaving voice mails and getting past secretaries and nurses by saying, "This is an urgent call about Jonah Gersten, and I need to speak with whoever now." Then I'd immediately add, softening my voice from powerful to genteel, "if that's possible." I got through right away to a fair number of the names, but by the time I began the D's, I'd learned only two things I hadn't known before. Jonah wished he'd taken clarinet instead of piano lessons as a kid. And about a month earlier, when he'd run into a friend from Yale, he'd said the biggest change with having triplets was that there never was a time he wasn't exhausted. I chewed on my knuckles for half a second as I listened to this, then got up the courage to ask, "Did he sound depressed?" Not at all. In good humor, actually, accepting perpetual fatigue as a fact of life.

Between each call, I'd close my eyes to blank out reality, but it was there anyway: I kept picturing the boys. Today would be all right, not counting the trauma I could be inflicting on them by playing down the terror I'd felt about Jonah not being in bed and them seeing through my act. Everyone said kids were so smart that even toddlers knew when their parents were faking emotion. They'd grow up not trusting me.

I worried about them in triplicate: as a threesome, as individual boys, and how each would affect the others. Closing my eyes, I got an image of Jonah and me making triplet sandwiches, snuggling the boys between us. If he didn't come back, would I have to explain those open-faced sandwiches with teeny fronds of dill they always serve at Wasp weddings, and wouldn't a Mommy canapé be fun? Would they think I was pathetic? I pictured furrowed-brow Evan growing closer with Mason, who would resume his thumb-sucking but still have enough security to give Evan a little boost, and Dashiell, who'd try to swagger through it all, being ostracized by the other two because they'd think he didn't care.

What could I do for my kids that I wasn't doing? That second, I wanted to embrace them, soothe them, though truthfully, part of me wished they could go visit Norway with Ida and Ingvild and milk reindeer until this nightmare blew over.

Except if Jonah didn't come back, it would never blow over. At that moment, I had a selfish or even depraved thought, which was: Did Jonah have enough insurance? I might even have worried that I'd have to sell the house, move to a garden apartment, and buy store-label toilet paper instead of Charmin Ultra, but then I thought, *No, my in-laws would help us out,* if only for the boys' sakes, because without them, Babs probably wouldn't care if I had to cut up *The New York Times* into four-by-four squares to keep beside the toilet, though without insurance, I wouldn't be able to afford home delivery anymore.

"Oh my God!" The words burst out of me.

"What? What is it?"

"My in-laws don't know!" I must have looked both pleading and stricken. I guessed I hoped that Andrea would respond: "Listen, your mother-in-law is not a piece of cake, and I know you work yourself up into a froth over dealing with her. So let me call her and explain what's going on."

She exclaimed, "'Oh my God' is right! Here you are, calling up everybody who knows Jonah! One of them—shit, so many doctors!—one of them could call Clive. You better call this *instant.* Which one? Him or her?"

Him, my father-in-law, was infinitely preferable. Clive wasn't nice, but on the other hand, he wasn't not nice. I'd never gotten beyond his blah-ness, but maybe that was because there was no beyond. So while no one, including his children and his wife, ever went to Clive looking for love, you could take being with him. You'd never have to fear getting worn down by high-pressure charm. Nor would you have to worry about getting hit with a Babs zinger. With my father-in-law, you never had to be on the lookout for hostility so gracefully disguised it sounded amazingly like flattery.

But with Babs, I never once said goodbye to her without feeling that some small but significant number had been deducted from the sum of my soul during the encounter. "Her," I said to Andrea. "If I don't call her, she'll think I was afraid."

Which of course I was.

Chapter Six

Babs sat on the dark red leather couch in our den, her elbows resting just above her knees, her hands veiling her eyes and cheeks. Her nails, coated with Gigi de Lavallade's Crème Caramel, precisely matched the hue of some new liver spots her dermatologist hadn't gotten to. She uncovered her face and said, "Of course you're doing everything that can be done, Susie . . ." I nodded, except she wasn't finished with the sentence. "But we're always here for you if you have any doubts. Never, ever hesitate to call on us."

Clive sat beside her looking at me, though I wasn't sure he was seeing me. He was swaying slowly from side to side, like Ray Charles keeping time to a ballad. I waited for him to add something, but he was silent. Then Babs took a deep breath that looked like preparation for a long sentence. But she didn't speak. So I did. "Right before you got here, I called back Detective Sergeant Coleman, the Nassau County cop who came this morning. I hadn't heard from him again, not even to say they hadn't gotten any leads. Maybe they don't do that—call to say they don't have anything to tell you. But since he'd said he—a detective—had been sent here instead of a regular cop because of Jonah's 'position in the community,' I figured I could push it a little." Clive stopped his swaying when he was at a 100-degree angle away from Babs. I waited for him to right himself. He didn't, so I continued. "I told Coleman that since Jonah spent so much time in Manhattan, there was a good chance that if, God forbid, something bad happened to him, it could have happened there. I asked if he'd been in touch with the New York police. He said yes. So then I asked him for a name."

"Good," Babs said. I couldn't tell if she was approving or thinking, *How come you didn't think of this five hours ago, asshole?* Not that she would use a word like "asshole." In a confrontation, I imagined that, since she'd graduated from Vassar, she would more likely say "unmitigated fool." She cocked her head at the same weird angle as Clive's upper body, as if they shared a choreographer. "And he gave you the name?"

"He said it might be in the notes he'd typed up, but he wasn't near a computer." My in-laws kept their gaze on me, though I sensed they were controlling themselves, aching to exchange a glance, maybe hoping I'd look away. Was I reading something into the situation? I didn't know. Yet their silence also told me they'd vowed to each other to be gentle: Families could split apart under this kind of pressure, and the Gerstens weren't that sort. I could hear Babs telling Clive on their drive out from the city, "I want this to be civilized. No recriminations. Even if we have to bite our tongues." And Clive, hands gripping and pushing against the wheel as if to fuse it to the steering column, murmuring in a choked monotone, "Unless she's making a complete hash of it and putting Jonah in peril. Then we cannot remain silent. Am I correct?" Clive came from a middle-class New York background, but when he did speak, his vocabulary was kind of grand, as if he had a screenwriter specializing in biblical epics writing his dialogue. He was so worshipful about his wife's privileged background, I guess he kept wanting to sound like the man he thought she deserved. Now, though, he had nothing to say.

Possibly what I was reading from their silence was my own tale, composed totally in my head, and they were simply waiting for me to talk again. "I got the feeling Coleman's 'not near a computer' might be some kind of delaying tactic. So I asked him, 'Could you do me a favor and just check that notepad you carry? Maybe you jotted it down.' And he waited, like, a few seconds too long. It could have been that he was hoping I'd tell him not to bother if it was an inconvenience. But I kept quiet. So he gave me the name."

"Which was?" Clive asked. He loosened the knot on his tie, an orange Hermès with teeny giraffes all over. Its cheeriness was making me uncomfortable, and I wished he'd worn something in a gray basket weave.

"Lieutenant Paston," I told him. "Gary McCorkle Paston. From the Nineteenth Precinct detective squad."

Babs leaned forward. "Did you get a chance to call Lieutenant Paston?" she asked with the sweet neutrality of a social worker, which made it sound like she'd sprouted a second personality.

"Yes, I did call him. He'd already gotten some details and the picture of Jonah I'd given to Detective Sergeant Coleman—I'm not sure whether he's called Detective or Sergeant or both because he only gave me his card. I don't think he said, 'I'm so-and-so.' Maybe he did. I guess I just wasn't paying attention." I was starting to sound ditsy, and probably not only to myself. I inhaled one of those conscious diaphragmatic breaths they teach you in yoga to relax. I could have used a few more, but then my in-laws might think I was acting weird or even on drugs. "Anyway, Lieutenant Paston asked if I had any more pictures, so I scanned a couple and e-mailed them to him. He said he'd call Gilbert John and Layne, and whoever else police call. A few of Jonah's other contacts. But he said the good news was that he'd checked: There weren't any reports of people resembling Jonah who were, you know. Unidentified."

Even though the den was the warmest room in the house, all

three of us seemed to feel the ice of my unsaid words: "morgue," "dead body." In the same instant, we each tried to get warm. Babs pulled the shawl collar of her taupe sweater tighter against her neck. Clive clenched his hands, brought them to his mouth, and breathed hot air on them. I lifted up my cup of tea, but its warmth was gone, and the aroma of the cold, smoky Earl Grey made me shudder.

We were quiet too long. Maybe because they were in my house, I felt obliged to say something, but I'd already gone the "coffee? tea?" route twice since they'd arrived. So I picked up the pad and paper I had ready to make a note or take down an address if I got a call. I wrote down Detective Sergeant Coleman's and Lieutenant Paston's names and numbers. "These are the Nassau County and NYPD detectives I've been dealing with. If something pops into your head that could be useful, feel free to call them."

I hoped they understood I was giving them permission to tell the cops anything they might know that they wouldn't want me to hear: that Jonah had experienced some bizarre mental disorder in childhood involving running away from home. Or that he had a girlfriend—who didn't have embarrassing parents—he was planning on leaving me for.

My father-in-law appeared grateful as he took the paper, though given those upturned corners of his mouth, he could be thinking the most horrible thoughts and still appear smiley. My mother-in-law pursed her Bronze Méditerranéen–glossed lips but overdid it. Instead of appearing reflective, she looked like she was about to give me a great big air kiss.

I wish I could say that one of us let our humanity shine through long enough to reach over and squeeze a hand, or stand and offer a long, comforting hug. But providing comfort didn't seem to pop up on any of our to-do lists.

Babs, who had been staring at the bare, dead-looking aerial roots of an Evening Star orchid I had on the end table beside her, turned back to me. Managing to keep any hint of dread out of her voice, she asked, "Are your parents coming over?"

Oh, shit! I thought. The idea of my mother and father—the very fact of their existence—simply hadn't occurred to me. "I haven't called them yet." I was sure Babs was relieved. "I didn't want to scare them and then have Jonah walk in."

She nodded and refolded the left cuff of her sweater as if it hadn't already been precisely folded back the same number of centimeters as the right. Like many Manhattan women, Babs was meticulous in her casualness. Her black hair with silver at the temples and subtle gold and platinum streaks shot through was blown dry, then artfully disarranged by Sabine, her hairdresser, every other day. God could have created my mother-in-law to counterbalance my mother's denial of adornments. Not that Babs was fussy. Her clothes were Armani and Jil Sander in black, white, and a narrow spectrum of pale browns. Jewelry wasn't a problem for her, either, as Upper East Side good taste discouraged all gems except diamonds and all metals but gold and platinum. Still, beside the pale green petals and violet red lips of the fully bloomed orchid she'd been staring at, my mother-in-law looked less chic than sick. Just the couple of hours of knowing Jonah was a missing person had been enough to bring out deep beige shadows beneath her eyes. Even her knuckles and wrist bones seemed mysteriously altered in the fading afternoon light in the den, so her hands looked like a crone's.

We hung out for another fifteen minutes, forcing conversation. At one point, I almost asked if they thought I should hire a detective agency, the way Gilbert John and Layne had suggested. Some mental censor clapped a hand over my mouth just in time. If they said no and I decided I needed one, they'd find out. No detective could call half of Manhattan (the upper half, where Jonah came from and worked) and hide it from my in-laws. And if they did think hiring an investigator was a dandy idea, they'd take over—Clive saying that John Doe of the Doe Agency, you know, international reputation, had a mother who'd been a patient. Then Babs would chime in that she'd gone to Fieldston with Jane Roe, whose husband had formed the Strategic Inquiries Group, or some Washington-esque name, after he left the Department of Justice, where he'd been Janet Reno's right arm.

Periodically, one of us would glance at the silent phone, which would give the others a millisecond of hope that there had been some kind of pre-ring in a decibel range just below their hearing. But then nothing would happen, so one of us would mutter a sentence or two to cover the embarrassment of our naive optimism.

My ears did pick up what theirs didn't: the crunch of one of the minivan's tires as Ida veered slightly off the driveway, which she did about 50 percent of the time, riding the pebbles that protected the bases of the boxwood and lavender shrubs that ran along the driveway from the street all the way up and around to the garage. The triplets coming in—the sudden clomp of Ugg boots, the thud of backpacks on the floor, accompanied by "I gotta pee," "No, me first! I gotta pee worse!" and "Apple slices with peanut butter!"— startled my in-laws, as if all the time they'd been in the house, they hadn't remembered they had grandchildren.

I got up to go into the kitchen. Clive and Babs stood also but stayed where they were, in front of the couch. "Do the boys know?" Babs asked.

"They know he wasn't here this morning. They get up at five-thirty. Jonah's always there, but they didn't seem to attach any real importance to it. If any of them had a clue at all, it would be Evan."

"He is very sensitive," Babs said, the strain already in her face growing more intense, as if her inner colorist had brushed on another coat of ashen concern. This time, however, she didn't get a chance for her usual "I do worry about Evan, though I know his sensitivity will be an asset in the long run" or "He's

like my brother Bill, with his nerve endings so close to the surface," because Clive cleared his throat. He did it so loud that it
made her flinch and cry, "Ooh!"

"Susie," he said, "we are not in any way criticizing you. But
we should be working together on this." Standing, I was taller
than either of them. My height never bothered Jonah: One of
his nicknames for me was Stretch. But I could tell Clive wasn't
so crazy about it.

What did he mean, "working together"? Sometimes I didn't
understand the dialect the Gerstens spoke. I got all the words,
but it was like one of those communiqués you hear on the news
about the State Department, where they say, "We had a full and
frank exchange of views, and warm wishes were exchanged over
cups of tea and the traditional almond cakes." The only way you
could comprehend what was going on was if you were an insider
and knew the lingo. We shared the last name, but I often found
myself longing for subtitles. "Working together?" The way he
used that phrase made me feel like something had grabbed the
intestines behind my belly button and twisted. But I knew I had
to be cool. I couldn't get elbowed out of the way in the search
for Jonah, yet I needed his parents to stay on my side.

"Of course we'll work together on this," I told him. "That's
why I telephoned you as soon as I saw . . . the lay of the land.
I mean, I didn't call my parents. I only checked with Jonah's
office manager to make sure he hadn't been called in for some
emergency. Then I notified the police." I didn't mention I'd
been at Florabella making calls and talking through everything
with Andrea. "Then I immediately called you."

"What we are trying to say," Babs said carefully, "is that perhaps going to the police so very soon might not have been—
how can I express it?—the quickest way to get an answer. It's
not that I'm questioning your judgment, Susie. It's that they are
a bureaucracy. And bureaucracies are notoriously inefficient."
Standing straighter, she kicked out one leg, then the other, to

align the pleats in her black pants. For an instant, she teetered on
one of her black alligator boots with its four-inch heel, but she
quickly righted herself.

"In this case, they seem to be responding pretty well," I said.
"Nassau County sent a detective, and he got the NYPD on to it
right away. I called the police in because"—I wanted to sound
authoritative, or at least like I wasn't a total screw-up—"the cops
have the power to get information from hospitals and police
departments, their own and in other places." The boys would
be racing around the house any second, searching for me, calling
out, "Mommy." I talked faster: "Were you thinking along the
lines of the investigative agency?" They nodded. "I agree with
you completely. It's something we should consider. As far as I'm
concerned, we should look into it today."

"One of my patients—" Clive began.

But he was cut off as Dashiell careened around the doorway
of the den. Dash's hazel eyes with their awning of thick brown
lashes opened wide: *Wow! So great that you're here!* their sparkle
seemed to say. I'd trained the boys not to demand "Got a present?" each time Babs and Clive arrived, even though my in-laws
came bearing gifts on every visit. Naturally, I'd asked them not
to. "Just little tokens," Babs had explained the next time as she
handed out packages artfully wrapped in high-end silver foil to
look like a giant Hershey's kiss. But the last time they were over,
Dash had hinted not at all subtly for a Webkinz bulldog. This
time he knew not to ask. He blinked once, then twice, trying to
come up with something interesting to say, a simple "Hi" obviously not occurring to him. I shook my head at him: *No. No
presents today. Don't expect . . .* But he cut off my silent protest
with a grin toward his grandparents. "I got a riddle!" he told
them.

"You've got a riddle?" Babs said. "Tell me, Dash."

"Guess who didn't go to bed last night?" he asked. He gave
her no time to answer. "My daddy!"

Chapter Seven

✂──

Other than sighing "Heaven!" over a hot fudge sundae or a great orgasm, ordinary people don't talk about paradise much. But everyone's heard a million definitions of hell. I remembered one of Jonah's fraternity brothers at Yale, drunk out of his mind, sweat streaming through his sideburns, across his jaw, and down his neck, yelling, "You know what the existentialists say hell is, cocksuckers? Other people! That means you!" And someone famous enough that I vaguely recognized the name wrote about hell being the torture of a bad conscience. Et cetera. But every hour or so over the next couple of days, I wanted to cry out, "Those definitions are crap. Hell is what I am living."

Not knowing if my husband was alive or dead. If he was pinned inside the smashed metal skeleton of his car after an accident, screaming in pain from crushed bones. If he was being held in a stinking basement, tortured by some psychopath like a victim on *Dexter*.

Once or twice I felt temporarily normal, like when I helped the boys make zebra cookies with chocolate and vanilla stripes for the Tuttle Farm school's zoo carnival. Then I'd be back to hell, picking up (or making up) Jonah's screams of unspeakable pain. I'd calm down, though only slightly, picturing him in an East Sixty-fifth Street town house sipping martinis with the shockingly rich, once-homely, now-stunning former patient he'd decided to leave me for.

After my in-laws went back to the city and I whispered, "Thank God," I had a long phone conversation with Gilbert John and Layne: What to say to Jonah's patients, especially the ones scheduled for surgery? Layne was totally against trying to take over the surgery themselves because it was too much pressure and they wouldn't have time to get to know the cases. Gilbert John was most concerned about managing what he called "the situation" in a way that wouldn't provoke gossip. He kept interrupting himself with a single cough either from something in his throat—peanut speck, post-nasal drip—or overtaxed nerves. Between coughs, his main point was Protect Jonah's Good Name. That might have been Gilbert John Noakes-ese for Protect the Practice, but it did make sense. So did his suggestion, which we all agreed on, to say simply that Jonah had had an emergency and they had to cancel his appointments for the time being.

The days began to take on a rhythm. Once I caught the beat, I began living a regular life. True, it was in an irregular regular life, like living in some war-ravaged country. You knew a bomb could blow you away a minute from now, but meanwhile, you were out of dishwasher detergent. I did only what needed doing, the basics.

I was responsible for the boys. Funny: One of Jonah's tender, ironic names for Evan was Killer, because he was such a high-strung kid. I worried he'd be the one most disturbed by his father's absence, but he didn't even get teary. On the other hand, Dash, who generally possessed the sensitivity of a dump truck, couldn't seem to stop talking about how Daddy wasn't there. Mason, as usual, was Mr. Moderate, neither unglued nor unruffled; a couple of times each day, he asked if Daddy would be home on Saturday to make waffles. I managed a bright "I hope so."

After the triplets' day at preschool was finished, I had the twins keep them out of my way. I needed a break from their usual "You're a poopy head!" shouts at one another. Even the thought of having to holler "No!" when they tried yet again to climb the bookshelves was too much for me. I was so exhausted and overstimulated. I felt one more decibel would kill me.

February was a lousy month for a husband to disappear, with its snowless days of cold wind and rain. The house seemed airless yet bursting, as if it wanted to break open and expel the boys into the fresh air. Me? I still had to deal with my parents. But when I tried to call them, fortified by many deep, relaxing breaths, I couldn't. The effort of picking up the phone and lifting it to my ear pushed me over the edge—a place I was getting used to.

I ordered myself, *Get it over with*, but I wound up half sliding onto the kitchen floor and sat there sobbing. My back pressed against the pantry door, my legs splayed out, and I, the Pilates queen, couldn't summon the strength to haul myself up. I stayed there on that wood floor for nearly thirty minutes, long after the dial tone had changed into the loud, high-pitched cry that signals the receiver is off the hook, my mind whirling in a vicious circle of crazy thoughts all those self-help books urge you to avoid.

First I kept imagining that when I'd been at Florabella the previous morning and sent the boys to preschool—with the twins in the Mommies' Room—Jonah might have come back briefly. Finding no one home, he'd decided to leave forever. The whys—where had he been? why would he do such a thing?— came fast. Madness, I decided. Madness induced by a hit on the head by a gun butt during a mugging. No, from eating a salad with "wild mushrooms" that were actually never-before-seen hallucinogens. All right, maybe not actual madness. Just a nervous breakdown from four years of mornings with triplets, afternoons operating on patients who were still whining that the cost of genioplasty should include a freebie chin cleft even as they were going under anesthesia. And, of course, evenings with too much of my "I think we should repaint the boiler room floor" and too little sex.

Then I thought that maybe Jonah hadn't come back when I'd been out. No, it was his kidnappers who'd dropped by to leave a ransom note. Finding no one around, they'd decided not to bother—just to kill him and snatch a richer doctor whose wife didn't go gallivanting on a day when she should have been home. On and on, sitting motionless on the kitchen floor on the balls of my ass, while my head swirled with frightening what-ifs.

The few seconds of silence between horrific scenarios offered enough clarity for me to glimpse not only the hugeness of Jonah's absence but its profound and awful mystery. That profundity business lasted only about thirty seconds; I'd never been the plumbing-the-depths type who knew from cosmic despair.

I finally got up and took a giant bottle of San Pellegrino and a water goblet from our Baccarat crystal that we'd registered for but never gotten a full set of, and I went into Jonah's study. Bernadine and her vacuum cleaner were approaching, and I didn't want to be sitting at the kitchen table when she turned on FOX News and then have to watch her clean between the two wall ovens with a Q-tip dampened with her own saliva even though I'd gently pointed out three times that it wouldn't be much harder to wet it at the sink. Anyway, Jonah's study was the most businesslike room in the house. It contained only a desk, computer, phone, and shelves of books on plastic surgery I never looked at because not only were they technical and boring, they were also filled with hideous illustrations of surgical procedures and, even worse, photographs printed on thick, glossy paper.

It was a calm place. I'd made it that way. The walls were covered in a watered silk the same color as the lightest amber in his bird's-eye-maple desk. The room emitted a golden warmth that avoided the decorator-trying-for-scholarly-humanist ambiance.

I called Manhattan Aesthetics and punched in Gilbert John's extension, grateful that despite my protests of "tacky" and "user-unfriendly," the practice had switched to a voice-mail system and I no longer had to speak to Karen, the receptionist who looked as if she'd been manufactured by the same company that had done Schwarzenegger as the Terminator.

Gilbert John took my call within seconds. Even though my first words were "Sorry. No news," he didn't sigh or tsk or indicate any disappointment. In fact, he was pretty compassionate, for Gilbert John. So while he wasn't oozing empathy, he sounded genuinely concerned, not just about Jonah but about how I was doing.

"Holding together," I told him. "I'd love to fall apart and have to be heavily sedated, but I can't."

"The boys," he observed.

"Yes, and also . . . I don't know. Maybe I can think of something, or at least have a working mind, if someone says something that has any potential."

"I understand. The toughest part for me is the worry," he said. "No, let me be more precise. The fear. And for you? I cannot begin to imagine." I could hear him take a deep breath to settle himself. "A nightmare. A heartache."

"Yeah," I agreed, then wanted to bite my tongue because I hadn't said "Yes." Jonah once told me that when I got emotional, I got Brooklyn, and he hadn't meant it as a compliment on being myself and not putting on airs. He could take only so much of my authenticity. "You're right," I said. "This whole thing is every word for awfulness you can think of. But I'll tell you what I would like. One or both of you mentioned something about hiring an investigator, detective, whatever. Can you get me a name or two? Obviously, the sooner the better."

"I'll get right on it," Gilbert John said, pronouncing each word as if the survival of properly spoken English rested solely on him. "Is there anything else, Susie?" I told him no and thanked him, probably a little too profusely.

Before I even hung up, I was pulling open the top right-hand drawer of Jonah's desk. True, I had watched Detective Sergeant Coleman search the desk. And I had seen for myself that he hadn't found anything. Then we'd moved upstairs.

During our entire search, neither Coleman nor I had found anything in the room to make me think Jonah was anything other than what I believed him to be. No pieces of paper with mysterious, scribbled phone numbers, no hate mail, no blackmail demands, no charge slips at La Perla for a G-string in size P. But I was hoping to find a clue that might prove at least a beginning. Maybe Coleman and I had overlooked something, the way you finally discover the Advil in your handbag that you'd failed to find after two thorough searches.

But with Jonah being as orderly as he was, there were no surprises. Even his paper clips in the top drawer's tray all lay on the horizontal, though I doubted he'd consciously arranged them that way. Maybe in the back of my mind was the belief that objects, like people, bent to Jonah's will. Not that he was a bully: It was just that his way always wound up seeming so reasonable.

I was about to get up and start leafing through his books, shaking them, too. Maybe something would fall to the floor that would make me go "Aha!" But the phone rang. It was Gilbert John with the names of two investigative agencies.

"I'm told these are the crème de la crème," he said, "although technically, I suppose only one can be the cream of the cream." I couldn't tell if he was correcting himself or if he thought I needed a translation. "In any case, I have contact names: David Friedman at InterProbe, though he might be in Dubai this week." I pictured a Jewish guy with a hundred-dollar haircut at a conference table with a bunch of Arabs in keffiyehs on the eightieth floor of a building overlooking a futuristic city like you see on the covers of science fiction paperbacks. I decided David Fried-

man might be a little too high-powered. "The other one is Lizbeth—*Lizzz*beth, with a Z, no E, no A—Holbreich at Kroll."

Lizbeth, it turned out when I called her, sounded pretty
high-powered herself, with a low-pitched, southern-accented
voice that conveyed the confidence born of an earlier life as Miss
Tuscaloosa or, more likely, a brigadier general in the army. She
had no trace of the flirty, rising inflection that turns southern
women's sentences into questions. In fact, her actual questions
sounded more like commands.

I spent nearly an hour on the phone with her, going over
a lot of the same ground I had covered with the police. Was
Jonah under stress? Going through a difficult time? She came
right out and asked if I thought he could have committed suicide. I told her, "Jonah is the last person in the world who
would take his own life." She wanted even more details than
the cops, data on everyone in Manhattan Aesthetics and information on Ida and Ingvild, our housekeeper, Bernadine Pietrowicz, plus people she called vendors, everybody from the guys
who picked up the garbage to the plumber. I swallowed hard
and agreed to a twenty-thousand-dollar retainer and faxed
permission for her to speak with our accountant, lawyer, and
stockbroker, and to examine the hard drive on Jonah's comput-
ers at work and at home. She said she would talk to Gilbert
John Noakes about getting the names of Jonah's patients to see
whether any of them were suing him (no) or were wack jobs
(yes). As we talked, I e-mailed her Jonah's cell phone number,
e-mail address, head shot, and the URL for his biography on
the practice's website.

"I don't want to frighten you," she said. "Well, any more
than you already are, which is more than enough. So let me be
clear that kidnapping is very, very rare in the U.S. Most of the
cases we deal with happen abroad. Even so, it's a good idea that
if the police haven't done it already, we get the FBI on this and
also put recording devices on your phone."

"In case of—" I stopped cold. This conversation was so far away from anything I ever thought I'd be talking about that it felt like I was being forced to read from a script meant for somebody else. "Are you talking about a ransom demand?"

"Yes. But as I said, that scenario is highly unlikely."

I didn't have the courage to ask what scenario she'd put her money on. But by the time we were finished, Lizbeth didn't scare me anymore. While not exactly in the ninety-ninth percentile for effusiveness, she sounded decent: Two or three times she'd said some version of "You must be going through absolute hell." And when she opened Jonah's picture, she'd remarked, "He looks like an absolutely lovely man."

Fifteen minutes later, I felt the urge to get out and go to Florabella. Andrea told me not to come in, saying that she would call in Marjorie, a retired florist who helped us out during busy times, squeezing us in between her daily Alcoholics and Overeaters Anonymous meetings. Still, I yearned for an hour or two of the mindless comfort that always came to me when I was using my hands, like greening out hunks of floral foam, covering them with leaves or moss as the basis for table arrangements. But now I was too scared to trust call forwarding; I worried that some vital message from the cops would not only go unanswered but not make it to voice mail. And I wanted to be home in case . . . I caught myself in what Jonah would have called "doing a Sherry," sighing my mother's *It's hopeless* sigh. He could do a hilarious imitation of my mother that included shaking his head in despair, followed by an "oy" and a few tsk-tsks, even though she never actually said "oy" and at most gave a single tsk. But how could I not sigh? With each hour he was gone, it got tougher to come up with a Jonah-coming-home fantasy powerful enough to divert me for longer than ten seconds.

Bleak. Every few years, Jonah would tell me I really should read his favorite novel, *Bleak House*. Except it was incredibly long and the title wasn't exactly a grabber. Also, it was by Dickens, and okay, maybe something was deeply wrong with me, because whenever someone brought up Charles Dickens, everybody else nodded with reverence and got that funny little smile that's supposed to signal "Literature has added so much meaning to my life." Except the only thing in high school I hated more than *A Tale of Two Cities* was *David Copperfield*. So I kept telling Jonah, "You're right and I'd love to. As soon as I finish whatever for my book club, I'm going to read it. Then we can go out to dinner, just the two of us, and really discuss it. Plus, I'll finally get to see what makes you so passionate about it."

The house was silent except for the occasional gust of wind that rattled the shutters. I walked purposefully from Jonah's study to the den, thinking that I would find his leather-bound copy. Maybe in the back of my mind I was picturing him coming home so quietly I didn't even hear his key in the lock. He'd find me reading *Bleak House* and be incredibly moved.

Except I passed the den, went into the kitchen, and made myself a sugar-free hot chocolate. I drank it standing up, leaning against the island where the stovetop was, thinking, *Bleak House? You want fucking* Bleak House? *I'm in it.* But I was barely halfway through the thought when I realized there was a house even bleaker, the one I'd grown up in. Not bleak from tragedy. Bleak from perpetual simmering, silent resentment. I decided I really had to call my parents.

Chapter Eight

My mother answered the phone. She always did. Her "hello," as usual, came across as a challenge, as if she expected every call to be a fund-raiser from some organization whose position she'd once been passionate about and then lost interest in: NOW, NARAL, Emily's List, Americans United Against Gun Violence, Greenpeace. She'd bought a T-shirt from No God 4 Me at an atheist street fair on Amsterdam Avenue, but she'd never gotten on any sucker list because she'd switched to her most recent cause, libertarianism, which she seemed to define as being at liberty not to do anything for anybody and listening to deeply unattractive people on C-SPAN talk about abolishing the Federal Reserve.

"Mom, it's me."

"Susan?" I was an only child. Her voice was frosty; I hadn't called her in over a week. Not that she ever called me, apparently being under the impression that the telephone was a one-way instrument.

"Yes. Listen, I have some . . . not-good news." Why did I expect a nervous intake of breath or a terrified "Are the boys all right?" Beats the hell out of me. I definitely shouldn't have, because after a lifetime of phone calls, I knew it was my job to set the tone of our conversations. I usually tried to be affectionate (extending an invitation to a Mother's Day barbecue) unless the occasion called for a little dab of melancholy (inquiring where Cousin Ira's funeral services would be held).

I'd always low-keyed it around my parents, even during my years of the usual teenage derangement, because their emotional gamut ranged from a high of not unhappy to a low of vaguely depressed. On the rare occasion when they were directly confronted with someone else's hilarity or heartache, they'd practically stagger, as if they'd been hit with a Category 4 hurricane. So I kept my hysterics to myself. Still, when I blurted, "Jonah's been missing for two days," I couldn't subdue my agitation vibes.

"Two days?"

"Yes."

She burped, and I let myself think the news was a shock to her system. "You don't have any idea where he is?" she asked.

"No. Nobody has any idea."

"Are you going to call the police?"

"I already did. So far I haven't heard anything."

"That's not like him," she observed. "Two days?"

"Yes."

The ball was in my mother's court, but she couldn't do any more than stand there and watch it bounce. "Effectual" wasn't a definition for either of my parents. Even when they sensed something was expected, they rarely managed to figure out what it was. If there had been a Rabinowitz family crest, *Think on your feet* would not have been its motto.

Now, however, my mother's silence lasted longer than usual. Another time (more in the interest of "Let's move it along" than out of kindness) I would have offered a hand to pull her out of her emotional hole. Why not? I'd been doing it most of my life, once I decided that, through either the grace of God or recessive genes, I had what they lacked: sense.

I'd grown up being their guide around Normalville. This time, though, all I could do was get angry and think, *Can't you even ask me, "Is there anything I can do?" Aren't there any limits to your insecurity? You're my mother, for crissakes!* Just then she asked, "Would you like us to come over?" I decided she was hoping I'd say, "No, don't bother." Before I could stop myself, I told her it would be great if they could. Maybe I was thinking that someday in the future, I'd be saying, "Listen, my parents are far from perfect, but when the chips were down, they were really there for me!"

There for me? Maybe I was fantasizing my mother calling my father at work and saying "Susie needs us!" then grabbing a cab out to Long Island and him driving eighty-five miles an hour from Queens to comfort me. Maybe—though I knew that despite her fifteen-year flirtation with feminism, she never went anywhere without my father. She'd flunked her driving test forty years earlier and found taxis too filthy and obscenely expensive. Public transportation was, in her view, too public: crowded with male riders who saw buses and subways as prime turf for humiliating women via the rush-hour penis prod.

Anyway, by the time my father left work, drove back to Brooklyn to pick her up, and crept out in rush-hour traffic to the house via the expressway, since side roads could still have ice from January, they arrived after six.

"Maybe he's at a medical conference," my father, Stanley Rabinowitz, suggested, "and just forgot to mention it to you." He was sitting at the kitchen table wearing one of his Mr. Rogers cardigans, this one a weary green covered with decades of pilling. Very little actual sweater remained, yet the tiny pill balls somehow hung together and seemed to have acquired balls of their own. I set a large plate of grilled cheese sandwiches on the kitchen table because naturally, they had shown up at dinner-time expecting to be fed. When I sat, they seemed taken aback that there was no soup or salad. My mother, glancing around at the place mats and finding neither forks nor spoons, reluctantly took a half sandwich.

The boys and Ida and Ingvild were in the den with their cheese sandwiches, apparently charmed by the sophisticated wit of Lenny the Wonder Dog, giving me time to bask in the warmth of my parents' company. My father always ate sandwiches from the outside in: His grilled cheese sat on his plate with even denture marks all around the perimeter, like a decorative scalloped edge. He picked it up and took another bite.

"He's not at a medical conference," I replied calmly. "First of all, Jonah wouldn't forget to tell me he was going someplace. Even if he did, he would have had to plan for going out of town. There isn't any sign of planning. He had operations scheduled, appointments at the office. He just disappeared. Didn't come home, didn't show up at his office or the hospital. His partners are as mystified as I am."

My father shrugged to show he was stumped, too. When no one else spoke up, he added, "Maybe foul play?"

"Maybe." Just those two syllables used up all the energy I had left.

My mother shook her head, a movement that communicated *Gee, too bad* rather than *Catastrophic*. When she'd come in, she'd given me her usual awkward hug, where her upper arms performed the actual hugging and everything else, from elbows to fingertips, hung awkwardly in the air behind me. Now, though, she seemed to realize some comforting maternal gesture was in order, so she reached across the big round table to squeeze my hand. However, her arms were short. In order to do my part and get my hand squeezed for comforting, I wound up stretching forward until, from the waist up, I was almost flat on the table.

"Thanks, Mom," I said.

She muttered something into her sandwich. It could have been "No problem."

My mother was short and chunky. Not a stylish combo, but short, chunky women can be tough/adorable or else little dynamos throwing off sparks of energy. Sherry was neither. She was belligerently unattractive, almost as if she'd been created in the late sixties by a male-chauvinist cartoonist as a malicious caricature of a feminist.

Periodically, one of my friends would tell me I was too harsh about her; that, okay, she would never win any awards in the mother-love department, but wasn't that because she thought herself less than lovable? Probably. Her own mother, Ethel, had walked out when she was eight. Little Sherry had been raised by her father, my grandfather, Lenny "the Loser" Blechner. After failing early on to be a nightclub singer, probably because he had a mediocre voice and kept forgetting to smile between songs, he'd become a bookkeeper for Calabro Brothers Flounder in the Fulton Fish Market.

"So," my father said, "where do you go from here?" An outsider would think he was wracked with emotion because his voice quavered so much, but I knew better. For as long as anyone who knew him could recall, he'd always talked as if the section of floor he was standing on were vibrating. Now and then some less than diplomatic soul would ask, "Hey, uh, what's with your voice? You got Parkinson's or something?" He'd reply, "Huh?" He never got it.

"I honestly don't know where I go next," I told him. "I want so much to do something. But the police are on it, and a private investigative agency. I wish I could think of something else to do."

"Terrible, terrible," he said. His eyes fell to his plate, and I sensed he was trying to come up with a suggestion, but nothing came to mind, so he picked up his sandwich.

Some people would call my father a nebbish. I certainly did.

Other than despising my mother, an emotion he projected mostly by flaring his nostrils whenever she spoke, he had few strong opinions. He was bald and colorless. Even if he'd committed some terrible crime, he would never be picked out from a lineup because it was impossible to remember his face. He worked as a salesman in a store called My Aching Back, although he wasn't particularly successful at it. As a kid, I had sensed his boss kept him on because even though he was only borderline competent, he was very reliable. Stanley was without ambition to be any better off than he was, so he was truly reliable. His commissions were enough for us to live on. Also, his shaky voice made some customers believe he was becoming emotional about their back pain, so he was never fired. I guess he liked his job; the only time I saw my father anywhere close to animated was when he was holding forth on sciatica.

"Maybe you should go on TV," my mother said. "All those missing women? You always see their parents on the *Today* show with their home movies of the one who's missing. The husbands sometimes do it, although ninety-nine times out of a hundred, you know what?"

"What?" I knew what.

"What?" my father asked.

"The husbands turn out to be batterers who finally went over the line and did what all the friends and relatives always knew they would." In case we weren't clear on what this was, she added: "Kill the wife. And then the relatives all have the chutzpah to say, right on camera, 'Oh, I *begged* her to get out while she still could, but she just wouldn't listen.'"

"I did give some thought about publicity," I told her. Her mock turtleneck was covered by some weird little capelet, squares of black and forest green that looked like an afghan someone had abandoned when they realized they hated crocheting. The capelet had captured a lot of sandwich crumbs and three orange teardrops of melted cheese. I went on, "I may have to resort to going public. There are even organizations that help you with PR. But right now it's only been two days. If something's happened to Jonah that he or I or his partners wouldn't want public, going on TV or whatever would put it all out there. Something embarrassing could mean the end of his career."

"Like what?" my mother asked. "What could he be doing that couldn't be public? He's not a drinker, as far as I know." I shook my head: No, Jonah wasn't a drinker. "So he wouldn't be lying in the gutter on the Bowery. Is there something you haven't told us?" She shrugged. "Drugs? You hear about doctors getting hooked because they have easy access. Homosexuality? Some other . . . whatever."

"No. To the best of my knowledge, which I truly believe is excellent, Jonah is what he seems to be: honorable and sober. And heterosexual." Since she looked as if she still didn't get it, I explained, "It doesn't have to be a major issue. Sometimes even the best people get into trouble."

Silence. Maybe someone else's mother would have clearly disagreed about not seeking publicity and told her daughter that finding Jonah was of paramount importance. "You have to risk bad publicity in order to find him. The more time elapses, the colder the trail gets."

But my mother had strong opinions only on matters with no direct effect on our lives, like what had been printed on her T-shirt the previous summer: SOCIAL WELFARE REVERSES EVOLUTION, which I'd spent half a barbecue thinking was an anagram I couldn't figure out.

"Well," she said, "I guess you know what's best."

The few good-hearted thoughts I had about my mother were like: *Okay, she's embarrassing, grabbing on to causes, letting the slogans on her T-shirts substitute for snappy conversation and a philosophy of life. Amazing. There is absolutely nothing she can do well or even competently—cook, clean, talk about a TV show, buy shoes, show affection (much less love). To be fair, she's like someone who had a terrible accident as a kid and can't walk. Her own mother abandoning her when she was eight was exactly like that—a terrible accident. It left my mother permanently crippled. She can't do all the simple, normal things in life that other people take for granted.*

That abandonment was obviously the central fact in my mother's life, and maybe in mine. If Ethel had left Lenny the Loser but kept little Sherry with her, my mother might have been different. Okay, maybe she wouldn't have been fun or kind or had a sense of style. But she could have been emotionally savvy enough not to need MapQuest to find her way across a room to hug her grandsons.

My mother had very little to say on the subject of her own mother other than "I hardly remember her." The times I pushed for more information, all I got was "I have almost no memory of her." No memory? The only memory she ever dug up for me was: "One time we heard her screaming at the top of her lungs. My father and I went running into the bedroom. She was holding a stocking in her hand, and she screamed at us, 'My last pair of stockings, and I got this huge run!' Then she went right back to screaming."

Eventually, I stopped asking my mother, but that was when I was ten or eleven, old enough to take aside some cousins nearer to my mother's age and ask them about the woman I thought of (with bizarre familiarity) as Grandma Ethel. Cousin Marcia told me she'd heard that someone had seen Ethel in a nightclub in Miami Beach wearing serious jewelry in the company of an Italian-looking guy. However, further inquiry by Cousin Danny led to finding out the man was Ethel's husband, Sidney Nachman, of Nachman & Company, distributors of wine and spirits. Cousin Naomi made a few calls to Florida and learned the Nachmans had no children. About ten years later, Cousin Marcia told me that her best friend from high school, who'd moved to Coral Gables, had sent her a clipping of Sidney Nachman's obituary from the *Miami Herald*: *Nachman is survived by his wife, Ethel, and a sister, Rita Umelitz of Creve Coeur, Missouri.*

And that was—almost—that. Although my mother never told me, I heard from assorted cousins that she knew Ethel was alive and well and wearing serious jewelry. However, she made no attempt to contact her mother. Maybe she was waiting for Ethel to make the first move. That never happened.

Just before my twentieth birthday, a half year after Jonah and I were married, we were on a flight to Miami for the wedding of one of his camp friends. I'd had a couple of vodka tonics to dull the sound of the engine (it was only the third or fourth plane ride of my life, and I was still terrified). In a what-the-hell mood, I said, "Hey, we'll be in Miami. Maybe I'll try to find my grandmother." I waited for Jonah to say, "Are you crazy?" When he didn't, I asked, "Do you think I'm crazy?" He said no, not at all, but I should be prepared for someone who was a total bitch and who would refuse to see me—and don't forget I'd made a hairdresser appointment at the hotel at four-thirty on Saturday.

Finding her wasn't as easy as it would be today; we were in the pre-Google era. But after an hour at the Miami Beach public library that Saturday morning, Jonah and I discovered Ethel Nachman had married Roy O'Shea, a man who owned several Honda dealerships in South Florida. The O'Sheas definitely had an active social life. As we sat looking into the microfilm viewer at newspaper photos of parties and benefits, Jonah kept saying, "I can't believe how much she looks like you!" I kept saying, "Oh my God!" I also said, "Do you think my mother remembered what she looked like and saw the resemblance and that's why she always held back with me emotionally?" Jonah said, "Everything doesn't need a psychological explanation." We went back to the microfilm and discovered that in the mid-eighties, "gregarious and charming socialite Ethel O'Shea" was high on a list to take over as the new host of a local late-morning TV show, *Talk of Miami*. Ethel got the job. Ethel was a hit. Within a year, Roy O'Shea was history.

I didn't get up the courage to call her—not that I had her unlisted number. But while I was at the hairdresser, Jonah called the TV station, said he was Jonah Gersten from the Yale School of Medicine and that Ethel O'Shea had asked him to mail something to her at her home address. Sadly, he'd lost it. Who would have believed a story like that? Anybody. I'd always told him I trusted everything he told me. Whenever I said that, he'd smile and say, "Why wouldn't you?" But most other people had that reaction to him, too. So at nine the next morning, four hours before we had to leave Miami to get back to New Haven, the two of us rang Grandma Ethel's bell.

"I'm . . ." I began to say to the woman at the door. She was me plus forty-something years—assuming a good dermatologist and a great colorist and plastic surgeon. Her jaw dropped. She barely looked at Jonah before turning back to me. Even without makeup, her eyes were her most beautiful feature: pale green jade. Her smooth skin was an almost completely unwrinkled pearly pink, and her hair an incredibly believable blond. She was built like me, too, tall and long-legged. Even though we didn't have any money yet, I already knew enough about fashion to realize the satin robe she had on was a Donna Karan.

"You're mine?" Grandma Ethel asked at last. She knew the answer. Before I could say a single word, she took my arm and brought me inside.

But my blocking out the reality of my parents' alternating grilled cheese and diet-ginger-ale burps with the memory of my grandparent ceased when my father boomed, "Excuse me!" It so startled me that I twitched, dropping my last bite of sandwich, a near-perfect circle, onto the floor. "I know this is a bad time for you," he said.

He does have empathy, I thought. "Thank—" I started, but

never got out the "you" because he cut me off: "Maybe you haven't gone shopping, but do you happen to have a piece of fruit?"

One navel orange and two decafs later, they left. Four hours after that, the police rang my doorbell.

Chapter Nine

On either side of the front door, there were tall, slender panes of glass, so even before I opened it, I could see Detective Sergeant Timothy Coleman looking down at the doormat. He stared with an intensity born of a desire to face anything but the person who would open the door. Beside him stood an African-American guy in his forties—the ex-jock type who looked like he'd discovered doughnuts, though only recently. He had on a gray overcoat and a long black knit scarf, the kind male models wrap around their necks a hundred times. It ended at his knees in a hysterical eruption of fringe. He studied me through the narrow window. It was nearly midnight, but he appeared more weary than physically tired, probably because he knew too well what the next hour would bring.

As if to live up to his expectations, I began to cry as I tried to turn the stiff, heavy lock. I clutched the brass knob, and it felt like forever before I was able to turn it.

"Mrs. Gersten," Coleman said, "this is Lieutenant Gary McCorkle Paston from the NYPD."

"Corky Paston," the other cop said.

It wasn't until the gusting icy wind made me shiver that I

realized my hand was still gripping the knob and the two men were outside. "Sorry. Please come in." I led them into the living room, though all I wanted was to stand right there in my bare feet on the cold marble floor of the hall and shout at them, "For God's sake, just say it! Get it over with!" I was still crying as we passed through the hall, yet when we got to the living room and I turned, a small part of me expected to see Paston smiling and giving the thumbs-up to signal, *Hey, no reason to cry. I'm here with good news. Your husband's fine: just a little worse for wear.*

"I'm sorry, but I have bad news," he said.

"Is Jonah dead?"

"Yes."

I didn't move. I didn't wail. I stared at his scarf and thought it looked hand-knit.

"We found him just a few hours ago."

"What happened?" My voice emerged as an awful croak. I got so busy clearing my throat again and again that I didn't notice Paston had guided me over to a chair until I felt the frame and seat cushion against my leg. But it was the wing chair, Jonah's chair, and sitting in it would have been indecent, like flag-burning or even idol worship. I stepped away quickly and moved to the deep corner formed by the arm of the couch. I motioned for them to sit. Neither went near the wing chair. Coleman took the chair he'd had the last time, and Paston sat on the middle cushion of the couch.

"I'm sorry to have to tell you: Your husband was murdered," Lieutenant Paston said.

"Oh my God!" I said, covering my face with my hands. "Oh my God!" I may have groaned. Shock: That was what was so weird. I'd spent so much time in the past two days picturing not just something terrible happening to Jonah but murder, specifically murder, in ten or twenty or maybe a hundred different ways. I made an awful grunting sound, but that was because the words "How?" and "Who?" crashed into each other as they came out.

The detectives' silence lasted way too long, and I realized they were waiting for me to say something. I uncovered my face and put my hands in my lap. A second later, I was crossing my arms and clutching them tight against my ribs: holding myself together. "What happened?" I asked Paston. His first few words didn't register because I got lost staring at the red blood vessels in the whites of his eyes. They were thin and twisty, like the lines indicating bad country roads on a map.

". . . in the chest."

"What? Sorry, I didn't hear what you said."

"Dr. Gersten appears to have been stabbed in the chest with a long, pointed pair of scissors."

I heard the words, but all I could say was "I'm sorry. I forgot to take your coats." Lieutenant Paston took off his scarf and stuck it in the sleeve of his coat, but it must have been Trauma Time, like during a car crash, when everything slows. I saw his hand grasp the scarf near his collarbone and imperceptibly make an arc behind his neck until three feet of black wool hung from either side of his hand. He slipped out of one coat sleeve, then another, in what seemed to be a series of jerky pictures—more like primitive animation than fluid motion. *Funny,* I thought, because he looked graceful, like one of those extra-large men who surprise you by moving like Fred Astaire on a dance floor. It was only as I got mesmerized watching him snake the scarf into a sleeve that Coleman's sheepskin jacket suddenly appeared in my hands. With that, time returned to its normal speed.

"Surgical scissors?" I asked Paston.

"No. More like the ones barbers use," he said. "Your husband seems to have been stabbed twice." Paston had even more of a New York accent than I did—his "more" came out like "maw." "It'll be clearer once an autopsy is performed." He lowered his voice to a funeral-parlor hush. "We'll let you know when that will be." I watched as he took a deep breath. I knew something I didn't want to hear was coming. "Then you can make your arrangements for . . . whenever you want to. I know at this point nothing can comfort you, but you ought to know—the doctor from the medical examiner's office at the scene indicated that after the second wound, it couldn't have been long at all."

I'll treasure that thought, shmuck, I thought. "I don't understand," I said. "A barber's scissors? Did it happen—"

"No, no." Coleman cut in so fast, it was clear that Paston running things wasn't sitting well with him. "That's just a description of the kind of scissors."

"Well," I snapped at him, "where did it happen, then?"

"Let me start at the beginning," Paston said, flashing Coleman a *This happened on my turf, so shut up* look. The little cop's lips pressed together to show a slash of resentment. "Naturally, we'd been working on your husband's being missing. But a call came in to the NYPD around six tonight," Paston continued. "Someone living in an apartment on East Eighty-seventh Street got home from work and called the building's superintendent. Said there might be a problem in the apartment next door."

One half of me wanted to stick my fingers in my ears and go *la-la-la* real loud so I wouldn't have to hear any of what he was going to say. The other half urgently needed to know every detail. "What kind of a problem did the neighbor report?" I asked.

"I haven't had a chance to speak to the individual, so I can't say for sure. In any case, the superintendent tried to contact the tenant but wasn't successful. He didn't want to enter the premises without permission, so he called the police. Two patrolmen came from the Nineteenth Precinct. He let them in. They found Dr. Gersten just past the front hallway."

"Was anyone else there?" I asked.

"No." Maybe he sensed Coleman was about to say something, because he turned, flashed him a beady-eyed glance, then continued, "The apartment is sublet to someone named Dorinda Dillon. Do you know her?" I shook my head. "Ever heard the name mentioned?"

"No. Who is she?"

"Actually, that's only one of her names. She changed it a few months ago. Before that, she was known as Cristal Rousseau."

"What?"

"Cristal Rousseau." He spelled it out. "That probably isn't her real name."

"What kind of a person would call herself Cristal Rousseau?" My voice was so loud it made me sit up straight. I tried to think of something more to say to show I was in control, but nothing came to mind.

"Ma'am," Coleman cut in, "would you like me to call somebody for you? A friend or family member? You know, just to have someone with you."

It sounded like the right thing to do. Except I couldn't think of anyone I wanted to be with me. No one in either of our families. Not any of my you-know-I-am-always-there-for-you Shorehaven friends who would try to hold my hand or hug me. If I'd said anything, they'd murmur "I hear you." Of course, the whole time they'd be making mental notes so their "I was with Susie Gersten the night she found out" story would be filled with rich insights and examples of their sensitivity.

"No one," I said.

"Are you a hundred percent sure, ma'am?"

No, not Andrea. She'd offend Coleman with a single blink of contempt at his low-end shoes; Paston by eyeing his slightly over-the-belt gut. The cops might forgive her bad manners if they got distracted by her body—basketball-sized boobs stuck on a lean, boyish frame. Once that happened, they'd quickly turn into admirers, especially once they realized her excessive blondness was natural. Andrea was okay for sexy comedy, but she wouldn't fit into a horrible dark story.

I shook my head. No one. But I realized they hadn't seen my dismissal because they were eyeing each other. Maybe glaring. Any second it could escalate into NYPD/Nassau County, black/white, big guy/mini-man hostility. I cleared my throat. "There's no one I want here now." Except Jonah. An insane thought flew through my head: Once he came home, I'd feel so much better. "Please, for God's sake, just tell me everything. Who is this Dorinda Dillon?"

Coleman opened his mouth to speak but then realized he didn't have anything to say. Lieutenant Paston leaned forward in his chair. "She's an escort," he said. I didn't react. Maybe I was trying to think of a way to ask him what he meant by "escort." Could it be a new term for someone who took around Europeans looking for plastic surgery bargains? But he dissolved any potential for sugarcoating: "By 'escort,' I mean a call girl. A prostitute."

I shook my head hard—no, no way!—even as I understood he was telling the truth. Jonah had been murdered in a call girl's apartment. "She did her work . . . ? Was that apartment her place of business?"

"Yes."

"East Eighty-whatever," I said. "That's a good neighborhood." Paston didn't say anything, and Coleman flexed his ankles to study the Velcro closings on his little brown shoes. "I don't mean that it's better to get killed on the Upper East Side than, say, someplace else." I realized I was babbling, but I didn't want Lieutenant Paston to get the idea that I was thinking, *Oh, God forbid! To be stabbed to death in Harlem.* "What I meant was that Jonah's office is in that area, so maybe he dropped in to see her on his way home. Maybe she was post-op. If there was some minor problem, he could check up on her without her having to go to the office."

"It's only been a few hours since we found him," Lieutenant Paston answered. Either he hadn't heard or didn't care about my "good neighborhood" comment. I decided that mentioning that Jonah had switched from Hilary to Obama early on would be tacky. "First thing tomorrow," he went on, "I'll ask someone at Dr. Gersten's medical office to check if she ever was a patient."

My mind kept going to stupid things. Should I offer them coffee? Could I ask Paston to tell my in-laws about Jonah so I didn't have to call them? Even if he did, I realized, I'd still have to let Gilbert John and Layne know.

Soon everyone would know. Soon everyone would be shaking their heads and saying, "Susie Gersten won't believe Jonah went to a hooker for sex. Is that willful ignorance or what? So sad."

Part of my mind must still have been functioning because I surprised myself by suggesting: "You might want to check at Mount Sinai, too. Jonah and his partners were sometimes on call for victims of domestic violence—" But then I cried some more. One of the cops must have gotten up; a moment later, the tissue box from the downstairs guest bathroom was set on the coffee table. I felt a couple of tissues being tucked between my thumb and index finger. I blew my nose and went on, "They do pro bono work for victims of domestic violence, women and children whose faces . . . Prostitutes, you know, they get abused. So if Jonah had any dealings with someone like that, I'm sure it was to help her."

"It's definitely a possibility," Lieutenant Paston said. His eyes moved from me to the table beside him, to an old green Derby tureen I'd filled with preserved yellow Dendrobium orchids and pale orange roses. I could tell he wanted to touch the flowers to feel if they were fake. "We'll look into it."

"Lieutenant Paston, if I could only listen to myself, I'd probably be saying, 'Poor thing. She is *so* trying to deny reality, swearing her husband wouldn't go to a prostitute for sex.'"

"Not at all," Detective Sergeant Coleman said.

"Except this is the thing," I explained to Paston, "I know my husband. You don't." He nodded. "But maybe, in a way, you know more than I do." Believing Jonah wouldn't cheat on me, especially with a call girl capable of calling herself Cristal Rousseau, was one thing. But now, to ask a specific question . . . I saw it as a test. Was my faith in Jonah the real thing? Or was it self-deception to keep the horror to a manageable size, as in "Sure, my husband may have been stabbed to death in a whore's apartment, but he was there for severe facial trauma, not a blow job"?

"Jonah had his clothes on, didn't he?"

"Yes."

I don't think I said "Thank God" out loud. "It wasn't like he was killed without clothes and someone dressed him."

"No," Paston agreed, "the wounds were made through his shirt. Mrs. Gersten, I'll be glad to talk to you about the crime anytime. But maybe this isn't the moment. Let me explain. Dr. Gersten's been missing for several days, so there must have been moments when you expected the worst. But no wife is prepared for the cops to knock on the door late at night and tell her that her husband has been the victim of a homicide. You're in a state of shock. It may be better to skip the details now. You don't need images of graphic violence in your head. Tomorrow, next week, next month: All you have to do is call and you have my word, I'll describe—"

"No. I'd like to know now." I crossed my arms again, tight. I needed my own embrace because the mere thought of not being held together, of resting my elbow on the arm of the couch or setting my hands in my lap, made me feel sick. "Let me try to explain," I said. "I'm a floral designer. My work is getting images in my head." Paston glanced at the orchids and roses in the tureen and turned back to me. I went on, "If I know what happened to Jonah, I can deal with it. I have to. But if there's a blank, I'll need to fill it in. I'll create a thousand images in my mind, and a lot of them will be more horrible than anything you can tell me. I don't want to go through that again, because I've been there since he's been gone. That's all it's been. I can't live through hundreds of wide-awake nightmares anymore. Let me deal with just one."

Coleman had been eyeing me, expressionless. Now the side of his mouth formed a curlicue of doubt. Not a good idea, he was guessing, giving details to the victim's wife. But he couldn't signal to Paston because the Manhattan detective was too busy thinking and nibbling tiny bits of skin off his chapped lips. Finally, Lieutenant Paston sat back in the chair. "Dr. Gersten was stabbed through his shirt. He was fully dressed in a tie and suit jacket, though the jacket was open. He may have been holding his overcoat because it was found near him on the floor."

"Doesn't that back up what I was saying?" I asked him. "About Jonah not being there as a customer?"

"You say you want to deal with reality now, so I'm going to take you at your word," Paston said. "If you're looking for the truth, you have to keep an open mind at this stage. We're just hours into the investigation. We know only a small percentage of what we need to know. It's too early for conclusions. For us, that's a definite. Naturally, how open-minded you want to be is up to you. Being fully dressed may be evidence that your husband wasn't using Dorinda Dillon's professional services. But the homicide might have occurred as he was entering the premises. Or as he was leaving."

I began nodding to show I was comprehending, though I was so tired I was still processing what he said. At last I asked, "When you say 'leaving,' you mean he might have been leaving after having sex with her and getting dressed again?"

"Yes. We'll know more once we get the medical examiner's report."

"You mean if he . . ."

"Yes." I was grateful to Paston for not saying "ejaculated" in front of Coleman. I wouldn't have minded if Paston had said it five hundred times—if Coleman hadn't been there. But there was something about the Nassau County cop's prissy politeness, and his looking at me like I was a piece of sculpture with jade eyes, that made me uncomfortable in my own living room. "I'll keep an open mind," I told Paston.

"Good," he said. I doubted he believed me.

"So you haven't found Dorinda Dillon?"

"No. It looks like she left the building the night Dr. Gersten was killed. We haven't found anyone who has seen her since. Her normal pattern is either working—men coming and going days, nights—or being up there by herself. The only time she seems to go out is in the afternoon, to have her nails done or to pick up a few groceries. Maybe get drugs, too. She's had two arrests for possession. Cocaine. Charges dropped the first time. The second time she pleaded guilty to a Class C nonviolent felony and got a suspended sentence."

"Do you think she was the one who killed him?"

"We don't know at this point."

"You're keeping an open mind," I said. Coleman's brow furrowed, but Paston didn't take it as a sarcastic remark, which was good, because I hadn't meant it to be.

"Yes. We need to be able to weigh whatever evidence comes in, so it doesn't make sense to close off our options." He stood and walked around the coffee table and over to the fireplace mantel. He was tall enough to lounge against it and rest his elbow on its ledge, but after a couple of seconds, he came back and sat beside me. "Had to stretch my legs," he said. "Sorry."

"It's fine." I shifted slightly to face him. When he spoke again, his voice was so soft I had to strain to hear it. Just the two of us: He wanted Coleman out. "Once we leave, a person going through what you have to deal with should have a friend in the house. A person to rely on. Sergeant Coleman says you have two Norwegian girls who work here. They'll probably be busy keeping those triplets of yours under control, right?"

"Yes. And they're teenagers. I wouldn't . . ." I wanted to ask him what I should tell the boys. He would know the right thing.

"So what Sergeant Coleman suggested, you calling a friend or a family member, you need to do that. At some point you're going to have to sleep. You'll need somebody with a good head on their shoulders to answer the phone, do what needs doing." I didn't say anything. "Your parents are alive?"

"Yes. But not them."

"Dr. Gersten's—"

I shook my head. "I'll call my business partner. She's my best friend, too. I didn't want to before because she can be . . . She's a little much on the cool, calm, and collected side."

"Got it. But some cool can come in handy at a time like this." He took a card case from his inside jacket pocket and handed me two of his business cards. Lieutenant Gary McCorkle Paston, Manhattan North Homicide Squad. The NYPD shield was flat. I imagined some New York City budget gap that had needed closing decades before had meant the end of embossment. "You can reach me day or night. If for any reason I can't come to the phone, there will be other detectives assigned to the case who can help you or get a message to me. If you think of anything that might help, or anyone it might be good for us to speak to, let me know right away. Don't worry about bothering me or calling with some small detail. We need whatever you can come up with." I nodded, although I didn't realize I'd closed my eyes again until I got startled when he spoke. "This is a shock and a terrible loss. Nothing I do can make it better for you. But I'll do everything I can to find out who did this to your husband."

"Thank you." Before he could say "You're welcome" or anything else, I added, "I feel confident having you on this case." Before he could thank me and we'd wind up in some embarrassing gratitude match, I said, "One more thing: Jonah's parents."

"Right. I heard about them. He's a big deal at Sloan-Kettering. She's a big deal at some makeup company."

He seemed to have gotten the picture before he even drove up to the house. Just to be clear, I said, "This is going to be devastating for them, too. They're very fine people, wonderful grandparents to our kids. But they're the types who are used to being in charge of stuff, respected. Also, they are very well connected. I'm sorry if this sounds obnoxious, but you should know: They probably know the chief of police and the DA and half the judges in the city. My father-in-law is involved with some charity with Mayor Bloomberg."

"I understand."

"Over the years they've come to like me, or at least have learned to live with me. Our relationship is . . . how would my mother-in-law describe it? Perfectly pleasant. But bottom line, they think Jonah could have done better, that I don't have enough class for him and that I'm not smart enough—except for me having the brains to reel him into marriage while he was still too young to know better." I was glad Paston didn't go into the "Oh, I'm sure that can't be true" business. "They may call you. No, they will call you. I'm telling you all this because although I'd appreciate it if you could talk to them, I don't want them pushing me out of the picture. I want to feel free to speak to you and find out—"

"I understand. I'll tell your husband's parents the truth, that you're the legal next of kin, and that means, while I'll speak with them, I deal only with you."

"Thank you." I didn't cry again. I just started to shake, pretty violently.

Coleman decided his help was needed, so he practically flew over and stood between the couch and the coffee table, so he was right beside me. "If you give me your doctor's name, ma'am," he said, "I'll be glad to call him or her. A sedative might—" He had sweat on his upper lip.

"Thank you, but no sedatives. I can't take drugs with three little boys in the house." He fell silent, though he didn't move. He just stood next to me, his shins an inch from my knees, as if he had a front-row seat to some all-star nervous breakdown. I wanted Paston to tell him to get the hell away, but he didn't.

After a few minutes, my shaking eased to mere trembling. My head cleared so I could remember Andrea's number. I gave it to Coleman so he could call her and tell her to come over. Only then did he go back to his chair to get busy on his cell.

"I didn't tell him the truth," I murmured to Paston. "About drugs. I actually have enough Xanax to calm a herd of crazed elephants."

"Good," he said. "You're going to need it."

Chapter Ten

Andrea must have arrived soon after Detective Sergeant Coleman called her. I heard her voice at the front door, followed by the purr of small wheels. She'd brought the small Vuitton suitcase she always kept packed in case Fat Boy finished some hedging deal early and called her to join him in Shanghai or Dublin. I saw her as she stepped into the room, and I watched as she came over to pat the back of my hand—the Andrea equivalent of a regular person's loving embrace. She said, "Oh, Susie, this is dreadful. I'm so sorry." Maybe I nodded, and I think I retreated farther into the softness of the couch's corner, where the overstuffed back met the fat arm. At some point the detectives left. For all I knew, they simply evaporated. I heard no goodbyes, no footsteps, no closing doors. "Tell me what you need me to do, Susie," Andrea said.

"Calls." I exhaled it more than I actually said it. "I need you to call . . . everybody. Not tonight. I think it's too late."

"Yes. It's almost one in the morning."

"Maybe you should go home, come back later. I don't know. They told me I needed someone to be here. I can't think clearly." My arms were still crossed so tight over my chest that my shoulders ached, but I couldn't seem to release them. "Do I have to call his parents now?"

"Yes, you do. Soon, I would think."

"What?"

"They can't hear this on the news."

"They're asleep at this hour."

"But someone they know might hear of it and call them."

"Oh God, I can't believe I didn't think about that."

One of Andrea's usual snotty retorts got to the tip of her tongue, but this time she stopped it before it came out. She didn't even look like herself. She was wearing just lipstick. Without other makeup, her eyes were almost lost under puffy pink lids and uncurled blond lashes. Her face seemed magnified, a white oval with a glossy brick-red mouth that appeared glued on, as if she'd cut it out from a Chanel ad. "And you'll have to call your parents. Unless you want me to do it."

I shook my head. The movement loosened up some words. "No friendship could survive that kind of strain."

"I can do it."

"No, I'll call them. Don't worry. They won't be able to cope with coming back out here. Most likely, they'll wait till nine-thirty or ten in the morning. That way, they can get the car washed before they stop at GNC because they're low on acidophilus. But then they'll be on their way."

"To offer their usual nonstop comfort," Andrea added. We'd been partners and friends long enough that I knew, even before she did it, that she'd start to look up to heaven but quickly avert her gaze, knowing that when it came to my parents, even God couldn't help.

"Well, when they do show up," I said, "they're bound to be wonderful with the boys." I knew I sounded bitter.

That was when it hit me: *I have children.* It must have been too awful to think about the boys immediately after I heard the news. I just blocked them out. I wished I could do that again.

The thought of Evan, Dash, and Mason missing Jonah while not truly comprehending what had happened was too sad to dwell on. And what about their growing up without a father? My head flopped down. I was defeated. "I can't take this, Andrea."

"You have to."

"Take your stiff-upper-lip Wasp bullshit and shove it."

"I'm not Anglo-Saxon, as you well know. I'm Dutch. And I don't expect you to stiff-upper-lip it, Susie. You should know that. This is beyond horrible. I'm only saying that you're eventually going to have to find a way to take it because . . ." She swallowed. "You're all the boys have now." Her eyes closed for what was either a very long blink or a prayer: *Thank you, God, that it isn't me.* "The good news is, they won't be up until their ungodly wake-up time. You don't have to think about them this second. You have other fish to fry now: your in-laws, your parents. And what about Gilbert John? Layne? You do have to call them tonight, don't you? Or can I call them and you call the others?"

I made all the calls. It was worse than I'd imagined because I had to live through everybody else's shock. I don't recall having even a milligram of compassion. I wished I could get away with "Listen, I hate to tell you this, but Jonah's been murdered. I'll know more tomorrow. Speak to you then," and hang up. Take three Ambien. No, two, because of the boys. Three wouldn't kill me, probably, but I couldn't risk even a little soothing brain damage.

If I could have made the calls and heard "You poor thing!" over and over again, I might have dealt with giving them the news. But I had to listen to my father-in-law's terrible groan, like that of a lion gone mad with pain, and Babs screeching in the background, "What? What? Tell me! For God's sake, tell me!" So I had to go into the whole thing, repeating large parts of it because they put me on speaker and then couldn't understand half of what I was saying.

And of course it wasn't "Your son was stabbed to death in the midst of performing some noble act." The answer to their wheres and hows was "In the apartment of a call girl named Dorinda Dillon, aka Cristal Rousseau, who'd had a couple of arrests for cocaine." With a pair of those long-bladed scissors you see in barbershops. All this interrupted by moans and cries and me saying, "I'm sorry, I'm so sorry," too many times to count.

Gilbert John Noakes, MD, FACS, didn't scream or groan. In fact, he was almost speechless except alternating in a shaky voice between "Good God!" and "I'm sorry, Susie" a few times. He didn't ask questions, and after I'd told him Jonah had been stabbed, I heard what sounded like a sigh filled with pain. "I don't know what to say. It's brutal." He sounded so wiped out that I couldn't bring myself to tell him about the call girl. At the end of the conversation, he said he'd call Layne, but I told him I'd do it, since I figured they had to hear the Dorinda details that, barring some international tragedy or celebrity overdose, would be on the news.

I hadn't realized Andrea had left the living room until I saw her coming back in. She handed me a mug and said, "You had some actual cocoa. This is true hot chocolate, not your diet shit. Drink it."

"Thank you." Andrea had to be thanked constantly, even at work, like when she was just handing you pieces of sphagnum moss every two seconds.

She said, "You're welcome. I brought Xanax. Do you want any?"

I shook my head, then said, "No, thank you." She gave me the raised-eyebrows, flared-nostrils look she gave to clients who were making a foolish decision, like wanting lollipops on ribbons in table arrangements for a First Communion luncheon. It worked 99 percent of the time. I added, "I don't need anything. I'm numb." I couldn't say "What I'd like is an overdose of

something so I can die and not have to face the rest of my life."
Not that I'd have done that: I knew I had to be there, as whole
as possible, for the boys. But it would have been nice to say it
and hear a passionate "I know it's terrible for you, but you can't
even think that way!" Except Andrea would have added, or at
least thought, *Don't be a self-indulgent ass.*

When I called Layne, she was on the other phone with Gilbert John, but she was back to me within seconds. She talked for
too long, but it was bearable because she spoke the way decent
people are supposed to, the way you see in the older movies
when you're surfing channels. "What a horror for something
like this to happen to such a fine, honorable man. A good man!
My heart . . . my heart goes out to you." She either swallowed a
lot or cried for a few seconds. "And your wonderful boys. Susie,
I don't have to tell you how much he loved all of you. You know
those office watercooler chats? Every single time Jonah and I
would talk, a light would come into his eyes. I always knew the
next sentence out of his mouth would be about one of the triplets. Or all of the triplets. He'd get this gleam — "

"Layne, thank you so much, but I have to tell you — "

"Jonah wasn't just a partner and mentor to me. He was a
great friend. When he was senior resident — "

"Layne." Not that I would actually tell her to save it for the
funeral home and the shiva, but one of the reasons everyone said
"Oh, Dr. Jiménez is such a fine, fine person" was that Layne
didn't stint on kindness. She was never too busy for a good
word — or, more to the point, words linked into paragraphs.
"Gilbert John sounded so shaken up that I didn't want to go
into detail," I began.

"And if you can't handle it, you don't have to with me, Susie.
Whenever you're ready . . ."

"You both need to know something now, before you hear it
on the news or anywhere else."

"What is it?" she asked cautiously.

"Jonah was killed in a call girl's apartment."

"No!" Her "no" came out so spontaneously that a huge sigh of relief escaped me. Thank God for that reaction. Clearly, I'd been dreading the overlong silence I'd be forced to translate into "Oh, you found out about his whore habit." Maybe I was misinterpreting. The "no" could have been pure reflex on Layne's part. But I grabbed on to it as if she were saying "He was too much in love with you to even consider any other woman, much less a call girl."

That was all the reassurance I was going to get, although I didn't realize it for another twelve hours. Andrea got a little pushy—in a good way, I guess, urging me to go up and get a couple of hours' sleep, or at least rest, before the boys woke up. If she hadn't been there, I probably would have spent the night on the couch.

I didn't want to go upstairs. I was afraid. Climbing the steps (right foot, left, right, as if I were on a Level 4 hike instead of walking up to the next floor) was too much effort. I was terrified. Spooked. I stood before the black rectangle of the door frame, staring into the unlit bedroom. I was sure I'd take one step onto the carpet, reach for the light switch, and suddenly— a gut-ripping noise, half howl, half shriek—and the enraged ghost of Jonah would boil the air an inch from my face. I didn't know why I was so crazy, or why, even if I didn't believe in ghosts, which I didn't, except maybe the week after I saw *The Sixth Sense,* Jonah's spirit would be anything but benevolent toward me.

Yet I had to force myself to lie down in our bed. My heart fluttered, then slammed against my chest in panic at the sudden, jarring silence when the heating system turned off. A second later, a current of warm air puffed across my ear and blew a strand of my hair onto my cheek. I suppressed a scream. Maybe that strand had been there all along. Yet the air above the bed felt agitated by invisible goings-on in some parallel sphere.

At times during the night, the fear vanished. I was in the bedroom I had once shared with my husband, although now I was a widow. I censored that line of thought not because of what it represented but because I'd always hated the word. It conjured up old ladies in shapeless black dresses gray with lint. Or those black spiders with gross hairy legs.

But I forced myself to stay where I was. I mumbled aloud what I knew of the Twenty-third Psalm—not much—again and again. If I couldn't whip it up for the Lord being my shepherd in the Valley of Death and getting me through this night of grief and hysteria, it would be the start of big-time bedroom phobia, a truly embarrassing fear. Because truthfully, how could I tell my therapist, Francine Twersky, that my dead husband's vengeful soul was whirling around the Regency bergère chair and that the very air of the bedroom stank of sulfurous fury? I could tell her—and doom myself to session after boring session of her getting me to understand that what was haunting the bedroom was coming from my head.

Speaking of heads, I covered mine with the duvet, then started worrying that if I suffocated, the boys would go to Theo, Jonah's brother. Jonah once said, "Even though my folks are hip enough to appreciate one sciencey kid and one arty one, they know I'm the winner and Theo is . . . They always try to act like he's my equal or a close second with the silver medal. But deep down? All four of us know he's the loser."

If something happened to me and Theo got the boys? Within weeks, one of his friends would convince him to coproduce a reality show—giving him the excuse it would be a public service. *TV Guide* would write, *Sparks fly in SINGLE WITH TRIPLETS when a young Maserati-driving Manhattan casting director gets surprise custody of his four-year-old nephews.* I rearranged the duvet so my nose and mouth were out in the air.

At five-thirty, the boys startled me awake, so I must have gotten a little sleep. "Come up on the bed," I said, patting the mattress. My chest ached from holding back sobs, though I didn't completely rule out a heart attack. "I want to talk with you." I had to wait while Dashiell used the bathroom. I made the mistake of telling him to use ours. Within a second, the other two were demanding the privilege. I got all choked up, so I nodded. They ran in, and even before the giggling became wild laughter, I could visualize the puddles of pee I'd have to wipe up. Jonah wouldn't be calling on his cell, bored in bridge traffic, and my "They're the Jackson Pollocks of urine" would forever stay unsaid.

When they returned, they were so high from the excitement of a triple toilet experience that I had to get up and grab them as they raced around the room. I plopped them hard onto the bed. By the time I finally caught Mason, I was screeching like the Wicked Witch of the West, "Shut up! For God's sake, shut up and listen to me!" over and over again. Naturally, I spent the next few minutes weeping and apologizing—"I'm so, so sorry, sweeties. Oh God, I'm so sorry"—and calming them down, especially Evan. His bony shoulders jerked with each of his sobs. Mason's eyes were still wide with fright at my rage while Dash stared at me with concern mixed with contempt.

I pulled them close, for the thousandth time envying mothers of twins, who had an arm for each kid. It was only then, as I was kissing one of their heads and trying to banish non-mournful thoughts like *He needs a shampoo* that I realized I had no idea what to tell them. During the days of waiting, imagining every terrible outcome except the one that had happened, why hadn't I turned on the computer and Googled "explain child death parent"? My eyes grew heavy. I so longed to go back to sleep with them, bony shoulders and smelly heads snuggling against me, even though their wakefulness and squiggliness were proof of what an idiot fantasy that was.

"I have something very sad to tell you," I said. All three of them looked downcast, but it struck me that they didn't understand that "very sad" had to do with Jonah's not being around. Their "sad" was more "Carvel has run out of rainbow sprinkles." "You know Daddy hasn't been home for a couple of days." I guess I expected children-as-seen-on-TV behavior: nodding, gazing up at me curiously. But all three of them talked at once.

"Where is he?"

"When's he coming home?"

"Where's Daddy?"

"Is he bringing us presents?"

"Can I—"

I said, "Shhh!" loud enough to drown them out. "Evan, Dash, Mason! Let Mommy finish. Okay? This is very important." I took a deep breath. I knew I had to say something fast, before they started babbling again. "Daddy . . . Something very sad happened to Daddy. He got hurt, really hurt. He died. You know what that means, don't you? It means—"

"He's dead!" Mason said, triumphant at having beaten out his brothers. "When somebody dies, he gets dead!"

"Yes. Very good. That's right. But it's also very sad because it means he's not coming back anymore."

"Jake's grandpa isn't coming back," Evan said. "He died. He got too old." Then he added hopefully, "Daddy's not too old."

"Daddy can go to the hospital," Dash said. "They'll get him all fixed. Then he can come home."

"I wish more than anything that could happen. But Daddy didn't die because he was old or sick. He got hurt so bad that . . ." I started to cry, which maybe wasn't so terrible; all the articles say that kids feel the passions that are swirling around them, even if they don't comprehend. So if they remembered this, at least they'd know I was talking from my heart. I did try to calm down a little, so I could keep talking. "When someone dies, it means their body got hurt—or sick—so bad that nobody could fix it. Not even the best doctors."

"Daddy's the best doctor," one of them said.

"I know that. He was the best doctor in the world. Except even Daddy couldn't get someone who is dead to come back . . . to be not dead."

I had to stop not because I was still crying, though I was, but because I couldn't think of what to say next. They hadn't asked me how he'd gotten hurt, and I didn't want to tell them it was an accident, because they might soon be hearing words like "killed" or— I prayed not, but I had no reason to believe that at some point they wouldn't run into a neighbor or relative who would be stupid or cruel enough to say something like "stabbed with scissors."

It definitely wasn't the time to explain that a very bad person had killed Daddy. Or a sick person, a crazy person. Instinct, along with four years as their mother, told me that right then the boys could deal with only one basic fact: Their father was dead. That was all the horror they could take.

Usually, they had the normal fears that came, went, and sometimes traveled from triplet to triplet: alligators under the bed; automatic flush toilets in restrooms; being the first belted into his car seat, at which point the minivan would slide shut its doors and, driverless, zoom off; Goofy Goober from *Sponge-Bob Squarepants* hiding in our basement. They didn't have to deal with the concept of bad/sick/crazy people who kill daddies.

"But we have to remember one thing," I said. "Daddy loved all of us more than anything. Do you know what he called you? 'Our miracle boys.' We wanted so much to have a baby, and Daddy said, 'God gave us a very special present. Not one baby—'"

"Three babies!" they sang out. We'd been through this story too many times to count, but they loved it.

"Three wonderful, gorgeous baby boys. And when Daddy looked at all three of you right after you were born, he said, 'I am the happiest, luckiest man in the world, because I am the daddy of these perfect babies!'" Actually, right after they were born, I'd been fixating on my episiotomy incision and whether the OB had been as careful as she'd sworn she would, so I hadn't been paying attention to whatever Jonah had been going on about. But this sounded good enough, although way too flowery for Jonah. "So even though Daddy won't be here to tell you how much he loves you, you know he did. Right? He always said 'I love you' when he kissed you good night."

"He said 'Go to sleep,'" Mason piped up.

"He said—" Dash began.

I cut him off. "But mostly, he said 'I love you.' So even though we won't see him again, we know how much he loved us. And every night before each of us goes to sleep, we'll think about Daddy, about saying 'I love you.'" If I'd expected tears from them, I would have been let down. But Dashiell said he was hungry as a bear, and Evan wanted to know if Jonah would come back when they were five.

Let me go back to sleep, I thought, wishing there was some way the boys could knock on Ida and Ingvild's door and say, "Mommy asked us to tell you that Daddy's dead and not coming back, and could you give us breakfast and take the phone, and she'll definitely be up by ten-thirty or eleven."

As I followed them downstairs, I felt overwhelmed by two warring emotions, grief and anger. Grief that Jonah would not see the boys grow up. Anger at Dorinda Dillon. What had happened in that apartment? It made no sense. What could have made anyone, even a crazy whore, want to kill a wonderful man like Jonah Gersten?

Chapter Eleven

Jonah had been wowed by our house before he saw it. Just as the real estate agent announced, "Here it is!" he realized he couldn't see anything except an old-fashioned green mailbox on a white post, two weeping cherries, and a row of rounded boxwoods, beautifully pruned, standing guard on either side of the driveway. Imposing yet inviting. Tasteful, too. Proof to his Manhattan parents that moving to Long Island didn't mean he'd chosen a life of LICENSED TO GRILL barbecue aprons.

When we curved around to the front of the house, Jonah, who'd been sitting in front next to the broker, leaped out to open the car door for me, mainly so he could whisper, "You can't see the house from the street!" I'd nodded but didn't really get into picturing his parents' dropped jaws. I was too hard at work being what I'd set out (and failed) to be, a landscape architect. Already my mind was sketching in . . . what? Oh, perfect! Lavender shrubs. That would soften the tight-ass formality of all that boxwood. It registered, though barely, that Jonah was being cool for the broker—giving the slate roof a critical eye, dilating his nostrils with displeasure at the perfectly fine lunette window over the door, even though his knowledge of construction was limited to the difference between a shingle and a brick.

Still, both of us must have been throwing off rays of excitement. From that second on, even before we walked between the white columns and stood on the grand front portico, the broker went from nervously chirping, "You okay?" every three seconds to acting so relaxed it looked like she'd been popping Valium instead of Velamints. She knew she'd made the sale.

So given that long, curving, upwardly mobile driveway, it took me a while to find out what was going on beyond our house. All had seemed quiet enough when I went to the kitchen with the boys shortly after five-thirty, gave them breakfast, and parked them in the den with a *Let's Learn Spanish with Frank & Paco* video. I didn't hear anything unusual when I went back upstairs just after six. I had to tell Ida and Ingvild about Jonah. Tears plus a lot of what must have been "Oh my God!" in Norwegian, and they kept taking turns hugging me, which did nothing except make me realize that Ida, who always looked like she'd just jumped out of a shower, wasn't very good at washing her neck. I finally slipped away so they could get dressed.

As I closed their door, I bumped into Andrea in the hall. "When did you get here?" I managed to gasp. "Who let you in?" I was so shocked that there was someone in the house I hadn't known about that I could hardly catch my breath.

"What are you talking about? I was here the whole night." She was already dressed—in pale pink cashmere pants and a matching sweater that had a cowl neck the approximate size of Cape Cod, the sort of getup you'd expect in a Neiman Marcus catalog, not in life. "Remember? I came over with my carry-on."

"Sorry. Obviously, I'm not thinking clearly. I guess I assumed you left after I went upstairs."

"Why would I do that? You needed someone here with you, right? That's what the detective told me when he said to come over. What if I'd gone home and at three o'clock in the morn-

ing you wanted to talk? Anyway, I went to the guest room and
looked through your eight hundred thousand *World of Interiors*
magazines and was fine."

"Was everything okay?" I asked. I seemed to be flying on
some sort of automatic pilot, making conversation that meant
nothing to me. I'd found myself comforting Ida and Ingvild,
telling them that Jonah had been so grateful to them for being
with us and how he'd thought the world of them, when in fact
he'd been pushing to get "a proper nanny," which showed he'd
been having too many hands-free chats with his mother during
his drive home from the city.

"The guest room is fine," Andrea said, "but you really need
to tell Bernadine to put fresh soap in the shower right after a
guest leaves. So she doesn't forget."

"I did tell her. She's like you, always making lists. I can't
believe she forgot. Her urge not to waste is probably stronger than her obsessive—" Automatic pilot must have stopped
working, because all my thought processes crashed. So I said,
"My husband's dead."

"I know," she said as gently as she could, which would be a
sensitive person's callous. "I didn't want to say, 'Oh, your husband's dead and we ought to sit down and make a list of what
needs to be done,' because . . . I don't know. It might sound
coarse. Speaking of coarse, Fat Boy is coming over with a few
things I need. But you don't have to look at him this early in the
morning. I'll get rid of him—"

"No, it's fine if he comes in."

The bell rang, but it was someone from Kroll, the investigative agency, coming for Jonah's hard drive. Since I didn't think
of saying it was too late because he was dead, I let Andrea take
him to the study.

When she came back, she was still on Fat Boy. "Don't say
it will be fine if he comes in. It will be awkward and horrible. I
know that, you know that."

While a nail-gnawing, socially buffoonish, three-hundred-pound, waxy-skinned man wasn't most women's idea of a dreamboat, Hugh Morrison wasn't that bad. All he ever wore, four seasons a year, were short-sleeved Ralph Lauren Polo shirts, but when he came in I noticed he'd put on a black one to show respect in a house of mourning, and the shirt was so spotless that I couldn't even guess what he'd had for breakfast.

"Hey, Susie."

"Hey, Hugh."

He squeezed my shoulder, and I could feel the wetness of his palm through my sweater. Andrea said he didn't hug or kiss other women because he was shy. I'd always thought the reason was he feared they might misinterpret a friendly gesture, assume he was coming on to them, and not be able to hide their distaste. "Sorry about Jonah," he said. He spoke so fast that it came out "SarboutJo."

"Thank you."

He held out a stuffed Vuitton duffel for Andrea. She walked to him with the dread and dignity of an aristocrat going to the guillotine, and they exchanged their usual greeting—puckering lips and kissing on the points of pucker. Then she grabbed the bag out of his blubbery hand. "Did you remember to ask Cora to pack the Louboutin Mary Janes?" He nodded. Side by side, the Morrison-Brinckerhoffs were a perfect ten, she a willowy numeral one, he a jiggly zero. Andrea seemed surprised and perhaps disappointed that he'd remembered the shoes, but she offered him a dour "Good work, Fat Boy."

For once I was able to resist watching the awful spectacle of their marriage, and I headed off to the kitchen. It occurred to me that I hadn't excused myself, but it didn't matter: Fat Boy shuffled up beside me. (Long ago, I realized I should think of him as Hugh, but my mind had accepted the name his wife had assigned him.)

"You got a problem out there," he said.

Comprehending any sentence of his usually took double time: First I had to break down the whiz of sound that came out into words. Plus, I was now so numb—or maybe paralyzed with grief—that there were whole minutes I really didn't comprehend Jonah was dead. I was down deep, drowning in pain, and I could make it to the surface, to reality, only when grabbed by someone and pulled up. "What?" I asked. "A problem out where?"

"End of the driveway." I panicked for a second: One of the weeping cherries had been uprooted by a blast of winter wind. Jonah would be beside himself because he loved those trees. Also, it would cost thousands to replace it with one of the same size, and we'd have a fight about whether that was necessary.

Then I realized Jonah was somewhere in Manhattan, ice cold, on his back in one of those stacked stainless-steel refrigerators like on *Crossing Jordan*. My breath blasted from me like a tire blowout, with such force that I would have careened into the wall of the hallway and crashed to the floor if Fat Boy hadn't grabbed me from behind. He held me under my armpits. When I glanced down, I could see his huge fingers sticking out, pale and porky like bratwurst waiting to be grilled. He propelled me into the dining room, pulled out a chair with his foot, and plopped me into it.

"Sorry," I mumbled.

"Forget about it. Y'okay?"

"I know you just told me something, Hugh, but I forget what it was."

"The end of the driveway. TV trucks and cameras and a bunch of reporters." My brain took far too long to get from *Why are reporters in Shorehaven?* to *Oh shit!* My face must have finally registered something close to comprehension because he started talking again: "Before I got out of my car, I called the cops. They can't keep the press off the streets. But they'll send a couple of guys over to keep them from putting a foot on your property." I nodded a thank-you. "Your tax dollars at work," he added.

Real crime, like big-time burglary or homicide, was handled by the Nassau County PD. But Shorehaven Estates was one of those privileged little incorporated villages that had a police force all its own for lesser offenses. It appeared to be made up entirely of white guys so shiny-faced and clean-shaven they looked like Mormons parachuted in from Utah. My only contact with them had taken place a year before, when I'd called asking what to do about a demented raccoon staggering alongside our house. They arrived three minutes later, shot it with a tranquilizer dart, and carted it away.

"What do reporters want here at the house?" I asked. "It didn't happen here." Had I been thinking straight, I wouldn't have had to ask, but I wasn't.

"They want whatever piece of Jonah they can get," he said. "Like you. You go to your mailbox, and you'll see yourself ten times an hour on CNN. And if they get a shot of the boys in the backseat of your minivan? Listen, Susie, they're pros for a reason. They're going to swear they'll go away if someone comes out and talks to them."

"A 'family spokesman,'" I said.

"Yeah. But they won't go." Fat Boy knew about media coverage. His hedge fund was in an overly glassed and marbled office building in Great Neck, fifteen minutes west, but he hardly went there. Not that it was such a depressing place: Unlike so many formerly smart financial types, Fat Boy had not been lured by skyrocketing real estate profits or exotic offshoots like mortgage derivatives. Instead of assuming all those investments were too sophisticated for him to understand, he'd told Andrea that the speculators and bankers "couldn't tell a pile of shit from a hot rock" and bet big against the boom. And of course he'd won.

Most of the time, his global dealings took place in the vibrating Barcalounger in his home office. With a headset blinking blue just over his right ear, he was commander of the six-line phone on a table beside him and the notebook computer on his lap. Four feet opposite him was a wall of TV monitors tuned to business and news channels, none of which were muted.

Fat Boy had the multitasker's dream brain, seemingly capable of absorbing every stream of data coming at it. Thus, he had the same total recall of Scott Peterson's murder trial as he did of Goldman Sachs's estimates for European metals and mining in 2005, and how many million hectares India was devoting to the production of soybeans. He said now, "They'll send in helicopters. Your house will come off so magnificent in an aerial shot it will make *The Great Gatsby* look like crap. You know what the crawl will say? 'Lush Long Island estate of Park Avenue plastic surgeon Jonah Gersten found stabbed to death in NY call girl's apartment.'" Had Andrea been around, this would have been when she snarled, "Shut your fat mouth, Huge." But she'd gone someplace—probably up to the guest room to put on her Mary Janes.

The thing was, Fat Boy hadn't meant to be cruel. He wasn't one of those financial freaks who specialized in tactless remarks and had zero knowledge of other people. Not that he'd ever win the Tobey Maguire Male Sensitivity Medal, but at his worst, he was simply a gauche guy who wasn't helped by being wrapped in layers of fat and decorated with swirls of sweat and splotches of snack food.

But, God, was he sharp. Fat Boy lived for data and assumed that the more anyone knew, the better. So right there in the dining room, two hours before I heard an awful *whomp-whomp,* ran outside, and saw the local stations' news helicopters circling over the house like mechanical vultures, I understood he was right: Jonah's murder was a nightmare for his family, colleagues, and friends, but it was a media dream. I had better be prepared that, besides being a personal and police matter, the story was public property. Anyone with a TV or computer could savor our tragedy.

"What am I going to do?" My hands were covering my face,

so my voice was probably muffled. Anyway, it was no big deal if I couldn't be understood. My question was one of those biggies to God, not an inquiry I expected to get answered.

"You need somebody to go out and talk to the press. A family spokesman."

"But you said that won't satisfy them that—"

"It won't." Fat Boy pulled out the dining room chair next to me. It was a nineteenth-century reproduction of an eighteenth-century Hepplewhite: in other words, a piece of furniture designed for slender aristocrats. I immediately put all my energy into not stiffening as he sat down. "Look," he explained, "nothing will satisfy them until a new scandal comes along. Meantime, you've got to deal."

"Okay, but can you do me a favor, Hugh? Talk a little slower."

"Sure, sure, sure. What I'm saying is, you need to deal—now. But hey, there's no law saying you can't do it from the bottom of the deck." He started cleaning under the nails of his left hand with his overlong right pinkie nail. "Here's the thing: You can have someone you trust strolling up your driveway to a bank of microphones three times a day. Except what will that get you? A guarantee to keep them here in Shorehaven throwing Starbucks cups into your storm sewer. No, you've got to give them a spokesman who'll say . . ." He put on what I took as his idea of a sensitive voice, high-pitched, all R's and T's articulated clearly. "She's devastated. Right now all she can think of is how to protect her kids. No, make that 'protect her three little boys.'"

"But isn't that giving them—"

"You don't do it, for Christ's sake," he said, cutting me off. "Oh, I forgot. I need to be really nice to you. Sorry."

"Don't worry about nice. Just tell me what you think I should do."

"Strategize. Give them their family spokesman. But . . . I'll tell you what. Give it to them in the city. That way most of them will be out of here in a day or two. The news outlets won't want to spend the money on two teams of reporters. You'll get the freelancers, the paparazzi, but between the local cops and a couple of weeks of hired security—I'll pay for it—you can probably deal."

"Thank you, but I can pay—"

"Hey, Sus, don't look a fuckin' gift horse. You know the exact balance of your checking accounts, what your credit card bills are? You know your net worth like you know your phone number?"

"No, but I do have some sense of what we have. And Jonah was great at details and on top of everything. So I'm sure—"

"Look, ninety-nine percent of women avoid reality because it isn't pretty." I would have said "That's such a dumb, narrow-minded remark from such a smart person," but Fat Boy talked too fast, and I barely had enough energy to think it, much less say it. "But your reality is that less than a week ago, you thought Jonah was Dr. Nice Guy and in a million years he wouldn't go to a hooker—"

"Listen to me. I am positive—"

"—and that he'd live to be a hundred-year-old stud without eye bags. So be positive, if that's how you want to play it. Believe what you need to believe. But just understand there's a lot about your life you may not know shit about. I'm telling you that as a friend."

He wandered into the kitchen. By the time he came back fifteen minutes later, covered with streaks of confectioners' sugar, I'd forgotten he was in the house. I'd been concentrating on who could be a family spokesman and was getting nowhere.

"You had some good cookies in the freezer," he said.

I looked at the powdery streaks on his mouth and fingers and said, "Lemon curd cookies."

"Hey, I thought they tasted lemony."

"They're better at room temperature," I murmured. "I was thinking about a spokesperson. I considered calling Jonah's brother, Theo, asking him to find an appealing older actress, you know, someone with a big, comforting bosom and a lot of authority to play the role. Do you think that's a possibility?"

"S-U-X," Fat Boy said. "Sucks. Let me draw you a picture, Susie. You get an actress who depends on Theo for jobs, and you'll get someone willing to spout whatever lines he and his parents want to put out there, which could turn out to mean making them look good and you look bad. And don't ask me"— he raised his voice into a falsetto—"'why would they want to make me look bad if we're all family?'"

"Every time you imitate a woman," I said, "it comes out sounding like the same profoundly irritating person."

"I'm sure that's a comment fraught with psychoanalytic insight or some shit, but you're changing the subject. Still, the actress thing isn't a totally stupid idea."

"Thank you."

"Sure. You do need a pro. Don't even think of your cousin Schnooky or someone who's going to become an egomaniac after two minutes standing in front of a microphone bank. You need a PR type who's not in PR, because that went over like a fucking lead balloon with the JonBenét Ramsey parents." Fat Boy closed his eyes in thought and twisted his watch, which had gotten caught on one of the fat folds on his wrist. Then he looked at me. "Listen, I'll find someone. If you do it, you'll make the wrong calls, or start crying and sound like a potential pain in the ass, or try to get them to work for twenty bucks an hour."

"I wouldn't do that."

"It doesn't matter what you do. I'll do it better and faster," Fat Boy said. "You'll have someone in time for the six o'clock news."

Fat Boy was true to his word. Late that afternoon, he actually walked the quarter of a mile to the house. He was exhausted and triumphant, as if he'd just completed the Ironman. His shirt was soaked, like laundry when the spin cycle doesn't work. I handed him a giant glass of water and even managed my hydration speech, which he seemed to enjoy; I thought it made him feel like a jock. He told me he'd gotten a family spokesperson for me, someone named Kimberly Dijkstra, who had done some freelance writing for his hedge fund. "She was a reporter for *BusinessWeek* a hundred years ago. Steel-trap mind but comes off as warm and fuzzy—with big, maternal boobs, which is what you said you wanted. I kind of always liked those kind. Anyway, Andrea said you met her at one of our tree-trimming parties, so Kimberly can legitimately say she's known you for years. Trust me: She's good. She lives on East Seventy-fifth, in a town house, serious family money—and her parents were nice enough to die young, so it's all hers. She'll meet the press, so to speak. Do it in front of her house, which makes a good visual. A tree, window boxes, wealth . . . you will like it." I told him fine, although right now I couldn't think of anything I wanted to say privately, much less publicly. "You don't have to think," Fat Boy said. "Kimberly will. And if she's stumped, she knows I'll have the answer."

Chapter Twelve

By the time of the funeral, I'd broken apart. Now I was two people. Naturally, there was Susie the Wreck, the new widow who slept two or three hours a night, who had to fight herself not to break into hiccupping sobs when she was with her boys. That wound up being twenty hours a day, since besides my not being able to sleep, Evan, Dashiell, and Mason each developed his own brand of insomnia.

In Evan's case, insomnia was plain not sleeping. I could see his exhaustion getting worse day by day. His endearing little-boy skinniness—ribs and vertebrae on display—went from healthy to skeletal. His fair, lightly freckled skin grew pale, then took on a greenish undertone. Red smudges appeared under his eyes, then darkened until he looked like a creepy character in a Tim Burton movie. In those rare hours I managed to fall asleep, I'd wake myself. *Evan? Is everything okay with Evan?* I pictured him lying on his side, eyes wide open, though not really seeing the stuffed animal sharing his pillow. My in-laws had brought one for each boy from their trip to Machu Picchu. I'd done the aren't-you-marvelous daughter-in-law bit: "What absolutely gorgeous llamas!" Even before the "ma" in "llama" was out of my mouth, Babs was shaking her head. "Actually," she said, "they're vicuñas."

Dashiell would wake up screaming. No words, just an endless shriek that slashed through the suburban night. One of Jonah's and my private names for him had been Blabbo the Talking Boy—Dash had been born with no internal shutoff device. But now, at night anyway, he'd become mute. "Dash, sweetie, tell Mommy what the bad dream was about." He'd suck in his lips and shake his head violently, *No! No!* as if he were certain an evil Someone was listening in to make sure he didn't break the code of silence.

Mason had never completely given up his infant sleep habits. It hadn't been that terrible; Jonah and I had taken turns getting up whenever he woke, going to his room to kiss his forehead. At worst, we'd have to sit on the edge of his bed for a couple of minutes, saying, "Shhh, go to sleep, Mase." After that, he'd be fine for another three hours. Maybe we should have Ferberized him early on, but he'd been the easiest of the triplets, so without even discussing it, we'd just allowed him the right to be a little annoying. Besides, our sleep deprivation had been so off the charts that our visits to his room barely registered.

Now, though, Mason was wide awake for at least a half hour each time he got up. I'd hold him and whisper "Easy, sweetie" or "Shhh." But no comfort could get him to stop pleading with me to come downstairs with him and wait for Daddy. I knew I had to be patient. I would explain exactly what I'd explained a few hours earlier: Daddy wasn't coming back. "Remember, honey? We talked about it, that Daddy died. And what did we say?" His head swiveled frighteningly fast. No, no, no. He wanted no part of reality. "When someone dies," I went on, "they *can't* come back. No matter how much we wish they could." No, no, no.

So there was that half of me, Susie the Wreck. But beside this exhausted, shaken, grieving mess, another me took form. Enraged Susie. "Enraged Susie" did sound ridiculous, even to me—Premenstrual Barbie meets Bride of Chucky. Except my rage had such power I was frightened by its destructiveness. What I couldn't deal with was the fury; I was consumed with flaming anger even when I had zero energy to drag myself from room to room. The tabloid headlines could barely get through the wall of my grief, yet at the same time, they sent me into a frenzy. I wanted to scream louder than any human being ever had. Neighbors, acres away, would call 911 in horror. The cops would hear my shrieks over their sirens as they sped from head-quarters.

Left to myself, shielded by Kimberly the Spokesperson and Fat Boy's gift of two weeks of security goons watching the house, I wouldn't have seen those headlines. From the morning I woke up and Jonah wasn't there, I let the *Times* and *The Wall Street Journal* rot in their plastic bags in the driveway. And was I going to drive to the newsstand at the LIRR station to get a look at *The New York Post* and *The Daily News*? I saw the headlines because relatives and friends had decided the widow of a mur-dered thirty-nine-year-old man needed to know what the world had to say about her husband.

DOC SHOCK Park Avenue Plastic Surgeon Found Slain

UNKINDEST CUT Cops Say Park Avenue "Face Ace" Stabbed.

NO TRACE OF "FACE ACE" HOOKER Cops Step Up Hunt for Missing Call Girl.

If I'd had a minute to reflect, I wouldn't have found the crassness of those front pages such a shock. A young, success-ful doctor, married, three kids, is stabbed to death in a whore's apartment. Was that a tabloid story or what? Sure, I would hate it. But no rational person would believe *The New York Post* would rethink its mission and decide, *Oh no, hawking this story would be cruel, to say nothing of tasteless!* But I hadn't had that minute to reflect.

I could have borne Susie the Wreck better if not for Enraged Susie. Sure, I knew about the connection between depression and anger; I'd had enough therapy to understand that just by pressing Play in my mind, I could hear the placid but breathy voice of my shrink, Dr. Twersky, saying: "Depression is anger turned inward."

"For God's sake," I told Dr. Twersky five hours before Jonah's funeral. "I am not turning my anger inward. I'm angry! I know I'm angry." There she was, in my kitchen, a shrink making a house call and at seven-thirty in the morning, so I could get to Manhattan in time. I'd been to the funeral home before: It was every Jewish doctor's last stop between New York and eternity, upscale, dowdy, but reassuring. The chapel didn't have crosses, though the vaulted ceiling had fluffy clouds painted on it. *Hey, don't worry,* the azure sky seemed to be reassuring, *there actually is a heaven, and you'll get in.*

"Inward anger is one thing," I went on. "Mine is outward!" Actually, I shouted it. But it was the sort of whispered shouting you do when you don't want to be overheard—like by your children. I'd made the mistake of telling Ida and Ingvild it would be okay if the boys raced their Hot Wheels trucks along the upstairs hallway. "What I'm feeling is actual rage!" Except by whispering it, I was coming off more like an angry Muppet than the near-psychotic I was. "Even if I wanted to keep it inward, goddammit, I couldn't."

"You just told me—" She always spoke slowly. Either she weighed her every word or feared making some hideous and eternally mockable Freudian slip. "—that you—" I watched and waited. She was wearing a pantsuit and hadn't wanted to take off the jacket. Now, as she sat in the straight-backed kitchen chair, the shoulders were riding way up. She looked like one of those overpadded, neckless football linemen, except in heavy navy tweed.

I didn't let her finish. "I just told you . . . what? That I'm depressed? Of course I am." I was on the verge of saying I felt like a dead person, but I stopped myself. She'd say, "Let's talk about what you mean by 'dead person.'" Instead, I said, "I feel like shit. Except shit would be an improvement."

Dr. Twersky nodded. Some weak sun made it through the window and shone on her reddish-blond hair. It lit up her frizzy corkscrew curls into something painterly. Usually, she looked like Little Orphan Annie's grandmother. "Feeling like shit . . ." she said carefully. "That sounds like an appropriate response to me."

"But if I'm feeling so dead and empty, plus on the verge of hysterical weeping, how can I also have all this rage? It's almost impossible to control. I'm so exhausted. I need it to stop. I'm afraid I'll lose it and start screaming. Or hurt everybody."

"Everybody?"

"Well, not the boys. But with everyone else, I get wild with fury at even the dumbest remark. You know, something just thoughtless, not even cruel. Or at least not intentionally cruel. I got crazed by people who were calling here to talk to me. Why the hell can't they wait for the funeral? Then I get angry at all the others, the ones who don't call: Do they have to stand on fucking ceremony?"

"And you say you have none of this anger toward the boys?"

"No, not toward them." I smoothed the ribbed cuffs of my sweater. I don't know how long I'd stood in my dressing room, debating what to wear for a shrink home visit on the day of my husband's funeral. Wool pants? No, too afternoony for such an early hour. I finally threw on jeans and a black sweater. But when the doorbell rang and I was running down the stairs, I thought, *Oh God, what if she thinks I'm going to wear this to the service?*

I hadn't wanted Dr. Twersky at the house. She'd called a couple of hours after the news of Jonah's murder got on TV, and started going on and on about how sorry she was. I wanted to pretend the connection was bad; if she thought I couldn't hear her, I could say "What? What? I can't hear you" and hang up. I did try to lose her with "I really, really appreciate your calling" and babbling about how I wished I could get over to see her but I really didn't have time because as soon as the medical examiner released the body—Jonah—we'd have the funeral the next day.

That was when she offered to come over, which naturally made me wonder, *Is she doing this because she just wants to get a look at the house?* Because when I'd gone on and on in one session about picking yellow alabaster for the countertop in the downstairs guest bathroom—even though I wasn't supposed to be, because talking about objects was masking a psychological issue I obviously wanted to avoid—I realized she was leaning forward. Yellow alabaster! Obviously high on Dr. Twersky's emotional resonance chart.

Then I kept worrying if this session was going to be a freebie because I definitely didn't ask her to come. She volunteered. Or would she send me a bill? Fine, it was a professional relationship, but what if she billed me for, like, time and a half because it was so early in the morning, or because it was a house call? Now, sitting with her at the kitchen table, that all-American place for honesty, I realized I couldn't get away with saying I hadn't gotten angry at all with the boys. Fine: I admitted to her that I was so wiped that I didn't have my usual resistance to their noise, and that Mason's inability to comprehend that dead meant dead after I'd explained it a hundred times was getting to me. It made me want to break down and cry. In fact, one time I did. But I left out how a couple of times I wanted to grab him by the shoulders and shake him until his head rocked and he cried "What? What do you want, Mommy?" and I'd scream, with spit flying out of my mouth, "Never, ever talk about Daddy coming back again!"

Then I changed the subject to how, within a few hours of the newspapers coming out, before they even got to the autopsy, I'd picked up the remote in our closet–dressing room area, just out of habit. FOX News came on because Bernadine, our housekeeper, was not only a right-wing nut but had a fixation on Bill Hemmer that went way beyond a crush. Just as I was about to turn off the TV, I glanced up. They were cutting from a reporter in front of the UN back to the news desk.

Behind the anchor—a woman who'd had serial face-lifts that made her mouth look like it was experiencing major g-forces on blastoff—was a giant screen. On it was Jonah's photo from Manhattan Aesthetics' website. And Awful Face-lifts on FOX was telling her male co-anchor, Obvious But Not Terrible Eye Job, that Jonah had been "stabbed to death in the apartment of a notorious Upper East Side prostitute." She went on about Jonah being known as "king of the tummy tuckers," which wasn't true; he did much more face and some breast work. Then she said he was "a well-known Democrat activist," which was true if that meant someone who'd gone to one cocktail party for Obama.

Then she got to the family: first, Kimberly the Spokesperson, saying, "Mrs. Gersten has no reason to doubt her husband's love for her and their little boys." Then they played a video of me and Jonah. It must have come from somebody's black-tie wedding, or maybe a Mount Sinai benefit, because I was in an Armani, a strapless cobalt taffeta, from about five years before, that had never fit in the bust after my pregnancy. Jonah's arm was around me, and we were standing in a group, but they'd put our heads in a highlighted oval. It made us not just more visible to TV viewers but look like some golden couple among grayed-out dullards. I couldn't follow much of what the anchor was saying beyond "wife and triplets, four years old!" as if the boys being four made Jonah's murder or his being at a prostitute's— whichever—infinitely worse than if they'd been three or five.

"And," I added, "they had a close-up of our 2008 holiday card, with the boys sitting on a beautiful horse. Light chestnut or something. From when we were up in Aspen, in a glen with Ponderosa pines and aspens all around. Well, of course aspens. There's a . . . I guess it's a lake in the background. I don't remember it, but it's there on the card."

Dr. Twersky gave a nod and said something. Maybe "Uh-huh."

"It was really strange," I went on. "I was so shocked at seeing all of us up there that it felt like my heart stopped beating. But I was too stunned to worry *Am I getting a heart attack?* And I didn't get at all angry then."

"Do you remember anything else you might have felt?" For the second time, I saw her glancing over to the cooking island. I'd hollowed out a giant Savoy cabbage and filled it with white roses and Genista. She was probably thinking how superficial I was, bothering about arranging flowers when I had a dead husband to worry about. To be fair, maybe she was thinking that it was healing that I could lose myself in flowers, even for a couple of minutes.

Once Dr. Twersky left (after an inordinate amount of time in the yellow alabaster guest bathroom), I spent the next hour making brown sugar cookies with the boys, for whoever came back to the house after the cemetery. I figured it would be a good way to get the three of them to calm down after their truck races and also let them feel they were participating in the day. Also, I wanted to give Ida and Ingvild a break; based on their kindness over the last few days, they could qualify for sainthood.

I cried so much that day. Not just from grief, because I'd been grieving since they found Jonah, and even before, in anticipation. This time my tears were from being in this packed chapel with almost three hundred people demanding face time to tell me "What a terrible, terrible loss." Many of them meant it. "Susie, I'm so sorry." It was like someone else's car radio you couldn't turn off; I was stuck with listening to their every word. Yet all I heard of the rabbi's eulogy was "We have a right to ask, 'Where is God in all this?'" The rabbi probably offered an answer, though I didn't catch it.

Apparently, he went on for a while. One of Florabella's best customers, Caddy Demas, came running over—or whatever it's called in stiletto heels with anorexic ankles—just as I was getting into the limo to go to the cemetery. Her gloved hand tugged at my coat sleeve. "Susie, I just have to tell you. That rabbi may have gone on for what? twenty minutes? but it was so incredibly moving that nobody cared." Her gloves were persimmon suede with black satin skirtlike things flaring out at the wrists, a look for the woman whose devotion to fashion was so maniacal she was proud to look like the fourth musketeer.

By that time, I was little more than a robot programmed to respond "Thank you" when spoken to. But Caddy had a standing five-hundred-dollar-a-week order with us, and so was capable of overriding my circuitry. I wound up saying, "Oh, Caddy, thank you *so* much for sharing that with me," a sentence I normally would not only refuse to utter but would make me gag. Maybe it wasn't that she was a valuable customer; maybe it was dawning on me that I needed to be nicer to people.

With three little kids, I was facing the world as a different person. Whatever points a widow inherited from her husband's status weren't going to guarantee me a spot on the A-team anymore. "Stabbed to death" might make for interesting conversation, but Jonah's demise at a call girl's apartment would be taken to mean that Susie hadn't been able to satisfy him. Or that someone like me had managed to score a privileged-attractive-charming-gifted-successful Yale doctor only because he was one deeply twisted dude.

Chapter Thirteen

"How has it been, dealing with her?" my brother-in-law asked. Our heads turned toward the living room and his mother.

"Fine," I said. Theo gave me a look, so I said, "Doable. But she seems to be avoiding eye contact with me. Normally, that would throw me. But I'm too far gone to be thrown."

"Let me tell you: When a person comes to the end of her rope and she's sure there are no more terrors life can hold, that's only because she hasn't met my mother yet. You're never too far gone."

"Your mother can be a challenge, to put it mildly," I agreed. "But she loved Jonah so much. She and I are going through the same hell now. The last thing I want is for her to withdraw from me. Trust me, Theo: I understand what your parents—and you—are living through now, what you went through from the minute Jonah was missing. This is just as terrible for you as it is for me."

Theo flipped his stylishly messy hair off his forehead. "No. Look, they lost a child, but he'd had a life: He accomplished, he gave them grandchildren. I lost a brother who was always great

to me, even way back, when I was *the* primo pain in the ass."
Jonah would not have put that completely in the past tense, but
I nodded. "For me, a brother like him was a perpetual reminder
that you don't have to be a shit or a bore to get where you want
to go. He was such a good man, but he didn't wear his goodness
like, you know, Thomas More in *The Tudors*. He was fun. But
for you: We're not just talking close relative here. We're talking father of your children, triplets, for God's sake. And your
lover."

"My dearest friend, too." My voice might have trembled a
little, but by late afternoon, I was cried out, at least until after
everybody left. "He understood me so totally, right from the
start. And he loved me a hundred percent. He wasn't looking to
make changes."

"Sucks," he murmured.

"And then some."

It was the third night of shiva, the weeklong period of mourning. Theo and I had successfully hidden ourselves in plain sight
in the hallway between the guest bathroom and living room.
Momentarily, we were safe from the damp kisses and messy
condolences from the almost two hundred visitors coming each
day.

The seven-day grieving period probably had been a brilliant custom for a sixteenth-century Polish village, where you
could spend a whole lifetime meeting fewer than two hundred
people. But in the twenty-first century, Babs, Clive, Theo, and
I were overwhelmed with visitors from the different universes
we inhabited. We had doctors, of course, smooth-browed plastic surgeons and rumpled oncologists. Babs's crew of cosmetic-
industry executives was discernible because they looked like
they'd inherited their eyelashes from a mink. The theater and
New York movie types from Theo's casting life reminded me of
academics—the only other group I knew who wore their scarves
indoors.

From my life, floral types set down flowers that could have been plucked from the Garden of Eden when God's back was turned. Event planners came bearing excessively inventive sympathy baskets. Someone brought French preserves, a wheel of Reblochon, and baguettes tied around and around with tricouleur ribbon probably left over from a Bastille Day party. Another came with a Limoges plate on which she'd arranged gargantuan dried apricots and pears into a giant rose.

Neighbors came, too, from all the Gersten territories, suburban Long Island, Manhattan, the Hamptons. So did our best friends from high school, college, and the present. Obscure third cousins appeared, insisting on drawing family trees on the backs of business cards. It was all too much.

Every few sentences, Theo or I would glance over at Babs. She sat so far back in the wing chair—Jonah's chair—that her black lizard Manolo flats weren't touching the floor. I kept waiting for her to inch forward, as she was in deep dialogue with her blue-eyed rabbi. It seemed like a one-way conversation—she talked, he leaned in to listen. But she sat straight, speaking slowly but intensely, her head pressing against the chair's high back.

"I'm glad I'm not a fly on that wall," Theo remarked. "I'm sure she's saying something that would infuriate me." He shuddered in a way that made his glossy, longish hair flop charmingly. "Or humiliate me beyond belief."

"Maybe just embarrass you," I countered.

"Not that 'embarrass' is a natural segue, but are your parents coming tonight?" Even when trying to hide distaste, a lot of people broadcast it through small gestures—nose wrinkling or corner-of-mouth twisting. Theo's giveaway was always over the top in its lack of subtlety. He would jerk back his head in distaste as if he'd just spotted a conga line of cockroaches. I thought it was hilarious, though Jonah had a theory that Theo's hostility level was so off the charts that while politeness required everyone else to hide their "What a loser" or "Outrageously cheap wine" comments, Theo had to let it out. His "your parents" and head jerk occurred in the same instant.

"No, they're not coming," I told him. "My mother had a sinus attack. From my flowers, she said. She disapproves of flowers inside houses. Right after I dropped out of school and moved to New Haven, she went through an environmental-activist phase. It lasted about three weeks. But that was just when I moved in with Jonah and landed a designer job with *the* best florist in New Haven. When I told her about it, she did her quiet 'oh' first. She just says 'oh,' then stops. Gives you enough time for your heart to sink. Then she said, 'There are some of us who believe nature is a not-for-profit corporation.' I had some brilliant response, like 'Huh?' She got this really huffy tone: 'Some of us might ask if the florist business is ethical. You have to admit it does rip off nature.' So I asked her, 'What about farmers?' She couldn't think of an answer, so she backed down.

"But a couple of months later, she was sitting next to a basket of dahlias and bittersweet I'd done. All of a sudden she started clearing her throat about a million times. Then she said, 'The doctor thinks I may have developed an allergy to flowers indoors, when there's no ventilation.' She still does her allergy act whenever she remembers. Sometimes she rubs where her sinuses hurt. Except Jonah said where she's rubbing would be for TMJ pain, not sinusitis. Anyway, my father offered to come by himself tonight, but I could hear the relief in his voice when I told him he should stay home, rest up."

A minute later, we glanced back into the living room. Babs had fallen silent. The rabbi looked like he was trying to recall Pastoral Relations 101, the lecture called "When Communication Is Awkward." Suddenly, Babs burst into tears. She patted her lap, blindly searching for her handkerchief, unfolded it, and pressed it against her eyes with both palms.

"You can't see from here," Theo said. "But I bet you anything her Gigi de Lavallade waterproof mascara is still working."

I stopped the smile before it got to my face and said, "Theo, stop!" My brother-in-law had the bad-boy appeal of a precocious kid. People were forever shaking their heads at his scandalous remarks while being charmed at his wicked assessments. With him around, I was the nice one, but we'd always enjoyed verbal tennis, volleying remarks back and forth. So in this brief, bright time-out from the darkness of Jonah's murder, I was on the verge of responding that Babs could use the mascara's reliability for a first-person "My Tragedy, My Mascara" ad campaign. Theo would like that one, but I couldn't take the risk. He could easily become a loose cannon, and my remark was great ammunition the next time he decided to zing Babs: "I know your mother is in terrible pain."

Theo leaned back, tilting one of the antique prints of ferns hanging in the hallway. Though he obviously heard the scrape of frame against wall, he didn't say anything like "Oh, sorry," the way most people would have. He just shifted and spoke, his voice relaxed yet somehow flat, as if he were chatting about an actress not quite talented enough to play the mother in a movie he was casting. "She's probably in pain because my father wants to go straight back to work and not take a post-shiva week in Saint Barth to console her, which means she's feeling pressure to go back to work before she's ready."

"So you're telling me not to go gently with her?" I asked. "I mean, if she's feeling pressured."

"No. Be however you want to be. Say whatever needs saying. Well, easy for me to say. I am her son, which I guess entitles me to special treatment from her. The Best of Babs: Good, Bad, Ugly. You know, I had an internship at a rep company out in L.A. the summer between my junior and senior years at Wesleyan. Okay, I'd been to camp and on teen tours, but that was the first time I was really away from my parents' world. Not that summer theater is the place to go if you're big on genuineness, but I felt so *right* there. What's really strange, though, is even driving out there, I went through Terre Haute, Indiana, and I thought how much easier my life would have been if I'd grown up there. I'd never realized before how—I don't know—complex, difficult, it had been living in my parents' world."

I could almost feel Jonah beside me, whispering in my ear, "See? You asked a question about you, and what did it become? All about Theo." He'd be smiling, less with pleasure than with satisfaction that he had his brother's MO down pat.

I had to get back into the living room. Heads were starting to swivel. Visitors were searching for me so they could say, "This must be such a nightmare for you!" and still have enough time to get home for *American Idol*. But my bro-in-law didn't want to let me go.

"I call it my parents' world," Theo continued, "but my mother rules."

I'd told Jonah once that Theo reminded me of those sprites or whatever in a Shakespearean comedy. Not gay, I'd added. He was definitely a hetero sprite, but he was unusually graceful and was always making delightfully wicked comments. Jonah replied that the problem was his brother often didn't see the difference between being wickedly witty and being a mean little shit.

I waved to Andrea at the far end of the living room, but she missed the urgency of my *Come get me!* signal and just waved back. I hoped a few seconds of silence would discourage him, but Theo wasn't going anywhere. I finally said, "You'd think with your father being an oncologist, he'd be more . . . not aggressive. Assertive. He'd know what's important in life."

Theo took over. "He knows cancer is important. But cancer isn't all there is in the world. The only other thing he ever knew was that being the son of a podiatrist with a plantar's-wart specialty wasn't a ticket to the A-list. More than anything, my father wanted to be a someone. He was like the Little Match Boy, staring in on people living—whatever—elegantly. He so wanted in, but he didn't have a key to the door. That's where my mother came in. 'This is the biography to read, the film to see, the primary candidate we should support. Wear a white dinner jacket for formal occasions between Memorial Day and Labor Day. Stop ordering risotto because risotto is so 2001.' It's all about surfaces with her. Look what she does for a living: marketing director for a cosmetics company. Can you get more superficial than that?"

Naturally, I didn't say "How about the last movie you cast?" *Call 666-SATAN* was not only superficial but supremely lousy. Also, as Jonah pointed out, totally miscast. Then again, Theo wasn't exactly coming home to voice mail from Martin Scorsese. He worked for deeply minor theater companies and film directors whose common goal seemed to be making bad imitations of successful horror, soft-core porn, and hacked-up teenager movies. So I said, "I don't know about superficial, but your mother is capable of love. You—" Theo shook his head: *No. She doesn't love me.* Arguing with him would have taken too much time, so I kept going. "She loved Jonah."

"Absolutely."

"She loves the boys. I know she sees them as individuals, not just the triplets."

"That's true. She—the two of them—are the quintessential doting grandparents. Granted, it's baby-boomer chic, being crazy about your grandchildren. But they are completely besotted. Well, she told my father he was completely besotted, so that's what he is. And that will be great for you."

I didn't get what he meant. Normally, to avoid the Gersten I-Must-Be-Patient-with-Your-Stupidity deep breath, I would have said sure, but I'd waited too long. As Theo inhaled, I was forced to ask, "What do you mean, great for me?"

"I mean she's not going to do anything to alienate you. Don't you see why? She's smart enough to know that, ultimately, alienating you would also mean alienating the grandchildren. You are the doorkeeper."

"What?"

"You control access to the boys. Also, if my parents didn't do right by you and word got out, they'd look bad. It's not comme il faut to fuck over your late son's widow."

Just as I was wondering if he meant his parents could deal with their son's murder but not with looking bad, Fat Boy came into the hall, double-timing it from the living room on his way to the bathroom. I noticed a macadamia nut drop from the huge fistful he was trying to hide by stuffing his hand into a too-tight side pocket. Since I didn't want to make him uncomfortable about having to squeeze by the two of us, I parted from Theo with "Later."

"Later" took quite a while, because I made the mistake of saying "Why don't we sit down?" to Gilbert John Noakes and his wife, Coral. She was a long-limbed Englishwoman. Though her looks made you think, *Oh, more graceful than a gazelle,* Coral lurched through life like a bad actor imitating a drunk, which I guessed she was. It was hard to tell, because all she ever drank in public was sparkling water, yet she showed the signs: Most of her sentences made you wonder whether you'd misheard—they were Britishly enunciated and probably grammatical, but they didn't make sense. Also, she was dangerous in any space containing antique vases and other people's feet—such as my living room.

Once we were seated, though, I was hardly able to speak to the Noakeses. People kept crowding around me like I was a Nancy Gonzalez sale table at Bergdorf's. I got that phobic feeling of *Oh my God, not enough air,* so I stood. That left the two of them gazing up at me, but at least I didn't feel like the oxygen was being sucked out of my lungs.

I sensed Coral and Gilbert John would understand my getting up, or pretend to, or not notice, and they wouldn't disappear from my life. I could look forward, unfortunately, to still being asked to their dinner parties. Gilbert John would invite a mix of doctors, potential patients, and what he called "interesting young people," which meant anyone under thirty who wore retro eyeglasses. Coral used a caterer who always served what Jonah had called "elderly chicken" with halves of grapes and a curdled white sauce. But maybe I'd be too tainted by the scandal of Jonah's murder to be asked to dine chez Noakes. They might take me to a restaurant every six months. Without the comfort of knowing I could at least laugh about them on the ride home, how could I bear it? Gilbert John would rake a fork tine on a tablecloth to show me the pattern of his newest mosaic, thereby competing with Coral's convoluted conversation about English gardens of her youth, though she could never remember the names of flowers: "The purplish ones with . . ." She'd fluff a couple of fingers outward, waiting expectantly, so I'd wind up guessing iris, anemone, cosmos. No to each. "Passionflower, echinacea?" Again a no.

At very long last, they stood to say goodbye. Gilbert John's chapped lips felt like an emery board against my cheek. "We'll speak soon," he said. Coral put her cheek to mine. As I kissed the air, she said, "If there's anything . . ." She must have thought she'd completed a sentence, because she turned and walked away. Gilbert John hurried to catch up and grab her elbow. He steered her across the rest of the living room so if she did trip over any feet, they would be her own.

I realized that by standing up, I'd become a one-woman receiving line for friends, relatives, and everyone else, from the long-retired coach of Jonah's high school tennis team to a Baptist minister who'd sat with me on the board of the Nassau County Coalition Against Domestic Violence. All the heartfelt words that came my way — "So very, very sorry" and "I know nothing I say can ease your pain, but . . ." — were offset by Buddy Gratz, a local pharmacist who elbowed his way into a knot of neighbors and in history's loudest recorded whisper confided to them, "Hey, can you *believe* the cops haven't found that hooker yet?"

Shudders passed through the room. But before the whispered "Oh my God's" that would mortify me even more got started, there was a Distraction with a capital D—as well as Drama. As "that hooker" still echoed, every head turned to a spot ten feet behind me. Right on the borderline between the entry hall and living room stood a tall, slim exclamation mark of a woman. Something about her drew attention, like the giant horseshoe magnets in science class that pulled in all those iron filings.

And there she was, Ethel O'Shea, my mother's mother, a woman I'd seen only twice in my life. Grandly, she swooped into the living room on the arm of her lover, Felicia Burns, whom everyone called Sparky. Halfway over to me, Ethel came to a halt. As we all waited for her to speak, she lifted her liposuctioned chin. In a voice that made Buddy Gratz's remark sound like silence, she declared, "Susie, dear girl! Grandma is here!"

Chapter Fourteen

For Babs, the blue-eyed rabbi became history. Like everyone else's in the living room, her gaze kept racing from Grandma Ethel to me and back again. For those who knew my family history, here, in pants and a black Malo turtleneck, was the anti-mom, the dreadful woman who'd walked out on her eight-year-old child. Heartless. But hey, did she look fabulous.

For the rest—showtime! There was the new widow greeting a woman who was practically her clone. Except the clone had called herself Grandma, so she must be, what? In her late seventies? Amazing, because the clone was simply not an old lady. She had fabulous hair, astoundingly lush for someone her age, deep gold and platinum—colors from a treasure chest. She wore it twisted into a soft knot pinned with careful casualness on top of her head.

Their thoughts were so loud I could hear them. *Look at her and Susie!* The same long arms and legs. Necks that came close to qualifying for swan status. Straight noses that Jonah once swore no plastic surgeon could replicate. Cheekbones like that of Mrs. Genghis Khan. And those mesmerizing eyes, so pale they were barely on the green side of white.

Seeing Ethel O'Shea was seeing the future me. Thankfully, since I was a superficial person, it was not a nightmare vision, though it didn't make me think, *Hey, I can't wait till I'm seventy-eight!*

I kissed my grandmother on the cheek, inhaling the Gardenia Passion I'd smelled the other two times we'd been together. I kissed Sparky, who was scentless. I'd met her about five years earlier, when she and Ethel had come to New York and Jonah and I had taken them out for dinner. My grandmother had introduced us by putting her arm around Sparky's shoulders and saying, "This is the love of my life." Sparky had grinned and said, "Ethel's got that line down pat."

"Susie, I am so, so sorry," Sparky began. She was a civil liberties lawyer. Every word she spoke, probably even "with milk and Splenda," came out loaded with passion and conviction. "Jonah was a wonderful guy. I only wish we'd had the chance to spend more time with him."

"He was beyond wonderful," Grandma Ethel corrected. "A total doll." Those in the audience close enough to hear her lines nodded in agreement. "You couldn't help loving him. He didn't hold back, you know what I mean?" Sparky nodded. Since she was the expert on how to handle my grandmother, I decided nodding was the way to go. "You know what was remarkable about Jonah? None of that 'Let me see if you're worth my while before I'm nice to you' crap. He was so decent. To everyone, even the waiter. Remember? Also, there wasn't an ounce of that bullshit gemütlichkeit successful men use to show they're not the arrogant putzes they actually are."

Compared to Grandma Ethel's greeting and what I'd come to recognize as her brassy talk-show-hostess style, her remarks were soft-spoken. Still, that didn't stop her magnetism. She didn't have to shout to draw all the attention in the room, even from those out of hearing distance. Babs, along with everyone else, was probably reflecting on the triumph of nature over nurture, as in: *The two of them have the same taste in clothes! Look at them. Black slacks, black turtlenecks, diamond stud earrings. True, the grandmother has about ten gold bangles on her right wrist, while Susie's wearing a wide gold mesh cuff. But that's more a generational thing than a different fashion sensibility.*

Finally, I sensed the *Oy!* and *Good grief!* reactions to the resemblance had gotten played out. Almost everyone in the room, Babs included, lost interest in me and got busy assessing the dynamics between Grandma Ethel and the woman whose arm she was holding. *That is definitely not the way an old-fashioned lady would take the arm of a hired companion or a good friend— not with her boob brushing the other one's upper arm.*

As for that other woman, mid- to late fifties. She's wearing a pantsuit. Wait, call it what it is: a suit that probably had GEN- TLEMEN'S CUSTOM CLOTHIER *on the label. Tropical wool, winter white. Worn with an open-necked white shirt. She looks like a sugar magnate in pre-Castro Cuba, minus the mustache, of course. She is definitely not masculine.*

Not that she's feminine, either. Though she, too, is wearing diamond stud earrings, hers are major, close to three carats each. By the time she gets to be the grandmother's age, her earlobes could resemble a beagle's. She isn't wearing a stitch of makeup, but she's good-looking in that "dark brown hair, sparkly brown eyes, tanned skin, pug nose" way. She could belong to any group that fell under the heading Caucasian, from English in a sunny climate to Sicilian with a nose job.

I glanced through the knots of visitors and watched my mother- in-law rising from her chair. Though only five feet three, Babs had that head-held-high posture that demanded deference: *I get intro- duced first.* She saw me looking at her and smiled a little—sadly, of course. Still, it was enough to tell me my social quotient had risen with the arrival of a stylish lesbian grandmother (carrying a Prada clutch under her arm). If, in the past, Babs had formed any men- tal picture of Ethel the Abandoner, it probably had been a crone version of my mother, Sherry Rabinowitz: Mrs. Potato Head but much more wrinkled, wearing a T-shirt that said DON'T CALL ME SWEETIE . . . IT'S BAD FOR YOUR TEETH.

"My grandmother Ethel O'Shea and Felicia Burns," I began, using the Spanish/Miami pronunciation Felicia preferred—*Fee-lee-see-a.* "This is my mother-in-law, Barbara Gersten."

Since shiva was not just a sad occasion but a religious tradition with its built-in formality, there was no follow-up of "Please call me Sparky/Babs." Grandma Ethel took Babs's hands in hers, closed her eyes for a moment as if searching, searching, for the perfect words. "Oh, Barbara. I am so sorry we have to meet on such a terrible occasion. But what a first-rate man Jonah was! Trust me. I've been around the block many, many times in my life, and I never met a better man than Jonah."

She was right. Throughout our entire marriage, I did believe there was no better man than Jonah. Still, I knew there was a 97 percent chance my grandmother's tribute was full of shit. Not that she didn't think positively about him—doctor/charming/ Gen X non-homophobe/nice pecs, not flabby tits—but that was probably as far as her enthusiasm went. Nevertheless, my mother-in-law, so wise in the ways of social fakery (having the ultimate insider's view), appeared genuinely moved by Grandma Ethel's words.

"He was wonderful," Babs agreed. "The best." She could barely get the words out because she was so choked up. "Thank you for saying so."

"I just met him once," Sparky spoke up. "But I knew right away, this guy is the real deal. I'm sorry that you, your husband, Susie, your whole family have to suffer a loss like this."

"I can't tell you how much I appreciate your kindness," Babs said. "Coming up here from Miami in the middle of winter."

"How could we not?" Grandma Ethel demanded. "We're family."

As Babs and my grandmother went back and forth, I watched

them with something between disbelief and awe. Grandma Ethel had spent twenty-five years hosting *Talk of Miami*. Even in the bit of it I'd gotten to see, in a single week, she could run the gamut of emotions from A to Z, then back from Z to A — depending on if she was interviewing a celebrity chef, a victim of ethnic cleansing in Rwanda, or a sixty-something actress who had written a memoir claiming simultaneous affairs with Adlai Stevenson and Grace Kelly. I couldn't decide if my grandmother felt all those emotions, or any of them. But she'd definitely acted as if she did.

And then there was my mother-in-law. Babs's life was dedicated to convincing women around the world that by laying out seventy-two dollars for a jar containing a buck's worth of petroleum jelly and chemicals, they would soon look like a million. She and Grandma Ethel shared two dualities: an ability to manipulate other people and a powerful ambition to be a somebody. Most likely, they also shared a common ruthlessness. What felt weird was watching my self-centered grandmother trying so hard to make my mother-in-law feel better — and my snooty mother-in-law reaching out to someone from my family, of all people, for the comfort and healing no one else seemed able to provide.

Just as I started to worry about what to do after their conversation ran its course, Sparky put her hand on my grandmother's shoulder. "Eth, honey, let's see if we can find a quiet spot so we can spend some time with Susie." She offered a brief, regretful smile to Babs, who offered her an *Of course I understand* nod. As Babs retreated, Andrea teleported over, and Grandma Ethel managed to simultaneously charm her and brush her off with a "Heard so much about you/loved meeting you" goodbye.

Sparky, definitely a take-charge type, herded my grandmother and me toward the piano bench and commanded, "Sit there." The living room was packed with people, and there was no seat for her. Glancing around, she decided Cousin Scott the tax examiner didn't need the chair he'd carried in from the dining room for himself. She had him bring it over and place it beside us, then gave him a thank-you that conveyed, without words, *Get out of here*—which he did.

"Is that nerdy man a relative of mine?" Grandma Ethel asked.

"No," I said. "He's a Rabinowitz. He's a semi-decent guy, actually."

"'Semi-decent' is not a ringing endorsement. Does your father wear hideous ties like that? What made someone think green and black ought to be combined into a houndstooth pattern?"

"My father's ties are hideous in a different way. He's into random splotches." I took a deep breath. "In case you're worried about my parents being here tonight, you can relax. They're not coming."

"I know," Grandma Ethel said.

"You know?—"

Sparky cut in, "We came up the second we heard about Jonah. But then Ethel thought our coming here might set off your mother, which would be rough for you, and—"

"We didn't want to give you any more grief," my grandmother said. "You have enough. So I looked up their number and called it the next couple of nights. No one answered. What's with them that they don't have voice mail? In any case, I called tonight, and she answered." I couldn't find the words to form a "And what did you say?" question, but she answered it anyway. "Naturally, I wasn't going to talk to her. I hung up. But at least I knew the coast would be clear for us to come here." She pulled back her head and gave me a haughty look. "What was there for me to say to her? 'Hello, little Sherry, this is your mother' would be awkward. And am I supposed to say 'I'm sorry I walked out and left you with that loser Lenny'?"

"What would be wrong with that?" I asked, amazing myself.

"Ethel's too ashamed," Sparky said, aligning the cuffs of her jacket. "And probably scared shitless."

"I am not!" Grandma Ethel snapped at her.

"Of course you are. The only thing in the world you're afraid of is your own child."

"I am not afraid! Except of being bored. When we had dinner with you and Jonah, Susie sweets, and you brought those pictures from your wedding, I took one look at Sherry and said—I think I said it to myself—that kid grew up to be one heavy piece of furniture. You know? Something in the middle of the room everyone wishes wasn't there but can't move."

"You just said you don't want to give Susie any more grief, Eth," Sparky snapped, "so why don't you zip it up about her mother?"

"Fine," my grandmother snapped back. She slid back on the piano bench to see me better, but we were still pretty close. Looking into her eyes was like seeing my own eyes in a magnifying mirror, except all the skin around them was covered with fine wrinkles, like a veil on an old-fashioned ladies' hat. "I wish there was something I could do for you, Susie," she said to me. "I mean it."

"Thank you," I said.

"Is there something?" I shook my head. She went on, "I wasn't kidding about what I said about Jonah, you know. Not my customary crapola. Good guy. Emotionally developed. Not your typical surgeon. And he was crazy for you. You know that."

"I thought so."

"Listen, sweet one, I'm an expert. I can smell a lousy marriage a mile away. Anyone's, not just the three stinkos I wound up with. But yours, it smelled like a rose. An antique rose, like you said the first time we met, when I wanted to know why roses didn't smell anymore and you told me about . . . antique and something else."

"Rosa rugosa, probably."

"Right. Anyway, the two of you were the real thing. You had a *marriage* there. Not just a husband."

Finally, I said, "Then why did it have to end like this?"

"You mean in his being killed?"

"Not just that. I could have dealt with Jonah dying, even with him being murdered. Painful beyond belief, a wound that would never heal completely, but still, I'd keep going. But to have him stabbed to death *there*, in an apartment of someone like her. It's too much." Somehow I was able to speak those last three words quietly, even though they wanted to be shrieked.

"It is too much," Sparky responded. She said it like an established fact, which for some reason made me feel better. "Are you getting a lot of 'You have to go on for the sake of the children'?"

"That's all I hear. 'Terrible, terrible, but you have to go on for the boys.' Like I don't know that. I want to tell them, 'You know, I was thinking of giving up and letting them raise themselves, but thanks to you, I'll keep going.'"

"People are shmucks," Grandma Ethel said.

"Some of them," Sparky agreed. "But others understand the awfulness of the circumstances. I'm not trying to make chicken salad out of chicken shit. Say, three quarters of the people in this room are loving the schadenfreude thrill, wallowing in the pleasure of someone else's misery; most of them also feel grief for you. Compassion, too." Sitting on the piano bench in the corner, I kept glancing one way to my grandmother, then the other to Sparky, whose vivid personality and wide shoulders blocked off the rest of the room. I'd temporarily forgotten the house was filled with people I should be paying attention to, though I couldn't think of a way to get up and say "Excuse me." Also, I didn't want to be with anyone else, just the two of them. "Listen," Sparky went on, "I'm a civil liberties lawyer. By nature and profession, I'm cynical. I fight for causes most people don't even want defended. But I've learned that too much cynicism can hurt you. If you let yourself be overly skeptical of other people's motives, all you'll do is isolate yourself."

"What Sparks is really saying," Grandma Ethel broke in, "is

that you might be . . . what's the psychological term for what you're doing? I forget. Transposing? Displacing? Anyway, you're putting what you're thinking on to them. Like you've got it in your head, *They're laughing about Jonah — happy husband, ha ha — getting killed by a hooker.* But you tell yourself it's what they're thinking because you can't deal with the anger, embarrassment, whatever. That he was with someone like her."

"Fuck off, Eth," Sparky said quietly. "That's not what I was saying. And not at all what I was thinking."

"Whatever you say, Sparky."

"And you shouldn't be talking that way in front of Susie." As there seemed to be zero comprehension on my grandmother's part, Sparky added, "She's your granddaughter, for God's sake. Act protective. No, excuse me. *Be* protective." Her eyes got an angry crinkle on the sides as she spoke. When her gaze returned to me, her eyes didn't exactly mist up, though they did soften into a sad benevolence. "She didn't mean to hurt you," Sparky said.

"What? Did I leave the room so you can explain me to my granddaughter?" Grandma Ethel demanded. She patted the top of my hand twice. Then, sensing something more in the way of maternal warmth might be called for, she offered a third pat. "Susie, I didn't mean to hurt you."

"I know." I took Sparky's word for it more than hers.

"The minute we heard about Jonah on CNN? I mean, it's good I've got a heart of stone. But right then and there, I knew I had to be with you. Not that there's anything I can do, but . . . I don't know."

"I'm glad you both came," I said. "I'm sorry I didn't think to call you, so it's extra meaningful that you just picked up and came on your own." Sparky nodded. My grandmother did an *aw-shucks* shrug/head tilt — as if auditioning for a cowgirl role — and gazed down at her suede ankle-high boots. I continued, "You're right about me being angry. Humiliated, too. I mean, God, Jonah being killed at a hooker's. But, Grandma Ethel,

I'm not taking my thoughts and sticking them in other people's heads. I read expressions. I overhear remarks." She looked up at me. I wondered whether her lashes had always been sparse or if she'd lost them with age. "Trust me: There are plenty of 'What do you think was missing in their relationship that made Jonah need a whore?' conversations going on. And comments like 'Susie is all about appearances, and with a crappy economy affecting Jonah's practice, he probably just wanted a nice, simple fuck without any pressure or demands.'"

"I'll take your word for it," Grandma Ethel said.

My back was hurting from sitting on the piano bench without any support. My neck ached from the weight of my head. Grandma Ethel, on the other hand, sat straight and looked supremely comfortable. I said, "My mind understands what Jonah probably went to Dorinda Dillon's apartment for. It has to, because it can't find any other explanation that it can believe. But you want to know something? My heart will never accept it. It's contrary to everything I ever knew or felt about him and our relationship." She nodded. I turned to Sparky. She wasn't nodding, so I added, "Maybe because not accepting it is the only way I can keep going."

"Then let me give you some advice," Grandma Ethel said. "Fuck logic. Why torment yourself? If your heart says, 'He was a good and faithful husband,' go with it. You have every right to tell yourself, 'Maybe he was in a whore's apartment, but not for sex.' Period. End of sentence."

Chapter Fifteen

Closer to eleven o'clock than ten, after all the goodbyes, I didn't feel just exhausted. I felt physically weak. When I got to the staircase, I had to clutch the railing with two hands, lean forward, and pull with all my strength to get up the first step. What kept me from sitting right there, resting my head on the third step, and sleeping like that the whole night was fear that Mason would wake up. Not finding me in bed, he would come rushing downstairs thinking Daddy had come back. Then I heard a scraping sound: footsteps coming out of the kitchen. I'd been sure everyone was gone. A surge of adrenaline I didn't know was in me rocketed me up. I was ready to grab the boys, lock us all in my bedroom, and call the cops.

Then I heard "Susie?" Theo's voice, but he said my name in an odd way. Had he heard me practically crawling up the stairs? I turned. He was holding what was left of my last organic Pink Lady apple; his mouth was full. "Anything wrong?" he asked, the words muffled by apple.

"No, nothing. I was going to check on the boys."

"I was waiting for you in the kitchen."

"Sorry, I thought you went back to the city with your parents."

"I told them . . ." He flipped back his hand in a *get out of here* gesture. A piece of apple pulp slipped from his mouth and onto his black silk shirt, but he didn't notice. "You said we'd talk later. I assumed you still needed to unload after everyone left and that you wanted me to stay late or stay over."

"I did!" I lied. I flashed what I hoped was more grateful smile than mere display of teeth. "Let me run up and check on the boys."

When I forced myself to come back down, Theo was stretched out on the living room couch. My hope that he'd fallen asleep was dashed when he popped up into a sitting position.

"Were you in the living room when my neighbor asked if the cops had any lead on the call girl?" I asked. "Lovely moment."

"No," Theo said. "I was hanging in Jonah's study with my father. But my mother caught it, so naturally, I'll be hearing 'Can you believe the unmitigated gall of that tacky, tacky man' for the next two or three years. What a dumb pièce de shit. Your neighbor—not my mother, who, as you know, is not dumb."

"I do know." Every part of me was so heavy with exhaustion I dreaded moving. If anyone else in the world had been stretched out on my couch, eating my last Pink Lady, I would have been honest and said I was vanquished, beyond fatigue, and—though I was deeply and profoundly sorry—if I didn't sleep immediately, I would drop dead. We'd have to talk tomorrow.

The price of Theo's charm was saying yes to whatever he wanted. He hardly ever got anything but yeses, since nobody could deal with what came after the no. If I gave the slightest indication that I wouldn't go along with what he wanted, I'd be in for any of fifty different responses, all of them unpleasant. He'd rage out of the room in angry silence, shout "You think you're the only one who's exhausted?" Pull a passive-aggressive "I just want to help, but if it's more than you can handle . . ." hurl the apple across the room, and then stomp out.

But I hadn't said "No, I can't talk," so he leaned back his

head against a pillow and gave one of those half-smiles that people get when recalling a nice moment. "You know," he said, "when your grandmother walked into the room . . . Amazing! I knew instantly who she was. I mean, God, the resemblance!" His eyes opened wide, and he mouthed a silent "wow." "And her lover. You've got to give both of them credit. It can't be easy coming into a living room full of suburban types. But your grandmother has, shall we say, a certain chutzpah. Maybe even a kind of courage."

"I guess so. But 'courage' is such a positive word. Is it courageous to turn your back on an eight-year-old kid, your own flesh and blood?"

"I don't know," Theo said. "How can we judge what the mind-set was pre-feminism? It was a different world. Anyway, what is the deep dish?" He gave me what I guess was meant as an expectant raised-eyebrow look, except, as with most people, both brows lifted. "Come on," he said. "You and Granny were next to each other on the piano bench with the girlfriend right beside you. Into heavy-duty conversation." I waited for him to say more, but he sighed, like he was giving up on me.

"There wasn't anything special we were talking about," I said quickly. "Just about Jonah. They really thought he was a wonderful guy. And my grandmother obviously wanted to see me, to say how sorry she was. I'm surprised by how moved I was when I looked up and . . . Grandma Ethel. And I like Sparky a lot. She works very hard—long hours—so it meant a lot that she came, too."

"She's a civil rights lawyer?"

"Civil liberties. First Amendment stuff, keeping government out of people's personal lives."

"Does it pay?" Theo asked. "Not keeping government out of people's lives. I mean does it pay financially?"

"Probably not a bundle. But if you remember, no one has to hold a fund-raiser for Grandma Ethel." Theo nodded. I continued, "Two really profitable divorces. Highest-paid TV personality in Miami for years."

"I remember you guys talking about it."

Jonah and I had described going up to my grandmother's endless white fifties-style ranch house on some elegant little island off Miami Beach. It had high double front doors with double knobs right in the middle. The brass back plates formed a two-foot sunburst. "When Grandma Ethel and Sparky walked in tonight, it was such perfect timing," I said. Theo nodded again. I could tell I had become boring with a couple of sentences. But he wasn't getting up to go, so I added, "Actually, I was talking to them about Dorinda Dillon." Theo exhaled a long "oh." I had stopped being boring. "This may sound hopelessly naive, but do you know what I was telling them?"

"What?"

"That I still can't get my mind around the fact that Jonah went to someone like her." Maybe Theo murmured a response. It was difficult to tell, because he sat up, taking so long to change positions that it became the Theo Slo-Mo Demo and I was momentarily distracted.

Finally, he turned his head toward me and said, "I hear you, Susie." Too many seconds—maybe three—went by before he found something better to say: "He really, really loved you."

"The thing of it is," I told him, "he never turned off me the way some husbands do over time. We couldn't have kids right away because he was in med school and I had to work. Then I had all those fertility problems. So we had more years to be honeymoonish than most couples. There aren't lots of opportunities for intimacy when you have triplets, active boys, but I never doubted that Jonah was, you know, drawn to me. Even when he looked at other women, he was appreciating them, like *Hey, she is really spectacular,* but it was more as a connoisseur than a guy actively lusting. Or sometimes he'd look at them clinically, like someone would think he was gazing into their eyes while he was saying to himself, *I could make her look so much better with a brow lift.*"

"I hear you," Theo said again. "Let's put it this way: If you had exactly your personality and looked like a dog, I don't know if Jonah . . . you know how he was. About clothes, decoration, art. He had a strong aesthetic opinion about, really, everything. And for him, you were the best. My parents finally accepted they could never change his mind about you because his attraction was so strong."

"Were they hoping he'd get bored with me and see me as I really was—not an aristocrat?" *You Gerstens aren't exactly bluebloods,* I so wanted to say. *What do you have that I don't? A two-generation head start on my family in upward mobility and maybe an extra twenty-five IQ points?*

"I don't know what they thought," Theo said. "I didn't ask. The way I saw it was I loved my brother and you made him happy."

"I did. Listen, I admit I want to believe that he wasn't at Dorinda Dillon's for sex. And I do believe it. But what I'm after is the truth, even if it's an ugly truth that forces me to face something about Jonah or our relationship that I don't want to look at. Theo, the times you talked to him, did you get the impression that anything was wrong?"

"I don't know." He caressed the gold band of his thirtieth-birthday Rolex, but he couldn't check the time because the watch face was hanging down now that it was hip to wear watches loose. "I don't think anything was wrong with him, but I think he felt pressured."

"Pressure from me? Supporting me, the whole house and everything, in the style—"

"No. Possibly that's my mother's theory, but not mine."

"I wasn't that terrible a drain. I mean, for all that I'm high-maintenance, I'm doing part of the maintaining. I work. Florabella isn't making a fortune, but it's doing all right. So even with the economy and people cutting back on elective surgery, I didn't feel like I had to put the thermostat down to sixty-five degrees or buy Vanity Fair panties."

"He never complained to me about you. Period."

"The kids?"

"Well, they are a handful. As far as they went, all he ever complained about—and it wasn't in any really bad way—was their noise level. He said there were never five consecutive seconds of silence from the minute they got up to when they fell asleep. But he said it in kind of an amused way or a fond way, like 'They are so fucking noisy, but they're mine, and aren't they adorable?'"

"Then what do you think caused the pressure?"

Theo turned up his hands in an *I don't know* gesture. "I'm trying to think. Maybe he felt pressure about work. He never came right out and said it, but I sensed he didn't feel he was getting enough support from his partners. He had all the responsibility, making all the business decisions, following up on everything. Does that sound right to you?"

"It does. I mean, I don't know how much pressure he was feeling, because Jonah never was one of those husbands who took up the whole night telling you about his day. But he did feel he had too much on his plate. Gilbert John was doing his Grand Old Man thing on the international conference circuit, plus his pro bono work and philanthropy stuff. And when he wasn't busy with his usual grandness, he was getting ready for a gallery show of his mosaics. Jonah said Gilbert John was taking out the most money but working as though someone had named him surgeon emeritus. And Layne? She's the ultimate sweetie. Great with patients, but she can't or won't exert any authority over the staff."

I had to get upstairs. I suppressed a yawn so enormous, my eyes began to water.

"I think there might have been something else getting to

Jonah," Theo said. "I'm not saying it was a conscious thing. I don't know."

"What?"

"At some level, he may have been angry at not being able to live life as graciously as he wanted to."

"What do you mean?" I asked, sensing that I was going to hear something I wouldn't like.

"You know, he loved beautiful things. He wanted beautiful things. And with him being the first child, *and* the most gifted, the fact of all the pressures in his practice and of earning enough to sustain the lifestyle he wanted . . . It pissed him off, having to work so hard and still not be able to get what he dreamed of."

Everything seemed to go silent except the ticking of the wall clock in the kitchen, which I could suddenly hear. "What did he want that he didn't have?" My fatigue gave my question a flatness I wasn't feeling, but I was grateful for being able to sound as cool as Theo.

"He said it would be great to be able to afford a driver so he could have some downtime between home and work. And he really wanted to get rid of those au pair twins who had to be treated like family and were always around—going out to dinner with all of you, even—and get a top-drawer nanny."

"He was angry over that?" I asked. The flatness was gone. If any word could describe my tone, it was disbelief. Yes, Jonah could get angry, but he wasn't the type to seethe over the injustice of our not having upscale servants. Theo's shrug meant either *I'm not sure* or *I won't push it because you're in total denial.*

He left a minute later. It was nearly midnight. I had to sleep fast. Given the boys' recent insomnia, along with their usual five-thirty rise-and-shine, I'd be lucky to get four hours. I would have been asleep before my head hit the pillow, but as I was pulling down the duvet, I noticed Lieutenant Paston's card. I'd stuck it among the pinkish-white Rosalind roses I'd arranged in Jonah's Yale tenth-reunion mug on my nightstand. Paston had said to call him any time if I thought of something. Midnight was definitely any time, but the number wasn't his cell, so it wouldn't be like I was waking him. And if he wasn't working the late shift, he'd told me someone familiar with the case would be on duty.

After a couple of minutes on hold, a woman's voice came on. "Mrs. Gersten, Sergeant Maureen Ferrari. I'm sorry about your loss."

"Thank you. I know it's late, but I haven't heard anything in a couple of days. Maybe I should have waited until the morning to speak to Lieutenant Paston, but—"

"No problem." Her voice was smoky, like one of those babes in old detective movies whose hair dips over an eye. But she spoke in a fast staccato, so she didn't come across as babelike. "I wish I had something solid to report. So far, none of our leads to Dorinda Dillon has panned out."

"She's the only one you're looking for?" I asked. "I mean, was there any evidence that somebody else was involved? Her just disappearing: You don't think she had an accomplice to help her get away? Or else—this may sound far-fetched—maybe somebody did her in because"—even to myself, I was coming across like an overambitious rookie detective on *Touching Evil*—"if she was caught, she could be persuaded to talk?"

"There's really nothing to make us think anyone else was involved," Sergeant Ferrari said. "But I promise you, Mrs. Gersten, this case is our top priority. We'll find her. She left in a hurry."

"How do you know?"

"Because we found a salable amount of drugs, cocaine. In a plastic bag in a frozen pizza box. She glued the box shut, so it looked unopened." She took a deep breath. I sensed an announcement. "If Dorinda had a personal phone book or a PDA, she took it. But she did have a pad in the kitchen with a list of her . . . appointments for that day. It said six-forty-five

Jonah. I'm sorry to say this, but it's written in the same way as with all her clients—first names and the time they were coming."

I closed my eyes. "How many names were on the list for that day?"

"Dr. Gersten was her third," she said. "Third and last."

Chapter Sixteen

The end of the week of mourning coincided with the travel agent calling to remind me that Presidents' Week was two days away and, "Heavens," she said, "this is sooo awkward to have to say, but did you happen to remember that Dr. Gersten got plane tickets and put down a deposit for a ski vacation in Utah?"

"Oh my God, I forgot! And he kept reminding me about some new ski wax with Teflon . . ."

Every time I was doing something ordinary and mindless—like at that moment, making tea and answering the phone—and Jonah's name came up, my heart stopped. It beat *lub*, but then I kept waiting for the *dub*, except it felt like it was never going to happen and my life wouldn't go on. My final act on earth—in this case, bobbing a Dragon Pearl jasmine tea bag in and out of hot water—seemed both commonplace and so magical that Vermeer should have captured it: *Woman Dunking Tea Bag*. I held the phone between my ear and shoulder and wrapped my hands around the hot mug. As I lifted it, the jasmine went straight up from my nostrils and saturated my brain with sweetness.

Utah? It wouldn't be the worst thing in the world to get away for a few days, give the boys a change of scene. Maybe I'd be smart to take some of the unasked-for advice people kept giving me: Do a Variety of Activities with the Kids to Create a More Meaningful Bond; No Major Challenges the First Year, but Do Take on Small Ones; Time Heals; Don't Let Your Exercise Routine Go Because You Need Those Endorphins.

In the time it took to tear open a packet of Splenda, I decided the combination of a twelve-hour-long altitude headache, seven days of anxiety over Evan feeling abandoned in ski school, and me schussing down a mountain, sobbing so hard I wouldn't see the ponderosa pine four feet ahead and—whoops!—leaving three orphans, did not sound enticing. Even Jonah had been having second thoughts about the boys being too young and also (being a surgeon) about his hands after a day skiing in fifteen-degree temperatures. I suggested to the travel agent that considering the circumstances, a refund seemed the way to go.

Her call back showed that all the revolting publicity did have one upside: The reservations departments of both the Deer Valley Resort and Delta Airlines had heard about Jonah's murder and, as my travel agent put it, "How could they not understand?" It also helped that the boys had only a vague concept of time—Mason and Dash still believed that "tomorrow" meant any time in the future—and wouldn't understand that the ski vacation Jonah had been going into raptures about was supposed to be happening now. So we spent Presidents' Week at home.

I had tiny flashes of fun, although in terms of elapsed time, they lasted as long as the flare when a match is struck. I discovered an ice rink nearly an hour farther east on the Island and signed up the triplets for Tots on Ice lessons. Ida and Ingvild came along. Considering they were Norwegian, it wasn't a shock that they skated. But as I watched them swirl around the ice, I was amazed: With their round faces and red down-filled jackets, they were roly-poly Frosty the Snowgirls. Who knew they had been on a synchronized-skating team in high school?

They wowed everyone at the rink with their athleticism, including a routine that involved skating backward, then somehow, spinning faster and faster with the tops of their heads touching—while doing arabesques.

They even talked me onto the ice, not easy after I'd spent twenty-five perfectly happy years off. Within a half hour, I recovered whatever ability I'd had when I was ten. Rhythmic movement—running on a treadmill, sex, gliding around the rink—almost always suckered me in. For moments at a time, I forgot I had on rented skates that had been worn by strangers whose unwashed socks reeked from toe cheese and sweat. Once, the movement of my freezing cheeks even let me know I was smiling. (Of course I immediately felt ashamed and punished myself with a flash memory of Jonah's grave just before they lowered the coffin; I'd been transfixed by the horrid nakedness of a tree root sticking out from the cold, packed dirt.)

We went back to the rink twice that week. On another day, I let each of the boys invite a friend over, gave them charcoal and paper, and had them draw portraits of one another. One morning we took graph paper and diagrammed a vegetable and herb garden for the spring and taped it to a window that overlooked the garden.

Grief is supposed to take you over. A bright memory may break through, but mostly, it's full-time misery. One thing's for sure: The pain doesn't kill boredom. I was so bored. Other than the months I took off just before and after the boys were born, I'd been working since I was eighteen. Floral design was never nine-to-five, but there was always something to keep me engaged.

But after what was no doubt the hysteria of Valentine's Day, which obviously I missed, Florabella was completely quiet. In a good year, Presidents' Week meant seven bud vases of red, white, and blue flowers at six bucks a pop for the Lions Club luncheon. So when Andrea said, "Don't you dare show your face at the shop," I'd felt grateful and nearly guilt-free. Except that being bored at work would have been better than having nothing to do in a house where Jonah's anorak was on a peg by the back door and his J was monogrammed on every towel.

I wound up watching a couple of runway shows from Milan on Fashion TV. Just as I was thinking I could probably give Dolce & Gabbana a pass forever, it dawned on me that the accountants still hadn't given me the word on my financial future. Even if I was as economically secure as they were "quite confident" I would be, Italian couture—or any couture—was unlikely to find its way into my closet or my life.

At the thought of money, a memory of the retainer I had sent to the investigator at Kroll popped up. *Twenty thousand dollars shot to hell,* I thought. Grabbing a Diet Coke—decaf, since any financial uncertainty fried my nerves—I headed for the golden calm of Jonah's study to call the investigator, Lizbeth Holbreich.

"I am so terribly sorry it turned out this way," she said southernly. While her style was too formidable for honeyed charm, there was something in the way she was speaking that kept me from my post-Jonah robotic response: Wait for the person to finish their condolence spiel, then offer a "Thank you, I really appreciate, blah, blah, blah," as if their expression of sympathy was not just profoundly moving but also amazingly original.

Not knowing what to say when I actually was touched, I went with "Thank you."

"Is there anything at all we can do for you?" she asked. "I was going to call, but I didn't want to intrude quite yet." Her "quite" came out "quaaat."

"I appreciate that." I was thinking she and I were both business types. In my work, if the bride or groom didn't show at the wedding, I'd feel terrible, but I couldn't give a refund. Florabella had paid for the flowers and done the labor. In Lizbeth's case, I had hired her company to find out whether there was some secret part of Jonah's life that had led to his disappearance— and where he could have gone. Since only a couple of days had passed before he was found, murdered, I couldn't imagine they could have had time to do much investigating. "At the risk of sounding cheap," I began.

"Your twenty-thousand-dollar retainer."

"I was wondering . . . can I get any of it back, Ms. Holbreich?"

"Call me Liz, please. Some of it, I'm fairly sure. I'll need to check. But we did do some work on your behalf. I took it upon myself to go ahead and write a preliminary report. I'd be happy to sit down with you and review everything. I'll gladly drive out so we can talk. Of course, if you'd rather, I could messenger it to you with a detailed letter. Once you read it—"

Considering this was my second phone conversation ever with Lizbeth Holbreich and that I'd never been comfortable with letting anything, from bra straps to emotion, hang out, I surprised myself by blurting, "Listen, I've *got* to get out of this house. It's like there are bars instead of walls here." My volume went too high. In a quieter voice, I added, "Sorry. I'm usually not like this. Would it be all right if we met in your office?"

"Of course."

"I promise, no big emotional displays."

Lizbeth Holbreich's office was austere yet comforting. The walls were covered in a pale gray sueded paper, a hue to soothe. If its texture was as luxurious as it looked, it was thick enough to absorb all clients' shrieks of outrage and crying jags. Liz's lacquered black desk was one of those midcentury designs, asymmetrical, somewhere between an artist's palette and a boomerang. The only part of her computer that was visible was the monitor, a black rectangle jutting from the wall on a jointed steel arm; it could be angled up, down, or side to side if you pressed the edges of a quarter-sized control to the right of the mouse. It was so high-tech, I would have believed it could access the Internet via mind control from a teeny Bluetooth device embedded in the frontal lobe. But Liz pulled out a hidden drawer in front of her desk that held a keyboard.

Liz Holbreich was younger than her voice, which sounded at least fifty. She was probably my age, mid-thirties, slightly imposing but not scary. She wore what I was 98 percent sure was an Escada, a peacock-blue suit, with pointy-toed pumps that had princess heels. Her shiny dark hair was cut chin-length. She had the powerful-woman-politician look. However, being small-boned in the extreme, she looked less Nancy Pelosi and more a modern-dressed version of the elf Viggo Mortensen married in *Lord of the Rings*.

"This way we can literally be on the same page," Liz said as she pressed a control and the screen angled more toward me. "Naturally, before you leave, I can give you a printout. And a CD if you'd like."

I nodded, but then I realized she was typing. "That would be fine," I said.

"Let me explain. What I'm showing you represents the work we did so far." I raised my head slightly to read what was up there: a table of contents with listings for items like addresses, names of relatives, education, employment history, professional associates, personal associates, credit report. "What isn't up there," she continued, "though the fact is noted in the intro, is that there is absolutely no evidence that Dr. Gersten had hidden any sort of criminal record or used any Social Security number other than his own legitimate one."

It bordered on hilarious, the thought of Jonah hiding a criminal record. But how could I laugh when, if anyone had told me my husband was going to stop at a call girl's place before he drove home to Long Island, I would have . . . well, laughed.

Liz Holbreich continued her rundown. "No record of litigation, either — no pending lawsuits, including malpractice, which, considering his specialty, is amazing."

"One of his patients did threaten to sue about a year ago," I said. "I mean, it happened just three weeks after surgery. She claimed one of her eyes was higher than the other. She even got a lawyer. Jonah told her it would be fine once the swelling went down. It was, and the lawyer called him to say they weren't going to pursue the matter. Like two months later, that same lawyer wanted to hire Jonah as an expert witness in one of his cases."

Liz didn't show any signs of being impatient, but I began to feel I was wasting her time with unnecessary talk. This business was all business. Floral design was so much about major events in people's lives that, along with showing pictures of centerpieces and pulling together a fast nosegay to demonstrate an idea for the cocktail tables, you heard the saga of the bar mitzvah boy's triumph over developmental arithmetic disorder. You and the client chatted about wonderful weddings and tacky ones; confirmation parties that should have worked but fell flatter than the crabmeat crepes; the issue of themed bat mitzvahs; the etiquette of floral displays at funerals. A bride, noting your style, sought your advice about what shoes to wear with a tealength dress, while her mother asked how to get rid of slugs in her hostas. You, in turn, admired the groom-to-be's riding boots but knew not to ask where he stabled his horse. In my world, business rarely felt like business. In Liz's, it definitely did.

She swiveled her chair to face me and leaned back. Not the usual leather office throne but a fifties-style chair that resembled one of those nut scoopers at Whole Foods. She rested her elbow on her desk, which I took to mean the meeting wasn't over.

"You gave us authorization, so we were able to get a preliminary look at Dr. Gersten's office and home hard drives, along with his e-mails and Internet use," she said. "Our findings and conclusions are in the report. There's also a good deal of backup data on the CD that I'll give you before you leave. Now, do you want the bottom line?"

Whatever "a state of suspended animation" actually meant, I was suddenly in it—a cone of silence that wouldn't lift until she spoke. Would I hear "He had no secret life"? Or would it be something that would change everything, like "Dr. Gersten secretly operated on bin Laden and made him look like Calvin Klein"? "Yes," I managed to say. "Bottom line."

"Nothing major," she said. I realized how tight I'd been clasping my hands only when I eased up; my knuckles ached from where my fingers had been pressing on them. "No evidence of an affair or sexual liaisons."

I couldn't feel relieved. "Anything with prostitutes?" I asked.

"Nothing we were able to find."

"Isn't that kind of a lawyerly answer?" I asked.

"I'm not a lawyer," Liz said. "But if you mean it sounds qualified, I'd go with that. Look, the conclusions in the report don't exist in a vacuum. We have to take into account real-life circumstances. Dr. Gersten was killed in a prostitute's apartment. It's entirely possible he was there for a purpose that had nothing to do with sex."

"But you don't think so."

Liz was wearing a large aquamarine ring on her right ring finger. She twisted it around a few times, more thoughtful than nervous. "Let's put it this way: Is it more likely for a man to be visiting a prostitute for sex or for an undetermined reason—perhaps a benevolent reason? And if the reason was to help her rather than to use her services, why would this particular prostitute, a woman with a criminal record, go into her own medicine cabinet, take out long-bladed scissors, and stab him?"

"But that's what I don't get. Isn't her criminal record for drugs? I mean, she wasn't in trouble for anything violent. I didn't hear she was ever involved in something where anyone got hurt."

"True," Liz said. "In any case, there is one more point I should make. An entry was added to Jonah's office computer calendar around eleven-thirty the morning of the day he was killed. According to the police, his calendar hadn't yet been synced when he died, because the event wasn't on his Black-Berry. But 'D.D.' was put in the office calendar for six-forty-five that evening."

"Was she on his calendar at any other time?"

"No. Unless it was under an alias both we and the NYPD didn't come up with in our database searches. We contacted the authorities once we heard about Dr. Gersten's death. They understand that in a case like this, private investigative agencies are there to support them, not work against them. The cops passed along the information they and the FBI had because we did the same for them."

"Do you know anything about Dorinda Dillon? Her background, where she comes from?"

"No. Not because we wouldn't be able to get that information. But because you hired us to try to find Dr. Gersten. Not to investigate his murder . . ." She stopped.

A second later, I realized she was waiting because my eyes had filled up. "It's okay," I assured her. "I get teary at least ten times a day. I'm so used to it that half the time I'm oblivious. Well, almost oblivious. Anyway, sorry for the interruption."

"On my own, no charge to you, I ran a quick search on Dorinda Dillon. It's on the CD. But since this case went from being a missing-person case to a homicide, we wouldn't go much further—and keep drawing down against your retainer—without your go-ahead. Actually, I did call you once or twice."

I swallowed and recrossed my legs, all the minor movements to cover social embarrassment. Beneath Liz Holbreich's busi-nesslike courtesy, I sensed sweetness. I said, "I vaguely remem-ber you leaving a message or two. But once I knew Jonah was dead, murdered, plus with dealing with the boys and his family, and then all the publicity. I wasn't . . . I couldn't return phone calls. I started making a list and then stopped. I even stopped checking voice mail."

"Please. No explanation necessary." A small sigh escaped from deep in Liz's chest.

I realized I could be wrong about her. Maybe Liz Holbreich wasn't a sweetie pie, just a cool and extremely mannerly investigator. With all that southern stuff, I could be misreading courtesy as compassion. How could I tell? In the past, I'd trusted my gut because, as guts go, mine was excellent. Now I was too messed up to rely on myself.

"She had just changed her name to Dorinda Dillon a few months before. From Cristal Rousseau. But Cristal's name had come up in a drug case. When the cops got to her apartment to question her—ultimately, it turned out that time she wasn't involved—the super told them Cristal hadn't moved away, just changed her name."

"I'm assuming what you told me is all there is," I said hopefully. "Right? There wasn't anything else?"

"If our investigation had run its course," Liz replied, "there were a few avenues we might have explored."

Now I didn't have any choice except to ask, "Like what?"

"Nothing to be concerned about."

Had I looked concerned? Even after all her reassurance, was I still fearful that she'd spring Percocet addiction, spying for Russia? From the moment of Jonah's disappearance, I'd left no nightmare unimagined—except for some horror I lacked the capacity to conceive of, the one that could kill my love for him. If he was capable of going to a prostitute, was he capable of something much worse? If a husband is alive and a wife learns something awful, she can confront him with "I'll never be able to trust you again." What about a great guy who was maybe not so great and who was dead?

"We found a few e-mails indicating . . ." Liz tilted her head to the side. Shrugged. *Get it over with!* I wanted to scream. "I wouldn't even call them fights," she said at last. "Squabbles. The routine disagreements anybody could have in business or family life. They might be overlooked in the normal due-diligence investigation. But if an individual inexplicably disappears, we need to go the extra mile."

"Can you give me an example of a squabble?"

"Everything's on that CD," she said. She touched the edge of the desk with the heel of her hand, and the bright computer monitor faded to black.

Being an executive at an international investigation agency, Liz Holbreich clearly understood the world in a way I never would. So although I was a reasonably chic, très-upscale sophisticate in my black Proenza Schouler skirt and jacket, I was feeling more like a hick in a purple velour warm-up suit.

"I get the impression there's a lot of stuff on the CD," I managed to say. "So I'd appreciate some guidance. Maybe you can tell me 'I would have looked into this' or 'I wouldn't have wasted my time on that.'"

"Sure. I wasn't trying to blow you off. I'm genuinely sorry if I seemed abrupt. If I was holding back, it's because I was hesitant about giving too much detail," Liz said. "You've been through such hell. It would have been one thing to look over your husband's shoulder in the normal course of events, watch him typing an e-mail, and say to yourself, *Wow, is he pissed*. It's quite another to read or hear about that same e-mail if it was written in the last couple of days of his life. It has a great deal more weight."

"If Jonah had dropped dead of a heart attack, it would be one thing," I said. "But because he was murdered, murdered in a place where I would never in all my life have believed he would go, I need to understand what was going on in his head—and in his life."

"Fair enough. As I said, no matters of great consequence.

There were a number of e-mails between Dr. Gersten and . . . I believe it's the manager of the medical practice. A Donald Finsterwald."

"Yes. Were there problems?"

"Basically that when the going got tough with the economic downturn, Dr. Gersten thought Finsterwald was turning to mush. Doing less marketing, less PR rather than more. Your husband discovered Finsterwald had turned down an offer for one of the three partners to go on *Today in New York* because it was a local show, not national. Finsterwald e-mailed back to Dr. Gersten apologizing profusely. Had there been a history of friction between them?"

"No. Jonah thought Donald was the ultimate suck-up with physicians but too uncaring with staff. Jonah didn't like him personally, but I didn't realize he was so annoyed."

"More than annoyed, I think. Sometimes it's hard to get a reading just from e-mail, because in any office setting, there are always conversations taking place between correspondence. But the last few days, it looked as though your husband was downright angry."

"Anything else with Donald?"

"Yes. Apparently, part of his job was tracking financial performance. Finsterwald sent several e-mails apologizing for not having weekly reports done, saying it was difficult getting numbers, what with Dr. Noakes doing so much pro bono work and traveling. The records were incomplete."

"Gilbert John was good with his medical notations," I said. "But he practiced by himself for so many years before taking on Jonah and then Layne that he couldn't deal with being accountable to partners. And with the practice's businessy computerized systems, he was technologically lame."

The light coming through Liz's window was beginning to soften. Instead of looking overbright, like an HDTV test pattern, her black hair, blue suit, and aquamarine ring were starting to appear washed out, almost fuzzy, more like one of those fifties movies you rent that was done by some cheaper process than Technicolor. "Does everybody call Dr. Noakes 'Gilbert John'?" Liz Holbreich asked.

"Yes. At least, I've never heard him called anything else. It's weird, because he's probably the most boring guy at Mount Sinai, which takes doing, but everyone plays up to him. Part of it is that he's a really good-looking man. But there's something truly formidable about his manner. Jonah always said Gilbert John had a brilliant reputation as a surgeon, and the grand style to go with it."

"Is he a nasty kind of guy?"

"Not at all," I said. "He just has—pardon me—a permanent stick up his ass. And Layne is just the opposite: 'I'm just a down-to-earth gal from Albuquerque, and don't bother calling me Doctor because, gosh, all that formality just isn't me, and now, is there anything I can do to make you feel better about yourself because you're a wonderful person?' My guess is that's why Jonah was so upset with Donald Finsterwald, because he'd been hired to ease the pressure and make it easy for the three partners not to have any issues." My left foot started falling asleep. I wriggled my toes, but as I was wearing pointy stilettos, all I could do was rotate my ankle slowly so Liz wouldn't notice. "You mentioned avenues you might have gone down if you had more time to investigate. Besides Donald and the practice, does anything else come to mind?"

"Let's see." Liz shut her eyes, doing a major *I'm thinking*.

"Please don't be concerned about hurting me. I do flowers. I don't have the background, the way you do, to evaluate what's potentially investigatable."

She nodded and did the pushing-back-cuticle-but-really-looking-at-watch business. Maybe she was thinking her shot at leaving early to check out the shoe sales at Saks would be lost if I dissolved into tears.

"You're absolutely right to ask for a professional's opinion, though in this case, I don't know what it's worth. I was only hesitating because it involves family," she said. I almost laughed because my first thought of family was my parents and assorted cousins, whose existence seemed way too mind-numbing to merit investigation, except by researchers into the nature of boringness. "Dr. Gersten's brother, Theo."

"Theo?" Definitely an interesting life. And a self-centered one. Aside from their being siblings, I couldn't imagine his life and Jonah's crossing in any significant way. Years earlier, when Theo was still trying to be an actor, he kept sending his friends to his brother for consultations, though they seemed to believe Jonah would not only work on them for free but take care of the anesthesiologist and OR costs. After Jonah told them—and Theo—all he could give was a discount, Theo stopped the referrals, but only after telling Jonah that he was appalled at the cheap fuck he had become.

"He recently asked your husband for ten thousand dollars," Liz said.

"He did? Like 'Hey, can you give me ten thou?'"

"He needed it to pay for some fire damage to his apartment building from a sauna he'd had installed. Illegally, it turned out."

All I could do was shake my head. It was so Theo. "Jonah didn't tell me about that one."

"I must say, you don't seem surprised," Liz said.

"I'm not. Unless Jonah gave him the money."

"No. He sent him . . . I wouldn't call it angry, but it was a strongly worded e-mail. Essentially, it said, 'You've got to be kidding, asking me.' Theo came back with 'If you can't see your way to helping me out, could you loan me the money?'" I felt that tennis-volley anticipation, waiting for Jonah's response. "He refused," Liz said.

"How did he put it?"

"Something about Theo already owing him the equivalent

of the national debt. Obviously, I don't know if he was being ironic or if Theo did owe him a large amount." Natural curiosity made her pause, hoping for an answer, but I didn't have one. I hadn't a clue that Theo owed him—us—money. "Us" because everything we had was joint. Still, I couldn't think up a way to make it sound like "Oh, Jonah told me everything." For whatever reason, that was what I wanted Liz to believe. "Dr. Gersten suggested if Theo couldn't get a loan from a bank, he should ask their parents. Then it was a great deal of back-and-forth: Theo writing that Jonah should go F himself and Jonah asking him why, since they're both in their thirties, he should have any responsibility for Theo."

What I couldn't get over was Jonah not saying a word about this to me, not even "Theo's being a pain in the ass again" or "Can you believe my brother put in an illegal sauna and it burned a ten-thousand-dollar hole in his apartment?" Maybe he'd gotten so angry at Theo's immaturity that he couldn't even talk about it—plus, he knew I'd get furious and then he'd have to listen to me, like an echo of his anger.

I took a deep breath. "When did all this e-mailing happen?" I asked.

Liz's voice was soft. "A couple of weeks before Jonah was killed."

Chapter Seventeen

Forget about *Get a life*. It had been almost a month, and even though I'd OD'd on reality, part of me still held on to the primitive, pathetic belief that Jonah would be found alive. "That wasn't your husband in the Gersten plot, three feet away from Grandpa Ben, after all!" I'd be told. There'd be some jaw-dropping explanation involving amnesia, but seeing me would cure it. All the papers and magazines would write editorials apologizing for their gross misreporting, and Rupert Murdoch would send a handwritten letter saying how sorry he was about FOX News and *The New York Post* being *the* most disgusting media about Jonah, and he'd offer his private jet to take me and the boys anywhere in the world for a healing vacation; we'd know he wasn't truly sorry, just afraid of a libel suit because Jonah hadn't been a public figure till his tabloid notoriety had made him one.

If I couldn't get a life, I at least had to muddle on. Those he's-not-dead fantasies were scaring me with their seductiveness. I had to deal. So, having done the only decent thing, giving Ida and Ingvild three days off after their above-and-beyond, day-and-night selfless devotion, I was dealing—and proceeding to go insane.

Worse, it was Saturday morning. I'd been all alone with the boys only eighteen hours. "Evan, get back here! Don't you dare open that door!" I screeched from the kitchen. I heard the *shoosh, shoosh* of his Power Ranger slippers skimming along the marble checkerboard floor of the front hall as he raced to answer the bell. Mason and Dash, lacking their brother's gregarious nature, were still parked on the rug in the den, yukking it up as they watched *Kung Fu Panda* for the fiftieth time.

So much TV. I was afraid of a call from the accountants saying, "We've been going over your expenses, and sad to say, we were overly optimistic. You can no longer afford video on demand. In fact, you can no longer afford any luxury in your life." Whenever I called Wollman & Rubin, LLP, Certified Public Accountants and Profitability Consultants, they tried to soothe me with voices practically dripping in anesthesia: "Not to worry, Susie," "Jonah seems to have been on top of things," "We're almost ready to sign off." But until they did—

"Evan, dammit, if you open that door, you can forget your playdate with Josh! Cross it off your to-do list because there's no way in hell—" Still screaming that last sentence, I careened around the corner and skidded into the front hall.

Lieutenant Gary Paston stood framed by the open door. He was telling Evan, "You shouldn't open the door unless a grown-up tells you it's okay."

"Into the den!" I ordered Evan, who ignored me. He was riveted as Paston flipped shut his gold shield with one hand. Paston obliged him by flipping it open and shut a few more times. "Evan." I forced myself to use my reasonable voice. "You know your brothers won't rewind. You'll miss the best part." He took off.

"Please come in, Lieutenant Paston," I said. It came out too ladylike, the tone you resort to when trying to make someone forget how you'd been shrieking like a shrew. A second later, any notion of graciousness vanished. Normality, as in "Can I take your coat?" was out of the question. Instead, I stood mute, staring at his black fringed wool scarf. It was the same one he'd worn on his other visit. An ordinary knit scarf, but seeing it brought back the moment I'd found out. It was like that guy in Proust who dunked a cookie in tea and got not just a memory but a total five-senses replay. All that hand-tied fringe bursting from Paston's scarf, and I was back in that awful night, when my hope had turned to dread and dread to despair.

A six-feet-something, football-player-sized African-American guy in a gray overcoat was standing framed by my front door, but I couldn't see him. All I could take in was the fringe on his scarf, the fringe of his eyelashes, and the knowledge that in a couple of seconds, he was going to tell me Jonah had been murdered. Post-traumatic stress? Maybe. Probably.

It wasn't until he said, "Mrs. Gersten? Are you okay?" that I realized I was rigid—like in the game the boys played, where one kid yelled "Red light!" and everybody froze. Despite my asking him in, I was blocking his way. "I owe you an apology," he said. "I should have called to see if it would be okay if I drove out. I just thought, *Well, it's a Saturday morning and—*"

"No, it's fine. Really. Please come in." We had an awkward couple of seconds of me wanting to hang up his coat, him saying not to bother, he could put it down somewhere. Then he noticed there was nothing in the front hall except a bombé chest, a mirror, and two antique Chinese chairs that looked like they'd break into smithereens with one good sneeze.

We wound up in the kitchen, where he put his coat on a chair and I got to make a fresh pot of coffee so he would think I was a decent person and not an alternatingly shrewish, catatonic homicide victim's widow. I pushed the button on the coffee machine, and as I turned back to him, he said, "We found Dorinda Dillon."

"Oh." That was all I could think to say.

"That's why I drove out. I wanted to tell you personally and also answer any questions you might have before . . ."

He stopped. Suddenly, I realized that was because I'd turned my back on him again. "Sorry. I just wanted to get down a couple of mugs. What do you take in your coffee?"

"Milk."

I set up the mugs and Splenda, and poured milk into a small pitcher. Then I took a mason jar of gerbera daisies from the windowsill over the sink and set it on the table. "I'll sit down now," I announced. "Sorry I cut you off."

"No problem," Lieutenant Paston said. I sat across the table from him. For an instant we looked at each other. The only sound was the dribbling of the coffeemaker. We had an ESP moment, or at least I think we did: Each of us found the other a decent, likable person, so we took time off—maybe five seconds—not to speak. We wished we could avoid the single awful subject we had in common. Then he said, "She was arrested around three this morning. Midnight in Las Vegas. I'll give you the whole story in a minute, but the department wanted you to be the first to hear it. There's supposed to be a joint announcement of the arrest, us and the Las Vegas police, but these things can leak. I wanted you to be prepared in case there were phone calls or reporters showing up wanting you to comment."

"Thank you." The coffee was still dripping. I was eager for the big hiss that came at the end of brewing so I could jump up to get the pot, not to get away from the table but to have something to contribute. "How did you find her?" I asked.

"We got cooperation from all three of the escort services she occasionally worked with."

"Occasionally?"

"They'd call her if their regulars were booked, away, whatever. If she had free time, she'd take the job, or if things were slow with her, she'd call asking for work. Anyway, none of the services had heard from her. But yesterday afternoon she called

College Girl Companions—the one she did the most business with. She told them she needed the name of a criminal lawyer in New York and tried to get them to advance her some money. She was broke."

"Advance her some money?" I asked. "They do that kind of thing?"

Paston shook his head. "I doubt it, especially when they know she's a person of interest in a murder investigation and isn't likely to be getting anything in the way of income for the next twenty-five years plus. We had advised the owners of all three escort services to stall her, talk, get whatever information they could. Luckily, the girl who spoke to Dorinda was smart, told her to wait a couple of hours, that she'd come up with the names of some lawyers and try to convince the owner to wire some money. We had a recording device on the phone. I heard the conversation. The girl did a great job: very sympathetic, finally got Dorinda to a comfort point where she gave the number of the motel she was at."

"You couldn't trace the call?"

"We did, to a pay phone in a Laundromat. I had one of the guys in my squad fly out to Las Vegas right away. By the time the local cops got to the pay phone, she was gone. No big surprise. But they staked out the motel and arrested her two hours later."

"Did she say anything? About what happened?"

"Initially, she claimed not to know about the killing." He shifted the knot of his tie about a millimeter to the left, then shifted it back. I didn't know why, but I trusted Paston more because he dressed nicely: no shirt gaping between the buttons; no strangely stiff tie that looked lined with cardboard; no fluffed-out mustache like those of detectives on TV shows—and in real life, on the news. A subdued rep tie, white shirt, and a dark gray suit. Not badly cut or old guy, but not trendy either. "She claimed she was in Vegas for a vacation, hadn't been watch-

ing TV, and was shocked to hear someone had been murdered in
her apartment."

"And then?"

"They didn't question her formally until my guy got there.
It went back and forth for a while: she saying she didn't know a
thing, my guy telling her, 'Do yourself a favor by cooperating.'"

"Did she have a lawyer by that time?"

"No. Listen, most jurisdictions videotape any questioning
of someone involved in a homicide case. So don't worry. Whatever we have is solid. It's on tape, her being read her rights.
She did ask for a lawyer—Legal Aid, public defender, whatever
they call it out there. One of the Las Vegas cops made the call,
and meanwhile, my guy and one of their detectives kept talking
to her."

More than anything, I wanted to ask if Dorinda admitted
knowing Jonah, but I didn't want Paston to think my only concern was that my husband had gone to a whore and I didn't give
a shit about justice. So I didn't interrupt.

"What got her talking a little was my guy. Irish, blue eyes,
thinks he looks like Brad Pitt when he smiles, which he doesn't,
but women are crazy about him. I'm sure it's on the tape, him
smiling and saying 'Give me a break' to everything she said."

"Did she confess?"

"No. She claims she doesn't know anything about what happened. It was when she went to the closet near the door of her
apartment to get your husband's coat." He said it matter-of-
factly, as if there had never been any doubt in the world that
Jonah was her customer. If Paston hadn't been with the NYPD,
but a private detective paid by me, he might have told me a little
more gently, allowing me a couple of seconds more to hold on to
an illusion, but this was the no-frills, publicly funded truth. "She
said when she opened the closet door, someone who had been
hiding there smashed her in the head with an electric broom she
kept in a corner behind the coats. She claimed she was knocked

unconscious. She didn't see her assailant. When she came to, Dr. Gersten was on her living room floor. He was dead.'"

"Do you believe any of what she says?"

"Absolutely not. But let me give it to you straight. If we're going to believe or disbelieve based on someone's status, we're not going to solve many cases. Prejudice gets in the way. So it doesn't matter if Dorinda Dillon is . . . what she is or if she's ambassador to the UN. And it doesn't matter if the victim is a homeless psycho or a high-class plastic surgeon. Those of us who investigate homicides really believe the old 'Thou shalt not kill.' We see our job as putting the scales of justice back in balance." Corky Paston rested his hands on the edge of the table. "But you know and I know we live in the real world. Right?"

"Right."

"So we wind up responding to its pressures. Do you know what I'm talking about?"

"I'm guessing here: a case that's gotten a lot of publicity, or where the victim has . . . Detective Sergeant Coleman mentioned something about Jonah's position in the community."

"Right. So this case, your husband's murder, qualifies on both counts. The words 'thorough investigation' really mean something here. We interviewed the doorman, but he didn't see anyone else come in. These doormen who work in rental buildings are pretty savvy. One look at a tenant like Dorinda Dillon—maybe the rental agent can't figure it out or doesn't want to, but the guys at the door know what she is before she even signs the lease. Same thing when they're standing out front. They can see a man walking down the street and know 'This one is going to the big dinner party in 6A,' and that other man a couple of feet behind him, dressed pretty much the same way, has a date with the hooker."

The coffeemaker gave its last steamy hiss. I brought the carafe over to the table and started to pour, then worried that Paston could be saying to himself, *I cannot believe she's going to serve me from Pyrex!*

"So what you were asking about, whether we believe what she says: The answer is no. There's nothing to back up her claim. No one else got past the doorman after Dr. Gersten asking to go to Dorinda Dillon's apartment. No one who even looked like a client type came around. Also, the doorman was sure everybody who got into the building that afternoon and evening was either a tenant or had some legitimate business in one of the other apartments."

"I see," I said. "Okay."

"The other thing is the closet." I wanted to tell him fine, enough was enough. I believed him. I believed the police did their job. For someone who'd had such a need to know, I was rapidly becoming the don't-tell-me type. Still, there wasn't any way I could make Paston stop. "We didn't find evidence that anyone had been inside the closet other than Dillon herself. There were some prints, a few hairs—long, dyed blond—that matched up with what was all over the apartment. The prints were hers, too. We have them on file because of her previous arrests."

It was weird, but I didn't remember, in all the media coverage, seeing any photo or mug shot of Dorinda, though I must have. For whatever reason, I hadn't imagined her as a blonde, not that I'd really had an image. That in itself was strange for me, because nearly all the time when people described something that had happened to them, or when I was reading, I got vivid mental pictures of what was going on. Jonah once told me, "You have an amazing visual intelligence," which was such an ego-boosting compliment, even if I wasn't totally sure what it meant: maybe my ability to visualize a design or room layout, or what wasn't right about someone's outfit, or why a piece of art didn't work. He'd said it when we were at a Calder exhibit at the Whitney after I'd told him why I didn't love Calder's work, even though I respected it.

"Now that she's in custody, we'll know for sure about the

hair when the DNA tests come back," Lieutenant Paston said, "but there doesn't seem to be any reason right now to think it was someone else's."

"I understand." He took a sip of coffee and seemed to be waiting for something more, so I added, "Sounds right to me."

"Now, as far as the electric-broom thing is concerned." At that point, I was hoping one of the boys—no, all of them—would come in and behave so obnoxiously that Paston would make his excuses and leave. He'd say, "I'll e-mail you the details." But obviously *Kung Fu Panda* was still entrancing. "The only prints on the broom were hers. There was no hair, no blood on it that would be consistent with someone using it to hit her over the head. Just the usual household dirt. Also, electric brooms are mechanical."

"Uh-huh." I wasn't sure what this had to do with anything.

"They weigh something. But most of the weight—this one was eight pounds—is toward the base, where the mechanism is. Eight pounds doesn't sound like much, but because it's bottom-heavy, it would be hard to grab and raise up as a weapon when somebody opened the closet door. Possible but unlikely."

"Thank you. Thank you for all you've done."

"Please," he said. "It's what we do. Before I forget. Speaking of her hair, or what we assume is her hair. There was one of them on Dr. Gersten's jacket, just to the left of the second stab wound." I couldn't really say thank you for that information, so I just nodded. "Oh, and there wasn't any cash in his wallet." I shrugged. All I remembered was someone saying the police had to hold on to his wallet, keys, and BlackBerry—"all Dr. Gersten's effects"—as evidence when I'd asked if I could get back Jonah's photos of me and the boys. "Not even one dollar," Paston added.

"I'm not sure how much he had. Most of the time, he never carries more than a hundred, a hundred fifty." Then I said, "I mean 'carried.'"

"He did make a withdrawal from an ATM near his office late that morning," Paston said.

"How much?"

His slight hesitation made me listen more closely than I might have. "Six hundred dollars."

"I see." How could I not?

"He had lunch brought into his office. Fourteen dollars and change. He doesn't appear to have left there before . . . before he finally left for the day. Of course, he might have paid cash for something, but we didn't find any receipts." I didn't ask what Jonah had ordered for lunch, even though I figured Paston probably knew. A couple of times over the years, Jonah and I had had that dumb conversation about if you knew something was your last meal, what would it be? Even though both of us hardly ever ate beef, I'd said a pastrami sandwich and a real Coke, not diet; he'd said a steak and hash browns from Peter Luger with their best bottle of cabernet.

As Paston headed to his car, I glanced out the window and noticed he had the slightly bowlegged walk of an ex-jock. He'd said, "Call me if there's anything more you want to know." How about why? Maybe Jonah's murder would always seem senseless to me, but right now I felt there were too damn many unanswered questions. I didn't expect Lieutenant Corky Paston and the entire NYPD to share my passionate need to know, but didn't the why of it make them at least a little curious?

Chapter Eighteen

I blessed the Tuttle Farm nursery school's four-hour day, its "yummy, nutritious, all-organic lunch," and its "wide range of exciting, individualized, optional after-school activities." The wide range was two: Yay for Yoga or Creative Clay. My three boys went for clay. Each indulged his unique artistic vision by making humongous plates with SpongeBob and/ or Squidward painted on them. So I was free, and with Ida and Ingvild off with another au pair to explore still more wonders of Long Island mall-dom, I had my Monday in front of the TV in the den watching Dorinda Dillon.

Not that there was much to watch except the perp walk. There she was at JFK, handcuffed, with a quilted jacket too big to be hers draped around her shoulders. Two female detectives for whom the word "strapping" must have been invented led her past a lineup of photographers and reporters who shouted to get Dorinda's attention: "Hey, look over here!" "Did you know him before that night, Dorinda?" "Over here, beautiful!" "Did you ever have plastic surgery?" "Yo! Dor! Why'd you kill the doc?"

CNN and MSNBC had slightly different angles. I went with

CNN's because Strapping Detective #1's shoulder wasn't blocking the camera at the moment Dorinda turned her head to the shoving pack of journalists and rolled her eyes in *Give me a break* boredom. Her expression was more what you'd expect from a celebrity-hounded eighteen-year-old hip-hop star than a handcuffed hooker with no makeup except atrocious blackish-red lipstick, whose shoulder-length hair (not the roots but the part that was still blond) looked like the hay they fed hansom cab horses around Central Park. Too bad for her that her chances of getting near a stylist, or even a box of Clairol Champagne Blond, were iffy—at least for the next twenty-five years.

I couldn't get enough Dorinda. I had recorded a bunch of evening and late-night local news shows so I could watch them first thing the next morning, the instant the boys left for school. After I'd seen them, there was nothing to do except wait for the perp-walk clip on CNN Headline News every half hour. Right after it ran, I'd race upstairs to my computer to check out online videos on a couple of Las Vegas TV websites.

Since I'd spent extra on a high-quality color monitor for viewing flowers, I was able to check out the style and eye-burning purpleness of Dorinda's halter sundress, which had been hidden under the borrowed jacket at the airport in New York. The purple had a sheen not just of the sleaziest polyester ever manufactured but also of newness.

I played those Las Vegas news segments over and over. As I watched them, parallel videos ran in my head. I pictured Dorinda getting to Nevada in New York winter clothes and spending twenty dollars of Jonah's fast-disappearing cash in a dreadful store with filthy linoleum on the dressing room floor. Maybe she thought she looked luscious in the dress. On the other hand, she could have felt miserable knowing such a trashy dress (all she could afford) would discourage the class of customer she wanted. Once or twice I imagined her shoplifting, stuffing the dress into her handbag, thinking she was smart: *This'll never wrinkle.* When she pulled it out, though, it had creases even the hottest iron could never flatten.

To add a little shame and disgust to my Dorinda imaginings—what fun was a fantasy without them?—I envisioned her running out of money and having to work: turning a quick trick, a hand job in an alleyway (assuming there were alleyways on the Strip), or a standup fuck in a place known to locals as the worst hotel in Vegas, beyond some slot-machine room in a corridor that still reeked from cigars smoked in the seventies.

The quality of the Las Vegas TV footage wasn't great. I tried to zoom in on her, see her expression, but even my high-res monitor couldn't get me a decent picture. Still, I saw enough to decide Dorinda Dillon was definitely not pretty. And not just by my standards; she knew it. Even under arrest, a woman who was aware that she was appealing could get paraded and handcuffed and yet hold her head at least a quarter inch higher than someone who felt unattractive. A pretty woman would hope her good bones or shining eyes would please the cameras, tame the ferocious media.

It didn't help that Dorinda was also a mess. Besides the wreckage that was her hair, her crappy bright purple dress sucked the color from everything around it, including her face. Her posture was awful, shoulders slumped, back hunched, which I assumed was what happened when you were in heavy handcuffs attached by chains to your ankles—though I couldn't see below her calves.

It struck me that even if there were a charity benefiting homicidal whores that gave Dorinda the full Day of Beauty package at the best spa in town, she would still be wrong-looking. Her nose was both long and unusually broad, so it pushed her eyes far apart and took up so much space that the sides of her face, reserved for cheeks on other people, were flat. Forget being able to tell the color of her eyes; I could barely see eyes at all, because they were little more than slits. Dorinda reminded me of Dolly, that sheep who was cloned, except without the sheepy dread-locks, which might have been an improvement.

It took me a weirdly long time running between the TV and computer to stop trying to read her face, maybe even her thoughts, and start thinking, *Oh, right, she's a prostitute. Her body is what's for sale. Let me see what that body looks like.*

It looked good. In the Las Vegas footage, I saw the sundress was short enough to show that unless something repulsive was going on around her ankles, she had great legs. The dress was tight enough to reveal a notably small waist. And not an ounce of fat stuck out over the top in back, unusual because the sad fact of life for most women, even thin ones with fantastic arms (which is maybe 3 percent of the world's population), was that the tight-bodiced halter dress was meant more for a fashion spread than a body. In front, the dress was cut low enough to display Dorinda's major boobs—maybe real, or at least well-done fakes, since Jonah had always said the soccer-ball look (those high, round mounds on either side of a canyon of cleav-age) were the sign of a second-rate surgeon.

A little before one o'clock, I decided I needed a break and sat down for my favorite lunch, cut-up apple and cheddar. I started leafing through the latest issue of *Fleur Créatif*, but I'd been on overload with "Idées pour Noël" since early December and hated trying to figure out half of the French words, which were probably on a second-grade reading level. I decided to get lunch over with, so I stuffed a whole bunch of apple slices and cheddar into my mouth.

But I didn't get up, and I didn't chew. Instead, I slid my chair over to a small patch of sunshine. I sat in the warmth with a full mouth and tried to be objective about how people would react to Dorinda. Most of them, I decided, wouldn't look at her and think, *Two-bit whore.* On the other hand, she wasn't exactly exuding gentility. Most neutral observers would take a look and think, *Cheap.*

I spat the apple and cheese into my hand and ate the pieces slowly. They were ooky, saliva-coated, and I wondered if I was already losing whatever polish I'd gotten by marrying up. But being a slob was better than having Ida and Ingvild get back from the Walt Whitman shopping center and find me choked to death on the floor. I ate the lunch in my hand tiny piece by tiny piece. As I did, I told myself, *Trust your gut. Does Dorinda Dillon look like a killer?* The answer seemed obvious at first. No. She did not look murderous. Just stupid.

Then it hit me: The impression she made didn't matter. Stupid or smart didn't matter. Neither did whether she was groomed or disheveled and dirty. All I needed to figure out was this: Could this slitty-eyed, big-boobed, horrid-haired, badly dressed, handcuffed hooker be capable of murdering my husband? This time around, I decided, *Of course. Now get on with your life.*

The next few days, I did get busy at work. Though our business was always slow from Valentine's Day until the week before Passover and Easter, I wound up doing everything from super-scrubbing every flower bucket to scanning all the photographers' proofs of Florabella decorations and arrangements that our clients had given us over the years. We'd tossed them into acid-free boxes and forgotten their existence.

At home, I kept occupied, working with the boys to prepare a Saturday-night dinner party for the four of us. We made pasta by hand, did menus on the computer. I had them create table arrangements from leaves, three dollars' worth of carnations, and things that should be thrown away from each of their rooms. Evan's showed actual talent: He entwined leaves and a blue ribbon all around a sneaker he'd outgrown; stuck more leaves, carnations, and two curled-up baseball cards into the shoe; and hung his Johan Santana Mets key chain from one of the Velcro closings. I was amazed: four years old, and somehow he understood you had to have a theme.

Even keeping busy on those Dorinda days, right after she

was arrested and brought to New York, were rough. War, famine, economic convulsions: None of them made headlines like Dorinda Dillon. First her perp walk. Then TV and the Web got busy with clips from a couple of soft-core movies she'd been in during the late nineties. Networks and cable stuck shaded ovals or rectangles over tops, tushes, penises, and pudenda. I realized how often I'd watched the clips when I began seeing an abstract dance of geometric shapes.

Maybe Dorinda had once dreamed of a film career. Forget about it. All she got to do was be naked, or almost; not a single line of dialogue. She was one of four pole dancers in a bar, an extra girl at what was supposed to be a Hollywood orgy, the second of two blondes climbing all over a guy in high pimp gear who went for the other girl while shaking off Dorinda as if she were a pesky, leg-humping golden retriever. Dorinda Dillon had played the porn equivalent of a wallflower. But a famous wallflower, at least for those few days.

The scenes took on an almost comforting familiarity. They felt like old family movies you've had to watch too often. No more shock, any more than watching (for the fiftieth time) Cousin Mindy curl her lip in disgust as Aunt Edith demonstrates the twist, or watching baby Hannah do absolutely nothing at her first birthday party, an unsmiling Buddha in a frilly pink dress.

The weird thing is, these home movies always take over and become the truest Truth. There may be a million memories in your head, but your mind's basic definition of Mindy is COUSIN WHOSE LIP NEVER STOPS CURLING. For the rest of her life, Hannah will be BLAH PUDGY GIRL. And Dorinda Dillon—Dorinda Before, with long, silky, teased porn hair, and the hay-headed Dorinda After—would, first and forever, come to mind not as prostitute/accused murderer/coke-dealing robber of cash from a dead body who happened to be my husband, but as FORMERLY BARELY-ATTRACTIVE SLUT WHO FORGOT IMPORTANCE OF GOOD GROOMING WHEN ON THE LAM. Even weirder, the image with a lifetime lease that now resided somewhere near Mindy and Hannah would make it feel like Dorinda was somehow part of the family.

Weirdest: A week to the day after Lieutenant Corky Paston dropped by to tell me Dorinda had been apprehended, my obsessive curiosity about her simply stopped. When I got back from Florabella after doing a few centerpieces for local dinner parties and sharpening all our knives, pruners, and deleafers, I switched the cable DVR list to find a *Cook's Country* show I'd recorded. When I saw my endless lineup of local news shows starring Dorinda Dillon, I had one of those *What was I thinking?* flashes. Then I erased them all.

Late that afternoon, my cousin Scott Rabinowitz came over, more to play with the boys than to keep me company. He was a couple of years younger than I was, but he had the social sophistication of a six-year-old. Naturally, that made him a favorite of the boys. The pleasure was mutual. Being an IRS tax examiner, Scott was accustomed to being detested by people. Also, being a pudgy accountant with a juicy lisp, he wasn't a guy's guy. As an extra attraction, he had a unibrow, so he was achingly familiar with the disdain of the glam women he was, unfortunately, attracted to. For a guy like Scott, being considered cool by Evan, Mason, and Dash was an ego-booster. I assumed that for him, a Saturday night building SpongeBob, Patrick, and a bunch of jellyfish from LEGOs was a small triumph and not a defeat.

Since I couldn't completely abandon my cousin, I put him and the boys at the kitchen table. I kept busy making whole-wheat dough and cutting out five-inch circles to freeze for future pizza nights. Now and then Scott and I would exchange a few sentences on how Cousin Kay, researching the Rabinowitz family tree, had discovered a branch of rogue Rabins in Indianapolis, or how it would take years for the IRS to remake the enforcement division after what the Bushies had done to it. Most of the time, though, the boys kept him too busy to make conversation. A good thing.

Suddenly, Dashiell began yelling at Mason for hiding some green LEGOs in his room. As the two of them stomped off to search, Evan sat quietly, ignoring us, balancing LEGO pieces on the backs of his outstretched fingers. Scott got up, looked in my refrigerator, and asked, "Don't you ever eat unhealthy food?"

"Of course. If I kept it in the house, I could eat pounds of it."

"But you don't really *desire* salty pretzel rods, do you? I mean, like, you want one so bad you would go out at three in the morning to a 7-Eleven . . . except they'd probably only have those twisty ones that don't crunch."

"Listen, you pick your poison. If someone said, 'They're selling English florists' bulbs from the Wakefield and North of England Tulip Society on a street corner in the Bronx at three A.M., but you'll have to fight off a gang of crackheads—trust me, I'd be there."

"Bulbs for planting, not eating, right?" Scott asked.

"Right. People don't generally . . . Well, onions are bulbs."

Times like this, I missed Jonah even more than I did at night when I was alone. I could cry then over my loneliness, though I'd be so exhausted from the day that no matter how bad the desolation was, sleep knocked me out. Talking about pretzels with someone who was nice enough but could disappear off the face of the earth and I might not remember he'd existed or been nice to the boys was a worse kind of loneliness.

Right after dinner, I sent Scott *time-to-go* thought waves, but he didn't receive them. Instead, he came upstairs while I bathed the boys—the fast bath, which meant they all stood in the tub while I soaped them, sprayed off the soap, dried them, and gave them each a star stamp on their separate Clean Guy charts, then did the hurry-up toothbrushing with all three around the sink at the same time, which got them another star stamp because they kept to the no-spitting-toothpaste-or-water-at-your-brothers rule.

"How do you do it night after night?" Scott asked after we put them all to bed. "Aren't you completely wiped?"

I took his question as a positive sign, that the boys had worn him out. So I censored "Not completely wiped, just your basic wiped," and offered him what I hoped was a weary smile as I led him downstairs. I made the mistake of turning on a lamp in the living room. He took that as an invitation to stay, plopping down in a club chair, leaning his head back, closing his eyes, and letting his arms dangle over the sides.

In defeat, I grabbed a fringed throw from the arm of the couch, wrapped myself in it, and sat in the corner of the couch. The throw had a pleasing verbena smell from a delicate-fabric wash I'd forgotten I'd bought.

Scott lifted his head and opened his eyes. Then he realized he had nothing to say but couldn't very well close his eyes again. So I told him, "You put on your sincerest voice and say, 'Tell me, Susie. Really. How are you doing?' Put a lot of concern into the 'how.'"

"Okay," he said. "I'll know for next time. So?"

"So, I don't know. Up, down, up, down. Never really up, actually. There's just low-key down and deep down." He nodded, which was fine because there was really nothing to say. "Sometimes I think it can't get any worse, but then I realize it can and probably will."

"Scary." He rubbed his nose with the back of his index finger. I pictured his knuckle hair rubbing against his nose hair.

"Scary on its own," I said. "But with the boys . . . and don't tell me I'm stronger than I think I am. I'm afraid I'll be in the middle of a normal moment a few months or a year from now, doing whatever but thinking about Jonah, and I'll break from the cumulative effect of all the memories."

"When people break down—"

"I'm not talking about breaking down. Breaking, period. As in shattering. Like a champagne flute."

Scott laughed. "A champagne flute?"

I got up, pissed at how he'd pronounced "champagne" with a French accent, as if my mere use of the word was pretentious. But I tripped on the long fringe of the throw, and I wound up right back on the couch. "Dammit! I was talking to you, one human being to another, opening up."

"Susie, listen, I know. I'm sorry. Honestly, I was listening, one human being to another. But we're Brooklyn human beings, and 'champagne flute' was never a word combination in Flatbush."

"Your part of Flatbush."

"Like your parents knew from champagne flutes. Anyway, it just struck me. Believe me, I wasn't—you know—making light of your troubles. Your pain."

"It's okay, Scott. Forget it."

"When I said 'breaking down,' I wasn't talking about you having a nervous breakdown and going to a psych ward or anything. For all I know, that could happen. Except you really are so strong. I was thinking that you got to be what you are not from marrying Jonah, who was a wonderful, wonderful guy. You know I always thought that. He was so nice to me. But you didn't become what you are now just through your looks or your talent or marrying a doctor. Look, I'm a tax examiner. I deal with some rich people. You know what I see? Some of them got where they are through inheritance or brains. Or dumb luck. Or embezzlement, tax evasion. There are loads of ways to make it. But you: You got what you wanted because you had a powerful vision of how you wanted to live. And you got there because of whatever gifts you have—and your strength. You didn't sit around eating bonbons and fantasizing. You worked your ass off. You built a business. You kept up with that fertility business for years, and everyone is in awe of how you deal with the little guys. You were a huge asset to Jonah in his practice."

"Then why would he . . ." I didn't even bother to finish.

"I don't know," Scott said. "But if you're clueless, maybe there's a reason. Maybe it had nothing to do with you." I shrugged. He went on, "What? It sucks if you can't blame yourself? Listen, you've always been the creative type. If you're looking to blame yourself, you'll invent a way. But come on. Was Jonah a shit who always screwed around?"

"No. Of course not. Well, it's possible, but it's so totally against everything I knew about him. He was so dependable. And moral. Also, I can't see where he could have found the time."

"Maybe he had some secret kink he managed to hide from the whole world, including you, that he could satisfy in five minutes."

I had to laugh. Maybe I even did. "Scott, give me a break."

He scratched his jaw. Even though he was in his early thirties, a pear-shaped man in unfashionably baggy jeans and loafers with black tire-tread soles, I still saw him as my kid cousin, so the rasping sound of his fingernails on his five o'clock shadow surprised me. "I don't know if I should be saying this," he began. "Probably not. But anyway, about being duped: People meet some slicko with a ton of hair gel and a bullshit story, and they say, 'That guy is a con man.' But that's not a con man, that's a loser with too much crap on his hair. The successful con man, white-collar criminal, guy who leads a secret life—someone with a big sex secret, or a spy—gives off waves of normalcy. They're nice guys, but not so nice that it calls attention to their niceness. I've been with the IRS for ten years, and you know when my antenna goes up? When someone comes in, tells his story, and my reaction is 'Whoever looked at your returns made a big mistake. I apologize that we wasted so much of your time and energy.'"

I leaned back to mull over what Scott had said. I tried putting my feet up on the coffee table, but Bernadine had moved it farther from the couch, where she believed it belonged, and my heels slipped off the edge. I sat straighter and said, "You're right, and it's the perfect viewpoint for someone working for the government looking for really clever tax cheaters. But it's different living with somebody. I know there are lots of wives who go into shock when they find out their husbands have been fooling around with another woman, or with a guy, for that matter, or that they're involved in some giant fraud. They're always saying, 'I can't believe it!' But almost all the time, if they've missed the signals, it's because they didn't want to pick them up."

"So you're saying you're not that way," Scott said. He sounded more matter-of-fact, as if making an observation, than doubting.

"Scott, I've thought this through again and again, and I can't remember any signals or signs of distress that made me draw back and tell myself, *Uh-oh, I don't want to deal with that because it would jeopardize the marriage or my lifestyle.* And okay, maybe I wasn't well-bred enough for him, or interesting on intellectual subjects, but I don't think it was anywhere near a deal-breaker. Even if it was, does a guy who wants to talk about history cycles go to a prostitute for conversation?"

"No. If Jonah was hostile that you weren't into history cycles, I can't see him taking that route."

"You know what I wish?" I said.

"What?"

"I wish there was someone who'd been Jonah's best friend, someone he really confided in, and that guy could say to me, 'Susie, I swear to God, that one night was the only time Jonah ever cheated on you. We told each other everything, and trust me, I would have known. It was just one stupid moment of weakness in a whole lifetime of love.'"

I could see Scott felt sad for me. Usually, that would have pissed me off, being the object of pity, but I didn't feel any condescension of the "naive little fool" variety that had been coming my way since the cops found Jonah. "Maybe there's something to say that would make you feel better," Scott finally said, "but I don't know what it is."

"Thank you. Listen, your coming over, hanging with the boys because you have fun with them, not because it's the decent thing to do—it means a lot to me. And so does your telling me how strong I am, even though I'm not so sure about that." We sat in what I suppose was called companionable silence. I broke it by saying, "When I tell myself, *All right, Jonah went to a call girl for sex,* and no matter what my gut says, it's a fact, I still hit a wall. I try and try, but I can't imagine a scenario where his being murdered there could happen. How could Jonah set someone off to the point where she'd want to kill him?"

"Maybe . . ." He decided to let it drop.

"You mean maybe he did something awful to her, or asked her for something that was totally disgusting?" Scott nodded. I continued, "But prostitutes get asked to do disgusting stuff all the time. See, that's what I don't understand. Men beat them up or ask them to do dominatrix stuff. All sorts of things that you think, *God, how could anyone be so bent?*"

At that moment, it occurred to me that I had no idea what my cousin did for sex, that maybe he shared a bed with a blowup doll named Titty Rabinowitz and I'd offended him.

"Maybe it wasn't anything Jonah did," Scott said. "Maybe Dorinda was crazy."

"She had arrests for cocaine. But nothing I heard from the detective or the DA's office made me think of her as a violent person."

"Did Jonah have a bad temper? Ever lose control?"

"No. He never screamed like a crazy person or anything. Once in a while we'd have a fight and he was really loud, but so was I. At his worst, he was overbearing, I guess that's the word. A control freak: my way or the highway."

"If she was really deranged," Scott said, "that's the kind of behavior that might have set her off."

"Could be." I guessed that made sense. At least it was an explanation, where none had existed before. I started with the *Time for you to go* thought waves again, but they were as unsuccessful as they'd been earlier.

"No," Scott said. "I don't think I'm right. Because if Dorinda was a total nut job, she would have—sorry to say this—killed him in a crazy way. He was stabbed, what? Twice?"

"Yes."

"It seems to me a crazy person would have stabbed him a freakish number of times. That's what happens if someone is wild with anger, out of control. Right? Doesn't that make more sense to you than just twice?"

"Yes," I said, "it does."

Chapter Nineteen

My conversation with Scott was keeping me up. For the first time since I lost Jonah, I wanted to talk more. Not with my cousin, though.

I could call Andrea, who would welcome any excuse—"Susie needs to vent"—to escape the California king she shared with Fat Boy. But we'd talked so long and so often that before our first word, I knew where we'd end up.

I adjusted my pillows against the headboard and considered my best friend from high school, Jessie Heller. I called her my human resource; she'd been in HR at Goldman Sachs before she had kids. But even though she was smart and practical and had been at the funeral and the shiva, it would take a half hour to bring her up-to-date.

Seconds later, Grandma Ethel's phone was on its third ring. That was when it hit me that she might not be thrilled with such a late call. What saved me from hanging up was remembering that old people are supposed to need less sleep. And I'd always felt that gay people led more exciting lives and so went to bed later than straights.

"I was just thinking about you a few minutes ago," she told me. "I saw the hooker on the TV."

"So how come you didn't call?" I said it in a teasing way, but when it came out, it sounded whiny.

At least I thought so, but my grandmother acted like she'd heard a regular question. "I didn't want to wake up your children."

"The children are boys," I said. "Three of them. Triplets."

"Did you call because you missed me or to give me a hard time? Because to tell you the truth, if you want to give someone a hard time, don't bother me. Call your mother."

I was about to make a snide comment, but then I thought that would be like telling Grandma Ethel, "Boy, were you lucky to get away from her." "Is this too late for you?" I asked.

"Are you kidding? I live in Miami. For half my friends, this is dinner hour. Now, as I used to say to the guests on my show, 'Talk to me, sweetheart.' You wouldn't believe the people I called 'sweetheart.' Cher. Archbishop Desmond Tutu."

"It's not so much about me talking," I said untruthfully. "I could use some wisdom."

"For that you need Sparky." My grandmother's voice sounded cheery and charming, the upbeat voice people use at dinner parties they're delighted to be at but surprised to be invited to.

"Actually, what I want now is grandmotherly wisdom," I said. No one could possibly call my voice upbeat.

She was obviously someone who knew when to leave the party, because when she spoke again, it was clear that she'd let go of the cheery business. "Sure, grandmotherly wisdom . . . if I have any. Tell me. Whatever I can do for you, I'll do it. And don't think that's just Ethel O'Shea's patented bullshit, because I almost never make offers like that." I was about to thank her when she added, "Maybe three times in my life. You don't make commitments, you don't have to back out of them. Know what I mean?"

This wasn't exactly reassuring, but after eleven at night, I couldn't be picky. "Sure."

"Good. Now talk to me."

"Okay. You know how when something bad happens, there's the story of what happened that makes sense to most people. And then there's all sorts of conspiracy theories?"

"Right," Grandma Ethel said. "You should've been around after the Kennedy assassination."

"From what I've seen, a lot of the conspiracy theories are crazy stuff—from paranoids and idiots. Then there are a few that come across as reasonable." I had been lying back in bed. Now I sat up and crossed my legs under me, which had the double advantage of being the posture of a heart-to-heart discussion and also keeping my feet warm. I was so chilled. I prayed the boiler wasn't having its biweekly collapse and I'd have to wait up half the night for the oil burner guy.

"You heard some conspiracy theory about Jonah that you're tempted to believe?" my grandmother asked.

"No. Not really. It's just that the murder case against this Dorinda Dillon is so open-and-shut, which is fine with me. Well, it should be fine. But every time I accept what happened, what all the experienced people like the cops and the head of Homicide at the DA's office say happened, I think, *All right. They're pros. Not emotionally involved. Now it's time to get on with my life*. And just when I do, something starts troubling me."

"What's the something?" Grandma Ethel asked.

"That's just it: nothing specific. It's always one bit of information or another that seems wrong. I keep wishing somebody— me, even—would come up with a conspiracy theory that would take care of all the little doubts I have."

"Tell me the little doubts."

I went through my talk with Scott, saying that if Dorinda had been crazed with anger at Jonah or plain crazy, how come she hadn't stabbed him over and over?

"You don't know for sure that's how a nutsy person would go about it," Grandma Ethel said. "I'm sure some of them would stab him a lot more than twice, but there's no book called *There Is Only One Type of Homicidal Stabbing Behavior for the Criminally Insane*. Right?"

"Right. But stabbing multiple times seems more likely. And even if she was a stab-twice-only kind of person, it doesn't explain why she went and got the scissors and killed him."

"Listen, I interviewed a madam and also a couple of call girls over the years. The madam, I forget her name—that's okay, there's not a chance in hell it was her actual name—she was smart. Well spoken, well put together, reminded me of Rita Hayworth, except not sexy. That was strange, because before her Call Me Madam days, she was a hooker. The madam, not Rita Hayworth, who I think started out as a dancer. Anyway, when I say her 'Call Me Madam' days, that was a Broadway musical. Ethel Merman. But not about a madam. The madam on my show was smart, made a good appearance. You could bring her to a luncheon at your club and not be at all embarrassed. But below the surface, I could feel there was something a little nuts. A cold beyond cold. It's one thing to sleep with a creep because he's rich or famous or you need a guy and he's the only one with a regular paycheck who'll have you. It's a completely different mentality to sleep with twenty, thirty, forty guys a week. What I'm saying is, don't go giving Dorinda Dillon a clean bill of mental health."

"I'm not," I said. I wished now that I could ask her to bring Sparky into the room and put me on speaker. That way there would be someone in on the conversation capable of saying, "Eth, you seem to have used up your daily quota of logic."

"Good, because from what I've seen of darling Dorinda on the television, she looks like she's got a few screws loose."

"Even if she's not a picture of mental health, it still doesn't explain her being a killer. Thousands of prostitutes go through their entire careers without murdering a customer."

I got into explaining what I believed in my heart, that while there were no guarantees in life, I was willing to bet Jonah hadn't had some kind of messy sexual secret, no fetish that could send a pro like Dorinda into a killing frenzy or frighten her into self-defense with a pair of scissors.

"Did he ever hit you?" my grandmother asked a little too casually.

"No! Of course not!"

"Okay, I was just asking. Don't bite my head off. Did he ever call you names or humiliate—"

"Absolutely not! Jonah didn't have an abusive bone in his body."

"Just to make sure I have the picture . . . He wasn't violent, no vicious tirades. Any throwing things, kicking over tables?"

I shook my head but then realized we were on the phone. "No."

"Was he controlling with money?"

"No, only with tight lips. As far as money went, he wasn't at all cheap. Maybe one of the reasons he was so uncritical of me was that he was really good at spending, too. And I was never out of control." I paused. "Well, once."

"What?"

"A red gown. From Valentino's last collection."

"No! Not the strapless with the double flounce on the bottom?" It was a question, but somehow she knew.

"Yes!"

"My God! They had a Valentino spread in . . . I think *The Miami Herald,* and my jaw dropped when I saw that gown! Good for you!"

"But usually, both of us were under control, for two acquisitive personalities. Jonah was never one of those show-offy guys, handing hundred-dollar bills to maître d's. It's weird, I was thinking about this last night, about Jonah and money. Whatever happened at Dorinda Dillon's, I can't imagine him being cheap or not fair. And he would never hold back on paying her, if that's a thing that could set her off. He told me a story over and over again about going out with his parents when they had a lousy waiter. His father left a dollar bill as a tip."

"It upset Jonah?"

"Incredibly. He kept bringing it up."

"He was right. It was petty and vindictive. Probably made him realize his old man was a shtunk." On the phone, I kept forgetting my grandmother was a woman of a certain age—old. Not only was her voice free from shakiness, but even though she was pretty good at digression, she didn't lose her focus. This was especially true when she wasn't being Unforgettable Character and concentrating on her own delightfulness but was focusing on a thought or another person.

"Jonah always said, 'Give someone the benefit of the doubt.'"

"So give Jonah the benefit of the doubt by asking the questions."

"Who can I ask questions? They closed the case. It's over."

"It's not over. Dorinda's in jail, she hasn't been on trial yet, so how can it be over? Go back to the cop or the district attorney and tell them you still have some questions."

"They'll think I'm a real pain in the ass."

"So? Big damn deal if they do. Listen, law enforcement has to cooperate with a victim's widow—unless she's an out-and-out lunatic, which you obviously aren't. They don't want to risk alienating you. You could go to the media and shed a few tears and tell them, 'I'm disappointed in how the police and the DA are handling my husband's murder case.' It would be a nightmare for them: a beautiful widow with three little boys who are also victims of this crime."

"I don't like the role of victim."

"But you've got it," my grandmother said. "This isn't 'victim' as in 'My parents wouldn't pay for a nose job, and when my first husband left me, he called me Pinocchio.' This is genuine victimhood, so you might as well use it. The world loves victims."

"I don't."

"Then be a pain in the ass, a thorn in their side. Be whatever the hell you want to be. But give your husband the benefit of your doubt. And while you're at it, toots, give that to yourself, too."

Chapter Twenty

✂——————————————————————————————

"You know the chief of the DA's Homicide Bureau's a woman?" my in-laws' lawyer, Christopher Petrakis, asked me.

"Yes," I said. My father-in-law also nodded. My mother-in-law acted as if all she'd heard was silence.

"Just so you know, because her name is Eddie Huber. It's a nickname, but I forget what her real name is." Christopher Petrakis adjusted his French cuffs by holding them at the very edge. This gave us a view of one of his gold scales-of-justice cuff links; a single diamond chip rested on only one pan of the scales, yet the two were in balance. "I call her Eddie Hubris. Obviously, not to her face." He seemed a little surprised that none of us chuckled. You'd have thought that, having once worked in the DA's office himself, he'd figure the parents and widow of a murder victim, who were about to go in to discuss the case against the accused, would not be given to chuckling.

The four of us stood outside the door to the chief's office. A secretary had met us as we got off the elevator, walked us through the hall, then told Petrakis, "She'll send somebody when she's ready to see you." The whole building was so run-down, I felt like I was breathing in not just dust but decades of suspended dirt that normal air currents could not pass through—mildew, tracked-in shoe crud, sneeze droplets from a 1967 flu outbreak.

When I'd called Babs and Clive to tell them I wanted to talk with someone in the DA's office, I didn't mention any of my assorted qualms about Dorinda Dillon. Still, from the moment Babs had asked, "Would you mind terribly if one or both of us come?" I'd said, "Of course not. I was hoping you would." That was immediately followed by Clive on speakerphone responding, "Excellent," but in a tone he might use to offer a dismal prognosis. So I knew meeting with the chief of the Homicide Bureau would be a snap compared to dealing with Babs and Clive.

Babs had called me from her office three days in a row with variations on "Don't you think you should wait until someone from the DA's office calls *you*?" I mumbled some bullshit that included "proactive" and "engaged in the process." She told me she was concerned that if we pushed too hard, the prosecutors might get the impression that we weren't satisfied with their handling of the case. "As you know, Susie my dear," she said, "they've been wonderfully cooperative about keeping us informed. But consider this: If we were seen in the building, word could leak out that the family was putting pressure on the district attorney's office!"

Pressure for what? I wanted to ask. To get them to railroad a poor, innocent hooker? Unlikely, since they were absolutely certain Dorinda Dillon killed Jonah.

My mother-in-law's calls were followed up by one from Clive, wanting to know if I'd have any objections if they brought along a lawyer. "We've got a first-rate man. Fine, fine reputation. He himself used to be with the DA's office. With a midtown firm now. Comes highly, highly recommended."

Their concerns about not wanting me to start trouble seemed over-the-top, especially because they had no clue about my agenda, to the extent that I had one. I wasn't about to confide in them how plagued I was by the small doubts that kept popping up, only to disappear into *How could I have been thinking that?*—moments when my own craziness made me cringe. But later, in those dull-witted hours between the kids' bedtime and mine, the doubts would pop up again, more powerful than ever.

Dr. Twersky, defying my principle (which, thankfully, I'd never mentioned to her in therapy) that women over fifty should never wear leather pants, had uncrossed her legs with a squeak and suggested my in-laws might be overcome with grief and anger at Jonah's death, made worse by the horrible publicity, even the social humiliation. Babs and Clive saw any questions about the case against Dorinda Dillon as . . . overstimulating, overwhelming, oversomething. The Gerstens wanted to let it be. They were older and more fragile than I was and therefore were at their breaking point.

It wasn't until I was driving home from Dr. Twersky's office that I'd considered she might be telling me I was being cruel to subject them to this; I was young enough to be resilient. I could eventually get over Jonah. The Gerstens didn't have that going for them. I'd asked Dr. Twersky if, when someone was feeling fragile, was the remedy to call a criminal lawyer? She'd gone on about them viewing a lawyer as a wise guide or perhaps a protector. Now I thought, *Protection against what? Me?*

I'd pulled over to the curb and parked in front of a tiny house dwarfed by a giant copper beech. I cried for a few minutes until I saw someone coming out of a house two doors down, walking one of the fifty thousand Labrador retrievers in Shorehaven, a community of thirty thousand people. Reasonably sure all my windows were closed, I'd yelled, "Go fuck yourself!" to either Dr. Twerksy or my in-laws, pulled out, and driven home.

Petrakis centered the gold Rolex on his wrist. Other than the watch and the scales-of-justice cuff links, he wasn't a flashy guy. His suit was a gray box, his tie black with unassertive white dots, his shoes black lace-ups that were neither scuffed nor shined. It looked like one person took charge of his jewelry, while another did clothes. "Any minute now," he told us.

"Thank you," Clive said. He turned to inspect the wall next to him. It was peeling, and long pieces of paint hung down like the drooping leaves of a spiderwort. But he was staring, intent, examining the strips of paint as if they were hung in an up-and-coming gallery.

My father-in-law's attire was a lot more elegant than the lawyer's, but then only one person—Babs—was in charge of dressing him. Jonah once complained his father looked like an assistant fashion editor's idea of a successful Manhattan doctor rather than an actual doctor. He'd laughed when I told him it was hostile to make it an "assistant editor."

Petrakis's arm made a sweep of the hall. "You can see for yourself. All the doors are open, so Hubris must be up to her eyeballs in work, or in deep conference with her door closed."

Clive and I nodded. Listening, I could hear the drone of conversation from the other offices, the clicks of keyboarding, phones that honked like geese. Babs didn't seem to have heard Petrakis and also seemed unaware of the noise of business. She stood pale and motionless, swathed in black. It was probably less for mourning than for the simple reason that black was the official color in her set, the Upper East Side's red, white, and blue. The outfit was by a designer whose work I didn't know: black pants that were almost leggings and a great deal of black jersey, somewhere between a dress and tunic, which fell several inches below the knee. All she needed was the face-veil thing to look like Mrs. ibn Saud, but I decided to compliment her on it to get some conversation going.

I was about to go over to her, but her posture stopped me cold. Her arms were rigid, as if she didn't have elbows, and tight against her sides. Maybe she sensed I was going to take a step toward her because her eyes, which had been staring ahead at nothing, now shut tight. Someone facing a firing squad, hearing "Ready, aim . . ." would stand like that.

I felt awful, sick to my stomach that I was making her go through this, because she really did look fragile. Both she and Clive seemed to have lost weight since Jonah died; in fact, they appeared diminished in every way. Then it hit me that coming to the DA's office wasn't a command performance. Babs had asked if one or both of them could come, and there was only one answer I could have given.

The door opened, and three lawyers—well, two women and a man, all wearing glasses and carrying binders—whooshed out of the office and flew down the hall.

"Come in, come in," a voice called. Petrakis tried ushering us all, but Clive held back to put an arm around Babs's rigidity and lead her slowly. He motioned to me to go ahead.

Eddie Huber was already up and circling her desk to greet us. "I apologize for keeping you waiting," she said. By this time, Clive had steered Babs into the room. Eddie approached her first, extending a hand.

I was nervous that Babs would continue with the catatonia business, but my mother-in-law shook Eddie's hand and said, "That's quite all right. It's kind of you to see us." She said it so graciously that I took a closer look at Eddie to see what could bring out that response from Babs. I didn't get it. Not that I had a mental image of the chief of a homicide bureau, but what I saw looked more like a woman in her mid-forties who taught Latin in high school in suburban Boston. She wore a plain sweater in a washed-out green that was probably called sage in the catalog she bought it from. The sweater was tucked into a wool A-line skirt in a wishy-washy color that didn't deserve a name.

After shaking hands with Babs and telling her how sorry she was about Jonah, Eddie did the same with Clive, then me. Her handshake was strong, but if I'd been wearing a ring on my right hand, it wouldn't have gotten squished. As she and Petrakis did the "How are you, Chris?" "Keeping out of trouble, Eddie" ritual, I noticed that her ballet flats looked like the ones from the fifties you see in vintage clothing stores—great leather but a little clunky in the sole-and-heel department. I wondered if she had some preppy/schoolmarm-style thing going. I might even have thought nun who works in the world except she didn't have a cross, and she wore minimal makeup: a touch of mascara and a hint of beigey-pink lipstick. Why she would go that far and not spend fifteen more seconds putting on a little foundation was a mystery.

My in-laws were seated, but Petrakis had to move a pile of file folders from a chair to the floor so I could sit. Eddie, meanwhile, went back to her desk, sat, picked up the phone, and said, "Now. One more chair." The words were snippy, but her tone was neutral, like that of an NPR voice announcing the time.

"Ms. Gersten," she said, looking at me and not Babs, "asked for this meeting so she could have a sense of how we're proceeding on the case."

Even though she wasn't short, it was hard to see more than her head when she was sitting behind her desk. Besides an old, bloated computer monitor, it was covered with piles of files, notebooks, legal documents with metal clasps, newspapers, and panda tchotchkes—wood, ceramic, metal, plastic—not one with any artistic merit as far as I could see. There were yellow legal pads and loose papers, some stained with circles of coffee. A few cardboard cups were balanced atop the piles. One lay on its side; the remains of the coffee left in it made a little pond on one of the few areas of actual bare desk.

"As you know, Dorinda Dillon is in custody. Everything points to her as the perpetrator. We expect her to be indicted soon, and she'll probably be brought to trial within sixty days." Before I could ask "Are you sure?" she continued, "Her prints are on the scissors that were used as the weapon."

"The scissors definitely were hers?" I asked. The door opened. Someone rolled in a secretary's chair for Petrakis, then left.

"At the time she was interviewed in Las Vegas, she wasn't asked. However, forensics has established that the scissors came from the medicine cabinet in her bathroom. The shelves there were full of dust from the compressed powder used in makeup, as well as regular dust and so forth. We found significant traces of that mix on the shank and around the finger rings of the scissors."

Eddie Huber glanced across her desk wreckage at my in-laws, who were seated directly opposite her. Then she looked at me to see if any of us had questions. We didn't. I was slightly off to the side and had to look past Clive to see Babs. What I saw was not encouraging. She was staring right at me, as if she'd been doing it for a while. Somehow she'd decided I merited more attention than the business at hand. Her hands, scarily white as they emerged from her long black sleeves, were gripping the sides of her chair as if she had to restrain herself from grabbing me.

I looked back at Eddie Huber and prayed for her to start talking again. She obliged. "We found what we posited was a strand of Dorinda Dillon's hair near the second wound, as if she bent over Dr. Gersten's body to examine it closely."

I expected a gasp from my mother-in-law just because she was a basket case. The phrase "Dr. Gersten's body" was pretty ugly, especially under the fluorescent lights in that pigsty of an office. But Babs was silent, and I was afraid to check again in case she was still staring at me.

"Are the DNA results in?" Christopher Petrakis asked. I got the impression that he wasn't as much genuinely curious as feeling the need to speak up and justify his five-hundred- or one-thousand-dollar-an-hour fee.

"Yes, we have the results," Eddie Huber said. "And the hair found was Dorinda Dillon's. All right, as I was saying . . ." While the two lawyers didn't seem to dislike each other, they didn't look to have great chemistry. She peered at a piece of yellow legal paper off to her right. "The doorman who was on duty that evening is willing to swear that no one came into the building whom he cannot account for. Ms. Dillon's last, uh, visitor left the building a few hours before Dr. Gersten's arrival."

"Did the doorman describe what that guy, the previous visitor, looked like?" I asked.

While she seemed surprised at the question, she answered in a polite way, which made me feel, despite my pounding heart, that it wasn't an unreasonable query. "An older man. Longish gray hair. The doorman thought he looked either theatrical or Eastern European, though he didn't notice any accent. He believes he's seen the man a fair number of times over the last year or two. Goes up, stays for a half hour or forty-five minutes, then out. Also, he saw no one else during his shift, four in the afternoon until midnight; no one else had any business in Ms. Dillon's apartment. She went for her usual late-afternoon walk and came back under an hour later—alone."

Petrakis spoke up quickly, as if afraid I'd beat him to asking something else. "Was the doorman who was on duty earlier that day also questioned?"

"Yes. He says she had no deliveries, no repair people of any kind. The only client was a regular—a man in his mid- to late seventies—who got there around ten o'clock and was out before eleven. That early-shift doorman saw Dorinda a little later, when she came down to check the mail, but she didn't go out." Eddie Huber had either a trace of a New England accent or that studied way of saying some words—"re-pay-ah" for "repair"—that I'd noticed with a couple of Jonah's friends at Yale. Jonah said it was the last gasp of what used to be the New England boarding school accent, the way Franklin Roosevelt and upper-class people used to talk.

I leaned forward to run my finger inside the back of my shoe, as if it were digging in near my Achilles tendon, but really to look at my mother-in-law. Thank God, her eyes were now on Eddie Huber, and though she was still holding the sides of her chair, her grip didn't seem as desperate. My guess was she had somehow determined the chief of homicide was an aristocrat, not someone working-class from New Hampshire. That was keeping Babs on her best behavior.

"Who's representing Dorinda?" Petrakis asked. "Legal Aid?"

"No. A lawyer named Joel Winters."

"Never heard of him." Petrakis rubbed his forehead. He would have been a nice-enough-looking guy except for his forehead and scalp, a few inches north. Earlier in his life, he must have had a low hairline, but what was left were tufts of fuzz, like bits of brown cotton balls, randomly growing between his forehead and the top of his skull. "Is he any good?"

Eddie Huber shrugged, which I thought was a pretty classy way of saying someone sucked. Maybe she actually was one of those blue-blood types, the kind who behaved as if they'd signed some code of behavior in Ms. Pomfret's penmanship class as soon as they learned script. I'd found that most people who considered themselves American aristocrats were no more honorable than anybody else. Some, in fact, flying first-class through life on family and school connections (not in a middle seat in row 37, where their own abilities would get them), had the moral code of hyenas. Even Andrea Brinckerhoff acted as if eight of the Ten Commandments were too annoying to be taken seriously.

"What's Dorinda's defense?" Petrakis asked, making me glad for the first time that he was there. Lieutenant Paston had given me some details, but I'd been so rattled when he dropped by that I wasn't sure I'd even heard everything he said, much less remembered it.

"She was unconscious. She opened the closet door to get Dr. Gersten's coat; someone was in there with Dorinda's electric broom and hit her over the head with it."

"When she says she opened the closet door," Petrakis said,

"did she mention whether whoever was supposedly in there had the broom raised in readiness? Or did the person pick it up when the door opened?"

"I don't think . . ." Eddie Huber raised herself a few inches out of her chair and leaned forward to one of the higher piles on her desk. She found what she was looking for a few inches from the top, papers held together with a large butterfly clip. Wetting her middle finger, she leafed through them, then put them down. "That was never asked," she said. "And now her lawyer won't let us near her. All right, so she claims she was unconscious. When she came to and discovered Jonah's body, she called a lawyer she had used on the drug charges: Faith Williams."

"Never heard of her, either," Petrakis said.

"Doesn't matter. Williams wasn't in, Dorinda left a message. While she waited for Williams to phone back, she threw a few things into a bag—just in case—though it's on the police video that when she was asked 'In case of what?' she was unable to say. She waited an hour. When Williams hadn't gotten back to her, she put on a pair of gloves, took whatever cash there was in Jonah's wallet, then left. She withdrew an additional four hundred dollars from her account at an ATM and took the subway to Forty-second Street, then the shuttle to Times Square. She stopped in a store, bought a curly red wig. Then she walked over to Port Authority and took the next bus to Las Vegas."

"Did the doorman see Dorinda leave?" I asked.

"No," Eddie Huber said. "Sorry I didn't mention it: Dorinda said she left the building via the service entrance that's off to the side."

I tried to picture it. "Is it, like, around the corner from the entrance to the building?"

"Sort of." I thought I heard the ultra-bland tone in her "sort of" that people put on when they're pissed, but maybe it was two-thirty in the afternoon and she needed another cup of coffee. "The front door of the building is mid-block, so the service entrance is technically on the same street as the front entrance. But it's a fairly large building, and the service door is set in a gap between that building and the one next to it. You go about six feet down an alleyway between the buildings to access the service door."

"So the doorman can't see it from where he stands," I said.

"It's monitored." Eddie Huber barely moved her lips as she said it, so much like a ventriloquist that I wouldn't have been surprised to see an assistant DA dummy perched on her lap. "The doorman has a console at his front desk with closed-circuit TV screens for the elevator, the lobby-level staircase behind the fire door, the service elevator, and the service entrance and alleyway. So he would see whatever is going on."

"Unless he's helping someone with packages or hailing a cab," I said.

"According to the building's management and all the doormen, the service entrance is always locked to the outside by a deadbolt. Of course, it can always be opened from the inside. When someone needs to get in that way, the doorman buzzes the porter. If he has any question about whether to let someone in, he calls the building superintendent."

"But Dorinda got out without anyone seeing her," I said.

Eddie Huber nodded. "Yes, she must have gone down the service elevator." Her thin, straight hair bobbed along with the motion of her head.

"So if the door is unlocked from the inside, it's possible that she or anybody else in the building could have let somebody else in earlier," I said.

"Technically, yes. Technically, anything could have happened. But we have overwhelming evidence, physical and circumstantial, that Dorinda committed the crime. We believe we have proof beyond a reasonable doubt. We wouldn't bring the case if we didn't think so. We also believe she was alone at the time of the murder, had no accomplices, and that's what we're going with."

Didn't you ever hear of anybody taping a lock? Or breaking it so they could get in from the outside? I was taking a deep breath to ask some modified version of that question when I heard the softest "Shh," like an exhalation through clenched teeth. And that's what it was, air through teeth. Not Petrakis, who I figured was annoyed that I was mixing in when he was there; it was my father-in-law, looking straight at me and shaking his head, warning me again to keep quiet.

"We wouldn't be proceeding with our case unless we thought it was not only strong but just," Eddie Huber said, making me realize I hadn't been quite as subtle as I'd thought.

"I think I can speak for all the Gerstens when I say we appreciate and value that," Petrakis said. "All we ask is that you keep us informed, either directly or through me. As I'm sure you understand, Eddie, the family has had more than its share of shocks and surprises."

"Absolutely," Eddie Huber said.

"Mrs. Gersten," he went on, "Mrs. Jonah Gersten, has been through an unimaginable nightmare . . ."

He babbled on, and at first I got steamed by the "Mrs. Jonah" thing. Every time we got an invitation saying "Dr. and Mrs. Jonah Gersten," I'd say something to Jonah, like, "This is enough to get me to put on one of my mother's T-shirts!" He'd start to laugh, and I'd go on, "Give me a break! Aren't I entitled to a name of my own? Is this 1907 or something? How much extra would they have to pay a calligrapher for a Susan?"

". . . a highly developed ethical sense."

I assumed Petrakis was talking about me. He was, because Eddie Huber gave me a nod of recognition, like *Good ethics. Mazel tov.* I nodded back, even though I'd never been totally sure what ethics meant (not counting medical ethics, which had been a huge deal at Yale) and whether they were different from morals.

Practically like the Rockettes, Petrakis and Clive made the same move simultaneously, inching to the front of their chairs, putting their right foot forward and leaning on it as they began to get up. So I said, "One quick question, Ms. Huber. Why would one of Dorinda Dillon's hairs near the second stab wound be proof of her, you know, examining Jonah to see if he was dead? Wouldn't it be even more likely to have gotten there in the course of . . . a prostitute cozying up to her client? I'm not saying you don't have a really good case against her, but—"

Maybe Babs would have yelled or cursed or even smacked me if she didn't believe Eddie Huber was the second coming of Katharine Hepburn, which struck me as showing she really was a total wreck and possibly delusional. Instead, she stood so fast Clive didn't even have a chance to get out of his chair before she was in the hall. My father-in-law hurried after her. I left more slowly because I sensed what fun awaited me. I knew I had gone too far for my in-laws. But not for me.

"How dare you!" Babs shouted at me as I came through the door. "What kind of sick, attention-getting game is this you're playing?"

"What . . . ?" It was such a blast that I staggered backward. It wasn't just her shouting in a public place, it was her shouting, period. The loudest she'd ever been was saying "Damn!" when she couldn't open the clasp of a bracelet. And while I was as familiar with her hostility as with her Gigi de Lavallade Ingénieux scent, it was always in the background, barely noticeable or low-level annoying, like elevator music.

"What are you talking about?" I asked. It sounded like a lame question, because most of the time when you ask it, you know very well what the person is talking about. But I hadn't a clue. A sick, attention-getting game?

"'What are you talking about?'" she mimicked, and the "talking" came out not only loud enough to bounce off the walls but as the meanest imitation of a New York accent I'd ever heard.

"Come on, Babs," Clive urged. He held her arm with one hand and placed his other on her back to maneuver her toward the elevator. "It'll be okay."

"How will it be okay?" she shouted. "Tell me—"

"Mrs. Gersten," Christopher Petrakis said quietly, "why don't we all go downstairs? We can talk outside."

"Why don't you go?" she snapped back. "This doesn't concern you." I was hoping she'd keep at him for a minute or two so I could get out of there, but at that moment she turned back to me. "You realize, I suppose, that your idiot questions could make them rethink the case against that disgusting whore. 'Oh, the poor little widow wants to be sure all the i's are dotted.' And for what? To keep the scandal in the news!"

"You really have to get her out of here," Petrakis told Clive.

"Don't you think I know that?" Clive snapped back. My father-in-law put his arm around Babs and drew her close. "Come, my dear. Let's go home. There are offices all around here, and they might think this is a security situation. We don't want them picking up the phone, calling the police, and saying—"

"You're raising questions about any stupid detail you can think of," Babs kept going at me. "You are in such denial. You really think you had the fairy-tale marriage, princess. You'll do anything to convince yourself that 'Ooh, Jonah loved me sooo much he wouldn't put his life in jeopardy without realizing it by going to a vile, druggy whore. It must be some CIA plot. Or he wandered into that apartment by mistake, and she just happened to be holding scissors and stabbed him.'" The door to Eddie Huber's office slammed shut, but my mother-in-law didn't take the hint. "You turned his life into a hell."

"If you can't deal with this," Petrakis said to Clive, "I'm going to have to escort Mrs. Gersten, the younger Mrs. Gersten, out of—"

But the older Mrs. Gersten wouldn't be stopped. "It was *you* who insisted on going through with having triplets. The doctor made it very clear to you that the pregnancy could be reduced to one or two. I saw the exhaustion in Jonah's eyes every single time we were together. There was *nothing* but tumult in his life. Demands and more demands. What I don't understand is how you can delude yourself that he wouldn't go elsewhere, just for a quick release, just to get away from the constant turmoil. And now you're rewriting history. You're asking questions to—"

I cut her off. "I have a question for you. Mason, Dash, Evan: Which one or two would Jonah have wanted to get rid of? And while we're at it, I've got another question. Did he ever once complain about our marriage? Or me? Or are you the one believing your own fucking fairy tale?"

I left as fast as I could. Only when I was outside did I realize that I had failed to ask Eddie Huber why Dorinda Dillon would have stabbed Jonah only twice.

Chapter Twenty-One

"Babs." Andrea made a noise halfway between a snort and a laugh. "What I don't understand is why her outburst surprised you. You can't expect good breeding from someone who contours their eyes with three browns for daytime."

"She went to Vassar."

"That's education, not class. By the time you're eighteen, you can't even learn how to imitate being polished much less be polished."

"Speaking of classy behavior," I said, "guess who said 'fucking'? I said it right to her face."

"If I stopped saying it, my mother-in-law would think I got run over by a truck and Fat Boy married someone else. Hand me the roll of cloth-covered wire, please."

We were in one of those huge echoing lofts in a nowhere section of downtown Manhattan, doing a wedding both of us hated to the same degree, a rarity. The bride's inspiration was "Make it look like a box from Tiffany!" Andrea's broad hint that this was not an original concept—some might call it trite—hadn't made a dent. Neither had my suggestion that the tiniest touch of red could take it to a whole new level. So, along with our part-timer,

Marjorie, and Tyrell and Nick, two tall Shorehaven High School seniors who helped us with installations, we were stuck decorating sixteen-feet-high structural columns with leaves, white flowers and tulle, aqua ribbon, and bushels of ivory hydrangea that had touches of greenish-blue. Andrea told the bride it was the *Hydrangea Tiffania*. A lie, of course.

I was making bows from six-inch satin ribbon. "When Theo was at the shiva," I said, "he told me I had nothing to worry about from his parents. They'd be good to me if only because I was the gatekeeper to the boys."

"Did I ever tell you he looks like a metrosexual Munchkin?"

"Many times."

"'We represent the Lollipop Guild,'" Andrea sang out in her highest voice. Tyrell and Nick, up on ladders, exchanged looks that said *I'm embarrassed for her*. "Theo was probably right," she went on. "I think Babs has broken under the strain. Nothing really bad ever happened to her. If you're sixty-something and have led a charmed life, you assume you have immunity. So Jonah's death has destroyed her whole view of reality." Andrea clipped a few lengths of wire, then glanced at me. "Don't look so stunned that I said something thoughtful."

"Sorry. I assumed I was hiding it. So, do you think now that my mother-in-law's hostility is out in the open, things can never be fine again?"

"They were never fine. You know that. But will they be okay? Probably, eventually."

"Do you think I should call—"

"Absolutely not! First of all, she owes you an apology. At some point she'll realize it. She'll go, 'Horribly, horribly sorry, Susie sweetness, but shock, breakdown, not myself, blah, blah, blah.' Meanwhile, she's too angry. And too threatened, probably at the thought of even more publicity. But who knows? Anyway, you'll have to accept her apology and move on. Even if you remarry, she'll always be in your life because of the boys."

I spoke quietly so if the high school boys wanted to eaves-drop—which was dubious, because they assumed Andrea and I had nothing interesting to say—they couldn't hear me. "Forget the 'remarry' business."

"I'm not suggesting this June," Andrea said.

"Listen to me: I know what my life is going to be. The accountants called me. It looks like I'll be okay financially. Jonah had enough insurance and pension stuff that it definitely won't be the way it was, but it'll be like ninety-eight percent of the world would like to live." I knew she was thinking what I was: *That's not good enough*. But at least we didn't say it. "You tell me, Andrea: What reasonably nice, semi-cute, single guy— who's going to have hundreds of women after him—"

"Unless he's really poor."

"—would get involved with a mother of three four-year-old boys? You've seen them do it time and again. Evan, Dash, and Mason come in, and they turn a room into a three-ring circus, except ten times noisier. A guy might want me. He might even want them—if he doesn't have kids and has a zero sperm count. But forget even a long weekend: Three hours with them and he'd run out screaming. And don't say 'not necessarily.'" Andrea might have been about to say it, but for once she thought before speaking. "I've thought about it," I went on. "You want to know what the word is for what my life will be? Lonely. My life will be so lonely."

She didn't say I was wrong.

True to what Andrea had predicted, my mother-in-law called to apologize four days after she exploded. She said it had hap-pened because she was a wreck, "an utter wreck," and also had an adverse drug reaction from a new antidepressant that didn't get along with her medication for arrhythmia. There was no way, she told me, to tell me how sorry she was; she only hoped that I would be generous enough to understand and, hopefully, forgive. I did the expected "I understand totally and there's no need to ask for forgiveness." Then I gave what I thought was a pretty moving speech on how I not only treasured my relationship with her and Clive but had always looked up to her as the model of what a wife, mother, and working woman should be. Of course I kept "except that you're a snob and a cold bitch" to myself.

I was trying to move back into the world. At home, whenever someone called, I tried not to think that he or she had put me on their Outlook calendar right after the funeral and forgotten me until—*Oh, dammit!*—the day popped up with *Call Susie Gersten.* When people left messages, I made myself call back, even a woman in my cousin Marcia's mah-jongg group with a terrible stammer who called everyone because in 1962 a speech therapist had told her that was the way to get over it.

I was so busy. I had tried to put Dorinda Dillon out of my head. Maybe the cops and the DA and Babs were all right about her. *The NewsHour,* which I still watched so I wouldn't get caught saying "Huh? Wha?" the next time a teeny country suddenly became important, didn't carry reports on killer whores. The *Times* might have had something on the case, but since the only section I read regularly was Style, I might have missed it. Since those first few days after Dorinda's capture, when I'd watched her perp walk about a thousand times, I hadn't Googled her or looked on YouTube: too addictive, too tempting to stay in that world and forget my own. Also, there was no one shoving a tabloid into my hands while telling me, "You need to see this." For all I knew, maybe some fact or new piece of evidence had come out that really sealed the deal on Dorinda's guilt. But I didn't read about it or see it. And there were definitely no calls from the DA's office or Gersten super-lawyer Christopher Petrakis.

One day, studying the olive oils at Whole Foods, I heard a woman in the next aisle tell someone, "I saw her! Dr. Gersten's wife! The plastic surgeon who got killed. No, *here,* in the store, a minute ago." I thought I'd gotten good at stuff like that, but I left my cart—with all its plastic bags of fruit and vegetables, Greek yogurt, and yet another box of organic cereal to challenge Froot Loops—and walked out.

Once I got the kids to bed that night, I filled my tub with the hottest water I could stand, determined to unwind until the water got cold or my finger pads turned to corduroy. I even dimmed the bathroom lights and lit a jasmine candle. I did succeed in forgetting "Dr. Gersten's wife!" Unfortunately, that left enough room in my mind to think about the photo of Dorinda that I'd seen in a magazine at the pediatrician's office.

It was a head shot with her looking into the camera, unsmiling. She was wearing heavy eyeliner and chandelier earrings, so it wasn't a mug shot. What struck me again was how dumb she looked, like someone who'd gotten lower than 400 on her combined SATs because she'd made too many wrong guesses. I opened my eyes and stared at the candle flame to hypnotize myself and clear my brain. But I couldn't not think. She might be dumb, but was she someone who could as easily stab her way out of a situation than think her way out? After all, she did have enough smarts to slip out the side door of her building and pass on taking a taxi to Port Authority because taxis keep records. She'd stopped in Times Square to buy a wig. True, maybe she'd stabbed Jonah in one insane moment and then was able to think clearly again. But was the DA's case really so solid, so beyond a reasonable doubt, the way Eddie Huber seemed so sure it was?

But where was Dorinda Dillon's lawyer? I wanted to know. If people can't afford a lawyer, they can only get Legal Aid. Dorinda, though, had hired her own lawyer, a guy named Joel Winters. Even if he wasn't any great shakes, and even without me sitting at the computer ten times a day to Google Dorinda Dillon, I should have heard something about Dorinda's side of the story. Okay, she was going to plead not guilty. The case would be going to trial. So why wasn't the lawyer out there defending her? All he had to do was go to the media, talk up some of the issues I'd been wondering about, like her not having a history of violence, like Jonah's personality: nonconfrontational, generous rather than cheap, a man used to putting women at ease and dealing with them directly.

And a couple of new thoughts. A prostitute and convicted drug offender probably wouldn't call 911. But if Dorinda really had killed Jonah, why did she bother calling that first lawyer, the woman who had once represented her for drugs? Why bother waiting around for a callback before getting out of her apartment? Why not just run? She'd waited an hour. Was she so stupid that it would take her that long to figure out to put on gloves, take the cash in Jonah's wallet, and decide it wasn't a cool idea to hang around with a dead body?

And what about the scissors? If you're crazy or threatened or in the mood to commit murder, wouldn't you go to the kitchen and grab a knife? Okay, maybe she didn't have a big set of Wüsthof, but she must have had at least one killer knife. Why would she instead think to go into the bathroom, open the medicine cabinet, and take out haircutting scissors she may have used—how often?—only every two, three, four weeks?

Dorinda probably wasn't paying Joel Winters enough to put a lot of time in. But this had been a high-profile case, all over the news. Wouldn't even a third-rate criminal lawyer recognize that it was a chance to get himself out there? Even if he didn't believe he could get his client off, why wouldn't he grab all that free airtime?

The water was still pretty hot, but I got out of the tub. When I blew out the candle, I was so upset that it was half air, half spit. I'd forgotten to take out a bath sheet, so, shivering, I wrapped myself in a regular towel and thought, *Why is Dorinda my problem?*

Chapter Twenty-Two

"I knew you'd be happy to see me!" Grandma Ethel announced, a display of either her self-confidence or her self-delusion, since all I was doing was standing in my doorway, my mouth hanging open in surprise. I hadn't asked to be made happy by my grandmother flying up to New York.

Just like before, she again showed up at my house without calling. Granted, we'd been speaking pretty often. I'd filled her in on both the briefing inside the DA's office and the drama outside. Sure, I'd wanted her take on it, but more than that, I simply couldn't stop talking about the People of the State of New York against Dorinda Dillon, aka Cristal Rousseau. Too often I found myself alternately fixated on the Meeting with Eddie Huber and the Big Babs Explosion.

Frizzy Francine Twersky definitely thought they were topics worth discussing—and better at two sessions a week. Now that I'd heard from the accountants that my budget could handle psychotherapy, I had no good reason to put Dr. Twersky off. Andrea was glad to talk about my obsessions, in part to satisfy me, but mostly because they appealed to her need for excitement. Entertainment, too. She gave it all her own spin, so instead of it being an episode of *Law & Order* with a gut-wrenching family subplot, she made it into a British drawing-room comedy, the kind on PBS. This one was complete with a social-climbing, overdressed mother-in-law, a charming and virtuous young widow, and a she-devil who happened to be the chief of the DA's Homicide Bureau. Clive and Christopher Petrakis weren't in Andrea's version. In fact, the only man in her cast was the one actor who couldn't make an appearance: Jonah.

Unloading to both your shrink and your best friend generally makes a good one-two combo, but I needed to explain things to someone more objective or maybe more distant. I wasn't looking for insights into my behavior or "You were right but much too nice to Babs." I hoped to analyze what I'd gotten, and not gotten, from my meeting at the DA's.

Maybe my phone calls made it sound like I wasn't so good at analyzing. All I knew was in the early evening of the day following my fourth or fifth phone call with Grandma Ethel, there she was, standing in my doorway—surprise!—telling me not to worry, she was staying in the city at the Regency because she genuinely enjoyed room service. Sometimes she loved going downstairs to the restaurant and seeing who was having a power breakfast. To be totally honest, she didn't particularly care for being a houseguest unless it was in a house with other house-guests and many servants. But I shouldn't take that personally, because when she'd gone to the bathroom during the shiva, she'd been struck with how perfect everything was and how clean—even with all that company!

We talked for almost three hours once the boys went to bed. The good news was that both they and she seemed to find meeting each other interesting. They vaguely understood that someone called Great-grandma Ethel was a member of their family. I was pretty sure they realized I looked like her because their eyes did the "Mommy Great-grandma Mommy" trip at least a dozen times. She gazed at them with some admiration, not hard, since they went from cute (Evan) to beautiful (Mason and Dashiell). She probably credited her genes for their good looks. I was amazed how unrattled she was by their noise and perpetual motion, though from time to time she looked apprehensive, as if she expected them to turn into vicious little monsters, like the Mogwais in *Gremlins*.

That night's talk comforted me. It felt relaxed, warm, fun at times, like a pajama party with your best friends in middle school. Mostly, we discussed what I should do about Dorinda Dillon.

"Do you know anything about ethics?" I asked her.

"Ethics?" Grandma Ethel repeated it like a new vocabulary word. "What about it? Yeah, I guess so. Someone on my show, a rabbi I guess, told a story about some medieval scholar. Jewish. Anyway, some evil king or an anti-Semite hooligan said to the scholar, 'Tell me about the Torah'—or maybe he said the Talmud—'while standing on one foot.' I guess what that meant was he'd have to stand for a long time, so it would be torture. But listen, it's not getting burned at the stake. So okay, the scholar stands on one foot. And you know what he says? 'What is hateful to you, don't do to others. The rest is commentary.' I forgot what happened to the scholar, but it probably wasn't good. It never was. So, Susie, there you have it: everything I know about ethics. It's the 'Do unto others' thing."

"Well," I said, "even though I talked to the prosecutor, I still don't feel comfortable about the case against Dorinda. I'm not saying she didn't do it. I'm sure it will come down to finding out that she definitely did. But what do I do with this being uncomfortable business? I told you about that meeting with the head of the DA's Homicide Bureau. Her bottom line is Dorinda did it. I don't see her—the prosecutor—being corrupt or lazy or anything."

"So she's got ethics?" my grandmother asked.

"I guess. But I wasn't worrying about Eddie Huber's ethics

as much as mine. What do I do? Do I have to do anything? If the cops and the DA's office say that this hooker killed your husband, that they did the investigation and have determined X, Y, and Z is what happened to Jonah, then I told them what was bothering me and they said, 'Okay, but she did it . . .' Isn't that enough? If I still think something feels wrong, even though I could be thinking it because I don't want to admit certain things about Jonah to myself, where do I go with that?"

"You mean, what should you do ethically? I don't know," Grandma Ethel said. "I'm at a loss. Frankly, when people think ethics, the name Ethel O'Shea doesn't usually leap to mind, as you might well imagine. It's a hard thing to think about, that's for sure. But listen, I'll tell you one thing: Don't be put off by authority. Now, call me a taxi and get some sleep or you'll get dark circles. God forbid."

That talk with my grandmother gave me the courage to call Eddie Huber the next morning and ask for a meeting—though I quickly assured her I wasn't bringing my in-laws or their lawyer.

After a long pause, but without any audible sigh, Eddie Huber agreed to my request. Only then did I add, "Oh, I forgot. My elderly grandmother is in from Miami. There's a very slim possibility I might have to bring her along. But she's going to be eighty on her next birthday, so don't worry about her giving you any trouble." Naturally, that conversation—with the word "elderly"—didn't take place in front of Grandma Ethel. I picked her up at her hotel an hour and a half later. By then, she'd had her fill of watching power brokers at the Regency schmoozing and brushing whole-wheat toast crumbs off their ties.

I needed Grandma Ethel along on my visit to the DA not just because her arrival had given me the courage to ask for another meeting, but also as a witness: Had Eddie Huber said what I thought she'd said, or was I misinterpreting? Was she telling the whole truth, a half-truth, or was she full of shit? Was she playing a game with me, and if the answer was yes, what was it?

"Boy, this place stinks like an unwashed twat!" Grandma Ethel announced as we waited to go through the metal detector in the lobby of the DA's office. In the same loud voice, she asked me, "Did I offend your delicate sensibilities or something?"

"A little bit with the volume," I whispered, praying we wouldn't be noticed. Talk about unanswered prayers: An almost-eighty-year-old blonde wearing a pink Chanel suit trimmed in black patent leather and wearing three-inch stiletto heels that showed off still-great legs could not go unnoticed in a hallway filled with lawyers, cops, and assorted shifty-eyed, slobby individuals who might or might not be criminals—especially when she said "twat" loud enough to be heard in all five boroughs. "It doesn't stink *that* much. It's just old."

"I'm old. This stinks. But I'll lower my voice." She did to the point that I could barely hear her. "I'm only here to make you happy," she said.

Of course, the danger of taking Grandma Ethel was that I couldn't predict how she'd behave; I didn't really know her. Having been the professional charmer hosting *Talk of Miami* meant she could be both smooth and savvy, but saying "stinks like an unwashed twat" in front of fifteen or twenty people, including the cop at the security desk, was neither. Still, part of her job had been knowing a little about almost everything; in a potentially hostile environment like the Homicide chief's office, having someone truly savvy and totally on my side was a plus.

Eddie Huber's jaw went momentarily slack at the sight of the "elderly grandmother" in bubblegum-pink Chanel, still a hottie at seventy-nine. Fortunately, she had no cause for complaint about Grandma Ethel's behavior. Neither did I, but it was only a couple of minutes into the meeting.

"I guess this must be a tough part of your job," I told the prosecutor. "Dealing with the families of homicide victims who need a lot of dealing with, when you have so many cases, so much legal work to do." I was trying to be ingratiating.

"This is as much a part of the job as going to court, and just as important to all of us," she said.

I tried to believe her. "Well, I'm very grateful, because I can see how I might be a pain in the neck." Using "ass" wouldn't have felt right. I glanced at Grandma Ethel nervously, grateful for her silence; her legs were crossed, and she was swinging the top one like a metronome, so at least she was occupied.

Eddie Huber was wearing the same bland green sweater she'd worn the time before. I didn't know whether to feel sorry for her or admire her. If someone like me had a second appointment to see me in my office, I would be constitutionally incapable of wearing the same thing. Maybe she genuinely didn't remember what she'd worn, or possibly, she didn't care. Or it could be Eddie Huber's way of sneering at me and my navy Prada pant-suit, which I didn't have on at this second meeting—it was now a white silk shirt and olive gabardine pants, since I'd realized the Manhattan DA's office was a dress-down kind of place.

I noticed I was twirling my wedding ring nervously, so I clasped my hands. "It might help me if I could find out more precisely what happened to Jonah once he got to Dorinda Dillon's." Eddie Huber's eyes moved to Grandma Ethel. "It's fine to speak freely in front of my grandmother," I assured her, just as Grandma Ethel offered her an encouraging smile.

"Can you give me an example of what you'd like to know?" Eddie asked.

"Do you have any idea how long he was there?"

"Difficult to say. When Dorinda was interviewed in Las Vegas, she was asked, and I believe her words were 'I don't know. Not that long.' Beyond that, without witnesses, there isn't enough evidence to make that determination."

"So it's not clear whether 'not that long' is two minutes or, whatever, a half hour or more?"

"We don't know. The natural assumption is that since Dorinda was going to the closet near the front door to get his coat for him, he was leaving after whatever business between them had transpired. What that was and how long it took, we simply don't know. Her interview with our detective and the representatives of the Las Vegas police was cut off after her lawyer arrived."

I took a deep breath. "In the autopsy," I said, "or in the evidence you found, was there anything that showed if . . . whether Jonah had ejaculated?" Out of the corner of my eye, I saw the pointy toe on my grandmother's shoe stop moving.

"It's not that simple," Eddie Huber said. I sat back, deflated. "I assume you mean was there an ejaculation following a sex act?"

"Yes."

"There was semen found on the meatus of the penis. The meatus is the opening of the urethra in the top thing on the end, the glans penis. But besides an ejaculation in a sexual situation, it's also part of what's called the autonomic nervous system. According to the medical examiner, finding semen is common. When someone dies, especially in a sudden, violent death, there is an ejaculation."

"But does that mean he didn't ejaculate before he was stabbed?"

Eddie Huber eyed my grandmother for a second and apparently decided she could handle the subject matter. She looked back to me. "From what I've learned in my experience with homicide cases, there is a little bit of truth in that if there's no ejaculate found, it may mean the man recently ejaculated—before death. But finding semen around the meatus doesn't guarantee Dr. Gersten did not have some sort of sexual experience with Dorinda Dillon. That's especially true in the case of someone being dead for several days at normal room temperature before being autopsied. When there is such a wait between death and autopsy, it usually cannot be determined when the last ejaculation took place. It might have been during a recent marital sex act. It might have been with Dorinda Dillon. An individual can die violently without any ejaculation at all before death and still show no evidence of semen on his glans penis."

I was working so hard trying to keep any thoughts about Jonah close up and impersonal, like cross sections in an anatomy text, that when Grandma Ethel did speak up, I was incredibly grateful. "Susie talked to me about the case in some detail," she said to Eddie Huber. "And on the flight up from Miami, I was reading some press accounts. I forgot where I came across this, but there was a mention about Dorinda getting clunked on the head with an electric broom when she went to get Jonah's coat. That's her alibi, that she was unconscious when Jonah was killed."

"Yes, that's her alibi."

"And you don't believe there's any truth to that?"

"No, we don't believe it. When such a heavy object is used as a weapon, it would have traces of blood and, considering it has bristles, a lot of hair. There was dirt, and I believe a couple of her hairs, which the lab said would be consistent with normal human hair loss. You know, picked up by the electric broom during regular cleaning."

Grandma Ethel rocked her head from side to side as if she were a balance scale weighing what Eddie Huber had said. "What if someone cleaned the blood and hair off the broom after they clopped her?"

Eddie Huber tapped the edge of her desk with her fingertips, either a sign of extreme irritation or a long-suppressed desire to play the bongo drums. "Then the broom would show signs of that cleaning. But there was only normal household dirt on it."

"If Jonah is dead and Dorinda is lying on the floor like a lox," my grandmother said, "would it take a genius to run the electric broom someplace not too obvious, like under a couch or a bed, to get it nice and normally dirty again?"

"It's possible, of course, but not credible. Believable."

"Thank you, but I am functionally literate. I know what

'credible' means." Grandma Ethel kept going, not giving Eddie
Huber a microsecond to respond. "Did anyone check her head?
If a blow was severe enough to knock someone unconscious,
there could be a bruise. Assuming, for a moment, that what
Dorinda claimed is true."

Eddie Huber didn't answer immediately. Maybe she was
counting to ten. She either did it very fast or stopped at five.
"There actually was a bump on the right side of her head, near
the crown," she said, giving her own head a light tap to show the
precise location. "But—and this is a big but—it could have come
from any knock, and she wove it into her story. Prostitutes do
sustain quite a few injuries because of the simple fact that a lot
of men are abusive to them. On the other hand, the bump could
have been self-inflicted."

"It's hard to imagine anyone being able to hit themselves on
the head that hard," I said. "I mean, they could think about it,
but doing it is something else."

"That is not the case, as it so happens," Eddie Huber said.
"Suspects have been known to crack their own skulls to fake an
alibi."

Grandma Ethel curled the side of her mouth into a *give me a
break* expression, then shook her head slowly, as in *I'm not buying it*. "That must have been one hell of a crack, to still be there
when Dorinda was found so long after."

"Or it could have been one hell of a crack sustained when
Dorinda Dillon looked out of her motel window, saw she was
surrounded by the police, and banged her own head. Let me
explain something, Ms.—"

"Just call me Ethel. Everyone does."

"All right," Eddie Huber said cautiously. "What I want to
say, Ethel, and to you, Ms. Gersten, is that there is no pristine
case. Details crop up. One piece of evidence seems to contradict
another piece of evidence, yet both seem solid. What we do, in
addition to applying the law in an evenhanded manner, is we rely

on the experience and judgment of our law enforcement team, cops, lawyers, forensic experts. It's not that we are ignoring the bump on Dorinda Dillon's head. It's that we've considered it and decided it was just that, a bump. None of her hair or blood was found on the electric broom, so there's nothing to back up her contention that she was knocked out after being assaulted with it. The bump has no meaning to us. It certainly cannot be used to exonerate her. It simply cannot deflect the evidence we have implicating her in the murder of Dr. Gersten."

She was a good lawyer. If Grandma Ethel and I had been on a jury, we would be nodding *Yes, right, I believe her*. Her argument made sense, but sense is what your mind appreciates, not your gut.

"What about her using a pair of scissors?" I asked. "Does that make any sense to you? Why would someone go into a bathroom, open a medicine cabinet, take out something she definitely wouldn't use every day, and choose that as the weapon? Why not go into the kitchen and grab a knife? It's more logical, more normal, in the sense that it's something a person would do. And a knife is easier to stab with than scissors, isn't it? It has a handle. And why stab only twice if she was so angry?"

"I have no idea why she chose a pair of scissors as the weapon. What I do know is that they did come from her medicine cabinet and that her fingerprints are on them. And it's not really relevant that she stabbed only twice."

Eddie Huber wasn't much good at hiding her body language, or maybe she didn't want to. Instead of leaning back in her chair, she sat straight and crossed her arms over her chest. She reminded me of an impatient teacher, annoyed at a disruptive student, waiting for the kid to quiet down.

"One more question," I said anyway. "Why do you think Dorinda called that lawyer she'd used in the past when she supposedly regained consciousness and saw Jonah lying there, dead? Why did she wait an hour for the lawyer to call back?"

"We don't know that she waited," Eddie Huber said. "She said she waited."

"If you can fix the time of the call from the lawyer's voice mail," my grandmother said, "then find out what bus Dorinda took at Port Authority, you might be able to subtract the earlier time from the later time and discover whether she really did hang around for an hour."

"First, even if she did wait an hour, it in no way proves where she waited, or that she didn't murder Dr. Gersten. Staying in her apartment for an hour would, to me, indicate a certain cold-bloodedness. If you came across a dead body, would you stay with it in a tiny one-bedroom apartment? Or would you want out?"

Grandma Ethel didn't take long to admit, "Out."

That was my reaction, too, and I nodded in agreement. Then I said, "Is there any way I could speak with Dorinda Dillon, ask her a few questions?"

I could have done without the recoil on Eddie Huber's part and without her mouthing the word "no."

"It's just that I'd like to know what happened before Jonah—"

"Absolutely not!" She stood and braced herself on her desk. I wasn't totally sure what that meant in body language, but I think she was saying *I am restraining myself from leaping over this crap-covered surface and throttling you, bitch.* "It would taint the entire case. I'm sorry for you, Ms. Gersten. And I admire your wanting to seek the truth. But there is no way I'll let you get in the way of my office doing what needs to be done."

Chapter Twenty-Three

Grandma Ethel's arrival meant trouble: From the moment she and Sparky had walked into the living room that night at the shiva, I'd known it was only minutes until some older cousin would search out a quiet corner to call my mother and whisper, "You won't believe who just came to see Susie!"

The evening following her appearance, my parents had shown up with a shopping bag full of the plastic containers they'd used earlier in the week to bring home a half-ton of smoked salmon, egg salad, and tuna salad from a platter someone had sent over. "Listen," I said as they'd come through the door, "there's something I need to tell you." As they walked through the house, my mother performed her sneezing/coughing/choking number at every vase she happened to notice.

Trailed by my father, she headed for the kitchen. Once there, she pushed up the long sleeves of her mourning apparel, a black T-shirt with an understated World Wildlife Federation logo, and started washing the plastic containers in my sink. As she pumped out enough Dawn direct foam to clean a 747, my father explained that their water in Brooklyn wasn't hot enough. "It's okay," I told him, "I'll put them in the dishwasher." My mother turned from the sink, shook her head, and told me the heat from the drying process would cause the plastic to release toxins that would infect the next food that went into the containers. I offered to take over the washing for her, or have our housekeeper do it first thing in the morning. When she shook her head emphatically, I suggested putting them in the recycle bin, where they could enjoy the company of all their little plastic friends. But she kept saying no, that I had enough on my hands, by which I assumed she meant Jonah's death, not bad smells.

"Mom," I said, resting my back against the side of the sink so she couldn't avoid looking at me, "your mother was here last night." She looked me in the eye, or nearly, and told me she didn't want to hear about it. If I desired a relationship with the woman, I should feel free, but she didn't want to know anything about it. My father chimed in that my mother really meant what she said, then asked me where I kept the dish towels. That was that: end of conversation.

But I knew more discussion was needed and now, having finally deposited Grandma Ethel back at the Regency, my car seemed to go on automatic pilot. It headed for Brooklyn and even found a parking space on Avenue O, around the corner from my parents' building. (If I'd had to go as far as Avenue P, I probably would have chickened out and gone straight back to Long Island.) I called and cut short my father's "By the time you get here, it'll be so late . . ." As I got off the elevator on their floor, I thought that if someone blindfolded me and turned me around a few times, like in Pin the Tail on the Donkey, I would have no problem walking a straight line to the door of their apartment. I'd rely on either the familiarity of having lived in that one place until I was seventeen, or the scent of garlic powder.

After I'd accepted a glass of store-brand seltzer with bubbles the size of my fist, we sat down in the living room. The only photographs were the ones I'd given them framed—our wedding picture and one of the triplets we'd taken when they were eight months and could sit up by themselves. For that one, I'd ordered anti-UV glass, so it was the only thing in the room not faded. The boys' blue, red, and yellow onesies, cute but ordinary, made them look like a riotous circus act in that dead brown room.

"I wanted to talk to you about your mother coming to see me," I told my own mother. Before she could object, I said, "I need to clear the air. Please view it as a favor to me. I'll be as quick as I can, and then I won't bring it up again unless you want to talk about it. Okay?"

"Do you have any idea what kind of person would walk out on, *abandon* her own child?" my father demanded. His voice had double or triple the emotion he normally expressed in his most passionate moments—debunking sciatica cures not sold by My Aching Back. "Do you, Susan?"

"Yes, I do have an idea. She'd be a person with terrible character or who's really disturbed," I said. Turning to my mother, I went on, "In her case, I vote for terrible character."

"Then why did you seek her out that time you went to Florida?" She often sounded angry, but that was everyday bitterness about glass ceilings, polluters, Al Sharpton, or pharmaceutical companies. This was a different anger; while she wasn't at all hoarse, her voice sounded raw. "It was early in your marriage, but I'll bet any amount of money looking for her wasn't Jonah's idea."

"I was curious."

"Curiosity—" my father began, but fortunately, he let it go.

"Your mother has always been the mystery woman," I said, "the subject nobody ever mentioned. I wanted to see for myself. Maybe it was wanting to look into the face of a monster. That visit came around the time everybody was getting into genealogy. It was a chance to see where I came from."

"You came from me!" my mother said. "And him." She

jerked her chin toward my father. "There was no mystery. What in God's name is the matter with you? Why is it a mystery when someone doesn't talk about a person who did them wrong, who put a blight on their whole life?"

"Maybe I wasn't mature enough to understand that." I tried to sound both soothing and sorry.

"Oh, please! A child could understand that. But no, you heard about her, that she was on TV. The big shot: 'Oh, *everybody* in Miami knows Ethel.' What were you doing, looking for a new mother?"

"No—"

"A rich mother who went to the beauty parlor three times a week?"

I had an awful feeling she was going to add "Someone you weren't embarrassed about?" and I would have had to lie and say "Don't be ridiculous." I quickly said, "I already had a mother. You, okay? Why would I have wanted another one?" There were several possible answers, but I kept going. "And of all the people in the world, if I were searching for a mother figure, why would I pick someone who had proved herself to be totally incompetent as a mother? Worse than incompetent: selfish and cruel."

All that was true. Yet walking around Soho with Grandma Ethel after the meeting with Eddie Huber, laughing at lace-sided pants and thousand-dollar military-style boots, then having Japanese beer and sushi and telling her about the weekend I'd moved in with Jonah, had been better for my spirit than any time I had ever spent with my mother.

"Now that she's an old lady, she wants a family?" my father wanted to know. "Don't make me laugh!"

Knowing that was close to impossible, I tried to tell them that Grandma Ethel wanted something or maybe wanted to do something. She was back in town. But my mother didn't give me a chance to talk. "You'll see," she said, "you'll be hearing from her again. She'll call, try to insinuate herself into your life. And then what? You want to know what?"

"She'll drop me like a hot potato," I said.

She nodded. I guess she meant to look wise, but it came off like a bad imitation of Yoda. "That's right! She'll charm the pants off you, then drop you for the pure pleasure of inflicting pain."

"I'll watch out for that," I said quietly.

"Look at the bright side," my father said to my mother. "Maybe she'll drop dead tomorrow and leave you everything."

"Stanley," my mother exhaled. "How can you be so naive? It'll all go to her girlfriend." She shook her head in sadness. "I was always a supporter of gay rights, but to think they can make a will any old way they want and completely cut out the family . . . Not that I ever expected anything." She turned to me. "I don't think I have any memories of her." She tugged at the neckline of her Air America FOR THOSE OF US LEFT . . . sweatshirt. "Is there any resemblance between her and you?" she asked me.

"Yes. It's pretty strong, actually. Same color and shape eyes, same bone structure, body type."

"Funny," she said.

"At least I didn't inherit her character," I said, no doubt fishing for an "Of course not!" All I heard was a grumble from my father's stomach.

Right after the kids left for school the next morning, I went back to sleep. It was one of those awkward situations when, because you don't know the person who's vowing to support you, you don't know if she means what she says. Grandma Ethel's "I'm here for you" might have been the truth; on the other hand, when she mentioned she hadn't been to Barneys in a couple of years, her voice had the wistful tone of someone who had a strong need to scrutinize avant-garde gloves. Still, on the chance she would call, I didn't turn off the phone ringer to avoid the "just calling to check how you're doing" calls, though their number had plummeted in the last couple of weeks anyway. Besides, my mother's warning was still fresh in my ears. It wouldn't have surprised me if my grandmother had simply picked up and gone back to Miami because she wanted to hurt me for the pure pleasure of it. Not that I really believed she would do that, but I couldn't rule it out.

So I was surprised to be wakened at a quarter to twelve when the bedroom door opened and Grandma Ethel, hand on the knob but facing the staircase, shouted, "Thank you, Bernadine sweetheart. I found the room." It was probably the first time in Bernadine's life anyone had called her "sweetheart," and she called back in a sugary voice I'd never heard, "Let me know if you need anything, Mrs. O'Shea."

"You need some more sleep?" my grandmother asked. "I can go read or tiptoe into your closet and try on your clothes. What size are you? An eight?"

"Yes," I said, sitting up and feeling with my feet for my shoes, "but more toward a six than a ten."

"I'm more toward a ten, but I know how to breathe in. You getting up?"

"Yes, but you can still try on my clothes if you want to."

"'Tomorrow is another day.' Know who said that?"

"Scarlett O'Hara."

"Right. So listen, that Eddie Huber? What's with the Eddie? I didn't pick up any signals." Before I could answer, she said, "I'll tell you what bothers me about her. Between you and me and a lamppost, like my uncle Morty used to say, I think she's part of a cover-up."

"Of what?"

I must have gasped "Of what?" because she quickly said, "Calm down. It's no major deal. Let me tell you." She tried to hurry me downstairs immediately. But whenever I woke up, I needed to brush my teeth right away. She followed me into the bathroom, just like the boys did, and talked while I brushed. "I think they all decided that Dorinda was the killer much too fast. That's what I think. What kind of investigation did they do? All they really did was send in a forensics team, do an autopsy—which of course they have to—and then try to track down Dorinda." I spat out the toothpaste, and she asked, "You don't brush your tongue?"

"Yes, I do. Usually my tongue and the roof of my mouth. Under my tongue at night. But we're having a conversation." I rinsed and went on, "But what is Eddie Huber covering up?"

"That the cops and the DA didn't do all that needed doing. They focused right in on Dorinda and said, 'Screw peripheral vision. We don't have to look anyplace else.' I'm not saying they're railroading her. I'm only saying that Eddie is one smart cookie. She's using her legal smarts to fend off any doubts about the case, because they're all committed to it. I admit it's a case that does make sense. And the sense is backed up with evidence. Our Ms. Huber is not going to open it up for more investigation based on your questions, your hunches. She made her argument to convince you, keep you on the reservation, put a million doubts in your mind about what you'd been thinking. But she also made it to convince herself because—it's just possible—some of your doubts sparked doubts in her."

I ran a brush through my hair, then we walked downstairs. "So in making the case to me, she's also working to convince herself how solid it is?"

"Right. She wants to believe their case is solid gold. She wants to show that asking why a call girl would up and kill a nice, paying client with hairdresser's scissors is a stupid question, like all the ones you've been asking. She's convincing herself the victim's wife has gone off the deep end and shouldn't be listened to. Heard out? Definitely, but that's all."

I was going to make a pot of coffee, but Bernadine was still sterilizing the kitchen. She beamed at my grandmother and offered to make us a pot and bring it into the library—a room everyone, including Bernadine, always called the den. She obviously was impressed with Grandma Ethel. I wondered if it was a new crush and if she'd stop watching FOX, waiting for a glimpse of Bill Hemmer.

"Listen, some lawyers do that," my grandmother went on. "They have to convince themselves of the rightness of their cases because that's how they do their best arguing. Sparky isn't like that. She's so cynical about everything. The only thing she believes in is the system. She can argue anything, any side of a case."

"It doesn't bother her when she thinks someone's wrong?"

"Absolutely one hundred percent not. Before she went into public interest law, her civil liberties stuff, she worked in a big law firm representing newspaper publishers, shitheads like you wouldn't believe. She says some of the people she represents now are no better, but it's *justice* she fights for, and these clients can't pay for it, like the newspaper shitheads can. She says everyone who deals with the system has to have someone arguing for them with passion, using everything the law allows. But your Eddie doesn't think like that. She needs to be Good fighting Evil. So when she believes 'Dorinda bad, Dorinda guilty,' she'll stay with it till her dying breath."

"If it turns out, which is a real possibility, that it was Dorinda, then I guess I'm lucky to have Eddie Huber on my side."

"On the case, toots, not on your side."

So where do I go from here? I thought. I looked over at a little settee Jonah and I had bought in Vermont the first time we went away without the kids. It had been pretty much a wasted weekend because we spent it reassuring each other that everything was fine with them, and if there was any trouble, his parents and the au pair we had then would call us. But we'd gone into an antiques store and seen some of those old pieces of furniture made for children, teeny rockers, itty-bitty tea tables. We'd spotted a Federalist settee, as much bench as couch, with a back made of three separate panels. We got it for half the asking price because the store owner said a lovely young couple with triplets deserved a piece like this, and also because sometime between, say, 1810 and 2005, it had been broken, glued, and repegged many times, something Jonah noticed and politely pointed out. I'd been so proud of his classiness that day, that he was direct but low-key and never made anyone feel he was backing them into a corner.

The boys used to love sitting in it together, but now it was becoming a little tight for them, and most of the time they grabbed throw pillows and watched the room's big TV from the floor. Soon it would be a settee for two, then one, then, off in a corner, something they could reminisce about to their friends. "Yeah, believe it or not, we all used to fit in it—with room to spare." Or maybe "Can you believe my mother paid good money for that fucking ugly piece of crap?" Or "That little couch thing was from before my father was murdered."

"Well," I said, "if Eddie Huber is Good versus Evil, and also right, then by the time the boys grow up and graduate from college, Dorinda will still be in jail."

"And I'll be dead," Grandma Ethel said. "Stop! Don't tell me 'You'll still be boogying at a hundred.' Dead. Or demented and tied into my wheelchair with surgical tape. The only attractive part of me will be my dental implants, and that's because they're made of titanium. But let me tell you something about then, Susie. I'll be gone, you'll still be gorgeous—and even if Eddie Huber was absolutely wrong, and Dorinda is telling the truth, she'll still be rotting in jail."

Chapter Twenty-Four

"What are we looking for?" I asked.

"The truth," Grandma Ethel said. "Or let's call it proof."

We'd finished our coffee in the den and then went into Jonah's study with a plate of uncategorized food Bernadine had put on the tray. The bottom line of the stuff on the plate seemed to be *small*, so maybe it was the Bernadine Pietrowicz version of teatime canapés: string cheese cut into one-inch lengths; half an English muffin with peanut butter sliced like a pie into six pieces, a dab of grape jelly on each; leftover mini–Danish pastries she'd frozen after the shiva, and now had almost defrosted; some almonds.

"Proof of what?"

"Beats the hell out of me," my grandmother said.

I sat in Jonah's chair, and as I tried to think of something, I ate a couple of the canapés. They were an odd combination, but either it was inspired catering or we were starved: The plate was empty in under a minute. "How about . . ." I said very slowly because I had no idea what I was thinking. "Maybe we should see what there is to be seen."

"That means nothing!" my grandmother said. "What are you, a fortune-teller at a carnival, mouthing gobbledygook? 'See what there is to be seen'?"

"No, seriously. Don't be a . . . whatever that word for old and cranky is."

"Curmudgeon?" Grandma Ethel asked.

"No, something else. Forget it. What I want to do is look at the stuff other people already looked at."

"You mean the cops?"

"The cops, but also that investigative agency, Kroll. I hired them when Jonah didn't come home. They only worked on it for a couple of days, but the woman who's like, whatever, my personal private detective or account executive—she gave me a ton of stuff they put on a CD. I've never looked at it."

"Okay," she said cautiously.

"I want to see if, when we look at all the information, we wind up with lots more questions that the cops should have asked, or if it's a collection of unrelated data. Because what you said about them deciding too fast that Dorinda's guilty, that rings true to me." I added, "We can do something else if you'd rather."

"What are you talking about?"

"I mean, if you want to talk, go for a drive, look at stores. There's a really upscale shopping center about fifteen minutes from here, with Van Cleef and Arpels, Bottega Veneta—"

"Stop! There are two things in life, style and substance. Okay? Do you think I'd drop looking into Jonah's death to go see those bronze woven-leather handbags? Well, you might think that. What the hell, I might do it. But not today. Not to you. So for now, I'm all substance."

Everything Jonah had on him when he was killed was still with the police or the DA, being held as evidence. That included his BlackBerry. I knew his password for it, f-a-c-e-s. I turned on his computer but soon realized I could access his office calendar only through the Manhattan Aesthetics website. Except f-a-c-e-s didn't work to enter the site.

Suddenly I had a *ping!* of irrationality, that all I had to do was call Jonah and ask what his password was. He'd tell me. I didn't know whether it was the subconscious or the unconscious popping up with such a thought, but it weirded me out that somewhere in my head a dopey smiley-face of a wish just kept rolling along, no matter how many times it crashed into reality.

After f-a-c-e-s, I tried other word-and-number combos we'd used over the years for our alarm system and ATM accounts: the boys' birth date, the last four digits of our phone number in New Haven, G-i-a-n-t-s because he loved football. I was getting into a sweat that all my tries would kick in a security warning to their webmaster. I'd wind up on a speakerphone call with Gilbert John and Layne saying, "Susie, you simply could have asked us."

Then I remembered before our wedding, when Jonah and I were discussing whether or not monograms were cool, he'd given me a wicked smile and drawn my married name in mock embroidery script with lots of ridiculous curlicues: SBARG, Susan B Anthony Rabinowitz Gersten. Sometimes he'd even e-mail me, "Hey, SBARG . . ." Those initials got me into the website. I brought around another chair so Grandma Ethel could see the monitor. While she went to get her reading glasses, I sat in the quiet room and looked at the calendar for the day he died.

I had no clear memory of our last time together. When I'd woken up and Jonah wasn't lying beside me, I'd gotten so caught up in fear that I'd lost any recollection of our breakfast together on the last day of his life. He said all my breakfasts were the same, that I had zero breakfast imagination—always Cheerios with a quarter cup of trail mix. But Jonah was his own creative breakfast chef. I didn't know why it was important to me to recall whether he'd made scrambled eggs or Irish oatmeal that final morning, but knowing would be a comfort.

I scrolled down to the early evening of his last day. Liz Holbreich had told me that Kroll's computer expert had discovered Dorinda's name and Jonah's appointment with her hadn't been entered until around eleven-thirty that morning; his BlackBerry had been synced earlier, so the Dorinda appointment was missing. Even though I knew it would be on his calendar, I shivered when I saw it: *6:45 pm D.D.* I double-clicked on the entry to see if there was anything under Notes. There wasn't, but I noticed he'd allotted one hour for the appointment, not that he had anything else on the schedule for that evening. I used Search to check the rest of the calendar, but there were no other entries for Dillon, Dorinda, DD, or D.D.

As Grandma Ethel returned with a pair of turquoise reading glasses that looked more old Miami than new, I switched from Day view to Month, as if I needed to minimize Jonah's disloyalty, though I did point out Dorinda's initials to her. As I clicked through each month, starting with the year before his death, I saw that nearly all his early-evening appointments were linked to the practice's patient database. The remainder I either knew about or could figure out. *Mac & Danny-drinks-YC,* YC being Yale Club. *Clean-Eileen,* an appointment with the hygienist in our dentist's office. *See Danny C,* his sports orthopedist, probably for his tennis elbow. Committee meetings, talks—a fair number to the men's groups that basically boiled down to "What to do when your double chin hangs over the knot in your tie." The clinic work he did at Mount Sinai, repairing facial injuries on victims of domestic violence.

"The more I look," I told my grandmother, "the more it confirms that he didn't have a secret life."

"Okay," she said, drawing out the word.

"You mean he may have had a secret life that he didn't put on his calendar."

"That *was* what I was thinking," she said. "But then it hit me that he did put 'D.D.' on it. Of course it was interesting that he only used her initials." Her lipstick had caked on the corners of her mouth, and she kept wiping them with her thumb and index finger. From the repetition, I sensed she was as deep in thought as she got and not doing a quick lipstick fix. "Okay," she finally said, "let's assume Jonah had a clean bill of health marriage-wise—except for Dorinda in the early evening."

"All right," I said. "Then we ought to go through the calendar and see what else he was doing during his days that wasn't linked to patients or something medical-surgical-business. But there are a lot of entries, and it's hard to tell what's what."

"You know what I'm thinking?" my grandmother asked. "I'll tell you. I'm thinking it's hard to interpret the calendar because even though you knew what Jonah did, you probably didn't know the minutiae of plastic surgery, the medical aspect—and the details of a surgical practice's business procedures."

"No. I mean, I have some general knowledge of the flower business just because I'm a partner in Florabella, but Andrea is the super-organized one, so I'm not up on the fine points. And Jonah's practice was so big and complex in comparison."

"I had a private investigator on my show a couple of times. Really easy to talk to, Cuban background, ran her whole operation herself. One of the things that struck me was she tried to learn as much as she could about whatever business she was investigating—wholesale jewelry, outboard motors, gift shops. She said the more she knew, the more comfortable she was in one world or another, the clearer she could see if there was any event or pattern that looked strange."

"That's interesting." *Must have been a riveting show,* I thought as I got busy aligning the keyboard with the edge of the shelf it sat on. "I'd feel awkward calling Gilbert John or Layne or the office manager to tell me about the ins and outs of running a plastic surgery practice. Anyway, Jonah was really unhappy with the office manager not being on top of things, so it would be doubly sticky."

She started working on the sides of her mouth again, even though there were no traces of dried lipstick anymore. When she pulled down, I could see how thin her skin was, how it was so much more loosely attached to her face than a younger woman's would be.

"I still have a little heat on in the house," I said. "It gets dry. Do you want some lip balm?"

"No, don't need it. But you're wasting your money on lip balm. Vaseline. It's the answer to a maiden's prayers. So tell me, what was the trouble with the office manager?"

"Jonah wasn't crazy about him to begin with. The guy's name is Donald Finsterwald. Jonah didn't like the way he sucked up to the doctors but basically didn't care if the rest of the world dropped dead. As far as I knew, he seemed all right at what he did, and he wasn't terrible with the staff. Just patronizing. I really didn't hear that much about him. But Liz—"

"The investigator," my grandmother said.

"Right. She said Jonah thought Donald was doing a lousy job and was really upset. Jonah had e-mailed him about it. With the economy, they needed to do more marketing and PR, but Donald was doing less. And Liz found e-mails from Jonah to Donald about him doing a bad job tracking the practice's financial performance."

I gave her a fast rundown on the personalities: Gilbert John Noakes, the Founding Father, who now expected to pull out major money for traveling to professional conferences and doing pro bono surgery around the world. "Jonah said when Gilbert John took him in, and then Layne, he made a speech about someday wanting to do less for himself and more for the world, but someday came sooner than Jonah anticipated. Gilbert John was doing more for the world, but he never got around to expecting less for himself."

"And the other doctor, Layne, didn't take Jonah's side?" she asked.

"No. She's a good surgeon and a sweetie socially, but she seems violently allergic to confrontation in any form. Jonah used to imitate her in this kind of high-pitched gentle voice: 'Isn't it pleasant to be pleasant?'"

"So," Grandma Ethel said, "you know more about his practice than you thought you did."

"But I didn't get it all from Jonah. I don't know whether he was keeping some of it to himself, so as not to upset me, or because by the time he left the office to come home, he was sick of it."

"The point is, you have some knowledge. It doesn't matter where it comes from. Let's see if anything on his calendar jumps out at us. Print out a set of monthlies so I don't waste what's left of my eyesight on the computer screen."

Jonah had only a couple of pens with dark blue ink, so I hit the boys' art supply basket and came back with a flat box containing a rainbow of thin-tipped markers. We decided to circle any questionable entry on the printed calendar pages. After a couple of minutes, Grandma Ethel found she had too many questionables and insisted I print out another set of calendar pages so we didn't have to share. She wound up finishing ahead of me because as I came to an appointment I couldn't make sense of, I'd switch to Jonah's contacts list and see if I could find something that came close.

I made pretty good progress, although even when there was a listing for the "Jun" who was on his calendar the first week in January at ten-thirty in the morning, it had only a Manhattan phone number. It looked as if Jonah was between surgeries at that hour, but I couldn't get up the courage to pick up the phone. Maybe I was thinking "Jun" was a "We'll gladly come to your office" prostitution ring.

Grandma Ethel reached across me, dialed the number, and

asked for Jun. "Hello. This is an official call," she said. I had no idea what that meant and neither did she, but it sounded important. "We found your name and number in the records of Dr. Jonah Gersten. You've heard . . ." The person on the other side of the line talked, then talked some more. Finally, Grandma Ethel said, "I see. Thank you. We appreciate your cooperation," and hung up.

"Who was it?" I asked.

"The guy who made Jonah's custom shirts. He heard about it, he's really sorry, and he made the shirts but decided not to send them because that might—I forgot his exact words—cause offense or hurt. There's no deposit or refund because Jonah had been a customer for five years. Jun would come to Jonah's office with fabric swatches. He said Jonah stayed the same size, never gained weight or got flabby. That's it in a nutshell."

"What are you not telling me?"

"Aren't you Little Miss Cross-examiner," she said. "What makes you think there's something I'm not telling?" I didn't have time to answer. "Nothing. In fact, it was complimentary in a way. Something to the effect that a fine gentleman like Dr. Gersten should not have to die that way. My first thought was, *If a guy was a redneck slob, he deserved to be stabbed to death?* But like Sidney, my second husband, said once too often, 'Ethel, that remark is beneath you.' Anyway, I wasn't keeping anything from you. I say whatever comes into my head. It's part of my charm. See? I tried to do something unnatural—censor myself— and you picked it up in two seconds flat."

One name started popping up early in November: Marty. The last Marty entry was eleven days before Jonah was killed. I couldn't tell whether the appointments were in or out of the office, but they were all between noon and one in the afternoon. Grandma and I each circled five Martys, which struck us as possibly pertinent, especially when I couldn't find any Marty or Martin in Jonah's personal contacts. There were four Manhattan

Aesthetics patients whose last name was Martin, one with Martin as a first name, and a Martino. Of them, only Brigitte Martin and Denise Martino were Jonah's patients, and I couldn't think of a way to call and ask "Did you have lunch or something else five times with my husband?"

Grandma Ethel was almost as tired as I was, so we called it quits. Bernadine's teatime goodies hadn't been enough, so I made us tuna-fish wraps on whole-wheat tortillas. By the time we were finishing, the boys and the twins had arrived. My grandmother looked from one to the other, not seeming at all appalled, but after being Fun Great-grandmother for fifteen minutes, she had me call a car service to take her back to the city.

As she left, I was on the verge of saying "See you tomorrow," when I realized I might be overstepping my bounds in assuming she'd be around. There probably weren't any such bounds with a sweet old granny you'd known forever. But Ethel O'Shea was not in that category. Besides, she had a life and a lover in another city, and whenever she mentioned Sparky, I could tell she missed her. Maybe I'd soon be on my own in finding the truth about Jonah's murder.

Chapter Twenty-Five

The next morning, since I was stuck in thinking-about-partners mode anyway, I called Gilbert John. I thought both he and Layne would be in on a Thursday morning, operating and seeing patients. I asked if I could come into town and meet with them. Gilbert John said, "Of course!" in his most mellifluous voice, but I could hear he was baffled about why I wanted to stop in. He asked if there were any papers or documents I wanted to look at that they could have ready for me. I was clearly an unscheduled annoyance, though he didn't intimate that. I told him I had no agenda. I wanted to see the two of them, talk with them.

Since Grandma Ethel's habit seemed to be hiring a car and driver to bring her out to Long Island and simply ringing the doorbell, I called her and told her I'd be in the city meeting with Jonah's partners. "Don't ask them directly," she murmured, as if she were cupping the mouthpiece with her hand to avoid being overheard by a crowd of paparazzi just dying to listen in on the conversation of a seventy-nine-year-old.

"Don't ask them what?"

"Don't rush me, I'll work cheaper. What I'm saying is you

shouldn't ask them up-front if there were any serious bad feelings between Jonah and that Donald person. It would only put
them on guard. Can you be subtle?"

"I'll give it my best shot." Then I added, "Even if there was
genuine hatred, which I can't imagine being the case on Jonah's
part, how could that translate into Jonah getting killed at Dorinda's place?"

"Are you having qualms?" my grandmother asked. "You
know what I mean. Qualms about questioning the whole rush-
to-judgment process." Apparently, being a person with qualms
wasn't an asset in my grandmother's book. While she didn't sound
pissed at the possibility, her inquiry couldn't be called neutral.

"No, no qualms. I just want to be clear in my head where I'm
going."

"Where else would you be clear if not in your head?" I was getting the impression that eight-forty-five A.M. was not Grandma
Ethel's finest hour. "All right, I'll tell you what. Call me on my cell
when you're finished with them. I'll either be out walking or having
my nails done. I'll tell you, I shouldn't have moved from New York.
A nail salon on every block, and so cheap compared to Miami."

Moved? I was tempted to ask. Like her leaving was a job trans-
fer or a yen for a warm climate? How about ran from New York,
abandoning your child to Lenny the Loser? Yet here I was, hoping this woman who had done something I considered perfectly
dreadful wouldn't fly out of my life. As for the woman she'd
done the dreadful thing to, who happened to be my mother, I
gladly would have given her all my frequent-flyer miles if she'd
move someplace else. Arizona, maybe, or some expat town in
Mexico for retirees with allergies and personality deficiencies.

"Whenever I'm done," I promised, "I'll call."

Manhattan Aesthetics looked like most other Park Avenue
upscale, highly touted plastic surgery practices: modern fur-

As Husbands Go   251

niture that went for wood over metal (warmth, genuineness); muted colors, mossy green and cream (tranquil, gender-neutral, conveying confidence that the patients weren't slobs prone to staining furniture); and soft classical music (elegant, calming, as in "Your tummy tuck will be as marvelous as Bach's Air on the G string"). In other words, it was somewhere between chic and inoffensive, but since every plastic surgeon I'd ever met thought he or she was in the ninety-ninth percentile of some Exquisite Taste aptitude test, the only opinion I'd offered was saying "Fabulous!" when their decorator was done.

Gilbert John Noakes and Layne Jiménez must have been buzzed the instant I opened the door because they swept into the waiting room together and gave me a duet of "Susie! Good to see you! Susie! We were so touched you decided to come in!" before I got halfway across the room.

I'd been so focused on talking to the two of them that it hadn't occurred to me how affected I'd be going to the place not just where Jonah had worked five days a week, but to the practice he'd helped sustain and grow. I knew nearly all the staff from holiday parties and from dropping in when I was in the city to meet Jonah, or just to use the bathroom and leave my packages between shopping and a museum. There were kisses, hugs, a gamut of handshakes and "How are you doing?" asked politely or with concern. Because Jonah must have had at least a thousand pictures of the boys and me in his office, everyone asked after them. Mandy, the woman I thought of as the supply/coffee lady although she had some other title, took my hands in hers and said, "There's a hole in my heart." Normally, that sort of comment made me want to stick my index finger in my mouth and mimic retching, but I could only squeeze her hands. If I'd tried to say thank you, I would have broken into sobs.

Since the hallways were big enough for two people walking side by side, or one and a gurney, Gilbert John fell behind and let Layne take me into the conference room. It wasn't really for conferences. The table could seat six and was covered in leather, so in spite of the decorator swearing it was treated, any emphatic gesture near an open can of Diet Coke would probably equal disaster. It was set for lunch with mirrored place mats, octagonal plates I was sure I'd have recognized if my tastes had gone to late-twentieth-century modern, and a platter of sandwiches. I looked at the seven- or nine-grain bread and wondered whether Jonah's death had freed them to give up salads or, if in the less than two months since he'd been gone, there'd been a revolution in Upper East Side lunch thinking.

After my "The boys are doing great, considering" and ten sentences on their spouses plus Layne's children, the conversation began to go slo-mo. Before it could stop totally, leaving us in unbearable silence, I said, "I should be the one giving you lunch, or giving you something. The two of you have been so decent throughout all this. I know it's been an ordeal for you, too, not just because of your professional and business ties to Jonah, but because when you lose someone you really care about at work, there's no kind of formal mourning process that helps you get over it. I just want to thank you for being so strong and so there for me."

Both gave me their version of thank-yous being unnecessary. Layne said a partnership like theirs was another form of family, and members of a family did for one another. Gilbert John quoted a poem, "'No man is an island . . .'" I'd heard it before and, frankly, didn't want to listen to it again. Then he came down to earth a little and said from the first time he'd met Jonah, when Jonah was a resident, he'd known he was superior: not just as a surgeon but as a man. He was gratified that they'd been able to form a special bond. In grievous circumstances like these, he would always hope to be able to reach out and offer help, but the boys and I were a very special case because we were part of what was Jonah.

Just when you thought Gilbert John couldn't go on and on

because he'd used up all the words in the entire universe, he'd stop, giving you hope that there was an invisible THE END sign. As usual, I fell for it, taking a deep breath in preparation for sighing in relief, but then the monologue continued, about Jonah's balance and how he'd fitted the various pieces of his life into a beautiful mosaic.

I tried to tune him out while I had a triangle of turkey and avocado and a bite of a grilled vegetables with hummus wrap that tasted like something you regret buying at an airport. Finally, I set it down, wiped my fingers, and said, "I've spoken with the chief of Homicide at the DA's office a couple of times." The two of them nodded politely. "Mostly, it was because I had some questions."

"About what?" Layne asked. She leaned forward, listening so intently that you'd think she was wishing she could grow another pair of ears to better hear what you were about to say.

"About their case against Dorinda Dillon." I glanced around. Someone, probably Mandy, had forgotten to put out water and soda, and I was thirsty. But I didn't want to ask for anything, because then they'd be upset that she wasn't doing her job. "I have some questions about the investigation, and also about how fast they focused on her being the one who killed Jonah."

They stared at me like I was a foreign movie and the English subtitles had disappeared. I didn't go into a lot of detail. I did mention Dorinda's lack of any history of violence and also the bump on her head that she'd claimed the real murderer had inflicted on her, though I left out the electric broom, as it needed too much explaining.

Without looking at each other, both of them reacted in pretty much the same way: tilting their head to the side and drawing their brows together in an *I don't get it* expression. Gilbert John straightened his head first and said, "I understand your being concerned that the authorities should do a thorough job."

"I feel uncomfortable coming here like this. It's not like me to go on about stuff like justice and ethics, but there are some details of the case that don't seem right."

Layne propped her elbows on the table and rested her chin on top of her entwined fingers. "This must make it even more painful for you," she said compassionately. "Of course you care about justice. You're a good person. That's one of the reasons Jonah loved you so much." She kept going in her lullaby of a voice. I started getting the feeling that Layne was intent on making me feel good because she knew about lots of other call girls in Jonah's life, to say nothing of seventy-five affairs with non-professionals.

When she finally finished, Gilbert John was pulling some excess roast beef from between two triangles of bread. He looked as though he wanted to pop it into his mouth, but he put it on the side of his octagonal plate. "It's impossible not to be touched by your concern, Susie. It does you great credit," he said.

"It was their total focus on Dorinda Dillon," I continued, feeling they needed more of an explanation. "If all they could think about was her, they weren't looking to see if anyone else was involved."

"I see," Layne said softly. "I understand where you're coming from."

"As do I," Gilbert John said. "You should never hold back on questioning authority. However . . ." He hesitated, probably because he was afraid of me reacting with this huge, hysterical fit. But he obviously decided to risk it. "In my opinion, only one person killed your husband. Dorinda Dillon. I'm sorry, Susie."

"I'm not so sure," I said. "I wish I were."

After I left the building, I called Grandma Ethel. She told me I should eat grilled vegetables only in four-star restaurants because lesser places served leftovers soaked in olive oil to revive them. Then she said it sounded like I needed company and to pick her up in front of the Regency in fifteen minutes. When

I did, a bellman was beside her with a huge, impressively aged Vuitton suitcase. "Don't worry," she said to me as the bellman, still thanking her for his tip, closed the car door. "I'll only stay a couple of days. Sparky has meetings in Atlanta, and anyway, you need me. If I get on your nerves, just sic the little tykes on me. Oh, excuse me, before you correct me: my great-grandsons."

While Grandma Ethel unpacked in the guest room, which was as far from the boys' rooms as it could be and still be part of the house, I went into my home office, a room the size of an inadequate walk-in closet, and turned on my computer. There was nothing in my e-mail that made me want to double-click, but I did notice the cursor seemed to be pointing out an emptiness in the Google box. It really was one of those "before I knew it" moments when, the second before, I was wondering if I could still order pizza for dinner, as I'd been planning. Suddenly, there I was, typing *Joel Winters* into the search box.

"Winters," he said. It wasn't necessarily worrisome that a criminal lawyer answered his own phone on the first ring—unless you were a client. The thought went through my mind that his secretary could be out to lunch, though four in the afternoon was a little late for that. Still, I considered she might have gone to the ladies' room and he, busy poring over law books where he would find an old precedent that would save a client from a lifetime behind bars, had been jarred by the phone and grabbed it. But there was something in his "Winters" that sounded both desperate and aggressive.

I hadn't expected him to get on the phone immediately, so my plan for what I was going to say wasn't fully formed. That was like saying a two-week-old embryo wasn't fully formed.

"Joel Winters?" I asked.

"Yeah."

"You're Dorinda Dillon's attorney?"

"Who's this?" I didn't see him showing up on my mother-in-law's guest list, even if she had an opening at the table for someone a little rough around the edges.

"Mr. Winters, my name is . . ." I swallowed, not buying time but because I knew I'd be lying. "Ethel O'Shea. I'm working on an article for *The New York Observer*, and I was wondering—"

"I read it all the time." Compared to his initial "Winters," this response sounded like someone had turned on an eighteen-light Murano chandelier inside him.

"Good, glad to hear it." I said it without too much enthusiasm, since that didn't seem to be a quality a journalist would have or want. "The piece is called 'Dialing for Death.' It's about call girls charged with serious crime."

"You want to ask me about Dorinda?"

I sensed a few of the lights in his chandelier had gone out, so I said, "This is my hook: It's the easy way out for the cops and the prosecutors to target a prostitute for murder. It doesn't require a lot of convincing."

"You know the guy was found in her apartment," he said. I couldn't see a best-selling biography entitled *Joel Winters for the Defense* appearing anytime soon. "But you're right. It doesn't take a lot of convincing. Just say 'The ho did it' and be done with it. Wipe their hands of it. Move on to the next case."

"I'd like to come in and talk to you," I said. "Get a sense of you and your work."

"I'm in the process of moving. My office is a mess."

"I'm not interested in how your office looks. I'm interested in what you have to say about your client."

"Let me see," Joel Winters said. "I've got an opening, a couple of openings actually, early next week."

"Sorry, I've got a deadline. I'd really like to be able to quote you, but it's got to be tomorrow or nothing."

"Okay, tomorrow. What time's good for you?"

Just as I hung up, my grandmother stepped into the room.

"'Dialing for Death'? That is *the* worst name for an article I've ever heard."

"Were you eavesdropping?"

"Were you lying through your teeth and using my name?"

"Yes."

"There you go. Let me tell you something here and now. I don't have many scruples. Three, maybe four, but not when it comes to eavesdropping. Anyway, what does this Joel Winters sound like?"

"Not quite the scum of the earth."

"But close?" Grandma Ethel asked.

"Close as they come."

Chapter Twenty-Six

When the phone rang a little after eleven that night, I tried to sleep through it. Having been married to a plastic surgeon, I'd learned to ignore late-night calls because 99 percent of them were from the answering service about ooze or a patient panicking that once the swelling went down, she would still resemble a duck-billed platypus. But my brain must have been wider awake than I was. It understood *No surgeon in bedroom anymore*. My eyes opened. I glanced toward the caller ID readout, half thinking it must be Sparky calling my grandmother, but it was glowing so brightly I couldn't read it. After a throat-clearing so my "hello" wouldn't sound like a death rattle, I picked up the phone.

"Hey, Susie," I heard. "I know it's late, but we need to talk." *Jonah!* I thought.

Of course I knew it couldn't be him. But still, that voice! With a giant *bam!* my heart seemed to explode. Tiny pieces of heart shrapnel shot through my body and, for an instant, filled me with joy. Nevertheless, even while overwhelmed with that euphoria, I was clear enough to ask, "Who is this, please?" Even though Jonah had been murdered, autopsied, and buried, I half expected to hear him answer, "'Who is this?' Susan B Anthony Rabinowitz Gersten, give me a fucking break!"

"It's Theo." I had been sleeping so deeply that I'd missed the big difference between his voice and Jonah's. Theo's perpetual peevishness always emerged within two or three words. Now I heard that touch of whine in his drawn-out "Theee-ooo." In all the years, I had never answered the phone and mistaken one brother for the other. Theo forever sounded like he'd just been given the smaller scoop of ice cream. "Are you okay to talk?" he asked.

"Yes. Sure."

"There's something . . . there's something I want to get some clarity on." Theo sounded agitated, but that was hardly a first. I braced the phone between my ear and shoulder and rubbed my eyes hard to get my depleted tear ducts functioning again. I guessed his issue was a major-major (as opposed to just a big) fight with my in-laws. Or, in descending order, career worries, money problems, women problems, drugs. "Are you all right?" I asked.

"I'm fine," he said brightly, so I knew another sentence was about to emerge to let me know me he wasn't fine. "I've got to tell you. I'm seriously concerned about my mother—her going off the deep end in the DA's office."

I gripped the phone and leaned back on the pillow. "Theo, I don't think you have to worry. Okay, she went off the deep end, but she came back. She offered me a really lovely apology."

"Good. I'm glad about that."

"So am I. I mean, all of us, our nerve endings are so frayed, so it's understandable. But all of us need each other's support to get through this hell."

"You know you always have had my support." It was true that he'd always been decent, never treated me as if any moment I might forget how to handle a knife and fork properly—the way Babs and Clive did—and muddy the name Gersten forever. "I'm on your side. That's part of what I want to talk to you about."

Beyond the built-in touch of petulance in my brother-in-law's voice, I thought I heard something else: strain, maybe anger. This wasn't head-on-pillow talk, so I sat up yoga-style, in a half-lotus position, and elongated my spine. I needed to be ready for whatever was coming, not tensed up.

"My mother's shit-fit outside that Huber woman's office . . ." Theo began. He seemed to be waiting for me to jump in with some comment.

"That's over."

"Look, the last thing in the world I want to do is hurt you, but I think there's a certain need for a reality check when it comes to your behavior." I didn't keep quiet out of any strategy but because I was so taken aback I couldn't think of anything to say. "I hate to say it, Susie, but my mother's mad scene—okay, it was over the top. But it was an appropriate reaction."

It was after eleven o'clock, for God's sake. Did I really have to stay on the phone with him while he worked up his monologue: "A Mother Driven Insane by Grief"? "Theo, you and I have always had a good relationship. We can survive a few bumps, so just tell me straight out what's on your mind."

A reluctant sigh. Theo had had enough acting lessons that it didn't sound theatrical, though I could sense it was a prelude to a rehearsed speech full of naked honesty. Or maybe tough love. I didn't give a damn as long as it was short. I could say "I'm sorry I didn't appreciate the profundity of your mother's anguish" and be asleep by eleven-thirty.

"I've held this in much too long. How could you *possibly* have expected my mother to maintain any semblance of self-control when faced with what you hit her with in Eddie Huber's office? Not just that you'd never given any of us a clue that you had these . . . these beliefs, but the utter irrationality of them. I don't know how to express how worried I am about you and your . . . let me just come out and say it: your delusions. You're seriously considering that the disgusting, cheap whore Jonah went to might not have done it?"

My mouth was open, but I wasn't talking. It was jaw-dropping, not only what he was saying but the harshness. It wasn't just his view of me that was getting me so upset but that he could be so blatantly harsh. I'd always thought of us as allies, the two members of the family his parents didn't approve of.

"Okay, fine," he went on, "maybe my mother shouldn't have been screaming in the halls of justice, or whatever they call that revolting place, but can't you begin to see the double horror of it for her? A murdered son. And then a daughter-in-law—the sole person in custody of her three grandchildren—who's desperately clinging to, quite frankly, an insane theory."

"How about 'a theory my parents and I strongly disagree with'?" I snapped. "And talk about insane: You should keep in mind, Theo, that I wasn't the one who completely lost control in public."

"Listen to me, Susie," he yelped. I may have heard a growl, too, because what popped into my mind as he spoke was our neighborhood psycho-dog, an Airedale that would strain on his leash, bare his teeth, and bark, unable to stop even as his choke collar began to strangle him.

"Calm down," I told him. "Just tell me what the problem is without using the word 'insane.'"

"The problem, Mrs. Gersten, is that with your barrage of questions and your pathological inability to accept the conclusions of more than competent professionals in the DA's office after a thorough investigation—"

"I have doubts about its thoroughness."

"You're jeopardizing the case against Dorinda Dillon!" he barked. "If it weren't for that, trust me, I wouldn't have brought this up. But the cops, the prosecutors, are acutely sensitive to public opinion. To them, you, with your endless questioning of their evidence and competence . . ." He was now so loud I had to hold the phone away from my ear. "You are just a time bomb they're terrified is going to blow up in their faces. And Jonah's killer could go free because of your craziness! You'd better get a grip, Susie. You better get a goddamn grip!" The line went dead as Theo apparently slammed down the phone.

I got so little sleep the rest of the night that the next morning I didn't even consider driving into the city. Though I probably could have found my way to Canal Street in Chinatown, the area of downtown Manhattan around the courthouses was a mystery to me. So I took the Long Island Rail Road and prayed that the subway directions to Joel Winters's office, which I'd gotten from the Internet, were right.

I was a total basket case. First of all, I was carrying my grandmother's old ID card from WPLG in Miami. Aside from the face on the card being decades older and ninety-five shades blonder, there was a resemblance, though not enough to convince any person with half a mind and/or the gift of sight. As the train sped and slowed through Queens and crept into the tunnel into Manhattan, I was dreading Joel Winters would not only ask for identification but actually look at it. Unfortunately, Grandma Ethel had not been very helpful, since her suggestion had been that I become a blonde. She seemed to believe that her picture on her ID and I were practically identical twins, so with me in light hair and bright red lipstick, we could pass for each other.

Right before I left, I'd remembered the Clarins tanning gel I'd bought the summer before and forgotten to use. I slimed it all over myself to get that *I use sunscreen, but hey, I live in Miami* color, but the directions said it took two hours to work. I prayed by the time I got to Joel Winters's office, I'd look like one of those hot bronze goddess statues everyone shleps back from India, not like a walking tangerine. Also, I'd pulled my hair into a ponytail, twisted it, and pinned it up; since all the photos of me in the news were with hair down, shoulder-length, maybe the change would help silence any she-looks-familiar bell.

Riding downtown on the subway, looking at faces, I remembered Jonah had talked about a rare kind of woman, one who was satisfied with how she looked. A plastic surgeon might think she could use several nips and a lot of tucks. That type of woman, though, would have been shocked to hear such a thing. It wasn't that she wanted to age naturally, without intervention. What he was talking about were the confident ones: pretty, plain, or even homely women who thought they were lovely the way they were. My grandma Ethel was one of them. She was truly pretty, but no one would call her dewy. Still, she was one of those who looked in the mirror and, at almost eighty, saw an ageless combination of Snow White, Cinderella, Ariel, and Anne Hathaway.

When I got to Joel Winters's office, I was surprised to find it had a working elevator and granite floors. My image had been so strong, and so Humphrey Bogart detective movie, that I'd been sure I would walk through a door with JOEL WINTERS, ATTY. AT LAW painted on its frosted glass pane: seedy, without the advantage of Humphrey in the role of Joel. Naturally, it wasn't at all like my other picture of a lawyer's office, which was the midtown firm where Jonah and I had made our wills after the triplets came: a forest of lacquered wood, legal pads, ballpoint pens, and mineral water, soda, and bottles of green tea on a credenza beside a stainless-steel bucket overflowing with ice. This place was a disappointment, probably not only to me but to its occupant. The small outer office did have a desk, chair, phone, and cup with a couple of pencils and a ruler, but there was no computer and no secretary.

The inner door opened and Joel Winters said, "Come in, Miss *New York Observer*. You're gonna have to forgive me, but I forgot your name."

"Ethel O'Shea." Here it was, the point he could ask "Can I see some ID?"

"Come in, come in. Sorry, my secretary's out on maternity leave." His office was about the size of the bedroom in our first Manhattan apartment. But that was where the resemblance stopped. With its dark beige carpet, light beige walls, and a medium brown desk, it managed to be unpleasant despite its aggressive neutrality. There were a couple of framed documents with foil seals, but they were hung so high it was hard to see whether they were diplomas or prizes in a pie-eating contest.

Not that he was fat. Winters was skinny—an old-fashioned word, but "thin" gives the picture of someone fit, or at least a person who knows about diet. From his rounded shoulders to his shuffle, Winters gave no impression of having any muscle tone. His walk was old-guy, but my guess was he was, tops, forty.

He gestured to a seat that looked like it had come from some dead relative's dining room set, then he went behind his desk. I pulled out a pen and a spiral notebook I'd bought in Penn Station and said, "Let me get a few particulars about you first."

"You're not taping this?" he asked.

"Oh no." I hadn't even thought to go tape-recorder shopping in Penn Station. "Even the newer ones are unreliable. Sometimes you get back to your desk and you listen and *nothing* . . . The new new thing is that most of the journalism schools have gone anti-digital and are requiring shorthand. Much more accurate." I'd made that up, and it couldn't be true, but Joel Winters was nodding, not only believing me but planning on using it as cocktail-party conversation if he ever got invited to a cocktail party. "I need a little bit of personal background on you," I said. "Age, what law school, how you chose your specialty—that sort of thing."

Obviously, my definition of "a little bit" and his were different. He passed the next five minutes talking about himself without, even for a single second, managing to be interesting. He would have kept going with great "Joel in Court" tales of brilliance and high hilarity, but I cut him off. "How is Dorinda Dillon doing?" I asked.

"You know. Holding her own. Hopes she'll be vindicated at her trial."

"Has there been any talk about a plea deal?" I asked, grateful that the thousand hours I'd spent watching *Law & Order* and *Son of Law & Order* had not gone to waste.

"No." He looked like he was about to add something else, but all he did was scratch behind his ear. It almost seemed like he had an on-off switch.

"What's your defense going to be?"

He gave one of those knowing laughs that sound like "huh." I thought it was supposed to mean *That's easy, and we're going to cream them,* but it just made him sound nervous. Finally, he said, "We're going with the truth."

"Which is?"

"Which is, Ethel O'Shea—great old Irish name, not that you're at all old, so please don't take that the wrong way—that she went to get the doctor's coat and there was somebody in the closet. He picked up the electric broom that was in there—"

"Did Dorinda see who it was? That it was a man?"

"No, actually. What do the politicians say? 'I misspoke.' She opened the closet door, I think got a look at the electric broom, though I'm gonna double-check on that. Then *whomp!* She got hit over the head so hard it knocked her senseless."

"And then?"

"When she came to, she saw the doctor on the floor. Dead. Naturally, she was shocked."

"How come she didn't call 911?"

"Look, Ethel . . . Is it okay if I call you Ethel?"

"Of course. Go right ahead," I said, though not too warmly. Maybe he was a sweetheart, but he had the look of a serious creep, and I didn't want to make him feel too comfortable with me.

"Dorinda may be a really nice girl, woman, but she's a woman who's a hooker and has—I'm not telling you anything here that isn't on the public record—arrests and a conviction on minor drug charges. Cocaine. It's not heroin or anything. Somebody like that isn't so quick to dial 911 about a corpse on her carpet."

I wrote a version of what he was saying in the spiral notebook, to appear reporter-like. When I glanced up, the overhead office light was shining on his hair, which was light brown coated with so much product that it looked like a piece of tinted, molded Plexiglas. "So the defense is that someone knocked her out and then killed the doctor?"

"Not just any doctor. A Park Avenue plastic surgeon." He shook his head sadly, as if this were an added burden he should be charging extra for.

"Does she have any theories who this killer could be?"

"No. None."

"Was there anyone else who had the key to her apartment?"

"The super has keys to everyone's place down in the basement but"—he smiled: humor on its way—"the keys are kept under lock and key."

"No one else has one? What about the person who lived in the apartment before she did?"

"Oh no, definitely not. When you're a hooker, you're into privacy big-time. She told me straight out that the first thing she did when she moved in was get a new lock, the really expensive kind. The keys got made on a special machine and had a number. If you wanted to get another one, you had to have the number. So this is not a case of keys floating around."

"It's strange, then, that she has no idea who it could have been."

"What did they used to say? 'Strange but true.'"

"Do you think that will go over with a jury?"

"It'll have to, Ethel. It's true, number one. And number two, off the record . . ." I put down the pen. "We're stuck with it. She talked. Not a lot but enough. In Las Vegas, after her arrest, and they videotaped it: her saying she got knocked out and woke up and there he was, dead."

"Off the record," I said, "if you weren't stuck with that, what would your defense be?"

"She doesn't pay me enough to come up with an alternate defense." Joel Winters had a good laugh about that one, and I joined in with a chuckle to prevent him from having a total ego meltdown. "We could go with the doctor being a real sicko. Self-defense."

I felt my now familiar shock reaction, a wave of nausea. Acid burned my throat, and I hoped I could heave and get it over with. "In what way was he a sicko?" I managed to ask.

"I haven't the foggiest notion," he said. "But if I was going for an alternate defense, I'd spend time with her, probing, maybe finding something we could work with." I nodded. While I now was merely queasy, it was too much to experience that rise of sickness and plunge of spirit, then snap out of it. I couldn't talk. I was desperate to catch my breath—except I was already breathing. "But that's neither here nor there," he went on. "We're stuck with what we have. The truth of the matter is, Dorinda did have a bump on her head when she was arrested. I just have to be convincing enough to the jury that she got it the night he was murdered, that she didn't take a hammer and go *bonk!* to back up her story, which is what the prosecutor is going to argue."

"What kind of sentence would Dorinda get if she saved them the trouble of going to trial and admitted to . . . whatever?"

"Ethel, that's what we in the law call a moot point. She says she didn't kill him, and she's sticking with that story. No matter what. If she pled, I could get her—if the gods were smiling that day?—five to ten if the victim's family would go along. The thing of it is, she just won't plead."

"Makes it tougher for you," I said.

"Hey, if I wanted easy, I would've been . . . I'll tell you what. A Park Avenue plastic surgeon."

Chapter Twenty-Seven

Sparky came into the kitchen while I was chopping a load of rosemary for roast chicken and said, "I'm so glad you convinced Ethel to stay here. I was hating the thought of flying in from Miami to spend two days on the Long Island Expressway, back and forth from the hotel."

"I didn't do any convincing," I said. "I picked her up at the hotel, and the bellman tapped on the window to get me to open the trunk for her suitcase. That was that, and she's here."

"Is she okay with the boys? I mean, is she behaving herself, not waving them away and saying 'Begone, you ghastly creatures!' or some such nonsense?" Sparky sat at the kitchen table, slipped off a loafer, and repositioned her sock. She had a great look: simple. She'd come from the airport in khakis, a white cotton shirt, and a dark blue suede blazer. Her only jewelry was a watch with a brown alligator strap and her giganto diamond stud earrings.

"She's fine. I mean, she's not getting down on the floor and playing with their Hess Oil trucks, but she's amazingly good with their noise. I wouldn't say she's enchanted by them, but she's definitely tolerant."

Sparky gave a small sigh of relief. "She said everything was fine with them and that they adored her. If you haven't noticed, she's given to overstatement."

"In fact, I did notice." I dumped the rosemary into a couple of spoonfuls of olive oil.

"Obviously, I don't have to explain it to you, but she's defensive on the subject of children. It comes out as a stand against a childcentric culture. Or as sarcasm."

"Four-year-olds don't get sarcasm," I said. "They are able to read people, though, even if they don't understand motivations. She's not giving off hostile vibes. I wouldn't go so far as to say they adore her. But she's tall enough to reach the shelf where I keep the cookies, and she doles out one to each of them—makes almost a ceremony out of it. I think they see her as an ally, maybe even a friend."

Grandma Ethel strolled into the kitchen. "Are you talking about me?"

"Yes," Sparky said, "though we were hoping a more interesting subject would come up. Any suggestions?"

"Did Susie bring you up-to-date on her trip to Dorinda's lawyer? She told him she was a journalist. Ethel O'Shea."

Sparky looked from her to me and shook her head in disgust. "Both of you . . . Why didn't you call me before doing something like this? That shmuck is going to be representing Dorinda in court. Do you know what he's going to do when he sees Mrs. Gersten take the stand and Mrs. Gersten is Ethel O'Shea?"

"I pulled my hair straight back," I told her. "Very severe look. Not like Grandma Ethel's photo ID, but I was planning on telling him that I'd let my hair go back to its natural color. He didn't ask for any ID."

"Except—correct me if I'm wrong—he did see you. It's not only that you pretended to be someone else. It's that you visited counsel for the defense under false pretenses."

"Is that a crime?" my grandmother asked. She sat at the kitchen table beside Sparky.

"I don't practice criminal law," Sparky answered.

"That's French for she hasn't a clue," Grandma Ethel told me. "Anyhow, the trial is still not set, most likely months away. Maybe he'll forget you, or you can have your shrink testify that you were acting under some sort of insanity."

Sparky was about to challenge her. I crushed a clove of garlic with the side of a knife and said, "Dorinda insists she didn't do it. She won't go for a plea bargain."

"She's going with the electric-broom story," my grandmother said. "You know, I was thinking. Maybe it was a burglar. It could happen. He knocked Dorinda out. Maybe she saw him, maybe she didn't. But she wasn't the threat. Jonah was, being a man. Maybe the burglar felt threatened, or Jonah could have even tried to stop him, and that's why he got stabbed."

"Eth," Sparky said, "a burglar would probably be armed. And even if he wasn't, why would he get scissors from the bathroom and not a knife from the kitchen? Or some other weapon—the proverbial blunt instrument? Or he could have used the famous electric broom on Jonah as well as on Dorinda."

"I don't think it could have been a burglar," I said. The oven dinged to show it had reached 375. "If it had been, how come he didn't take Jonah's watch? It was a Cartier tank. A burglar would know it or figure out it was worth something. And why didn't he take the money in Jonah's wallet? Dorinda was the one who did that."

"If she'd killed him to rob him," Sparky said slowly, "which would have been completely crazy, it being her apartment . . . But if robbery was her motive, she would have taken the watch. She didn't, which leads me to believe all she wanted to do was get the hell out of there and needed some quick cash."

"She went to her ATM after she left the apartment," I said. "She got another four hundred dollars."

Sparky turned to look at my grandmother. "I don't buy the burglar theory. If a burglar is going to break into an apartment, all he has to do is take one look inside. From what I read and saw on TV, it wasn't a luxurious place. Just the basics, although I think I read something about a carpet in a leopard-skin pattern. But what was there to steal? She didn't seem to go outside wearing a lot of jazzy jewelry. She was a recreational drug user, maybe dealt a little, but she wasn't a dealer with a ton of cash on hand."

I gave the big roasting chicken a rosemary rub and stuck it in the oven. "I'm with Sparky on this," I told Grandma Ethel. "I don't see her having a lot of money. I'm sure her rent wasn't cheap, and there wasn't a line outside the door waiting for the pleasure of her company. She did okay, but I don't know if it was much better than that. She needed to supplement her own clients by freelancing with escort services. And even though she's not using Legal Aid, she can't afford a top lawyer. The guy she's going to couldn't even be called third-rate."

"She would have been much better off with Legal Aid," Sparky said.

Grandma Ethel began, "She would have been much better off . . ." She dropped it, but we all knew she was going to say "not killing Jonah."

I decided to go with roasted sweet potatoes. My grandmother said she'd set the dining room table. She asked, "With Ida and Ingvild, how many? Oh, eight, and you don't have to tell me no wine for the boys."

That was Friday. By Sunday, I was exactly halfway between regretting that Grandma Ethel was leaving with Sparky and rejoicing at having the house to myself—or my version of myself, which included the kids, Ida, and Ingvild. Just as my in-laws arrived on their way back from Water Mill in the Hamp-

tons, exchanging excited hellos and air kisses with my grandmother and Sparky in the manner of the mutually sophisticated,
Grandma Ethel informed me she had canceled the suburban
taxi. She was taking my car to drive Sparky to La Guardia, then
returning. "You're not ready to be on your own yet," she told
me when she pulled the car keys from my hand. I had no idea
what kind of a driver she was, but I decided that if Sparky was
willing to put her life on the line with my grandmother behind
the wheel, it might be okay.

I was tired from a weekend of cooking, so for my in-laws, I'd
defrosted a vat of meatballs I'd made in December. I had a brief
fantasy of saying "Why don't I go out and you can enjoy the
boys' company by themselves?" They'd say "Wonderful!" and I
would rush out to Main Street before my grandmother got back
and go see a movie, any movie, a Jackie Chan or something sensitive from Hungary, and finish off a giant bucket of popcorn.

When I offered to give them quality time alone with the
boys plus meatballs, they asked me please not to go, they really
wanted to spend time with me, too. In spite of my fantasy, I'd
known that would happen. The older the boys got, the more
reluctant most people were to be alone with the three of them.
I felt Babs and Clive viewed the triplets as if they were wild
horses: beautiful but uncontrollable—rearing up unexpectedly
and galloping around stirring up great clouds of dirt.

After dinner and the boys' baths, my in-laws took them off
to bed to read to them. I stretched out on the living room couch
and prayed that either Sparky's plane would be late taking off or
my grandmother was a slow driver. That was the last I recalled
until I heard Babs and Clive coming down the stairs, saying "So
adorable!" and "What a vocabulary that kid has!" to each other.

I sat up and was smiling expectantly when they came into
the living room. I felt like I was giving off waves of charm and
totally down-to-earth, nondelusional goodwill.

"We'll only stay a few more minutes," Babs said.

"Please, stay as long as you like."

"That grandmother of yours is a charmer," Clive said. "And I like Sparky, too. What's her real name?"

"Felicia."

"She's much more of a Sparky," Babs said. "Felicia has such a languid sound. So your grandmother's staying on?"

"I guess so. She seems to think I need her, but it may be that Sparky's preparing for a big trial and is working really late every night."

"Maybe she's trying to somehow make up for the fact . . . with your mother." Babs paused, perhaps worrying that her analysis would set me off.

"I think there's a lot to that," I said. "But every time I bring up my mother, just the simple mention of her—not that the two of them should get together or anything—my grandmother changes the subject."

My in-laws nodded their understanding. Then Clive, quite casually, which he wasn't very good at, asked, "Do Ethel and Sparky share a room?" I must have looked at him like he was nuts because he quickly said, "I assume they do. I was just wondering, and you can put it down to my old-fashionedness, if it would have any kind of a negative impact on the boys?"

"You think gay is contagious?" I asked.

Clive smiled—a little. With him, it was hard to tell. Babs didn't smile. "Susie," she said carefully, "it's not that we care one way or another. They are a marvelous couple, which is amazing, because there's such a big age difference. My only concern, our only concern, is the boys. You grandmother is really incidental because she won't be staying that much longer. But with all due respect to you, because you're doing such a magnificent job with them, the boys' lives have changed so drastically. Don't you think they need all the stability they can get?"

"Absolutely." I wanted out of the conversation and was on the verge of offering to make coffee, slice a pineapple, anything to escape them for a few minutes. But I couldn't find a way out. So I sat up absolutely straight, maybe mimicking Andrea's I'm-an-aristocrat/stick-up-the-ass posture, and said, "Tell me what you're thinking about when you're talking about stability."

"To be perfectly honest, we know what a huge job this is for you," Babs said.

"It is pretty huge," I agreed.

"And as a woman who worked all through her children's growing up, I certainly wouldn't ask you to give up the wonderful business you and Andrea have created," she went on.

"Good" was all I could think of to say.

"My question is this: Do you honestly feel that two teenage girls, sweet, lovely girls, I'm not saying they're not, are enough help for you? Enough for the boys? When Jonah and Theo were growing up, we had Margaret. Well, of course. You've met her. When she started with us, she was well into her thirties and had superior credentials. Experienced. Trained. She was a proper nanny. You know, I was talking about this with Jonah—"

"Listen to me." I looked first at her, then at Clive, and sat even straighter. Slumping was a signal of defeat, and I was on the offense. I took a deep breath to calm down, because I didn't want to seem offensive. "I know you spoke about this with Jonah, about us getting a so-called proper nanny. He and I discussed it. And you know what? We rejected it, at least for the time being. But let's put that to the side for a minute." They were about to break in, so I kept talking. "We've all had a loss that's unbearable. Maybe it's bearable, because that's the only way to go on. But you know what I mean." They both looked away from me but not at each other. "The boys are what's left of Jonah. My sons, your grandsons. We can disagree over how I should raise them, and there are going to be times you'll be right and I'll be wrong."

"Susie," Clive said. His mouth, with its upturned smileyness, looked more inappropriate than at any time since the funeral. "It's not a question of right or wrong."

"Fine. But let me be blunt, though you can call it coarse, which apparently is my *spécialité de la maison*. You're concerned about the boys. I know you genuinely love them."

"We do," Babs said.

"But what have you done for them?"

"What would you have us do?" she asked in her cold voice, which, with me, didn't differ too much from her warm one.

"I'd have you spend time with them. If you can't take all three at once, how about one at a time for two or three hours? As for a proper nanny, Ida and Ingvild are two of the finest, most proper people I've ever met. They've worked harder than I would ever dream of asking them to. They are loyal beyond loyal, and they've never once complained. They love the boys, and the boys love them."

"We're not saying—" Clive started.

"Right now I'd rather be the one talking," I told him. "The twins' visas expire in May. I'm already talking to the agency that found them for me. The agency has another set of twins, a brother and a sister, who sound great. So either I'll be getting them or two others like them. If that doesn't sit right with you, if you really, truly feel a proper nanny would be better, then all right." They took a fast glance at each other, then turned back to me. "I'll go along with a proper nanny as long as it's someone who meets my standards, and I'm not just talking background check. I'm talking about someone who will be loving to the boys, strong enough to deal with them, and easy for me to have in the house."

"We wouldn't expect you—" Babs started to say.

"Hold on; that's not all."

"What else?" Clive asked.

"If you want this kind of person, then it will be the two of you who will pay for this kind of person. I'll be glad to contribute, but I'm not going to squander our resources paying for proper."

Clive looked at Babs. She didn't even glance his way. "We'll pay," she said. Then she cleared her throat. "And I *never* called you coarse."

The three of us were in the kitchen having decaf espresso when Grandma Ethel pulled into the driveway. Moments later, there were hugs and more air kisses as she came in and they went out. A half hour later, I was alone, taking off my makeup and feeling something needed doing. I just didn't know what.

The next morning I knew. I called Joel Winters and asked him to put me on Dorinda's visitors list. "That's right. O apostrophe capital s-h-e-a."

Chapter Twenty-Eight

I couldn't believe what I was doing. But I'd asked for it, and now it was happening. In preparation for meeting Dorinda Dillon, or at least getting in to see her, I went to the hairdresser and got the Ethel O'Shea makeover. I saw my hair, light brown with gold highlights, go so light some might call it blond, while gold highlights slid along the precious-metals graph closer to platinum. That was Tuesday morning. Though I'd explained to the boys what I would be doing, I was prepared for an afternoon of hysteria when they saw me as someone other than their light-brown-with-gold-highlights mother. Evan and Dash didn't seem to notice. Mason motioned me to lower my head. I sat on the floor with him. He took a handful of my hair, rubbed it between his fingers, decided it was still hair, and asked for a stick of cheddar cheese.

That night Grandma Ethel asked, "Are you sure you want to go through with this?"

"Listen, I won't use your ID."

"How are you going to get in? Spray mace at them and steal their keys? This is jail you're going to. Use my ID. What do I care about the station anymore? The bastards canceled my show. They should all drop dead."

Despite her protest, I told her that if anyone caught me using her ID, I'd say I'd stolen it from her wallet. "They're not going to arrest me or prosecute me," I said. I hoped I sounded more confident than I felt. "I've been through too much. The worst they'll do is be really, really unpleasant."

"You don't have to say you stole it. I'm a seventy-nine-year-old woman with three gorgeous great-grandsons whose father was brutally murdered. Do you think they're going to arrest me?"

The answer was no, but TV credentials can get you only so far. Other than by committing a crime or being employed by the NYPD or the New York City Department of Correction, it was not easy getting into the Rose M. Singer Center on Rikers Island.

But I'd made two decisions that turned out to be good ones. One was not driving my own car, registered in my name; I took a cab. The second one was leaving my handbag home. I took Grandma Ethel's ID card in one pocket of my jeans; a smaller spiral notebook I'd taken to Joel Winters's office in my other pocket; and two hundred dollars in tens and twenties in my jacket. The only jewelry I wore, since I'd read online that visitors had to put all their belongings, down to their earrings, in a bin that went into a locker secured by the police, was a Swatch with a plastic band that I always wore when we went to the beach.

The guards said in less than trusting voices, "You forgot your wallet?"

I told them I'd intentionally left my handbag at my hotel but forgotten to put the wallet in my jacket. "I'm so sorry," I said. "But what can I tell you? I swear, this is not your usual 'I forgot my wallet' story. I came up from Miami to do background for a big piece, except my plane was late. Once I got to the hotel, I was in such a rush I wasn't thinking."

They weren't buying it. I asked to speak to their supervisor. Though she was wearing a uniform, she reminded me of female guards in concentration-camp movies, big and boxy, with weird, watery, bulgy eyes, as if they were staring out from a fish tank. I wasn't going to win her heart or her mind with a smile. So I didn't smile. I told my story and said I had to catch the four o'clock plane back to Miami, so there wasn't time to go to the hotel and return.

Maybe she caught my exhaustion and frustration, maybe she liked the cut of my True Religion jeans, maybe she was a racist and was giving me points for being light-eyed and white. At least she didn't catch my desperation and near-hysteria. But after a blessedly fast glance at the ID and a check that Ethel O'Shea was on the visitors list, she finally ordered the guards to pat me down, give me my own special tag, and let me through.

I'd been picturing movie scenes with prisoner and visitor sitting opposite each other, separated by bars, and talking into a phone or a stub of a mike. Or another scene where a guard stands blocking the door, legs apart, arms crossed over chest, face like a particularly stupid bulldog's, while prisoner and visitor sit on stools or crummy chairs across the bare room from each other.

I got something else entirely. Teleconferencing. I was so unprepared for being stuck in a tiny room in which someone had recently sneaked more than one cigarette that I almost cried to be let out. The guard turned on a TV monitor and said, "They'll be bringing her into the booth in a minute. Have a seat. If you get any trouble with the audio, bang real hard on the door. This here is soundproof, so even if you yell, I won't hear you. And bang when you're done."

A couple of minutes later, some movement on the screen made me look up. Dorinda Dillon came in, sat, and stared at me. The only thing keeping my heart from rocketing out of my chest was that it didn't seem to be a stare of recognition. Just a dumb stare. Without makeup, her eyes seemed not only less human but even farther apart than in her pictures. Her hair had been cut short since her arrest and was mostly brown except for the bottom couple of inches. At first it looked like she had a rosy glow, but then I saw her face was chapped. Still, she looked . . . not exactly like a little lost pink lamb, but a lost sheep, one who definitely did not look pretty in pink.

"Hello, Ms. Dillon. My name is Ethel O'Shea. Did your attorney explain why I wanted to see you?" I asked.

"I got a message," she said. I don't know what I had expected, but what struck me was that it was such an ordinary voice, not breathy or husky. She just sounded out of town, like an operator at an 800 number.

"Would you like me to explain what my piece is about?" I took out my notebook and pen. She shrugged, so I went into my story about how prosecutors leap to judgment when—I said "someone with your background"—is involved in a serious crime.

"I am not a call girl," she said. "They kept calling me a call girl on TV."

"What do you like to be called?"

"An escort. Right now I don't look my best, but I'm a real escort." Except for a whine, her voice had no emotion. "A guy can take me out and be glad to be seen with me on his arm."

"I understand what you're saying," I said.

"Not that I'm arm candy."

"No, I'm sure you're more than that."

She was wearing a short-sleeved blue coverall, not the orange I'd expected, and once she said "arm," she started rubbing her right arm just above the elbow. "Some bitch pinched me," she said. "Last week, and it's still bruised. Look." She put down her hand and pointed. I thought there might be a black-and-blue mark, but I couldn't be sure. "It still really, really hurts."

"That's too bad."

"Can you see it?" she asked.

I hoped she was too dense to set a trap for me, but I wasn't sure. "Yes. Awful," I told her. She nodded, as in *Awful is right*. "With all this happening, are your friends standing by you?"

"Yeah."

"Have they been visiting?"

"Not yet." It seemed clear that she didn't have friends, but also that she didn't feel terrible about it. She gave her arm another gentle rub to soothe herself. I thought that somebody who complained so much about a several-day-old pinch was a major kvetch. Considering what prostitutes were supposed to do, she probably could take some kinds of pain. But I couldn't imagine her hitting herself hard enough on the head to cause a bump that would last for weeks. "You'd think that shit lawyer Winters would visit, but all I get is messages. He said we'd spend time together when they set a trial date. Like, what the fuck? What am I paying this guy for?"

"Tell me about the bruise on your head. I heard that when they arrested you in Las Vegas, you had a big bump."

"That's because I got hit. I got hit when I opened the closet door. Someone was in there, and they got my electric broom. The next thing you know, I was out cold. And when I came to, the guy was dead."

"Had you ever been with him before?" I asked. My mouth was completely dry. I truly would have given a year's income for a sip of Diet Coke.

"No. He was new. He was a very big plastic surgeon. I guess you know that."

"Yes. He told you he was a plastic surgeon?" I couldn't believe Jonah would give out information about himself like that. He was so discreet about talking about what he did, mostly because people were always asking his opinion on the work they wanted to have done, or whether he thought they needed a certain procedure. He hated being out for an evening and getting cornered by someone displaying arm flab. Also, he said that in most people's minds, plastic surgeons were fabulously rich, and especially when we were out with the boys, he didn't like people thinking of him as wealthy. He said it was simple discretion. I'd

always thought he was afraid someone would kidnap the triplets. Possibly even demand a triple ransom.

"Maybe he told me. I forget. I don't think he talked about it,
but maybe he said something."

"Did he pay cash?"

"Yeah. Private clients always pay cash. Up-front. With an
escort service, they can charge."

She looked more annoyed at her situation than fearful or
angry or anything else a person in a blue prison outfit might be
feeling. "What did he want done?" I asked.

"He was kind of crazy," Dorinda said. At that moment, I
didn't dare ask anything. If she had a train of thought, I wanted
her to stay on it. So I kept looking at her. Then I made some
scribbles on the pad. "He kept saying he heard I was a miracle
worker. A miracle worker? What the fuck? So I asked him what
kind of miracle he wanted. And he said something about his
hand."

"His hand?" I asked. "What about his hand?"

"I don't know. So I went over, and he started acting funny. I
told him not to be scared, to let me help him." She caressed the
bruise on her arm again. "Then I brought him into the bedroom
and said, 'Why don't you take off your shirt?' So he unbuttoned
a couple of buttons."

"And then?"

"He was slow, so I started to help. All of a sudden he got
really snotty and shitty and said, 'What the hell are you doing?'
I thought it was part of his game, so I slipped out of my dress.
Then he said, 'Get me my coat,' like he was the biggest big shot
in the world. And he started buttoning his shirt, so I went out to
the hall to get his coat."

"And?"

"And then nothing. I got hit. When I came to, when I finally
stood up, there he was. Dead. With scissors."

Chapter Twenty-Nine

So Jonah hadn't had sex with Dorinda Dillon. Thank God! The news I'd been hoping for!

Except he was dead.

Every once in a while, like now, waiting in the wholesale flower market later that afternoon while my favorite peony dealer finished haggling with Miss Northern Westchester Floral Design Queen—who was doing everything except carrying a riding crop to show where she was from—I would discover a new way of missing Jonah. This time it was looking at Willie, the exasperated peony guy, sleeves rolled up, punching numbers into his calculator, trying to make the sale and get rid of Miss NWFDQ. It was late for the market, midafternoon, and he'd probably lost most of his patience by nine in the morning.

The hair on his forearms, wet from working with unboxed flowers, looked dark red against his ruddy skin. Seeing it transported me right to our pool. Jonah and I were in the deep end facing each other, our arms crossed and resting on a white float. Just talking. I reached out and smoothed the hair on his arm so it would all go in one direction.

Another punch in the gut. I started crying, not just tears, but with my shoulders going up and down, like I was bouncing. I turned the other way so Willie wouldn't see. Except I was face-to-face with some Dutch bulb mogul I'd seen at a lot of the New York flower events, a young guy with a face full of brown polka dots that looked like age spots. So I turned back and cried facing Willie's face and his customer's horsey ass.

From the beginning, I'd known in my heart that Jonah was what I'd believed he was, loving and true. But along the way, my head had serious doubts. Okay: Not to feel overly guilty, most heads would do the same. Now I knew my heart had been smarter. But aside from feeling so grateful and relieved by my new knowledge, what could I do with it?

"I don't want to hear any explanations," Willie told me once he was free. "You got what to cry about, okay?" He looked around and handed me some green tissue paper to blow my nose in. I probably looked a little too directly into his eyes because I wanted to avoid seeing his arms. "Go ahead, honk away, but don't blame me if you walk out of here with a green nose." Then we did our Florabella business, Willie pushing a dark pink peony, the Edulis Superba, so hard I finally gave in.

Being in the flower market was usually the great joy of my job, in Manhattan in jeans and work boots, sipping coffee that got cold fast from the chill of all the refrigeration. The colors, the smells, the relationships that weren't quite friendships but came close: It all made me feel part of the world where nature and commerce met, maybe what a farmer felt when he hauled his potatoes to market.

But when I stopped crying, the flower market held no charm for me. I could have been in an office with fluorescent lights and no windows. All I could think of was sheepy Dorinda talking in her flat 800-number voice, saying, "He heard I was a miracle worker." And then "something about his hand." Why hadn't anyone asked her about this before? I knew the answer. They had all assumed Jonah was there for sex.

One thing I now was sure of: Dorinda Dillon had not killed Jonah. It simply didn't add up, in either my head or my heart. I believed what she had said. He was a new client. They had hardly gotten beyond the hello stage. She had no reason to kill him. Sparky and I had pretty much demolished Grandma Ethel's burglar theory, but did I have anything to replace it with? A random-intruder theory?

I finished with Willie and a couple of our other dealers and had the flowers and a couple of buckets of the floral preservative we liked loaded into the Florabella truck that I'd parked in a nearby lot before taking the taxi to Rikers Island. It was an old Chevy panel truck we'd bought mostly for its color, a lovely celadon green, a case of foolish business thinking that had actually turned out well. I was heading toward the Midtown Tunnel when I decided to take a look at what I'd been picturing for so long: Dorinda's apartment building. I headed up Third Avenue and turned past her apartment building, a large box with windows, probably badly built in the sixties. As I drove by, I noticed the side entrance about fifty feet from the front door. Just then a doorman walked out in a long gray military-style coat, looking like some character from *The Nutcracker*.

I drove into a garage a block away and talked the guy into taking the truck for fifteen minutes even though he said, "We don't take trucks." Charm and a twenty did it. Walking down the street, I felt at a loss because I was so used to being "done" when I went out: hair, makeup, nails, accessories. My casual was somebody else's wedding day. Jeans, shirt, old quilted vest, hair in a ponytail wasn't the way I dealt with any world except jail or the flower market.

"Hello," I said to the doorman, knowing I couldn't say "Excuse my outfit." "My name is Joan Smith. I'm a social worker from Manhattan Human Services." He didn't look impressed, but on the other hand, he didn't look unsympathetic. "I'm doing some background on Miss Dillon."

"And?"

So he wasn't exactly friendly. I didn't know why, but I got the feeling that his "And?" had zero to do with me and a lot to do with Dorinda Dillon. "All I'm trying to do right now is get a sense of her." I had a flash of worry that he wouldn't believe the Bloomberg administration would be paying for a social worker to get a sense of an accused murderer, but he nodded like he had a parade of social workers dropping by every day looking to get senses. "Did you know her?"

"You might say that," the doorman said. His sleeves were too long. They covered his knuckles, and I wanted to tell him to take his coat to a tailor and ask for a three-inch hem. "I was the guy on duty when the doctor came."

"Do you remember him?"

"Yeah, sure. Well dressed. An East Sixties kind of guy, except I heard he lived on Long Island."

Since the doorman was in a chatty mood, I decided to check out what either Eddie Huber or Lieutenant Paston had told me. "Was he one of her regulars?"

"No. Never saw him before."

I realized I had to start sounding like a social worker, except I wasn't quite sure what one sounded like. "I'm trying to get a picture of her character." He made a face that came close to a smirk but wasn't. I gave him my mega-wattage plastic-surgeons'-convention smile and said, "I'm not asking about deep-down goodness or honor, just what she was like on a day-to-day basis." He seemed a little hesitant, so I added, "Don't worry. I've been at this job over ten years. I stopped getting shocked after three months."

"Bottom line on the character?" he said. "Not so great. Didn't even bother saying hello unless you said it first. Like who did she think she was? A duchess? And another thing: Like you said you've been doing your work over ten years. I've been doing mine for almost thirty." I did the *Omigod! You couldn't be that old* gape, which he seemed to appreciate. "So over the years, in these rental buildings and condos, I run into a fair number of girls who do what she does. Most of them go out of their way to be friendly—friendly in a nice way—because they don't want trouble, they don't want a doorman hassling their johns or even being not polite. And Christmas? They're right at the top of the good-tipper list. You can predict it. Big tip, nice card with a thank-you. You know what I got this year from Dorinda Dillon? Fifty bucks in old crumpled-up bills. The day after Christmas. She hands it to me like it was five hundred in nice crisp bills."

"No card?" I asked.

"No card."

I sighed and shook my head sadly.

"Doesn't that say everything about her character?" he asked.

"Loud and clear," I said. I waited while he let in a tenant with a baby in a stroller, a shopping bag of groceries, and some forsythia branches in cellophane that looked like they had two more days to live. "So how did it work with her clients? Did they just come to the door and ask for her?"

"Right. And I have to ask all the time, 'Who shall I say is calling?' because I have to buzz her. And they all say they're Mr. Johnson, which is what she has them say. And so I let them up."

"Besides the doctor, did anyone else go up there that day?"

"A few hours earlier, the other doorman let in a regular. An old guy. Came and went. And another regular earlier in the day. But nobody else when I was on duty. Not even another girl for a threesome. Maybe I shouldn't say that."

"Please. You should hear some of the things I hear. I'm unshockable."

He smiled. "You must have a tough job."

"Sometimes. I love learning about people, about their lives, so overall, I enjoy the work. You know what the hardest part is?" I asked.

"What?"

"Walking and walking." I lowered my voice. "And if you'll excuse the expression, finding a bathroom."

"Don't I know it. Used to be, you could walk into a bar or restaurant anywhere in the city, do what you had to do, say thank you and goodbye."

"Not these days," I said. "Can I ask? What do you do?"

"Oh. It's no problem. They have a toilet in the basement right by the elevator. They got a buzzer down there. I lock the front door, and if the tenants or someone needs me, they press the button. I'm gone for a minute, but at least it's right here in the building."

"I'm jealous," I told him, and we smiled at each other.

I filled in Grandma Ethel after dinner but begged off her suggestions about researching hand fetishes on the Web or, as her alternate fun-filled evening activity, turning on some station that was having an Audrey Hepburn festival. Instead, I went to bed with a copy of *Vogue,* but I couldn't concentrate on the articles, so I just looked at ads. I must have fallen asleep about nine-thirty because when the phone rang a little after ten, the sound startled me awake. I grabbed it, and my "hello" came out like a chicken's squawk.

"Susie?" Theo. "How's it going?" His bedtime calls were becoming an unpleasant habit.

"Fine."

"I hope I didn't wake you." Without giving me a chance to offer a polite "Oh no, you didn't," which I wasn't going to, he went on, "I spoke to my parents after they dropped by your house on their way home from the Hamptons. They say you're doing so much better."

"It was a nice visit," I said. Clearly, he wasn't going to refer to his last nasty phone call.

"Susie, I know you'll think what I'm about to ask is terrible. But I just want you to understand I really don't mean it in any bad or selfish way."

"Okay," I said. Knowing Theo, I realized a little extra was necessary, so I added, "I wouldn't think that at all."

"Here goes," he said in his smoothest voice. "A while back, Jonah and I were talking. It was around the time you guys asked me if I'd be the guardian for the boys if God forbid you died, and I said yes. Anyway, Jonah said that besides the guardianship thing, he was going to remember me in his will. So I was wondering—you haven't said anything—if he left me any kind of keepsake."

I still hadn't shaken off all the sleep, so I almost said there wasn't any particular keepsake. But I stopped myself, because I realized that when he said "keepsake," he wasn't talking about a memento. He was, as always, talking about money.

"Jonah didn't have anything in particular as a keepsake for you," I told him.

"Oh."

"Is there anything of his you'd like to have?"

"You choose something," he said, like he didn't really care.

"How about his plastic bar mitzvah clock?" I wanted to ask. "Theo, let me think about it, look through his things. I want to choose something that meant a lot to Jonah and will mean a lot to you. I'll get to it over the weekend, I promise you."

Surprisingly, I fell back to sleep almost immediately, probably because my brother-in-law's request was a total nonshock. Jonah and I had debated whether he was needy or greedy or both so many times that we'd finally stopped because we really didn't care. The possibility of his guardianship of the boys had seemed so remote when we'd done our wills. I realized now that we hadn't thought it through. I needed to make a new will. Soon.

My first call the next morning was to the delightful Joel Winters. I told him that I'd had a good interview with Dorinda and, shoveling a little more fertilizer onto his ego, asked what he would do if he could change the criminal justice system. While he talked, I sat in the bathroom in front of a magnifying mirror, holding the phone between my ear and shoulder, and tweezed my eyebrows. When he stopped to take a breath, I said, "I do need one favor from you. I know you can get a message to Dorinda. I really need to find out who referred the doctor, the plastic surgeon who was killed, to her. Unless you know offhand." He didn't. "Was it through one of her own clients? She said he was a private client. I'm a little rushed on this, so I appreciate you getting back to me as soon as you can. And by the way, I know my producer will love what you were just saying about mandatory sentencing."

Since Grandma Ethel was not one of the early risers, I did something I should have done days before: I got out the CD Liz Holbreich had given me with all the materials she and her colleagues had collected during their brief investigation. I loaded it on the computer, but I couldn't figure out how to search through the documents to see if I could find the Marty who'd shown up on Jonah's calendar.

That wanting-to-throw-something rage that comes with computer frustration overtook me, but since I was down in Jonah's study and didn't want to damage anything, I tried to take deep breaths. It worked enough so that actual thinking could take place. I called Lizbeth Holbreich and asked her to help me find Marty.

"I've thought about you so often," she said. "I'm glad you called, because I wasn't sure whether or not to call you. I hope you're doing . . . I suppose I should say 'I hope you're doing as well as can be expected.'"

"I am doing all right. The missing him is much worse than I ever imagined at the beginning, but the day-to-day stuff is coming along."

"And your sons?"

"There are problems, but lots of times they're fine, normal. I just want to strike the right balance between keeping their father as a good memory and not continually poking them and saying 'Hey, don't enjoy yourselves too much because you have a dead father.'"

We talked for a few more minutes, and while I would have loved to get Liz's reading on my whole Dorinda on Rikers Island saga, I asked how to go about finding a name on the CD she'd given me. I made notes that seemed simple enough, but when she said, "Tell me what name you're looking for. I have the information on our server and . . ." I waited under a minute.

"Marty," I said. "The name was first on Jonah's calendar last November, though I only searched back a year. The last time he was on it was eleven days before Jonah was killed."

"No last name, I assume?" Liz asked.

"No last name, no address, no phone numbers. I checked Marty and Martin. There were Martins and a Martino who were patients, but patients were connected with the Manhattan Aesthetics database."

"If you ever give up flowers, you could come and work for us. Give me a moment. Let me see what I can find." This time she took a lot longer than a minute, but I had no desire whatsoever to tweeze my eyebrows. I thought about Theo and why someone with well-off parents, a good education, and an okay career as a casting director would expect his brother to leave him a "keepsake" of money in his will when the brother had a wife and three children. "There's an Anello and Martin, Rare Books and Texts," she said.

"He had started collecting some old medical books," I said.

"And there's a Martin Ruhlmann at a 212 number, no address. Hold on. I'll check him out." It didn't take much longer than a few clicks of Liz's mouse. "Martin Ruhlmann, certified public accountant. A forensic accountant," she said. "But now that I look at the name, it's vaguely familiar. We have forensic accountants here at the agency."

"What do they do?"

"They're auditors, but they bring an investigative mentality to an issue. A good one will have a combination of financial expertise, knowledge of fraud — and fraudsters, too, you might say — and real savvy about how businesses operate. You'd find them working on cases like Enron, or cases where a corporation is involved in a deal it has questions about."

"Why would a plastic surgeon need a forensic accountant?" I asked.

"Any number of reasons, I suppose," Liz said. "But . . . I'm just thinking out loud here. Maybe it was somehow connected to those e-mail exchanges Dr. Gersten was having with his office manager." She must have clicked another couple of times because she said, "Donald Finsterwald. Did you read those e-mails on the CD?"

I hadn't, but I would.

Chapter Thirty

The guard at the security desk in the lobby of Martin Ruhlmann's building smiled at me and Grandma Ethel and said, "You girls must be sisters." I guessed Grandma Ethel was thinking something close to what I was, like *Cut the shit, you creep,* but as he and an elevator were all that was standing between us and the forensic accountant, we smiled with delight.

Martin Ruhlmann and Associates might have been full of accountants, but it wasn't a green-eyeshade sort of place. It had the English-club look, right down to a male receptionist in a suit and tie sitting behind a huge mahogany desk. The walls in the waiting room were covered with antique lithographs of what I thought were drawings of rooms in old English clubs. "You have good eyes," Grandma Ethel told me. "Look. The stuff in the frames hanging on the walls. No, the pictures inside the pictures up there. Are they pictures of more rooms in English clubs? Are you supposed to think, *Hey, maybe it goes on forever.*"

"Maybe."

"Like anyone gives a shit. Oh, I forget to tell you: Sparky says either this Ruhlmann is the one man in New York who hasn't heard about Jonah getting killed, or he's treating whatever information he had about whatever Jonah went to him for as confidential."

"It's possible that the police tracked him down already, and whatever he had to say wasn't important," I suggested.

"Maybe."

A secretary, a woman in one of those dress-for-success suits from the seventies or eighties, except without the stupid little tie, led us into Martin Ruhlmann's office. He stood and, like a proper English gentleman, did not try to shake our hands until we offered ours. Well, mine, because my grandmother was too busy eyeing a grandfather clock in a corner, barely managing not to sneer at it.

We spent the first few minutes on what a fine man Jonah had been. Ruhlmann was unreadable. He might have thought Jonah was terrific, or he might have loathed him, but his words said nothing except every cliché about someone who'd recently died. There wasn't any body language to read, either, unless staying behind a desk with his hands in his lap said everything.

I decided to get to the point. "Could you tell us what the investigation you were doing for my husband was about?"

"This is a fairly complex, technical undertaking," he said.

"Try us," Grandma Ethel told him.

I couldn't get over how his mouth moved when every other part of him remained frozen like a still photo with animated lips. "Essentially, I was asked to look into the use of the practice's surgical suites. The use that was reported did not appear to be in keeping with the gross quarterly revenues."

"Was it Jonah who hired you, or was it the partnership?"

"Just Dr. Gersten."

"Do you want to explain what you mean by the use of the surgical suites?" my grandmother asked.

"I really wouldn't feel comfortable doing that," he said.

"Why not?" I asked.

"Dr. Gersten had a legitimate legal interest in the business of Manhattan Aesthetics."

"And doesn't my granddaughter, who is Dr. Gersten's sole heir, have a legitimate legal interest?" My grandmother, in her pink Chanel once again, looked like she should be wearing storm-cloud gray.

"I would have to look into that," Ruhlmann said. "Or rather, have our attorneys look into it."

"When can you do it?" I asked.

"I can have the answer for you within the week. Possibly a little longer, but I'm sure once they get going on it—"

Grandma Ethel cut him off. "Not good enough."

"I'm afraid, Mrs. O'Shea, that while I can certainly appreciate your interest and your granddaughter's, and your desire to know any details as soon as possible, I have to see that this is looked into in a proper manner as soon as possible."

Grandma Ethel rose in one graceful swoop. "Mr. Ruhlmann, you're obviously a gentleman, and I hope you think we're ladies." He nodded. "Good. Then let me tell you something about dealing with ladies of our caliber. Don't fuck with us."

As we got into the elevator, my grandmother asked me, "Coarse enough for you?"

"Yes," I said. "Thank you very much."

"Susie, I know you're worrying that my behavior might be counterproductive. It might be. But dollars to doughnuts, sweetheart, it'll work. I know how to deal with guys who think they can get away with repro grandfather clocks."

By the end of the week, we still hadn't heard from the forensic accountant. I couldn't believe Jonah had called him Marty or anything less formal than Mr. Ruhlmann. Then it occurred to me that if he hadn't put down an address or a phone number, maybe he'd been concerned that someone might be looking at his calendar. Donald, perhaps? Or someone else at the practice? Late Friday afternoon, I told Grandma Ethel I was going to call and prod Ruhlmann. She said, "Tell him you've got to see him Monday morning, and you'll be there with your lawyer."

"I don't have a lawyer—except the one who did our wills, and her partner, who did the closing on our house. There is no way I can get a lawyer between now and Monday, so I'm not going to give any ultimatums like that."

"Sparky will be here tomorrow morning. She can stay till Monday night or Tuesday, okay? You can't ask for a better lawyer. NYU. *Law Review*. Need I say more?"

At a few minutes after ten on Monday, Sparky Burns was sitting in the chair closest to Martin Ruhlmann's desk, but she leaned in even closer. "I admire prudence," she told him. "But you and I know there is no professional privilege of confidentiality for accountants unless you were working under the direction of an attorney." Ruhlmann cleared his throat, and she said, "What we are asking of you is not imprudent. Dr. Gersten paid you for your services. Mrs. Gersten would like to hear what you found."

"You mean what he hired me to look for," he said. Granted, my grandmother's toughness might have put Ruhlmann off a tad, but even before that, he had been about as aloof as a guy can get without actually being nasty.

Sparky centered the large, round face of her wristwatch on her arm and studied it. "We can have this discussion now. We have no intention of staying for lunch. Or we can come back after an extended period of filings and depositions. You call it." She sat back in the armchair and flashed a look at my grandmother that could not have meant anything but *Keep quiet*. My grandmother, without a word, opened her handbag, rearranged her wallet and compact, and snapped it shut.

Ruhlmann had perhaps hoped to outwait Sparky or give her the silent treatment, but finally, he said, "I have a meeting outside the office at eleven-thirty."

"Shall we begin, then?" Sparky asked.

"A check arrived in the mail at Manhattan Aesthetics made out to Dr. Noakes for thirty-seven thousand dollars. No one could figure out where it came from, because the checking account belonged to something called the GP Fund. Dr. Gersten consulted with his partners, Dr. Noakes, of course, and later, Dr. Jiménez and the office manager, a Mr. Finsterwald. None of them had any idea what the GP Fund was or why it would have sent a check made out to Dr. Noakes. Apparently, the envelope was lost or thrown out, so there was no return address." Ruhlmann took time to adjust the points of the linen handkerchief sticking out of his jacket pocket. "When Dr. Gersten was reported missing, and then found dead, I was still in the process of trying to track down who or what the GP Fund was."

"Why didn't Jonah give the check to the practice's regular accountant to trace?" I asked. For a second I felt uncomfortable, like I had tried to steal Sparky's scene, but she didn't seem to notice.

"I believe he wanted to investigate the matter himself. He was hoping to discover where the check came from and whether its existence was some sort of a mistake, a bookkeeping oversight, or perhaps something—part of something—devious. He was curious about what the GP Fund was. He wanted to see if the check could be the tip of a very unpleasant iceberg."

"So you were hired to explore where this thirty-seven-thousand-dollar check came from?" Sparky asked.

"It wasn't only the check that was troubling him. There seemed to be quite a bit of inventory shrinkage from the surgical suites in the practice's office."

"They did most of their surgery there, not at the hospital," I told Grandma Ethel and Sparky.

"In retail sales, 'inventory shrinkage' can mean shoplifting or employee theft. But in a medical practice, Dr. Gersten was concerned with much more than dollars and cents. What was missing, as I found out, was not at all what he'd expected. It

was not easily marketable drugs that had been stolen, but instru-
ments, supplies, anesthesia itself. He couldn't understand why
and wanted to know if there was a black market for that sort of
thing."

"So no one else in the practice knew that he came to see you?"
I asked.

"I don't believe so," he said. "I was to speak only with Dr.
Gersten, no one else. My instincts tell me no one else knew, but
my instincts don't bat a thousand."

"When you heard about Dr. Gersten's murder, did you contact the police?" Sparky asked. Ruhlmann didn't answer. "Did
you get in touch with either of his partners?"

"No," he said.

"I'll tell you what I need from you before we leave," Sparky
said. "I need your notes on the inventory shrinkage. I want a
copy of the thirty-seven-thousand-dollar check and whatever
information you did manage to get on the GP Fund."

"I have very little on the GP Fund."

"I have a suggestion," Sparky said. "You need to get cracking
on the person or persons behind GP."

"I'm really not interested in pursuing this matter beyond this
meeting," Ruhlmann said.

"You listen to me!" Sparky snapped. Ruhlmann moved. His
head snapped back against his leather chair, and his jaw dropped.
It was the equivalent of someone else having a major seizure.
"There is no excuse—Don't interrupt me with some line your
lawyer fed you. There is no excuse whatsoever for your not
notifying the police about Jonah Gersten consulting you. Interested or not, you are still on this matter. I might suggest it's your
highest priority."

Chapter Thirty-One

When Martin Ruhlmann called that night, it was clear he regretted dropping his jaw. He sounded like he had such a stiff upper lip—to say nothing of his lower one—that I had trouble understanding what he was saying.

"The GP Fund is not an entity of any sort," he said. "It's the bank account of a woman named Phoebe Kingsley. I believe she's a socialite. Her husband is Billy Kingsley."

"Is that a name I'm supposed to know?" I asked, but very politely.

"He owns StarCom. He's considered one of the great figures of the . . ." I couldn't comprehend what he was saying because people don't speak clearly when their jaws are clenched. I asked him to repeat it. "The telecommunications industry. I gather he and Phoebe Kingsley are separated and a divorce is in the works. But that's neither here nor there. Does that conclude our business, Mrs. Gersten?"

"My lawyer will let you know, Mr. Ruhlmann. Thank you for calling." *Phoebe Kingsley?* I thought. I pursed my lips, furrowed my brow, and waited for the name to ring a bell. It didn't.

Grandma Ethel and Sparky passed on pizza and went out

to an Indian restaurant. After I put the boys to sleep, I roamed
around the house and wound up in each of their rooms, gazing
at them. That peaceful euphoria mothers are encouraged to feel
each time they look at their children came to me once in a blue
moon, almost always when they were asleep and incapable of
shrieking, hurling their Spider-Man accessories, or crayoning a
mural on a silk-covered wall.

I walked down the second-floor hallway into my office
and Googled Phoebe. There was much to Google. Somehow
I'd missed her in those party pictures that appear in the *Times*
and all those *Town & Country*–type magazines. Maybe it was
because she always showed up in group pictures, never by herself. Billy Kingsley was rich enough to have his wife noticed, but
apparently, he didn't care enough to bankroll what it took to be
so exquisitely dressed and so philanthropic that reporters and
photographers cannot resist coming to your fifty-two-million-
dollar home in Southampton to cover your party for the Friends
of the South Fork Water Birds Foundation.

But I zoomed in on her again and again, and finally, in one
photograph that happened to have an incredible number of pix-
els, I could see her face clearly. No, I had never met her. Phoebe
and I ran in different circles. She was, as Andrea would have
said, a type, or at least doing her damnedest to become one. Her
hair was coiffed in one of those neo-helmet-head styles socially
ambitious women were wearing again, maybe hoping people
would take them for the reincarnation of Brooke Astor. She
was slim, pretty enough. From the little I could see in the photographs, she wore elegant, safe couture clothes well, and she
smiled with every tooth she owned.

What really impressed me was her face. Smooth and unlined.
Almost perfectly symmetrical. It was what Jonah called the
Gilbert John Noakes signature face-lift. I'd learned to spot one
years earlier. Flawless yet natural, except for two slight inden-
tations on the temples near the hairline, less obvious than but

a little like the forceps marks you see on some newborns. The dents could definitely be seen; Phoebe Kingsley's helmet hair was full, high, and swept off her face.

I wanted to get her out of my head, not so much because she was upsetting me, but if I could stop thinking about where she fit into the overall picture, maybe something would come to me. To change my mind's subject, I got into bed with an envelope of pictures from a vacation we had taken two summers before, in Chatham, Cape Cod. I'd taken photos of Jonah and the boys on the beach, the best photography I'd ever done. The sunlight had been perfect, illuminating the mist in the air so that all of them—alone or in groups of two, three, or four—looked like they were surrounded by an aura. Better than an aura: more like a head-to-toe halo. I kept going through them, about fifteen photographs, again and again. I didn't cry. Maybe I was melancholy, but I had the feeling you get from looking back on any good time that's gone with no possibility of a do-over. As I drifted off to sleep, I was thinking I could smell the ocean.

I woke up sometime during the night. When didn't I? No dreams startled me awake. No kids were crying. Instead, I recalled an evening Jonah and I had gone out to dinner with Layne and her husband, Mike Robinson, an OB/GYN. Jonah made it a rule never to gossip about one partner when we went out with another. That night, though, Gilbert John was mentioned. Jonah and Layne were deep in conversation about some fat-lasering procedure that Gilbert John had observed and deeply disapproved of. Mike murmured something to me about how he'd hate to have Gilbert John disapprove of anything he did. I'd laughed, partly because it felt like such an illicit conversation for the two spouses to be having about Gilbert John Noakes. I told Mike I didn't know anyone who wasn't intimidated by Gilbert John. He said Layne once had told him that early in her career, when she was assisting Gilbert John during surgery, he'd given her a dirty look for something minor she'd done wrong. Mike said he'd laughed when she described those disapproving eyes glaring over the surgical mask, but Layne was never able to. She'd told him it was like having all the presidents on Mount Rushmore angrily staring down at her.

Mike had been on something of a roll, and he wasn't at all a drinker, so it wasn't alcohol talking. I figured this was a conversation Jonah would rather I not have, so I tried making it a foursome again. But he and Layne were still going on about lasering in the kind of surgeons' shoptalk that gets pretty revolting. Mike hadn't moved on from our conversation, though he'd transitioned to Layne being upset about Gilbert John's lifestyle.

Gilbert John wasn't bringing in anywhere near as much business as he had been. We all knew that, right? Right. So why should Layne and Jonah get stuck subsidizing his house on the ocean in East Hampton and his ski lodge in Steamboat Springs when he was putting less time into the practice and doing more traveling and pro bono work? I kept quiet about Gilbert John's new Bentley convertible, an Azure, which was so big it could almost qualify as a yacht.

Mike was telling me he approved of doctors giving back. He himself was in a program where he was assigned high-risk obstetrics patients who had no insurance and no money. Mike thought Gilbert John's enormous number of good works was a great thing for a plastic surgeon to do toward the end of his career. Layne and Jonah each had their own pro bono causes. But Gilbert John's pro bono time was way out of proportion.

The memory of that dinner with Layne and Mike was still with me the next morning. I was doing busywork, cleaning out the freezer, getting rid of pesto marked *Aug 07* and containers of ancient cookies, when Grandma Ethel and Sparky came downstairs. Sparky asked me if it would be okay if she stayed another day or two.

"You have to ask permission to stay on?" my grandmother demanded. "I'm family, so you're family."

"Grandma Ethel," I said, "if you'd given me one nanosecond more, I could have been the one to tell Sparky that."

"You'd better work on your reflexes. Speaking of which, I heard the phone last night, but you must have grabbed it right away. Any news from the Rialto?"

"It was your boyfriend," I said. "Martin Ruhlmann."

"Eth," Sparky said, "if you want him, I won't stand in your way."

As they took breakfast, I filled them in on Phoebe Kingsley. Then I segued into my waking in the middle of the night, thinking about that dinner with Layne and Mike. I couldn't understand what about the conversation had been so significant that it suddenly came back, considering I'd forgotten it not long after it had occurred. Naturally, I'd mentioned it to Jonah, but he'd come to Gilbert John's defense; it was Gilbert John, after all, who had brought him and Layne into one of the city's most prestigious practices and therefore was entitled to earn a little more than his fair share of the proceeds.

"Maybe it's the connection," my grandmother said. "You know what I mean?"

"Not exactly."

"The connection," she said again, more impatiently, like I was deliberately trying to outdo the dumbest kid in the class.

"I give up," I said. "What connection are you talking about?"

"If I knew, I wouldn't be asking. The connection between Layne and her husband with that Phoebe Kingsley." She reached over to Sparky's plate and helped herself to half her bagel. "You hear from Ruhlmann about Phoebe, then a few hours later, you're remembering that dinner. We'll need to work on why you're tying the two together."

Before I could work on it, the publicity-hungry Joel Winters called my cell. "Dorinda got the client who referred Dr. Gersten through College Girl Companions," he said. "I gave them a call, but they don't talk to anybody. 'Our business is based on trust.' Can you believe that? Like there's a lawyer-client, priest-penitent, and madam-of-a-whorehouse-john privilege." Joel Winters seemed not just annoyed but upset at not being able to get me the information I'd asked for. I sensed he was worrying that his fifteen minutes of fame would be canceled.

"Who's in charge at College Girl?" I asked.

"Her name is Cleo. Maybe Clea. She's one cold fish. Ice water in her veins. The last thing she wants to do is talk to a reporter, so save yourself some time."

"All right, Mr. Winters, how about this? Let me have your e-mail address. I'm going to send you a photo of someone. I need you to take it to Rikers—"

"Listen, Ethel—"

"This will be a great story. I guarantee it. And it could make you . . . I don't think I have to draw you a picture. You'd be the guy who did what everybody else said couldn't be done—you saved Dorinda Dillon. Okay? Please ask Dorinda if she ever saw the man in this photo. One more thing: I need you to do it fast."

I had to get my grandmother away from Sparky for a few minutes to tell her what I wanted to do next. Sparky was the kind of lawyer who would tell both of us, "Forget it. You absolutely cannot do this." "Grandma Ethel," I said, "I have some lower-heeled Manolo slides that are too narrow for me. Want to look?" She did, of course, and Sparky didn't. When we got upstairs, Grandma Ethel seemed extremely aggravated by my shoe ruse because she'd already entered the Manolos into her "Assets" column. "Please, I needed to get you away from Sparky, because she does the ethics thing twenty-four/seven. Listen, stick with me now. Be with me. I'll give you any pair of shoes in my closet. Two pair."

"Do you think you have to pay me to be with you?" my grandmother asked.

"No. Of course not."

"Good. A couple of years ago, when we came up to New

York and had dinner with you and Jonah, you were wearing a pair of Manolos. Remember? I admired them, and you said you'd gotten them at an outlet. Sling-back, white and taupe stripe, two- or three-inch tapered wood heel. If I didn't have ethics, those are the ones I'd take."

I called back Martin Ruhlmann to get Phoebe Kingsley's number. On my cell, which had caller ID blocked, I reached her in one ring. I held the phone slightly away from my ear so Grandma Ethel could hear.

"My name is Marianne," I said. "I'm the bookkeeper at Manhattan Aesthetics." I heard a big-time tremble in my voice, but my grandmother gave me a smile of approval. "We're having issues about your check to Dr. Noakes." I spotted the striped slingbacks on a high shelf and reached for them. I got only one; the other flew off the shelf, beaned my head, though not too hard, then fell to the floor.

"I sent another check to his home address," Phoebe said, sounding irritated.

"Made out to him personally?" I picked up the shoe and handed the pair to my grandmother.

"Yes," Phoebe said. It came out as pissy hiss. "He was supposed to tear up the other one *personally* and mail it back to me." She took a deep breath. "Can I ask you something, Miss Bookkeeper? How many goddamn face-lifts am I supposed to pay for? I only had one." Phoebe Kingsley didn't sound low-class, but her voice had a raspy hardness, like a diamond nail file. "I can't have my checks floating around where some clerical type could deposit two of them. Listen, I asked for it back. Christ on a crutch! Two times! Do we understand each other?"

"Not completely," I told her. "I'd like to know—"

"That's it," she said. "I am not discussing this anymore!" She slammed down the phone.

I put down my cell and motioned to Grandma Ethel to keep silent because I sensed she was ready to make a noble speech renouncing the slingbacks. I closed my eyes for a moment and chewed on my knuckles. "Okay, let me try this out on you," I said. "It seems to me Phoebe Kingsley's check *was* for Gilbert John. There was no mistake. When Jonah found it, or maybe it was brought to his attention by one of his staff—I don't know—Gilbert John obviously couldn't admit what it was and cash it. So he called Phoebe Kingsley and told her there was a problem with *that* check and she'd have to write another one."

"He told her he'd send back the one made out to him torn into pieces," Grandma Ethel said. She was cradling the shoes in her arms the way someone else would soothe a baby. "But he couldn't because Jonah was probably holding on to it. So, like I used to say on *Talk of Miami,* 'I need to think.'" She smiled into a nonexistent TV camera. "Give me one hundred and twenty seconds, and I'll be back with an answer for you." She walked over to the bergère chair in the bedroom, put the shoes on the floor, then sat, and in under five seconds said, "Okay, tell me if you agree. Phoebe sent Noakes—what the hell kind of stupid name is Noakes?—another check. But she didn't get the torn-up check back. On the other hand, it never got cashed, did it? My guess is she probably forgot about it until just now, when you called. That's what happens when you're in the middle of a divorce. It takes all your energy. I was so grateful when Sidney dropped dead—I couldn't just leave him like I'd left Lenny the Loser, because he was a popular guy and I didn't want to alienate half of Miami. I love Miami. Anyway, if you ask me, and even if you don't, you can safely bet that Phoebe's GP Fund was money she'd socked away for incidentals, like a new face. And probably, when she got closer to going back on the husband market, lipo and new tits." She tried on the slingbacks. They fit.

We went downstairs to tell Sparky that Gilbert John Noakes's pro bono work most likely wasn't so pro bono. If Phoebe Kingsley was any indication, his on-the-sly surgeries were what was causing the inventory shrinkage that had so upset Jonah. We were careful not to let Sparky know how I'd gotten the information.

"The check to Noakes from Phoebe Kingsley's fund shows Gilbert John taking money under the table," Sparky said. "My guess is he's doing side deals with some old patients, friends he trusts, along with their friends. He gets the check made out to him and pockets it. He puts in for the anesthesia and surgical supplies as part of his pro bono work." I must have looked pathetically hopeful because Sparky said, "Susie, if this were reported and substantiated, it probably would be a good case for prosecuting him on tax evasion. But I'm sorry to tell you, this does not prove Gilbert John Noakes committed murder."

Chapter Thirty-Two

✂——————————————————————————————————————

"Maybe she'll offer you a job," Andrea said brightly. "Maybe I'll take it." Not so bright.

We'd gone to a luncheon at a private club in Manhattan for a client's fiftieth birthday. Now Andrea was dropping me at a brownstone on West Fiftieth: not one of those pretty places with geraniums in window boxes. Crummy, in fact. College Girl Companions was upstairs. A nail salon a few steps down looked like a place to go if you were interested in taking home a toenail fungus.

The building was not a place that had seen better days ever, though it might have watched its final tolerable ones fly out a dirty window in 1908. Now it was just another sad subdivided space badly in need of a sandblasting it was unlikely to get. This wasn't a block for gentrification. On one side was a locksmith. On the other was an Italian restaurant; its canopy was torn, and the ripped piece flapped crazily in the wind.

College Girl probably needed a midtown address to reassure tourists, but I couldn't imagine many people set foot on the premises. Why would a client want to go to a place like that, much less be seen there? And despite the "College Girl," I couldn't picture a bunch of academic whizzes like Dorinda Dillon sitting around a lounge and reading *Paradise Lost*.

"I'll find a place to park and wait," Andrea said.

"Don't bother. I don't know how long this will take, and you'll wind up getting stuck in rush-hour traffic. I'll grab a cab and get home by train." Our ride into the city, and then being at the same table at the luncheon, had been enough of Andrea for me for one day.

"You are not going home on the train during rush hour." Andrea wrinkled her nose like I'd suggested taking a bath in a vat of pig shit.

"It's okay," I murmured, opening the door of her latest car, a Jaguar convertible.

"It's not okay. I'm going to stay here. You're going to a whorehouse."

"I'm going to the offices of an escort service. What do you think, it's like a dorm and they have cubicles with beds up there? Go on. Go home."

"Susie."

"Andrea." I got out of the car. So did she. "Hey, you're double-parked," I said. "You're holding up traffic."

"I want you to keep your phone on. I'm going to call you in fifteen minutes. If you don't answer, I'm coming in with the police."

"What police? You'll go running to the corner screaming for a cop? You know what will happen? You'll get a ticket for double parking. I'll be fine. And please don't go calling me, because my phone may not work in there, or if I'm talking to someone and getting information, I don't want to be interrupted."

She put her hands on her hips. She'd looked so cool at the luncheon—killer stilettos, a Carolina Herrera dress and coat in gray—but having a snit beside her convertible on this seedy street, she looked bizarre, a deranged rich lady from another neighborhood who'd taken a wrong turn. "Hear me!" she said. "I do not want you to do this."

"Andrea—"

"What? You don't give a rat's ass what I want? Too bad. You can't go."

"Let me explain one last time. I'm trying to get some information so I can have something to push the cops and the DA to reopen the case. The only way I can think of—"

"Forget that I'm your business partner and have a strong financial interest in keeping you alive," she said.

"You can stay here and block traffic if you want." I turned to go upstairs. "I can't worry about you now."

"I don't want you risking your life!" The idea of me risking my life by going to an office was so over-the-top that I wound up smacking myself in the forehead, that *I can't believe it* gesture lusty ethnics do in old movies. But Andrea wouldn't let up. "Susie. You have three children. What if something happens to you? Who are you going to leave them with? Theo, that ridiculous, selfish Munchkin bastard? And if *I'm* calling someone selfish, you can just imagine!" I really couldn't. "Listen to me, Susie."

"I'm listening, and I understand what you're saying. But the only possible danger I can imagine is that they won't let me in. If I thought for one momen—"

"I'm going up there with you," Andrea said.

"No, you're not."

"I swear on all that's holy, I'll behave like the lady I am. I'll even keep my mouth shut."

"No. Anyway, you can't leave your car here."

"Do you think I give a shit about getting a ticket?"

"They'll tow it!" I was shouting as she came around the Jag to stand next to me on the sidewalk.

"So what? Fat Boy will send somebody to get it back. And if it gets dented, I'll get another one. Don't pretend to be appalled. That's the kind of girl I am." She grabbed my upper arm and pulled me toward the brownstone's stairs. "Come on. Let's see if we can make the cut at College Girl."

Once I had seen that College Girl was in a brownstone with a locked door, I'd come up with some sketchy excuses I could use after I pressed the button near the outside door. I needed to be prepared when a voice called out, "Who is it?" The inner door, probably warped, was closed, but the latch hadn't engaged completely. After we read COLLEGE GIRL COMPANIONS and SUITE 3 on the nameplate, we simply hurried up two flights of stairs. Despite our heels, neither of us touched the banister, probably sensing it was coated with decades of secretions from the palms of prostitutes not given to hand washing.

When we knocked on the door, a voice called out, "Who is it?" It was low-pitched, a woman's voice.

"Hi," I called back. "It's Susie."

I heard a chair scraping along a floor. Then the door opened a crack. I did my high school flutter-fingered wave. I must have appeared sufficiently adorable and nonthreatening because she opened the door.

"Hi," I said again. Andrea seemed to be taking her vow of silence seriously; all she did was smile.

The woman holding the door open about four inches was neither a college girl nor an escort anyone but a Boy Scout would touch. She looked like she was past forty and flooring it to forty-five. A fringe of deep vertical scratches radiated from her lip liner, a too thick band of crimson. Her saggy skin seemed to be pulling open her pores. "Are you Cle . . . ?" I asked, dodging the end of the name, not sure if it ended with an O or an A.

"No," she said. "Who are you?" She glanced at Andrea but decided she didn't need an S on "you." Then she looked back at me.

"I was hoping to speak with her for a minute."

"You're who?" she asked.

"I know she's so busy. I won't keep her long."

Without consultation, obviously, Andrea and I broke into our client-winning "You're Never Fully Dressed Without a

Smile" act with so much fervor it would have been impossible for the woman not to smile back. Actually, she began to, but it quickly disappeared into an "Ooh!" of recognition.

"I know who you are," she said to me. "You're his wife. I saw you in the papers. And on TV in an evening gown at some party. With him." Just as it occurred to her that the door would be better off closed—with me and Andrea on the outside of it—I pushed. Not a hostile push, like a break-in. More like a *I know you want me to come in except you're not moving fast enough* push.

"Honestly," I said, "I just want to speak to her for a minute. A quick question and I'm out of here."

"You know, the police thanked Clea for her cooperation on the case." Her voice was soft, a little husky but not a phone-sex voice. More business than pleasure. "Maybe they didn't tell you that, but she cooperated. They made a special call just to thank her."

"They did tell me. I really, really appreciate it. Look, I don't want to make trouble. I swear to you. You know the story: I'm a widow with three little boys. If I make trouble, what's going to happen to them?"

I felt sorry for her. She was overwhelmed. Maybe she'd been coached on how to deal with an obnoxious client, but she clearly didn't know what to do with me and Silent Andrea. "I'm not lying," she said. "Clea's not here. She hardly ever comes in. She monitors the calls sometimes, that's all."

"I'm told you keep records on customers." She was already shaking her head. "I know for a fact that the records are pretty extensive—for Clea's own protection."

"The records aren't here," she said, but ever since that body-language article, I'd watched out for the rampant blinking that signals a lie. *Blink, blink, blink.*

"They are here," I said calmly.

"No, they're not."

I wasn't going to get into a "They are, they're not" game that even the triplets were too sophisticated to play. On the other hand, I couldn't think of what to say next.

Not that I was conscious of it, but I must have been thinking what Grandma Ethel would do in the situation, because what I finally said was so not me: "I want to find out if at some point you might have done business with a certain gentleman. I could give you the gentleman's name, and if you would—" She was shaking her head. "If you can get me that name and show it to me and give me a copy . . . Come on, stop shaking your head. Let me finish. You can make an easy five hundred. We'll leave. Then you'll leave, say, a couple of minutes later. Just tell me which ATM to meet you at, and I'll be there. Bring a copy of whatever record you have with you, watch me withdraw five hundred dollars, and we'll do the exchange right there."

She took a long, quavering breath. She wanted the money. But then she started shaking her head again. "I can't risk it."

That was when Andrea decided not to keep quiet. "Another five hundred from me," she said. The woman barely had time to draw in her lower lip to chew on it in indecision when Andrea added, "Forget the thousand dollars. Within a few minutes, you can have *two* thousand in cash. Or a long afternoon to think of all the things you could have done with two thousand dollars. You decide."

"What's the gentleman's name?" she finally whispered.

"Gilbert John Noakes," I said. "Dr. Gilbert John Noakes."

Chapter Thirty-Three

Andrea and I nearly had twin heart attacks waiting for Ms. College Girl to show at the ATM. When she finally scurried in, head down, obviously avoiding the security cameras as if she were there to rob money rather than receive it, she opened a giant faux–patent leather tote bag that made horrible plastic-on-plastic squeaks. She handed me copies of three MasterCard statements for August, October, and November 2006 with a list of payments to College Girl. Talk about naming names: Noakes, Gilbert John. Twice he had paid five hundred and once seven hundred. I didn't want to know why the price had gone up.

That night, after a dinner featuring brisket I'd found when cleaning out the freezer, frozen after Rosh Hashanah 2008 but that everybody had loved, I put the boys to bed and met Grandma Ethel and Sparky in the den. While they watched me from the couch as if I were a one-woman play, I called Danny Cromer, the orthopedist Jonah had used for his tennis elbow, a guy he'd gone to medical school with; his name had been on Jonah's calendar. I spent a few minutes, too many, thanking him for the beautiful condolence letter he'd written. I sensed he was on the verge of telling me he had an emergency on the other line, so I said, "Danny, the last time Jonah went to see you . . ."

"Yes," he said cautiously, as any doctor in his right mind would.

"It wasn't about the tennis-elbow business, was it?" Counting on all the years of friendliness that would make him reluctant to give me the usual confidentiality speech, I quickly added, "It was the thing with his hand. He told me about it."

"Right." Still cautious.

"I don't want to put you on the spot, but I'd like to be able to reassure his parents. He told us it was nothing to be concerned about, since it wasn't anything like, whatever it's called, that bad-hand thing. But they keep talking about it. It's not exactly rational, but none of us have been lately."

"Rheumatoid arthritis? Is that what they're worrying about? I know his father's a physician. Rheumatoid arthritis can be passed down from parent to child. He's probably worried about your boys. No, this was osteoarthritis. Look, it can be a problem, especially for a surgeon who does the kind of work Jonah did."

"I didn't sense he thought it was affecting his doing surgery." I thought, *I can't believe he didn't tell me,* but then I thought, *I can believe it.* Jonah would want to know the whole picture before letting me in on it. Control. And knowing I was an anxiety queen, he wouldn't want me to agonize unless there was a need to agonize. Also, he'd been so smart about people. Not that we'd ever talked about it, but he would have known I worshiped him a little. Maybe he was afraid to seem vulnerable. Gods didn't get arthritis.

"I didn't find any loss of mobility," Danny Cromer said. "I gave him a shot and some medication for the pain. He was supposed to come back . . . Oh, Susie, I hate to be saying this. He was due to come back. We were going to go over options for treatment. Did he mention anything about how it was feeling after he saw me?"

"He said it was a huge improvement. He was so grateful."

After I thanked Danny and said goodbye, I turned to my audience. "Osteoarthritis," I told Grandma Ethel and Sparky.

"Are you going to call that Eddie back?" my grandmother asked.

"And say what? 'It turns out my husband had arthritis, and that's what he was talking about to Dorinda Dillon when he was complaining about his hand, a conversation I know about because I talked my way into Rikers Island and interviewed her under false pretenses'?"

"So what are you going to do?" Sparky asked.

For a while, all I could think of was picking at the welting on the arm of my chair. Then I went to find my handbag and returned. I searched until I found the card Lieutenant Corky Paston had given me. He answered the phone with "Lieutenant Paston."

"Hi. This is Susie Gersten. I know you probably think I'm crazy, at least if you've been talking to Eddie Huber. But let me tell you what I found out."

He wasn't having any of it. "Mrs. Gersten, you're a really nice woman. No one could have handled the situation you were in any better."

"Thank you, but—"

"To be perfectly honest, I think you need psychological counseling."

"I'm getting it." Then I told him what I'd gotten from College Girl, the copies of printouts with Gilbert John Noakes's name on them.

"Are you crazy?" The way he said it, it wasn't a half-humorous question equivalent to "Are you kidding?" "You actually went there?"

"Who else was going to do it? Now, listen, please, Lieutenant. You seem like a nice person, too. And definitely not crazy. Reasonable. Down-to-earth. So do me one favor." I heard the muffled sound of a phone being covered and him muttering to someone else. "Can't you have someone go back to Dorinda Dillon's building and take the picture of Dr. Noakes from the practice's website? Besides the doorman, there might be a porter or some other building employee who might have seen Gilbert John or dealt with him."

"I'm sorry. I really can't," he said. "The case isn't in my hands anymore."

"It can be your case if you'd just—"

He cut me off. "I honestly wish you well, Mrs. Gersten." At least he sounded regretful. But that was the end of the conversation.

After I related what Paston had said, Sparky got to wondering out loud how to get around him—there had to be a way. Grandma Ethel, on the other hand, took his "I honestly wish you well" to mean "You have my blessing in whatever you do, even though I can't officially condone it."

Fifteen minutes after Sparky's "You're beyond absurd, Eth" rejoinder, she was behind the wheel of my car, driving my grandmother and me into the city. As she pulled into a space beside a fire hydrant one block from Dorinda's apartment, Grandma Ethel told her, "Sit tight, because if you pull into a garage, it'll wind up costing fifty dollars, and it might have security cameras, so there would be proof we were in the neighborhood. Stay in the car, because you don't want to be anywhere near us. In case there's any unpleasantness, Susie and I have a fallback: We can say she's mentally unbalanced and I'm senile. But you could wind up getting disbarred in Florida for pulling a fast one in New York."

My grandmother and I strolled up and down Dorinda's block between the corner and the alleyway with the service door, trying to appear casual when turning midblock to avoid passing the doorman. After ten minutes, it began to get boring. After twenty, when all we'd done was decide the only passerby with any style savvy was an Asian deliveryman with a smartly tied black bandanna riding a bike, we began rethinking our plan. Fortunately, as we were approaching the alleyway for the thousandth time, we saw a guy in a janitor's uniform hauling out a huge can of bottles for recycling.

"Okay, you take him," Grandma Ethel said. "I'll distract the doorman." As she hurried toward the front door, walking as sure-footedly in dagger-heel leather pumps as if she were wearing Nikes, I headed down the alley to meet the porter halfway.

"My name's Ethel O'Shea," I said, and flashed my grandmother's press ID open and shut. Maybe I sounded nasal, because I wasn't breathing through my nose. Though the recyclables were in clear plastic bags, the janitor's hands were in giant leather trash-hauling gloves. I knew all I needed was one whiff of decomposing V-8 juice and I'd gag—not the best way to make friends. "I'm a reporter," I added. He had time to give me only one shake of his head—*No way I'll talk to you*—before I went on, "Sir, I truly want to keep you out of trouble."

"What do you mean?" His eyes moved beyond me toward the street, as if expecting trouble with a capital T to be loitering on the sidewalk. He looked like he was from some unhealthy Eastern European country, heavyset and pasty, with skin dotted by the faded mauve of bygone pimples.

"Look, I found out some of the details about how you let that guy into Dorinda Dillon's apartment. If you tell me the whole story, I won't name names." It occurred to me that he might not have done anything, that there might be some alternate porter or building employee. It didn't help that I couldn't read his expression, because there was nothing yet to read: He appeared to be a majorly slow thinker. "I'm sure whatever help you gave him, you didn't mean any harm by it. You seem like a very decent, honorable man."

"It didn't have nothing to do with the doctor getting killed," he said. He was hard to understand both because he was a natural-born mumbler and because his accent squished words: "Din ha' noth' t' do." "It happened at least a week before that." I nodded sympathetically. "Seven, eight, maybe ten days. And this guy—"

"*This* guy," I said, and showed him the picture of Gilbert John Noakes that I'd downloaded from the Manhattan Aesthetics website. I had a few others in my handbag, photos taken over the years at various conventions and parties, in case the formal portrait drew a blank. I'd made copies for Grandma Ethel, too. But this one was all I needed. The porter was already nodding.

"Yeah, that guy. A hundred-buck haircut if I ever saw one. But I felt sorry for him. He was panicked. He left some important papers up in Dorinda's apartment. I didn't call her Dorinda to her face. I'm just using that with you."

"Right."

"The guy was scared. What if she threw them out? The papers, I mean. What if she tried to sell them to the competition? I felt bad for him, and I said, 'Okay, wait till she goes out for her walk. Tell me where they are, and I'll run up to get them.'"

"Did you?"

"No. He said not to because he didn't know where she could have put them. If he looked, he'd recognize the envelope they were in right away, but I wouldn't, because it didn't have no writing on it. So could he please just get the key, and he'd go in and out fast. He swore if it took longer than three minutes, he'd come back down even if he didn't find them. He said, 'Trust me. I'm very neat. She'll never know I was there.' I did trust him because, you know, he was a really class act. Expensive coat. That's how you tell. Some guys pay a thousand bucks for a suit but buy a crap coat. Not him."

"So he waited there until—"

"No," the porter said. "I told him, 'She goes out every day late afternoon, so get back here at a quarter to four, and you'll be okay.'"

"So he came back?" I asked.

"He came back. Said he might not recognize her if she had clothes on . . . kind of funny, but I understood what he was saying, you know? So I should be on the lookout and signal him when she went out the front door and down the block. He stood across the street, but like right opposite here, because he couldn't go through the front door, past the doorman. He had to use the service entrance. It was better anyway, because I could go right to the room where we keep the apartment keys and give him Dorinda's and then take him up in the service elevator."

"Did you wait for him in the service elevator on her floor while he went in with her key?"

"Strange you should say that. That's what I wanted to do. But give him credit: He was shrewd. He said I should wait outside the service door, right at the end of this alley here, by the sidewalk. That way I could watch the front door, in case she came back early. I told him she never did, but he said, 'You can't be too careful.' Anyway, he gave me his cell number and said I should call him if I saw her."

"Do you still have the number, by any chance?"

He gave a loud "Huh!" like he was reading an instruction: *Insert laugh here*. In case I didn't get the humor, he added, "You gotta be kidding."

"No, I'm not. I even think I could convince my editor to come up with something for it if you do."

He considered the proposition by resting his mouth on the back of his hand—which was covered with the garbage glove. Finally, he said, "No. I threw it out. I mean, the guy came back down in two, three minutes. What did I need it for?"

"Did he find his papers?"

"Yeah. In a plain white envelope, so I wouldn't have found it unless it was the only envelope in her apartment. But he said he knew it right away and it was where he'd left it."

I nodded. "Just out of curiosity, did he give you something

for the trouble you went to?" He didn't say anything. I smiled. "You said he was a class act."

He smiled back. "A little something."

I'd already used a smile, a tossing back of hair as it fell into my eyes: your basic Flirting with Repulsive Guys When You Need to Get Something from Them Fast 101. But now, before the porter lifted the giant can filled with recyclables and started shlepping it toward the street, I had to get beyond the fundamentals to practically graduate-level. That meant a longing gaze that would display the wonders of pale green eyes and long, thick lashes and also would communicate the realization that I was so amazed by his masculinity, I was on the verge of falling in love. Add to that some nibbling of the lower lip to express a mix of hesitancy and embarrassment. It was a feminist mother's worst nightmare.

After the nibbling business, I said, "I don't know how to ask you this."

With something approaching grandeur, the porter said, "Go ahead."

"I've gone totally blank on your name."

"Oh. Pavel. Pavel Ginchev." He even spelled it for me.

Five minutes later, Grandma Ethel and I were walking back to the car. "I got bubkes from the doorman," she announced. She sounded both dispirited and surprised, as in *Life should offer more in the way of excitement.*

"I got a little something," I said. "Like Gilbert John getting the key to Dorinda's apartment and going in there alone."

"Wasn't it one of those special security keys you can't get copied unless . . ." She paused. With a great smile, she added, ". . . unless you're a high-class guy who can intimidate a lock-smith—and make him your friend for life with a few hundred bucks. Or a few thou. *That* would get you the key to anywhere you want to go."

Chapter Thirty-Four

"Nothing's wrong," I told my cousin Scott Rabinowitz the following night. "I'm healthy. I'm strong. Okay?"

"Okay," he said. Whatever the gene was for drama, he did not have it.

"But I need to ask you a favor . . . with you knowing I'm in really good shape."

"Okay."

"I need to make out a new will."

"Right. You should. Whenever circumstances change—"

"This is a huge thing I'm asking, Scott, so take as much time as you need before answering. You don't need to tell me now."

"Okay."

"Right now, if anything should, God forbid and all that, happen to me, the boys would go to Theo, my brother-in-law. I don't think he's steady enough to take on a responsibility like that."

Scott shrugged. "I don't really know him, but if that's what you think . . . Oh, you mean you're asking me to take the boys?"

"Yes. But I need you to feel free to refuse if you can't see yourself in that role, or if you can't take that kind of responsibility because you have other plans for your life."

"You think I could handle it?"

"Not counting me, you handle them better than anyone." What I left out was that I'd called Liz Holbreich and asked her to look into my cousin's background — and told her the reasons I was asking. When she got back to me, she said she'd found absolutely nothing to rule him out. I went on, "The chances of anything bad happening to me are . . . Well, you're the accountant, so you're better with numbers."

"You're likely to stick around for a while," Scott said.

"Please take time and think about it. And if you say no, I'll find someone else, so don't let that be a concern."

"I'd have to take off a few pounds," he said. "So I don't strain my heart. I couldn't afford to be one of those guys on the D train who drops dead standing up during rush hour because there's no place to fall."

And then he said he was honored that I thought so much of him. He was crazy about the boys. And I should live and be well, but yes, he was willing.

Late that week, I decided I was going to see if Eddie Huber and the forces of justice would take the copies of Gilbert John's MasterCard payments to College Girl seriously enough to check them out. I knew that having told Lieutenant Paston, he wouldn't keep it a secret. He was a pro. He'd want to look into it. So what was going on? Bureaucratic constipation? Being pathologically afraid to commit a mistake? Could Eddie possibly think I was so crazy that I'd made up a story and forged the statements? I needed to do something to get her to move. If not, I would have to hand over my information to my underemployed family press spokesperson, Kimberly Dijkstra, and let her make it public. I had to act.

At some point while driving between Shorehaven and Park Avenue early that Saturday, maybe I came up with a plan. I could have had one before I left. But a few minutes after ten, as I was picking through Jonah's key ring and trying each one on the private entrance into Manhattan Aesthetics' office, I suddenly wondered, *What am I doing here?* It wasn't reassuring that I couldn't come up with an answer. Except for emergencies and treating politicians and celebrities who didn't want to risk being seen within a mile of a plastic surgeon, the offices were closed on Saturdays.

The private door, down the long corridor and around the corner from the official entrance, was for the doctors, so they could avoid walking through the waiting room and getting waylaid. Naturally, it was the exit of choice for bandaged post-op patients who looked like they were starring in *Revenge of the Mummy*; they could be led out without traumatizing prospective surgical candidates.

The keys jingled as if they were trying to get the attention of all New York. Finally, the fourth one I tried not only fit into the lock but turned it. I was in. The buzzing alarm that greeted me was no big deal, because whenever I went into the office with Jonah, he'd mutter 3-3-3-3, his passcode. I'd once said, "You'd think someone would figure out a guy with triplets would use threes." His answer had been tight lips.

Only after the third 3 did it occur to me: *Oh God, what if they deleted Jonah's passcode from the system?* The alarm kept ringing: one second, two seconds, much too long. There I was, in some bizarre fight-or-flight paralysis, when . . . at last, silence. By the time I could breathe again, I had already turned the corner and was walking through the long corridor toward Jonah's office. The usual lights, a gentle, flattering pink, were dimmed to near-darkness, giving the pale peachy-beige walls a spooky glow, as if they were alive.

I didn't know what to expect once I opened Jonah's office door. I was clutching the keys in my fist so they wouldn't jangle, and

I slid out one key with my thumb. As I put it into the lock and grasped the knob, the door opened so fast that I stumbled inside. I ran my hand along the left wall for the light switch, the standard place, but all I felt was a wall sanded to a baby-skin finish appropriate for a plastic surgeon's workspace. The dim light from the corridor didn't shine into the room, but I could see the big things were still there: Jonah's Eames desk with its multicolored panels, chairs, a computer monitor so thin it looked two-dimensional.

I patted and stroked the wall for what seemed like hours until I discovered the light switch, ridiculously low on the right-hand side, as if it had been designed to be reached by preschoolers. As I switched it on and closed the door behind me, I had one of those irrational widow moments when I said to myself, *Don't forget to ask Jonah why the switch is in such a crazy place.*

When I walked over to the desk, I knew immediately that other people had been there. Of course the police would have. The pens in the cylindrical wire cup leaned this way and that; for Jonah, they'd stood at attention. There were papers, too, in reasonably neat piles, though if Jonah had ever left papers on the desk—a dubious proposition—the outer edges of every side of every sheet would have been in perfect alignment. I couldn't make myself sit in his chair, but I stood leaning against the narrow oak rectangle that was the top of the desk and checked out the papers. Nothing unusual: printouts of his notes on patients, a report from a journal about impending thrilling developments in dissolvable sutures. The desk had only one drawer, for files, but even though I looked carefully from A through Z, I found nothing but the alphabetical file dividers themselves.

I'd made up my mind before I got to the office that if Jonah's computer was still there, I wouldn't turn it on. Too big a risk, because there might be some record on the server or network or whatever they called it that would flash an alarm: *Dr. Gersten's computer has been accessed by unauthorized person or persons unknown, but I'll bet you a hundred it's the wife.* I walked around the cool, modern office, angular and spare, so unlike our house, but Jonah always said that his office was like his work, precise and carefully thought out—though he hoped that, unlike his surgery, it wasn't sterile. He said it was great, returning to the warmth, tradition, and layered complexity of the house. I'd laughed and said I'd always dreamed of a husband who could say "layered complexity" and not sound like an ass.

I barely looked at his walls because I didn't like the painting, some streaks of color and scribbles by an artist trying and failing to be an abstract expressionist like Cy Twombly; when I said something diplomatic like "It's pedestrian," Jonah told me he'd already paid for it and told me I was hypercritical and should understand there was a difference between office art and personal art. I'd said something like "bullshit," and that was the end of the discussion.

The only thing left to look at was his narrow built-in closet, a woodworking craftsman's elegant interpretation of a high school locker. I stood before it, I guess looking a little bit like the apes staring at that big black monolith in *2001*. It looked so plain, spare even, yet so scary. There was no knob, but as I reached out to the door's edge to pull it open, my heart was pounding, as if to warn me: *Don't!* Maybe I half expected a dead body to keel over, or a jack-in-the-box with a giant U of a smile painted on his face. When I did pull the door outward, all I found was an umbrella and the pair of black rubber pull-on boots Jonah kept there in case it snowed. God, I hated that he'd died in the winter and never gotten to see the spring.

Just so I wouldn't be angry at myself later, I felt inside the boots. Jonah had been a great one for hiding cash or keys under the orthotics of his sneakers, on the theory that even second-rate burglars wouldn't look in smelly places. The boots were empty. Then I took the umbrella and, turning it right side up, opened it only a little because of the superstition that it was bad luck to open an umbrella indoors. I was thinking, *Yeah, I never opened*

*an umbrella inside in my whole life. Did it bring me lots of luck
in the husband-longevity department?* As I started to close it,
something floated out: a news clipping from *The Wall Street
Journal.* The headline read, REDLEAF CAPITAL'S GRAYSON ASKED
TO RESIGN. The dateline was—even I could do the math—six
days before Jonah was killed.

It was no big story, just another financial hotshot getting
payback for making lousy investments with hundreds of millions of dollars of other people's money, though at one point
Redleaf Capital's holdings were "well over $1 billion." As far
as I knew, there was no Grayson in Jonah's life. Still, that didn't
mean very much, because why would Jonah—if it was indeed
Jonah who'd neatly cut out the article—want to hide something
like it in an umbrella?

In one of those out-of-the-clear-blue-sky moments, it hit me
that when I'd been taking Detective Sergeant Timothy Coleman
around the house, I'd looked in the Einstein biography on Jonah's
night table. He'd had a list, with razor blades and shoe polish on
it and a note, *check red cap.* I'd assumed it meant red capsules.

I pulled out my cell and called Andrea's house. I knew she
would be at Florabella, but I didn't care, because I also knew it
was the one phone line Fat Boy would answer.

"Hey, Hughie," I said, "it's Susie. Did you ever hear of something called Redleaf Capital?"

I realized I should have said "How are you?" but my lack
of graciousness did not appear to be noticed. "Hey, Susie, my
wife's working while you're lounging around eating chocolate
truffles? How y'doing? Redleaf? Fucking loser hedge fund,
one of the greatest of the great Greenwich loser hedge funds.
Something in the Connecticut water, maybe. Or all those Irish
Catholics and Jews trying too hard to be Wasps up there caused
massive brain damage."

"You know how Jonah and you sometimes talked about
investments?"

"Sure."

One of the things I liked about Fat Boy was that he made no attempt to think of what he should answer about a guy who'd been murdered. He just said it right out. "Did he ever say anything about investing in Redleaf?"

"No, why would he do such a stupid thing? Anyone who knew shit about money would have the brains to stay away from that stinker. Even when it was good, it was bad. Not that it ever really was good." Fat Boy took a fraction of a second for a diplomatic pause. "He didn't put his money there, did he?"

"No, not that I know of. Not from anything I've seen from the accountants or that Jonah ever mentioned."

"So why are you asking me about a fund that was headed for the crapper two, three years ago and everyone knew it except the fund manager and the investors?"

"Did that guy Grayson do anything criminal?" I asked.

"No. Just dumb, arrogant—the usual stuff. So fucking predictable. Listen, I'd be shocked out of my mind if Jonah—"

I said, "I have to go," because just then the door opened. And there was Gilbert John Noakes.

Even under the best of circumstances, he had a right to be livid about my being there without consent. I, of course, had a right to be scared shitless over what might happen. For too long a moment, nothing did.

Just as he was saying "Susie" and taking a deep breath, I became more alert than I'd ever been in my life. Every cell in my body, simultaneously, was on duty. There was just him and me, which I knew was really he and I, but either way, that added up to only two. His words, all but frozen solid, came out: "Is there any possible explanation for you . . ." I realized two wasn't a good number because it was Gilbert John against me. If he had nothing to do with Jonah's murder other than a history with Dorinda Dillon, then I was destined for more boring, elderly chicken dinners with Coral and him. If all the law-enforcement people were wrong and I was right, I was in major danger.

Something inside me told me I had to up the number from two to three. So I brought in somebody else and talked so fast I might have taken lessons from Fat Boy: "I was talking with the forensic accountant Jonah went to see." That got Gilbert John's attention. It also let him know there was at least one more person in the equation. "He was telling me about a thirty-seven-thousand-dollar check that turned out to be from—"

"Phoebe Kingsley," Gilbert John said. "I would like to discuss that with you."

"Fine."

"Might we go, sit perhaps, someplace else. Unless you would be more comfortable here in Jonah's office. I would understand completely."

On one hand, I was scared that if we walked into the corridor together, he might have a couple of hired goons waiting to do something terrible. He might even hit me over the head with one of his exquisite mosaics that lined the walls. Naturally, my mouth went dry with that dirty-penny taste, even though I couldn't remember ever sucking a penny, so how would I know? On the other hand, could he possibly let anything happen to me if he realized somewhere out there was a forensic accountant who knew about a check made out to him by Phoebe Kingsley? And I did want to get out of Jonah's office. It felt wrong to be in here talking with this man, almost in a religious sense, a desecration, like when you drop the Bible on the floor.

No goons, no Attack of the Mosaics. We wound up in the employees' lunchroom, a small area with a table and chairs, refrigerator, and a soda machine I'd always felt was cheap—Manhattan Aesthetics could offer employees free sodas—but Jonah said they had to charge fifty cents each or . . . I couldn't remember what, just that it had sounded lame.

Gilbert John sat in a not too terrible plastic scoop chair and said, "I have to confess to something."

I nodded and managed to say, "Please, go ahead." I wished more than anything that Grandma Ethel could be sitting beside me, squeezing my hand, signaling, *You're doing fine.*

"The last discussion I ever had with Jonah was an argument about that check. I was sick at heart after it happened, and when Jonah went missing, and then we found out . . ." Gilbert John was pale, that greenish white people turn when they're sick and dizzy. Still, if he had started crying or gotten really emotional, I would have almost laughed. Instead, he said, after swallowing hard and seeming to get a grip on himself, "Jonah was a very balanced individual and a very responsible one. But he was also under a great deal of pressure. Sometimes I felt I was adding to his pressure by not being as active in the practice as I had been. But more and more, Jonah had a tendency to rush to judgment—though fortunately, not when it came to his patients. He was a fine, thorough surgeon."

"What was the argument about? What do you think there could have been about the check that made you think he rushed to judgment? Because I've known him longer and better than you have, I've seen him in every possible situation, and I never once witnessed a rush to judgment."

Maybe I sounded angrier than I meant to sound, because Gilbert John said, "Jonah was an extraordinarily rational man, but if I may contradict you in one small way, you did not see him in much of his professional life, only in its, shall we say, social aspects, in which a spouse is appropriate." I kept looking straight at him; if he'd had half an iota of sense, he'd have realized I was thinking that his spouse, the lovely Coral, was never appropriate. "Jonah was short on time, as well as patience. I believe I might have been traveling when this check arrived. Rather than waiting until I returned, or even phoning me, he took the check that indeed was made out to me to a forensic accountant. This was Jonah Gersten, a man I mentored, brought into my practice, cared for very . . . much."

"But can't you see—"

"No, I really can't. I've tried. Not that it matters anymore, because it was one small incident in a long and deeply felt relationship. But had he asked, I could have told him Phoebe Kingsley was—how best to put it?—a somewhat unbalanced woman. She kept harping, 'People will talk.' Nothing I said could convince her that our nurses, the office staff, are fully aware of the value of silence and of the patient's right to privacy. I explained, in the most conciliatory way possible, that we had dealings with patients far more celebrated than she and that none had any cause for complaint either with the results of their surgery or with our discretion. Mrs. Kingsley was under the distinctly mistaken impression that the way to ensure her surgery being hush-hush was to make out a check to me, to me personally."

"Did you ever explain that to him?" I asked.

"Of course I did. In that last conversation. Alas, Jonah's so-called forensic accountant discovered Phoebe Kingsley had some sort of secret fund, and from there the matter took on a life of its own in Jonah's mind. By the time he came to me for an explanation, he did not want one. All he seemed to want to do was accuse me of dirty dealings." Gilbert John rose from his plastic chair in his elegant fashion, as if from a throne. "All through this talk now," he went on, "I've wanted to say to you, 'Jonah was like a son to me.' I held back because it sounded so fatuous, so histrionic. The truth of the matter is, he was like a son to me." He seemed about to come toward me, but then he turned, nodded goodbye, and hurried from the room as if on the way to an emergency.

What began as a morning head-clearing walk the next day, Sunday, while the boys were at a birthday party, ended with me ringing Andrea's doorbell, the chimes of which would have been appropriate to Westminster Abbey. When I heard the heavy tread coming down the stairs, I almost turned and ran. Either I flaked out for a few seconds, or Fat Boy was faster on his feet than I'd thought.

He opened the door and said, "She's at some hotel, Four Seasons, Ritz-Carlton, in the city because some old ladies from France who embroider things come every year and she has to pick out new linens. What is that, sheets or tablecloths?"

"Probably both," I said.

"Economic stimulus. Who needs the Treasury or the fucking Fed when Andrea Brinckerhoff gets going?" He scratched the gargantuan belly beneath his lavender Polo shirt and invited me in.

We sat upstairs in his office in front of all his TV screens, Fat Boy in his recliner, his bare feet with little curlicues of blond hair on top of each toe hanging over the footrest. I sat a foot away, in a smaller chair that also reclined, although I didn't take advantage.

I filled him in on what had happened with Gilbert John and asked him what he thought. He said, "It's like this with coincidences. One, okay. More than one, a James Bond movie. Get what I'm saying?"

"Not totally," I said.

"Not at all, you mean. So let me explain. The Phoebe check, okay, maybe, could be. But then College Girls and Dorinda? Then add to that Redleaf Capital, because ten minutes after I got off the phone with you, what do I have up on my monitor but a list of Redleaf's investors, past and present. Not to toot my own horn, because I don't have to with you, you knowing I'm . . ." He shrugged.

"What are you going to say?" I asked. "'Aw shucks, well, I'm darn smart'?"

"I was trying to be charming. That well-socialized-modesty

shit. Forget it. I'm brilliant. You know it, I know it. But brilliance is one thing, and getting a confidential list like that in ten minutes on the weekend is fucking off the charts. You've got your dumb look on. You probably lost your train of thought, which people do all the time with me, so this is where I'm at. I looked at the list. Jonah was never a Redleaf investor. No Gersten in the history of the world was ever an investor with them, which speaks well for the family. Now, I'll tell you who was and is an investor in Redleaf Capital: Gilbert John Noakes. Not a high-rolling investor like a lot of the shmucks who sank their money into that fund. But Noakes's original investment of two point five mil has a current value of three hundred thousand and change. With a guy like him, that's real money, a real goddamn fucking hit. And for a guy like me, this information is just another deposit in Gilbert John's ever growing coincidence account. The guy is feeling short of cash. Desperate, maybe."

"But there was something very believable when he said that Jonah was like a son to him."

"Susie, ever hear of filicide?" He didn't give me time to answer, which I might have in an hour or two. "Filicide. The killing of one's child."

Two days later, Eddie Huber finally called to say my copies of Gilbert John's MasterCard payments to College Girl checked out. The last time he had used the service was 2006. But two weeks before Jonah died, Gilbert John had called and said he'd wanted a new girl, someone he hadn't used before. He'd arranged to pay cash. He didn't want anything charged to a credit card, even though it would appear as College Data Research Services.

They got him Dorinda Dillon. A few hours before their scheduled date, Gilbert John called the service to say he couldn't make it. However, there was a 20 percent cancellation fee, so he had a street-level messenger service deliver an envelope with the cash. He hadn't gotten any sex from Dorinda. He hadn't even met her. But he had her name and address.

"We'll keep you advised on the progress of the case," Eddie Huber said to me. Not that I was expecting a thank-you note, but she could have said something like "Good work" or "We would appreciate your not mentioning our little investigatory oversights to CNN."

The life that I was stuck with and blessed with went on. I worked at Florabella, went back to my book group, where, luckily, I'd missed the session on *The Idiot*, interviewed several nannies from what Babs called "the only possible agency" in an effort to replace Ida and Ingvild when they went back to Norway. One nanny seemed really great, but after she met the boys, she said she didn't want to work on Long Island.

After Passover at my in-laws', where Dashiell climbed their bookshelves to toss down a few pre-Columbian statues so the three of them could play a Baby Moses game, I took them and Ida and Ingvild to a hotel in South Beach for the rest of the vacation. We spent half the time at Grandma Ethel and Sparky's. I fantasized, briefly, about opening a Florabella Tropical, but I knew I had to go home. Before I left, I tried and failed to convince my grandmother to have some sort of reconciliation with my mother.

"Fine," she said. "I'll call and say, 'Hello, Sherry, this is your mother. I'm sorry I left you with Lenny. Have a nice life. Goodbye.'"

"Don't you feel—"

"No," she snapped. "I don't feel."

Grandma Ethel came to New York a week later and sat with me in Eddie Huber's office. Gilbert John Noakes had agreed to plead guilty. But as part of the deal, he had to sit with me, face-to-face, and tell me what had happened. The other part of the deal was that during his fifteen to twenty-five years in prison, he would be allowed to do mosaic work for four hours a week, as long as he maintained good behavior.

Grandma Ethel and I were led to chairs across from Eddie Huber. Her desk was bare, and she seemed vulnerable, like a soldier without a weapon. I guessed it was a security precaution. Gilbert John was seated on one side of the room, about eight feet from us. His posture had initially appeared relaxed, close to lounging, especially considering that besides being handcuffed to the arms of the chair and wearing irons on his ankles with a very short chain between them, he had a cop on either side of him, another in front of the window, and a fourth guarding the door. But something in his head must have pinged, *Ladies present!* and his back reflexively straightened.

"I can't tell you how sorry I am about this," he told me in his rich, gentlemanly voice.

"Tell me what happened," I said.

"Where to begin?" Maybe he had an inner voice-over saying, *Everyone leaned forward expectantly,* because when no one reacted, he sighed and said, "It's like this. Over the years, Jonah and I had talked about holding all our tension in our hands." He folded his hands into fists and squeezed them. I had no idea if he was aware of what he was doing. "I saw Jonah rubbing his hand in the offices several times and could see he was in pain."

"Did you know Jonah was suspicious of you?" I asked.

"I wasn't sure. But I pride myself in being perceptive. I knew he was concerned about our inventory shrinkage. And then there was the check from that dreadful Phoebe woman. Do you know what she told me the GP Fund stood for? Gorgeous Phoebe. I knew it would be only a matter of time before . . . I suppose there's no need to go into detail. I realized Jonah was putting it all together, which, as you can imagine, was quite troubling to me. I had no idea he had already begun looking into it in such an organized fashion. In passing, I told him I knew a brilliant massage therapist who had studied in India and did ayurvedic hand massage on the top surgeons of New York. I said I myself had just been to her and that I couldn't stop raving. No one could."

"And then," Grandma Ethel said.

"I bribed the building's porter to get in and get the key. I made an imprint in modeling clay. I knew it would be dangerous to tape a door latch closed. That's how the Watergate burglars were discovered, taping back the locks—a piece of historical trivia. But I did use a high-viscosity skin adhesive to glue the latches of the doors on both the service entrance and the room where they keep the tenants' keys. Marvelous stuff. And it readily cleaned off with a solvent, acetone. However, the debossment of the key in the clay was sufficient, though at the risk of sounding crass, it cost me a fortune to get a copy." He leaned forward to me. It burned me that they had allowed him to put on his own clothes, that they hadn't brought him to the DA's office in a prison jumpsuit. "I know you think I'm terrible. You're right."

"Keep talking," I said.

"I told Jonah I had my secretary make an appointment for him, but I did it myself and entered it on his calendar. I was terribly nervous he might refuse to go, or might not show up. The day before Jonah's appointment with Dorinda, when she went for a walk—the porter told me she went out once a day—I let myself in and looked around."

"Weren't you worried you'd run into the porter?" Grandma Ethel asked.

The small smile that made its appearance and quickly vanished was one I'd seen so often during the years of Jonah's partnership with him: Gilbert John, self-satisfied. "One has to take risks in this sort of enterprise, but risks can be minimized. I called the doorman from my cell phone, taking care to press star-six-seven. That blocks the caller ID, you know. I told him, 'You need to get the porter up to the tenth-floor trash room this minute!' in a very irate manner. I waited three minutes and then took a deep breath and hurried in via the service door. No porter, as I'd expected . . . or at least hoped."

"All right, so you got up there," I said. "Then what?"

"I found her scissors. I sharpened them. The following afternoon, when she went out again, thank goodness, I waited down the street a bit, coat collar up, brim of an old felt fedora lowered so I was not recognized. Finally, I saw the porter. I knew I would eventually. Again a risk, but he was slow-moving, to say nothing of slow-thinking. When he came out the service door with a huge can of recyclables and was setting it on the curb, I rushed down the alleyway, let myself in, and took the service elevator upstairs, taking care to send it back down. I secreted myself in Dorinda's front closet. I'd planned on sneaking up on them, knocking her out with a stun gun, then quickly slitting Jonah's carotid artery with a blade of the scissors." He paused. "I'm awfully sorry to burden you with these details, Susie, but I was told that I had to be completely forthright. What surprised me was that Jonah caught on so soon to what Dorinda actually was. He was so quick-witted. Dorinda came back to the closet incredibly fast to get Jonah's coat. The stun gun fit too tightly in my coat pocket, and I couldn't get it out fast enough. Instead, I knocked her out with the bottom of the electric broom."

"You cleaned off the broom, didn't you?" Grandma Ethel said. "And then vacuumed somewhere it wouldn't show to get the brush dirty again."

"Yes!" He sounded pleased that someone was recognizing his cleverness. "Actually, I dumped out the vacuum's contents and swept them up again." Then his eyes returned to me. "Certainly, I have no expectation that you will approve of me in any way, but I hope someday you recognize that was fast thinking."

"It was fast thinking," I agreed. "But it wasn't good thinking. If it had been good, you wouldn't be in leg irons now, facing four hours a week of mosaics followed by . . . what? Freedom after twenty-five years with no money and jailhouse dentures?

Death." He tried for a nonchalant shrug, but the handcuffs threw off his balance so only one shoulder rose. I went on, "You'll have your art. But most likely, they'll give you cheapo grout."

I sketched that picture, if unconsciously, knowing Gilbert John was at least as visual as I was. He wouldn't be able to resist coloring it and filling in the details: the inferior, gritty grout; the no-deodorant-for-me prison guard coming to take him back to his cell even though he had hardly begun to work.

"Come on," Eddie Huber said to him, "you know the parameters of our agreement. Tell Mrs. Gersten what happened after you struck Dorinda Dillon with the electric broom."

I was annoyed to see Gilbert John's back relax into a slumped C in relief at her interruption. He said, "After hitting the woman, as you might imagine, I was very shaken. Jonah was strong, younger, but he was not prepared. As it turned out, neither was I. I was unable to open the scissors to slit his throat. So I had to stab him. Is there anything else you'd like to know?"

I didn't answer. I just gave him a look I hoped he'd never forget, though I knew he would. I couldn't manage a thank-you to Eddie Huber, but I gave her a nod. Together, Grandma Ethel and I walked out.

Outside, in the bright sun of early spring, I said, "This knowing doesn't make anything better."

"Did you think it would?" my grandmother asked.

"No. But I had to hear it."

"Please, you don't have to explain to me. How could you allow that sociopath in bespoke suiting to get away with murder and not have to face you? Not just you, the wife. You, the person who wanted to know the truth about what happened to Jonah."

"It wasn't so much truth-seeking as I couldn't stand the thought of that repulsive, stupid, useless, innocent hooker rotting in jail . . . not that she'll ever do any good on the outside. But I had to do something."

"I guess that's what ethics are," she said. "Or is it 'what ethics is'?"

"I think it's 'are,'" I said, "but I'm not sure."

"If I still had *Talk of Miami*, I'd have an intern look it up," Grandma Ethel said. She was downcast for an instant, but then she took my arm and smiled. "So, what's the best restaurant around here? I'm talking four stars. I'm paying."

"I don't have much of an appetite," I told her.

"It doesn't mean you don't eat. Life goes on, toots, whether you like the way it goes or not. The best a girl can do is mind her ethics—and eat a nice lunch."

Acknowledgments

True, this is a work of fiction. The novelist needs imagination, the passion to write the story she most wants to read, and talent. Facts, too. Make an avoidable error and some knowledgeable reader will smack palm to forehead in annoyance—and at the same time be pulled out of the universe of the novel. Facts also matter because, as author, the more I know about an aspect of the world I'm creating, the more authentic and authoritative my writing will be. So thanks to the following generous and patient individuals who answered all sorts of questions. However, when their facts did not fit my fiction, I went for the story. The inaccuracies are mine, not theirs.

Joan Smith of Joan Smith Flowers in Port Washington, New York, is a gifted floral designer whose work is gorgeous and sophisticated yet cheery. When I decided to put Susie Gersten in the flower business, I began by asking Joan about her work. Through her generosity, I actually wound up "helping" in the back room of her shop, learning some of the lingo, getting hands-on experience. What fun! I loved the work—plus Joan is a hoot and a half.

I can write short and long fiction, screenplays, op-ed pieces, and book reviews, but I learned I cannot write a clever tabloid headline. After I turned out a series of clunkers, I called Andie Coller—journalist, pundit, and former headline writer—for help. Not only did she do what I could not but she did it expertly and breathtakingly fast.

Jules B. Kroll, founder of the global risk-consulting giant Kroll Inc., told me everything I needed to know about missing persons and private investigative agencies. He was thoughtful, patient, and a charming raconteur. He also was kind enough to introduce me to his former colleague Annie Cheney, who offered me some sound insights.

When my great pal from high school and college, Suzy Sonenberg, told me her son Dan was going to be the father of triplets, I knew his wife, Alex Sax, was someone I needed to ask, well, what it's like to be pregnant with triplets. Alex was informative, knowledgeable, and delightful. (And their three sons are adorable!)

I'm indebted to my friend Adrienne Arsht for reading a draft of my manuscript. She is not only smart about life and art, but about dangling modifiers. And thanks to my pals Victoria Skurnick and Bob Wyatt for prodding me until I came up with this novel's title.

I'm also grateful to Dr. Andrew Jacono for answering my questions about how plastic surgeons work. He is a certified good guy, the national chairman of the Face to Face Committee for the American Academy of Facial Plastic and Reconstructive Surgery, which offers pro bono consultation and surgery to victims of domestic violence. For the past six years, he has chaired About Face: Making Changes, an annual Long Island benefit for survivors of domestic violence.

Also, thank you to Dr. Janice Asher, Dr. Gerard A. Catanese, Samantha Zises Cohen, Susan Lawton, Anthony Lepsis and Brian Whitney of North Hills Garden Design, Lara Zises, and Susan Zises.

The following people made generous donations to charities by "buying" characters' names in this novel: Maureen Ferrari, Lizbeth Holbreich, Gary and Corky Paston, and Chris Pierce (for her mother, Eddie Huber).

I am lucky to have two of the greats of the book business on my side: Nan Graham, my editor, and Susan Moldow, the publisher of Scribner. I'm also indebted to Katherine Monaghan, Paul Whitlatch, and their colleagues. Giga-thanks also to Susanne Kirk; she was a blessing in my life.

I am grateful to the staffs of the Port Washington (New York) Public Library and the Brooklyn Public Library.

My assistant, Ronnie Gavarian, has been a professional caterer, legal assistant, and jewelry maven. In my house we say "Ronnie can do anything." And she does everything, from copyediting to research to cake decorating, brilliantly.

Richard Pine is a super literary agent and a gracious human being. I'm glad he's in my corner.

I keep learning from my wonderful children and in-law children: Elizabeth and Vincent Picciuto; Andy and Leslie Stern Abramowitz.

In ancient days, writers of comedy had Thalia. My muses are Nathan and Molly Abramowitz and Charles and Edmund Picciuto.

And after two score–plus years, my husband, Elkan Abramowitz, remains the best person in the world.

About the Author

Susan Isaacs, novelist, essayist, and screenwriter, was born in Brooklyn and educated at Queens College. Her twelve novels include *Compromising Positions, Close Relations, Almost Paradise, Shining Through,* and *Past Perfect.* A recipient of the Writers for Writers Award and the John Steinbeck Award, Isaacs serves as chairman of the board of Poets & Writers and is a past president of Mystery Writers of America. Her fiction has been translated into thirty languages. She lives on Long Island with her husband.

About the Author

A Bonus Essay by Susan Isaacs on Her Inspiration for As Husbands Go

She began as someone for whom bravery was defined as electing to wear wide-leg pants in a season of skinny crops. Was there a way for such a woman not only to think courageously but to act it? Or was it simply too late?

I've got a license to daydream. Being a novelist is the adult version of a kid creating a make-believe world. But unlike a child, a writer of fiction has to come up with a structured story, one that has as much meaning for others as it has for her.

There is no "right" way to begin a novel, but for me, plot has to wait. The character comes first. Some new person comes strolling into my head asking I write his or her story. If I ignore them they insist. If I mutter, *I don't think so,* even the quietest ones get pushy: *Just do it!* They're convinced they picked the right writer for the job and they don't like resistance.

I guess I picked them, too—no matter who they are or how unlikely a character-author pair we seem at first. Slowly, we form a working relationship. They begin to confide in me. I listen, ask questions. Gradually, it becomes a conversation that continues throughout the writing of their (fictional) memoir.

Having said all that, *As Husbands Go* didn't happen that way. The would-be protagonist who came striding into my consciousness made me want to plead with her *For God's sake, find some other novelist!* But I couldn't whip up the courage because—I'm almost embarrassed to say it—this new, ultra-cool character in my head was too intimidating to challenge.

Not that she seemed hostile, loathsome, or even unlikable. In fact, she was the 2010 version of the American dream, female division: devoted mother (of four-year-old triplets, no less), loving wife. She had a successful, non-husband-threatening career as a floral designer, along with great looks and an enviable body. Money was no problem. Oh, and she had sublime taste. She stirred up every idiotic insecurity I'd experienced between sixth grade and my fiftieth birthday. Looking at her, my mind's eye flickered uneasily. Talk about statuesque! I noted that her height and model-sleekness were enhanced by Jean Paul Gaultier jeans and Louboutin stilettos. My normal protection against such blatant elegance would have been to embrace the Me = Genuine, She = Superficial defense, which allows me to congratulate myself for not being the sort who'd spend eight hundred dollars on shoes.

What kept me interested in her was puzzlement. Why was some empty suit (albeit a Prada) bothering me? I was a novelist, after all, not a stylist. And why did I need her? Did I want to spend the next two years growing progressively wearier of her 'tude, sublime appearance, and overt self-confidence? How could I explore the depths of a character when there seemed to be only shallowness?

Still, she got me wondering (not for the first time) what it must be like to be able to get along on your looks. Is it a perpetual high? Do women like this character merely glide through life, never experiencing the rough patches necessary for developing moral fiber? Were the people she charmed so preoccupied with her surface that they never challenged her ideas or values—letting her remain an exquisitely wrapped but empty package? Or were beautiful people no different from everybody else—aside from being capable of finding pleasure when shopping for bathing suits?

Our culture now places more emphasis on the visual than ever before. I needed to check out whether our greater-than-ever fascination with beauty, fashion, celebrity—style in general—keeps us from looking below the surface.

In case you're wondering, my being intrigued and somewhat daunted by this character did not arise from some lifelong "I look like Quasimodo with a wig" anguish. I'm okay. Nevertheless, "gorgeous" would never appear on any Top 10 List of Adjectives Most Frequently Applied to Susan Isaacs. Furthermore, I couldn't imagine writing a novel about someone who had that "g" word, along with "stunning" and "chic," on hers.

One microsecond later. Or maybe it was two weeks. Hard to tell, as my Susan-the-novelist mind often does its work on its own while Susan-the-person carries on with what non-novelists refer to as real life. However long it really was, when the beaut next appeared in my consciousness, she was no longer someone to be intimidated by or condescended to. She was clear to me. Amazingly, I liked her. (Not that you need to like or even respect your protagonist. I can't imagine Dostoevsky thinking, *Gee, that Raskolnikov is a total sweetheart*.)

I knew my protagonist's name was Susan B Anthony Rabinowitz Gersten and—surprise!—she was going to show everyone the stuff from which she was made: a lot more than sugar and spice and La Prairie makeup. I couldn't wait to write about her.

Best of all, I wasn't observing her from the outside. I was inside her head. Not only was I comfortable in there, I felt at home; Susie and I had undergone that magical author-subject merge. We'd become one (though not to the point of my being able to wear her clothes).

From the inside looking out, I comprehended what it was like to be self-assured and pretty, just a tad away from beautiful: it felt good. Okay, that sensation was not enough to create a fully realized protagonist. But I now understood that Susie's preoccupation with appearances was the key to her inner life. Her own prettiness and presentation were always works in progress. The world beyond herself was subject to similar scrutiny. She'd been born with a sense of order and style. For me, seeing the world with that artistic eye was so challenging. I'd never been the sort who instinctively knew which car or chair or abstract expressionist painting had intrinsic worth. I rarely had the urge to rearrange anyone's furniture.

What was it like to be supersensitive to fashion, art, or people's appearances? I had my own supersensitivity—to nuances in language and behavior—but I wanted to experience the world through the eyes of someone who had the Eye.

After I had that insight into Susie, the rest of the novel fell into place fast. Her background: She'd been born into a rather boring, mildly depressed family—a swan among ugly ducks. I could see her growing up in a dreary Brooklyn apartment, yearning for some quality in her life. Okay, some of that yearning turned into banal social ambition, the desire to be in a position where she could own the lovely things she believed were necessary for fulfillment and status. But Susie also needed to create beauty for others who didn't know how. I got a flash of her arranging roses in a bowl, inhaling their sweetness, getting pleasure from the process as well as the results. Bingo! She became a floral designer.

And who would be the man of her dreams? Jonah Gersten, a plastic surgeon, a man who also had the Eye, the aesthetic sense, as well as the need to make things beautiful. And since life is never perfect, Susie's backstory included a struggle with infertility that did have a happy ending: as the novel opens, she and Jonah are the exultant though frazzled parents of four-year-old triplet sons.

Backstory is dandy, but I needed a front story. I later realized it had been waiting for me from the moment I took on the voice of someone who is all about surfaces. What would happen when something occurs, something potentially shattering, to demolish a gorgeously constructed existence? Could Susie face the truth, no matter how awful? She might be willing, but would she be able to stand up for this truth, fight for herself and her family? Was there substance beneath the style?

Also, with all the current chatter about values, family and otherwise, few people truly have to put up or shut up. But here was my protagonist, thirty-five years old, someone who'd never given morality a thought beyond the vague understanding that it has to do with the Ten Commandments (of which, maybe, she could recite five). Facing what might be a major injustice—the wrong person being convicted of a crime—could she act? Was it even her responsibility, considering that all the authorities considered the prosecutor's case a slam dunk? Can someone whose lifetime thinking about morality probably totaled two minutes develop a sense of ethics, along with the courage to actually do the right thing?

So that's how I began. I joined with my new companion, Susan B Anthony Rabinowitz Gersten, saw through her eyes, thought her thoughts, comprehended all she was up against. Now I could finally do what she'd asked of me: set down her story.

As Husbands Go

Introduction

When renowned Park Avenue plastic surgeon Jonah Gerston is found stabbed to death in the apartment of a second-rate call girl, his wife, Susie, is left with a lonely McMansion in a tony Long Island suburb, fatherless four-year-old triplets, and a host of nagging questions about her charming, successful, and seemingly loyal husband. The product of a modest Brooklyn upbringing who climbed her way up the social ladder into the world of Manolo slingbacks and antique bergères, Susie had always felt secure in both her marriage and her posh lifestyle. But now, with tabloid reporters crowding her manicured lawn and the police convinced they have an open-and-shut case, she is left questioning everything she's ever believed in. But she's also got a gut feeling that all is not as it seems.

Luckily for Susie, her plucky, glamorous, and long-estranged grandmother Ethel has suddenly emerged, ready to take on the NYPD, the DA, Jonah's intolerable parents, and his former business partners, who would all rather just sweep this scandal under the rug. Their eagerness becomes a bit suspicious. With Ethel in tow, Susie embarks on a quest to reveal the truth about her husband's murder, hoping to find a way to validate her past and forge a new future.

Questions for Discussion

1. Early in the book, Susie reflects on her personal growth, or lack thereof, since the death of her husband: "Maybe I'm still shallow, just deluding myself that after all that's occurred, I've become a better person" (p. 2). How does Susie's character progress throughout the novel? Do you think that everything she has endured has made her a better person?

2. Jonah's friends, family, and colleagues all seem surprised that he might be cheating on his wife, and they repeatedly describe him as decent, honorable, and kind. What was your gut feeling about Jonah's murder from the very beginning? Did you believe that he had been buying the services of this prostitute, and did your impressions change at all as you were reading? Why or why not?

3. Susie seems to have always taken unabashed pleasure in her happy marriage, while her friend and business partner Andrea views her own marriage as a vehicle to the lifestyle that she wants. Compare and contrast Susie's and Andrea's views on their husbands and marriage in general. Do you think Susie married for money and simply chanced upon happiness with Jonah?

4. Throughout the book, Susie lovingly reflects on the household items that she and Jonah collected, from the ornate bergère to the antique settee from Vermont. In the midst of mourning her husband's death, she maintains, "I knew if I were sitting in a repro Regency covered in polyester damask, I would feel worse" (p. 25). What is her relationship with these objects of luxury? Do you think she is truly fulfilled by her life of material wealth? And do

you think Isaacs is being ironic when she says that sitting on polyester damask would make things worse?

5. As much as Susie clashes with her in-laws, Babs and Clive Gersten, she seems to revile her own parents even more. Discuss the depiction of the Rabinowitzes. How do you feel about Susie's attitude toward them? Do you believe they are truly as selfish and miserable as she makes them out to be, or is she resentful of her humble upbringing?

6. Susie struggles to reconcile her mother's perception of Ethel as a selfish absentee parent with the alluring, openhearted woman she knows today. What is your opinion of Ethel? Do you see her attempt to establish a relationship with Susie as penance for her past actions, or do you believe she has simply chosen a glamorous granddaughter over a misfit daughter?

7. On page 139, Isaacs writes, "[Babs] and Grandma Ethel shared two dualities: an ability to manipulate other people and a powerful ambition to be a somebody. Most likely, they also shared a common ruthlessness." Discuss the strengths and shortcomings of these two characters. Why do you think Susie seems so repelled by Babs and so enamored with Ethel, despite their apparent similarities?

8. Susie relentlessly investigates Jonah's murder even as her friends, family, and the police encourage her to move on. On page 148, she states, "What I'm after is the truth, even if it's an ugly truth" and at the end of the book she explains, "It wasn't so much truth-seeking as I couldn't stand the thought of that repulsive, stupid, useless, innocent hooker rotting in jail" (p. 338). Do you think that she is driven by the desire to clear Dorinda's name, her husband's, or both? Does her motivation evolve at all as the novel progresses?

9. Were you surprised to discover who the murderer was? Did you have any other suspects in mind?

10. Susie relies on an eclectic support group of friends and family, from Andrea and her husband, Hugh "Fat Boy" Morrison, to tough-talking Ethel and her lover, Sparky. Which of the novel's characters is your favorite?

11. What do you think lies ahead for Susie and the triplets? Will Ethel remain in their lives now that the mystery has been solved?

12. Reread the novel's epigraph from Walt Whitman's *Leaves of Grass*. How do you think this quote applies to the novel?

Enhance Your Book Club

1. Try your hand at Susie's trade! Take a floral design class with your book club at a local craft store or flower shop.

2. Grandma Ethel first appeared in Susan Isaacs's *Any Place I Hang My Hat*. Read this for your next book club meeting.

3. Find out more about Susan Isaacs by visiting her website, www.SusanIsaacs.com, which includes a list of her other titles as well as biographical information.